A BITTERSWEET STORY

A Historical Novel

by

Carolyn Tyree Feagans

A Bittersweet Story
by
Carolyn Tyree Feagans

Second Printing

ISBN: 978-0-9842516-3-6

A Bittersweet Story is a novel, interwoven with local, national and international factual events. However, all characters and names of characters are fictitious.

The front cover was captured on The Skyline Drive—
a profusion of Bittersweet in late autumn.

Warwick House

Publishing
720 Court Street
Lynchburg, VA 24504

In memory of all those displaced…

and dedicated to the beautiful Blue Ridge Mountains of the Shenandoah National Park …

and to their Creator!

PROLOGUE

The reader is asked to step back in time, not once, but twice, and both encounters emit passionate emotions.

Years ago, as a teenager, I was made privy to another's shouldered burden, and the alluring secret stuck with me for decades, popping up ever so often. Why? I cannot answer. Perhaps it will finally lie at rest–once I spin its tale–though largely embellished. But its inspiration, a war-torn casualty, was the unfortunate catalyst for the pages that follow.

As for the bigger story, I was compelled to write it, as well. Just as the mountain hiker in the sixties saw the occasional remnants of the giant chestnut trees that no longer ruled the forest, those of us in the twenty-first century witness the tall, skeletal hemlocks scaling the mountain ridges.

Everything has its turn–even the mountain folk who once peopled the Blue Ridge that is now known as the Shenandoah National Park.

Intrigued by the hidden past of this unique park, I decided not only to research its worthy story, but also to pen it through the eyes of one mountain family. Though the Ralston family is fictional, their story and experiences are based on true happenings in the Blue Ridge at this particular grim time.

As with my previous books, I have attempted to humanize an important slice of history, carefully following the calendar-line of events. Obviously I have understated and overstated, and for that I humbly apologize, but who can adequately do justice to such an enormous occurrence that painfully affected so many lives?

It has been said that history is the great educator and that one learns from it, but do we?

CHAPTER ONE
(Introduction—1966)

Private First Class Cory Blackenstaff and his mother drove down the long, straight stretch of Route 460, away from Petersburg, Virginia. They were headed east, back home to Sandbridge, a coastal community also in the Commonwealth. He was dressed in his sharp blue uniform at her request. She loved to see him in it, and she had wanted Aunt Callie to see it, too. Her heart filled with pride just looking at him, and he was whistling. He always whistled when he was happy, ever since he was a small boy, but she wished he wasn't whistling now. A knot formed hard in her throat.

How could she destroy his happiness?

The early spring morning also attested to this happiness, with birds randomly flitting across the sun-drenched highway, and trees lining it that were just beginning to come to life with reddish buds barely visible.

They reminded Cory of his childhood and the occasional spring trips they had made up this way, pleasant outings with his parents to visit his mother's aunt in Petersburg. She had lived then in a small bungalow in the old city. Its front porch hung heavy with wisteria, twisted vines laden with bunches of lavender blooms, but that was years ago, and his father was living back then.

The thought of his father left him with an unsettling mood. Maybe if he hadn't been an only child, things would have been different. There would have been others to share his aloofness, his coldness. Who knows? Still it was hard to believe that it had been almost three years now since his father's sudden heart attack, and yet he didn't really miss him.

He glanced over at his mother. She was staring out the window at the passing fields, some freshly plowed, others already leafy green. He knew she loved watching the sweeping stretches of furrowed rows in their varied phases of growth.

"Cornfields, I guess," he posed, noticing stubs from last year's crop.

She nodded.

He glanced to the opposite side. "And soybeans over there or maybe peanuts." It was difficult to tell with new growth, but once up a foot or so the thick lushness of the soybean was easily recognizable, with its quivering leaves blowing in the warm, southern breeze, and easily distinguishable from the low-lying peanuts that took up so many of the wide-open fields along the highway.

She nodded again without turning her head.

He wished she weren't so solemn. His mother was usually a high-spirited talker, never at a loss for words. A tractor-trailer loomed up behind them, and he sped up. He couldn't wait to get back home, back to the Bay. He had lived there all his life, but never tired of it. His mother had lived there all her life, too, as well as his grandparents. He glanced at her again. It was hard to believe that she was forty-one. She had always looked so young for her age, strikingly young in fact, especially with that pale blond hair, but he had to admit that today she looked more her age. Maybe she was worried about his going to Vietnam—no maybe about it! So was he, but he must not let her know. He was determined to make the most of his leave.

He looked at the clock on the dash. If he made good time, they would be home soon enough for him to hit the boardwalk. Lately, he and Sammy, his old high school buddy, who was also headed to Vietnam, had been doing this about once a week. It was as if they shared an unspeakable secret. They would live for the moment and enjoy every second, for who knew what the future held. And though it was early spring, the chicks were already up on Virginia Beach, and they loved a uniform! In fact, he had planned on going over yesterday, but he was glad he'd taken the time for his mom. He remembered how sad she had looked when they left Aunt Callie. The poor old lady didn't have a clue of who she was, and much less who they were. Alzheimer's. It had to be especially hard on his mother. She had always cared a lot for Aunt Callie, though they hadn't seen her that often since she lived so far away. She was a sweet lady, sweeter than his grandmother had ever been, he thought guiltily, but it was the truth. It was hard to believe that they were even sisters.

They drove on in silence for a while, and then his mother cleared her throat and turned to him.

"Cory…I have something to tell you…something I probably should have told you years ago…but the time… somehow never seemed right…."

He could see the strain on her face. What in the world could it be? Obviously this wasn't any trivial matter. She clutched her large, black pocketbook, visibly worked up, and leaned forward as if summoning inner strength.

"…it's been a burden I've carried with me all my life."

"Mom, it couldn't be all that bad—"

"Just listen, Cory, you need to listen…."

She stared out the window again, and he suddenly realized that's why she had been so quiet since they left. It wasn't Aunt Callie after all or Vietnam. Was this the real reason she'd planned the trip and insisted on him coming?

The warm, morning air was blowing in through the open windows, and her voice had dropped low. He could barely hear her say, "A terrible secret it's been…and I don't want to go to my grave carrying it."

"Mom, I don't think you're exactly ready for the grave yet," he chuckled, trying to lighten the mood.

"Cory…please…."

Goose bumps popped up on his arms by the tone of her voice, and he realized how serious she was. What could she be talking about? He drove on, staring straight ahead, but he could tell that she was watching him now with that intense worried look lining her otherwise pretty face. His mother had always been pretty, slim and willowy, almost ethereal at times. He could remember back as far as he could—seeing men, young and old alike, gawking at her, and he used to wonder why they were staring. Only when he grew older did he understand and he was proud of her good looks.

Tears now blurred her eyes, but he couldn't see them, for she had turned back to the window. He waited impatiently for her to reveal the mystery or whatever it was, and then she uttered those unforgettable words.

"*Cory…you have a sister.*"

The forbidden secret echoed in the strained silence that followed and hung there, filling the space between them, expanding and expanding, jamming the sedan as they sped down the highway.

He stared at her open-mouthed.

She was looking at him now, and he could see the tears.

"I know…I know," she cried. "It sounds crazy, but it's true." With a choking in her throat, she continued, "It all happened years and years ago…when you were just a baby."

He tried to keep the car in the road while staring at the mother he thought he'd known all these years.

"It was during the war, a terrible time, and your father was gone." Her voice was more subdued now, actually resigned. "I know it doesn't make it right, far from it, but I was so young and lonely…grasping at any fleeting moment of happiness. Everything was so uncertain during those days…."

He glared at her. Tears were streaming down her face now.

"…so young and lonely," she repeated sadly. "And the baby…" she was looking out the window again, wiping her eyes with her hand, "…was a little girl."

"But…but what happened to her?"

"I gave her to the father."

Cory glared in disbelief at his mother, and she turned back to him with a wretched expression, a look pleading for understanding.

But he could only stare at her.

"He named her Rayna."

"But…but what happened to her?" he repeated.

"He took her away."

"Took her away…where?"

His voice didn't sound like his own as he searched his mother's tearful eyes, but she hesitated, looking out the window again. Why wouldn't she look at him? Why did she keep staring out the window? He felt himself growing angry at this sudden revelation and confused, so confused.

He glanced back to the road just in time to see the lumbering farm truck loaded down with huge, round bales of hay.

The head-on collision was earth-shattering, deafening, a devastating crash with a tremendous exploding impact. Cory's head was spinning and pounding like someone was beating him with a hammer as he peered up from the twisted metal in front of him. Only his sense of hearing was acute as he listened to the eerie sounds of the settling wreck, creaking, popping, twisting and cracking and slowly dying to a frightening hush. Shreds of hay were sifting through the broken windows, softly floating in the smoky air, and he tried to clear his head, to escape the captive fog that enveloped him. But all he could see was glass and metal everywhere, and smoke rising up from the smashed hood that was bent up against the windshield, and something was cutting into his side. It was the door, and his legs were pinned beneath the crushed steering wheel. He jerked around.

"Mom!" he screamed.

She was gone. The passenger door was ripped off.

Struggling to free himself from the wreckage imprisoning him, pressing down hard upon him, he continued to scream, "Mom…Mom…Mom!"

He had to get out!

Where he found the sudden surge of strength, he would never know, but finally breaking loose, he managed to crawl over the twisted seat and cutting glass and out the other side of the car. To his horror, he saw her. She was lying in the ditch, all crumpled and limp. He got to her, dropped to his knees and fell over her, bawling like a baby. Her eyes were closed, and he clumsily cradled her in his arms the best he could. His heart was racing. This couldn't be happening!

"Mom!" he cried. "Please Mom…wake up…don't die!"

Slowly her eyes opened, and he heard her whisper, "…*Shenandoah*."

Cory sat in the sterile hospital room beside his mother. Periodically he looked out the window at the dazzling sunshine and maple trees lining the parking lot outside, a subtle, hazy red they appeared. Soon the tiny buds would burst open and turn a tender green. They had always loved spring, both he and his mom, taking long walks down by the Bay in the early days of April. The trees would look just like they do now, he thought miserably, and some would be bending out over the marshes, over the waters.

He leaned forward, the pressure suddenly excruciating, for his knees were black and blue, and he was painfully sore, but still he had come out practically unscathed. He stared at his mother. She was so still. She had not said another word, but had lapsed into this coma or whatever it was. The medics with the ambulance couldn't revive her, and now they were here.

He got up and limped to the window. The grass beneath the budding trees was a bright green, the way he remembered it at Easter time before being mowed. A picture of his mother hiding eggs suddenly hit him like a bullet. He couldn't think of Easter! Instead his mind reeled in red-winged blackbirds perched atop the trees, surrounded by waving cattails and singing their hearts out, in hopes of finding a mate. She had pointed them out to him when he was a small kid and showed him how they proudly spread out their wings, displaying their scarlet shoulder patches in their dramatic courtship. He stifled a sob. It felt like a dream—a horrible dream!

How could his world have crumbled to pieces this quickly? When they left the motel this morning, they were happy setting out for home just like always. At least he thought so until she dropped the bomb!

A sister?

Then the big, old farm truck that had come out of nowhere…and now his mother was lying at the point of death.

"Sergeant Blackenstaff?" A heavy-set nurse filled the doorway.

"That would be nice, ma'am, but I'm just a Private First Class."

"Well, I wouldn't know the difference. I'm Nurse Smithers, and I'm here to check your mother's vitals. The doctor will be in shortly."

He nodded as she entered the small room, pressing in between him and his mother, and began checking all the paraphernalia hooked up to her. An IV bag hung from a wheeled pole, flattened and almost empty but still dripping slowly. There was a tangle of tubes connecting her to mysterious machines that constantly blinked on and off and made weird sounds periodically. It was all quite intimidating to say the least, and he didn't understand any of it.

"The men…the men in the farm truck…how are they?"

"Some broken bones, cuts and bruises, but otherwise they're doing fine," she answered.

"Thank you."

"You're welcome," her voice softened.

He still couldn't figure out what had happened. All he knew was that the truck was suddenly in front of him, on his side of the road, or at least it had appeared to be. Now he wondered. But it wasn't important. He vacantly watched the nurse take down the limp IV bag and replace it with a swelled, full one, and then she punched certain buttons on the machinery and wrote down some numbers on a chart. She straightened the rumpled sheet and pillow in her efficient but nurturing way. He could feel his world silently slipping away from him, and there was nothing he could do but sit here and watch. That was the most frustrating part, so excruciatingly frustrating.

"You doing okay?" she asked, nodding at his visible bruises and swollen eyes.

"Yes, ma'am." He was still picking glass splinters out of his head and arms, but so what? If only that was all she had, bruises, glass and broken bones instead of this coma and only God knows what else.

But Lorna Blackenstaff was not in a full-fledged coma, and she was not in the world of reality either. Floating somewhere in-between, she was tediously balancing the tightrope that separates life and death, in a blurred, hazy world. It was all very strange, and every once in awhile she seemed to hear someone calling.

"Mom...Mom...Mom...."

Who was calling her?

There were green-painted walls in the haze and white-coated people scurrying about, hurrying down vague hallways, and a gurney—a gurney recklessly veering down long corridors. The corridors were cold, sterile and frightening, and she didn't like them, and there were piercing needles and tubes and pain. She wanted to cry out but couldn't, but that was all right. She was drifting away from it all anyway, and she was glad. Yes, she was drifting…drifting…where was she drifting? Oh, she could hear it now.

The seashore!

She could hear the restless roar of the ocean and feel the warm sun on her back, and laughing gulls were soaring above her. She could tell their distinct cries, their unique shrieks piercing the salty air as they tenaciously wheeled overhead. Laughing gulls had always been her favorite, and she felt as free as one of them.

CHAPTER TWO
1942

She stood on the sandy beach watching them swoop up and down over the tumbling waters. She studied the endless waves, rolling and crashing onto the shore. So many times she had stood there doing the same thing, stood there contentedly, but today was different. She was restless like the wide-open sea before her.

Why couldn't Hayden have been a Coast Guardsman like the ones that patrolled the beach at night, watching out for the enemy? They were out there, the German U-boats, mining the entrance to the Chesapeake Bay and declaring war on the shipping and military boats. Already several ships and tankers had blown up with enormous displays of fire and smoke, all within sight of the boardwalk at Virginia Beach. She hadn't seen such, but others had. She and her friend, Jill Scarborough, had come down here to the beach at Sandbridge one evening and watched two of the Coast Guardsmen in uniform marching up and down the dark coastline in a somberly fashion, blatantly reminding them that the country was at war.

Of course, she didn't need to be reminded—Hayden's absence was proof enough. But it had been awfully exciting watching the marching guardsmen as the last of light gave way to darkness, and all they could see were two shadows barely silhouetted against the vast sea. But when she mentioned it at home, her father had exploded and ordered her not to go back.

"It's dangerous down there at night and no place for a young lady after dark, especially now," he'd blasted. "We're at war!" It was no denying that, living on the coast. After the declaration of war, things had changed immediately. Fort Story, on the north end of the oceanfront, doubled in size. The U.S. Army had moved into Camp Pendleton, a short distance from Sandbridge, and there was talk of building a Naval Air Station very soon in nearby Oceana. Folks living in and around the coastal area were constantly aware of the dire situation, and some had even witnessed the sinking of ships within a few miles of the shoreline.

Still, life went on as normal as possible, and Lorna for one wasn't going to let it take away all her fun. She smoothed out the faded quilt, brushing off the sand from its frayed corners. Sandbridge Beach was remote, tucked away from the hoards of tourists that descended upon nearby Virginia Beach every summer, their bags stuffed with novels to read, the latest trendy swimsuits and postcards for home. Though only ten miles south of the more popular beach, it was basically obscure—known only to the locals, and there weren't many of them. It was a narrow strip of land approximately fifteen miles long situated between the Atlantic Ocean and the Back Bay. Sand dunes separated the ocean from the narrow road and marshland that bordered the Bay. The beach was practically desolate. Lorna had been coming with her parents to its natural, unpretentious shore since she was a toddler. Her mother had quit coming years ago, after that it was just her and her dad, and they would spend long hours surf fishing.

Her mother's nagging voice rang in her ears. "Watch out for those boats, Lorna. You know the German boats are out there, and don't go near the fish camps either."

"I won't, Mother. I have my own private little place."

She really didn't, but what her mother didn't know wouldn't hurt her. Besides, the fish camps were nothing to worry about anyway, especially now. Even the fishermen were scarce. Her mother was referring to the temporary shacks built from driftwood washed ashore and used by the fishermen during the spring and summer. They stayed there overnight sometimes. Some were just holes dug into the sand dunes to camp in, but they seemed more like caves to her. They had been doing it for years, as long as she could remember, and nobody paid them any mind, but, of course, her mother would.

"And don't stay out in the sun too long either," she had called out as she straddled her bike. "It's bad for your skin. Take my parasol."

She glanced down at it lying beside her now. Her mother didn't understand—she wanted to get some sun! But then, her mother didn't understand a lot of things. She never had, and ever since Cory was born, she expected her to stay home all the time. She expected her to find total contentment in feeding him, washing him, tending to his every need. And she did love to do all these things, but yet she missed the carefree lifestyle that had been whisked away from her—her school friends, the laughter and fun, and occasional party.

But mostly, she missed her husband. It still seemed strange to verbalize the word *husband*, probably because it had all happened so fast. Their whirlwind courtship, only eight months, their hasty marriage and just ten months later—little Cory. Then the call to duty! That's what Hayden called it. Hayden Blackenstaff was in the Navy. He was on a ship somewhere out in the Pacific. There had only been a couple of letters. Oh, she knew it was hard to get mail, but that didn't stop her from wondering. Did he miss her as much as she missed him? He had been gone for several months already. Maybe he was forgetting her! Things like that happened. But she also knew he was not one for showing his emotions, much less writing them down. She had found this out during their short time together, before he was shipped out, and she wondered why she hadn't seen it before when they were dating. What did they say? Love is blind? Maybe so.

She stretched out on the quilt, feeling the lumpy sand beneath her. The sun was warm and soothing. Caressing, she thought, like Hayden's touch. She wondered if he was thinking of her, or was he staring at some sexy pinup like the one of Betty Grable that she had seen in a magazine the other day. So she was the GI's favorite pinup! No wonder with those long legs and stunning swimsuit! Who could compete with that? She wished she could buy such a swimsuit, but her mother would have a conniption, and there was no money for that anyway, maybe after the war.

Oh, Lorna, you're totally ridiculous! She scolded herself and pulled out her book. Hayden is probably praying for his life right now, out there in the middle of the ocean. Scourged with guilt, she stared at the cover of Hemingway's brand new book. Oh well, she slapped it down in front of her and picked up where she had left off: *"Not for me," Pablo said. "I am tired of being hunted. Here we are all right. Now if you blow a bridge here, we will be hunted. If they know we are here and hunt for us with planes, they will find us. If they send Moors to hunt us out, they will find us and we must go. I am tired of all this You hear?"*

War!

It may be the Spanish Civil War, but it was still war! Why would she want to read a book about war for Pete's sake?

But it was the book her mother had given her, shoved it into her bag actually, and she knew darn well she'd better read it or she wouldn't hear the end of it. It might be the rage for the intellectuals right now, but she wasn't an intellectual, and she was doggoned tired of war!

She slammed the book shut and stared out at the rolling waves. She remembered watching them for endless hours as a kid while her dad fished. He never seemed to tire of waiting for a bite, and she had loved coming with him. She would build elaborate sandcastles, sandcastles that rose and fell with the endless waves. Life seemed so simple back then, and happy. She had found total contentment building those sandcastles and then knocking them down, only to rebuild them over and over again—for hours she would do that. Sometimes she would purposely carve them out near the water's edge just to watch the encroaching waves lap at them until finally they gave way to its compelling force.

Other times she would lie on her stomach on the warm sand and watch the ghost crabs pop out of their holes, very cautiously, and scoot across the sand sideways, their stark, black eyes ever alert for danger. And if she were to move, they would dash back to their havens. She especially enjoyed watching them dig out their holes, tossing out the sand as if they owned miniature shovels. She would slide on her stomach up to a hole and watch and wait until the job was finished, and the proud owner would pop out, only to duck back in upon seeing her giant image hovering over.

Childhood is a splendid thing, she mused, no responsibilities, simply days upon days of pleasure. Too bad it had to end. She glanced back at the book lying on the quilt. Well, she might as well read it. Her mother would certainly be asking about it, and maybe it would take her mind off Hayden.

The sea oats were waving atop the dunes when Greyson Ralston climbed them. He peered through—the strong, salty breezes catching his breath—and he was suddenly awestruck with what he saw. But Lorna was unaware that someone was watching. She was alone on the beach except for a young lad absently skipping off in the distance with a fishing pole in one hand and tossing seashells high into the air with the other. Every so often the lad would spin around effortlessly in the sand, obviously delighted to be on his way fishing.

But Greyson stood mesmerized on the sand dune.

He hadn't even noticed the boy that was now fading into the ocean's vapor as he distanced himself. All he could see was Lorna lying on the beach in that striking black and white swimsuit, her pale blond hair shimmering in the dazzling sun. He had never seen anyone so stunning in all his life! Maybe it's the seashore, he thought to himself. They say it does strange things to one's mind. He shook his head, his sandy locks whipping in the strong outer banks wind, and then glanced down at his fishing pole and can of bloodworms. He climbed over the dunes and down to the shore, planting distinct shoe prints in the wet sand and stopping at the water's edge.

He had only arrived the day before from the Shenandoah Valley and was anxious for some fishing. It was his first time to see the ocean, and he was more than impressed.

His friend, Lester Walters, had invited him down for a couple of weeks. They had met a few years ago when they were both enlisted in the CCCs and ended up on the same assignment at Skyland, a resort located at the top of the Blue Ridge Mountains in the Shenandoah National Park. They had made fast friends and had remained so, sending postcards to one another from time to time. Lester had grown up nearby and spent many a day fishing the coastal waters. He'd often bragged to the guys at camp about the nice flounder and spots that he reeled in. In fact, they used to rib him about his fish tales, accusing him of enhancing them, but Lester didn't mind. That's what Greyson liked most about him, how he seemed to take life in stride—didn't let anything bother him. He had often wished he could be that way.

Lester had first taken him to the more popular Virginia Beach, where he had marveled at all the shops and people and activity. The lively crowds were something to see, although he learned that it was nothing like it used to be before the war. But here is where Lester preferred to fish, in the Back Bay waters where he caught more large-mouth bass than he could dream of. At least that's what he claimed, and Greyson planned to put him to the test. However, he wanted to try surf fishing first, and the Atlantic spread out before him, heaving and swelling its squally waves and spewing out a foamy white spray, something that even he, with his vivid imagination, could never have pictured.

However, he was alone today because Lester had to work, but that was all right for he had found his way back down to the Bay, though not without a few wrong turns and having to stop and ask for directions more than once. It was nice of Lester to let him use his truck, but he wondered how anyone ever found this place. There were no signs, just narrow, twisting dirt roads weaving in and around trees and marshes, until suddenly you came out of it all and were facing the wide open Atlantic that lay out as far as the naked eye could see. It was like a fairy tale with a grand ending, he thought to himself.

He baited his line and cast out, feeling the jerking force of the undercurrent, something definitely new to him. But fishing wasn't new to him. He had been throwing out his line in the mountain streams ever since he was a lad, and as he reeled in a bit, he experienced that familiar sense of manhood, that sense of power, that sense of man's purpose on earth. He remembered feeling it when just a boy, but this was even more exciting, more challenging. The ocean's tumbling waters were absolutely alive with motion, and it was hard to tell whether he had a fish on the line or whether it was just the strong currents pulling on it.

He glanced to his right. She was still there reading her book, and a certain fidgety sensation stirred within, but then he felt a definite tug on his line.

Lorna rubbed her smarting eyes. The sun was glaring on the page as she held it down against the ocean breezes. She looked up and saw the young man reeling in a fish.

Where did he come from?

His short-sleeved shirt stretched taut against his muscled, broad shoulders as he strained against his catch. It had been awhile since she'd watched someone fish. Hayden didn't really care for it, and her father didn't fish so much anymore since he'd gotten older. Now the young man was pulling the fish out of the water, a large flounder it appeared to be, and it flopped back and forth in the surf. He turned to her with a proud boyish-smile, and she ducked her head. Embarrassed to be caught watching, she fell back to reading, but not before she noticed how handsome he was with a shock of sandy hair falling over his forehead, and even at a distance, she could tell he had arresting eyes.

She grappled with the book, but the words wouldn't register.

After awhile, she gave up, figuring she'd better head home anyway, though she hated to leave the sunny beach, but Cory would be waking from his nap and looking for her. She scrambled to her feet, gathered up her things and purposely avoided the young man who was still fishing and discreetly glancing her way from time to time.

She started up the beach, and he waved to her. She nodded self-consciously and headed for her bike, parked up against a dune. She picked it up and stuffed the book, sandy quilt and awkward parasol into the basket, and pedaled furiously up the path, guilt chasing her on. But she couldn't help it if he was fishing on the same beach. Still she wondered who he was. She had never seen him before. Must be one of the Virginia Beach tourists, she figured, lost or something.

Oh well, she pedaled on, feeling a bit light-headed as the ocean breezes whipped her hair into her eyes, and the laughing gulls cackled overhead.

The next morning she was hard at it helping her mother with the weekly wash, but as the warm summer sun spilled onto the back porch, her mind kept straying to the beach and drowning out the ramblings of her mother, who was visibly wound up over her new washing machine.

"No more bending over a scrub board for me!" she crowed. The hefty thing, along with its large galvanized tubs, took up half of the porch.

Lorna was also intrigued watching the wash flatten out as it slid through the sturdy wringer—a marvelous contraption it was! And they were sure lucky to have gotten it. Her father's boss had actually given it to them, and it was practically new. It had belonged to his sister, who had just died.

"I hate it that the old lady had to pass on," her mother reasoned while bringing out another armful of dirty linens. "But everybody has to die sometime another, and the timing sure is nice! We've been needing one of these for ages, you know."

Cory was lying on a mat at the other end of the porch, his chubby legs kicking feverishly at the warm summer air. His bright blue eyes studied the slight movement of the myrtle leaves that brushed up against the screen door, and Lorna watched his little mouth curl up at the edges into a crooked smile. Already he was pushing himself over and around on the mat. They had to watch him closely or he would roll right off the porch and down the steps. Three months old, she mouthed silently, and his daddy doesn't even know him. Maybe that's why she felt that he was all hers.

"Wanna walk over to Mrs. Ratcliff's when we finish?"

Lorna looked up. "I was hoping to go back to the beach for a little while."

"Thought you got enough sun yesterday."

"Well, Dad said it's supposed to rain tomorrow."

"What does he know? Only the good Lord knows when it's gonna rain!"

Then her mother recalled how discontented she had seemed lately. "Of course, you probably would be bored to death over at old Mrs. Ratcliff's. She does go on and on about her particular ailments, and she's got a passel of them, too." She peered around the raucous machine that was bouncing up and down, practically dancing out in front of them, the clothes agitating in a riotous fashion. "No, you go ahead to the beach for a while."

Lorna's face brightened.

"Do you good so long as you don't get too much sun. Cory will be fine. It's almost his nap time anyhow."

Lorna brushed her long, thick hair until it shone, and then she pulled it back and tied it with a thin, yellow ribbon. She swept a bit of powder across her nose to disguise the faint freckles that always popped up every summer and annoyed her to no end. She applied the deep red lipstick and smacked her lips together, knowing that this would initiate an unwelcome censure for sure, but she was able to slip out without being noticed.

Riding on her bike, the bracing wind whipped at her face, and she shook off the feeling of guilt that rode along with her. She was just going to the beach, for Pete's sake! She had a right to go to the beach if she wanted to. She pushed the unwanted rider away, determined to enjoy the beautiful morning and smiled up into the beaming sun.

The day would be nice, much like the day before. In fact, it was typical of most summer days on the Virginia coast, sunny and breezy, that Lorna loved. But what did she know? She had never been anywhere else! Most of her friends had at least been out of state, to North Carolina maybe, but not her. Her friend, Joan, visited Atlantic City every summer with her parents. But her folks were homebodies, and they didn't figure on changing. Not that she wanted to leave for good, but just to travel, see places, something other than the coast. Sometimes when she got on her bike, she felt like riding on forever, but that was foolish thinking, she knew. Her mother told her so. "Lorna, you need to settle down," she'd say, but she didn't feel like settling down, she felt alive, full of life!

She parked her bike in the same place, leaning it up against the wet, sandy dune and pulled her balled-up quilt and book out of the wire basket. It had rained a little during the night, and the sand was dimpled. She breathed in the delicious salty air and headed to the beach. As she topped the dune, she spied him, a lone figure midst the sand, sea and wind. He was busy casting out. She pulled off her sandals to feel the sand between her toes and trudged up the shore to the same spot where she was yesterday. She noticed that he was in the same spot also.

He saw her coming out of the corner of his eye and silently watched her spread out the old, worn quilt. She painstakingly arranged her belongings on it, and then pulled off a long white shirt, exposing the same black and white swimsuit. She aimed herself directly at the glaring sun. He suppressed his enthusiasm and continued to fish. Somehow he had known she would show up. Lester had caught him more than once daydreaming over dinner and peppered him with questions. But he kept her to himself, not wanting to share this enchanting creature even with his friend. As he repeatedly cast out and pulled in, his anxiety increased. Suppose she thwarted him? Or ridiculed him? The old fears set in. Why did he always feel this way when it came to girls? Because of it, he had avoided them for the most part. Just once had he even come close in high school, only to shy away when things turned more serious, but he knew why. He angrily pushed the thought away. He didn't want it spoiling the bliss he was experiencing.

Almost an hour passed before she pushed up and strolled down to the water's edge, poking her toes gingerly into the cold surf. He knew it was cold. He had tested it out yesterday after she left, jumping in headfirst, only to come up sputtering like crazy and spitting out the bitter water.

He decided then and there that he preferred the calm rivers back home without the salty taste and burning sensation in his eyes.

She waded on out but only up to her waist and reached down to splash water onto her face and arms while the waves pummeled her, and then turned and started back up. He gave up and reeled in his line. The fish weren't biting anyway.

Stretched out on her stomach and cooled down from the water, she saw him approaching but pretended to read.

"Hello, back again, I see."

Her smile lit up her whole face, and he was suddenly speechless. She was more beautiful than anything he'd ever seen.

"Any luck?"

He shook his head, finally able to speak. "No…not even a bite!"

"What're you using?"

"Bloodworms."

"Yucky…I hate those things. My dad always used cut bait, and he had pretty good luck, too."

"Is that right?" He couldn't believe he was standing here alone on a deserted beach with such a lovely creature…discussing bloodworms and cut bait!

"You're not from around here, are you?"

"No, ma'am, I'm not."

Her whimsical giggle floated out into the salty breezes. "You don't have to call me ma'am."

"I'm sorry." Blushing in spite of himself, he explained, "I'm from Elkton, just visiting a friend."

"Where?"

"The Shenandoah Valley."

"Oh, I've heard of that. Never been there, mind you, but I've seen pictures of it, beautiful pictures."

"It is beautiful…but no more than this."

Lorna nodded, looking out to the ocean. "Yeah…but sometimes I wish I could get away…there's nothing here, and it gets pretty boring at times."

"That's hard to believe."

"Not if you'd lived here all your life…nothing but fishermen, farmers, and hunters."

"What's wrong with that?"

She shrugged her bare shoulders. "Nothing, I guess if you happen to be a man."

His laugh was happy, full of gusto, and she smiled up at him. "What I mean is…there's nothing for us girls."

"What's your father do?"

She tossed her wind-blown hair out of her wide-set eyes, pale gray like the winter sky over the mountains, Greyson thought to himself.

"He's farmed mostly and fished, but he doesn't fish as much as he used to when I was growing up. He did the big fishing back then with nets and all, and sold his catch, hauled it up to the train station at Virginia Beach and then shipped it on to Norfolk."

"I've never seen anyone net fish."

"Really? Everybody used to come down to see what he and the others would haul in with their big nets. It was exciting, at least I thought so then. Some of the kids dragged the fish up and put them in the boxes, but not me. I didn't want to touch them. I never liked the feel of slimy fish. When I went with dad, he always took the fish off for me."

"Is that what that shed is about?" He was referring to a small shed he had passed on the way.

"Yeah, it's used for packing and icing the fish, and also those fishing shacks you see over there." She pointed to the rather rough-looking structures made out of driftwood. "That's where some of the fishermen camp out." And she hoped they wouldn't show up today.

"Maybe I'll get to see some big fishing before I leave."

"Maybe. Most everybody fishes around here...well, almost everybody. But dad has slowed down, and he doesn't hunt anymore either, and I'm glad of it. I hate to see them shooting all those pretty ducks."

Greyson recalled Lester telling him about the popular duck season and how hunters flooded into the Bay waters every year for it.

"Do you?"

"What?"

"Hunt?"

"Not really, not anymore. I used to go with my brothers when I was a kid, but I don't like...killing things." His brother William's chiding instantly surfaced in his mind, *Sissies don't hunt...you want to be a sissy?*

"I can understand. There's enough killing going on with the war." She quickly changed the subject, and he was glad.

A week later, they sat watching the shore birds skitter along the lonely beach. The sun was brilliant that morning, bouncing off Lorna's tiny birthstone on her right hand, the emerald her parents had given her on her sixteenth birthday. Her other hand was noticeably bare, but unconsciously she slid it beneath her and asked, "Did you bring it?"

He nodded. "It's in the truck. Lester said it hasn't been ridden in awhile, though. The tires needed pumping up, but otherwise it looks pretty solid. You ready?"

"In a bit." She was reluctant to leave the comfort of the warm sand and the soothing sound of the waves breaking gently on the shore, especially with him sitting so close beside her. But they had planned to ride down on the Refuge that morning. The Back Bay National Wildlife Refuge was just a ways from the beach, and Lorna often biked down to it, to enjoy its natural, unspoiled character. After learning about it, Greyson was anxious to see it, too, and she had agreed to accompany him.

He settled back on the sand to wait, though he was eager to set out. "How long has it been open?"

"Not long. About four years, I guess. There's thousands of acres and nothing but wildlife, and they can't hunt down there anymore either."

"I know all about that," he commented. "I mean about the rules concerning national parks and refuges, too, I suppose."

She picked up on his serious tone but didn't comment.

"Lester said the CCCs did a lot of work on it. In fact, that's where he started out before he was sent up my way, said they built the dunes too."

"Yeah, it used to be all flat here, but they cut down trees everywhere and piled them up with all kinds of scrub bushes. You never saw so many trees and brush! That's why they're so high. They just finished up about a year ago, and you can see it didn't take long for the sand to cover them."

Greyson studied the mounds of dunes, spotting the dead tree branches poking through every now and then, but figured in time with the never-ceasing wind and blowing sand, all traces would eventually be gone.

Lorna hopped up. "Let's go."

They trudged up the beach to the bikes and shortly were on their way. The ride was bumpy but invigorating, and soon they entered the Refuge, pedaling down the sandy dirt road that wound through the wind-swept dunes and marshland, brackish streams and lakes of water. Large turtles stared at them, still as statues, their necks stretched out as far as they would go. They were perched atop fallen branches that lay out upon the rippling waters, sunning themselves, and their wet, hard-shelled backs glistened black in the sunlight. But if they pedaled too close, they swiftly slipped into the shallow water and all that was left was a ring of widening circles.

Dwarfed, odd-shaped trees flanked the sandy road, severely pruned by the salt-laden, ocean winds.

Lorna suddenly pointed up ahead, and he caught a fleeting glimpse of one of the wild ponies that she had told him about, the ones that roamed freely along the outer banks, from North Carolina and on up the coast of Virginia. Its dark shadow vanished into the thick bay myrtles, and she turned and smiled at him and then coasted on down the flat, winding road.

After awhile, they entered the woodlands, oak, cedar, and yaupons. The sandy road darkened in their shade.

She pedaled on, and he followed, watching her pale blond hair blowing in the wind. He wondered about her, and he wondered if he was doing the right thing, taking this ride. The place was desolate except for the silent turtles and gulls soaring overhead and birds swooping down into the marshes with their lively chirps. It made him think of the settlers who had arrived on these Virginia shores so many years ago; they probably found it much the same. Primitive beauty, he thought. It was all very interesting, captivating in fact, but did he really need to be down here all alone with such a lovely creature?

His two weeks of vacation passed before he knew it, vanished with the strong coastal winds, two of the most breathtaking weeks of his life. It was as if he had been lifted up on some bountiful cloud and suspended there effortlessly between the blinding sun and the shimmering waters of the vast Atlantic. He was in love, and the whole world shone in brilliant colors just for him and his sweet Lorna. Vivacious colors of the alluring east coast—soft sky blues and iridescent yellows blended with warm, sandy hues that wrapped him up in a sphere of mystery.

Lester finally gave up and left him to his secret adventures. It was obvious his friend had met someone somewhere, but wanted to keep her to himself, and though miffed by this overt silence, he decided to give him his privacy. They had always shared everything, well, almost everything.

But all too soon, the summer clouds burst.

Greyson pushed himself out of bed and stumbled into the small bathroom, squinting into the clouded mirror, and puffy, bloodshot eyes stared back at him. He splashed cold water onto his face covered with a day's stubby growth of beard, and a sickening ache formed down in his stomach. Larger and larger it swelled until he felt nauseous and thought he might vomit. He leaned heavily over the sink.

How could he leave her?

But how could he not? His train left today, and he was glad, but still the mixed feelings vacillated between love and hurt and then out-and-out anger. Why didn't she tell him in the first place? When he first met her? Before they biked down to the Refuge? Before he lost his senses?

The cold spigot water sent shivers up and down his spine—he had to get away! He had to get back home, back to the Shenandoah. This was no place for him anyway with the bright, beguiling sun and salty air and constant roar of the sea. Somehow it had tricked him into thinking he was some Casanova, some white knight in shining armor come to whisk Lady Lorna away from her boring life.

He, of all people!

How could he have been so foolish? The radio was blaring in the living room. Why hadn't Lester turned it off when he left? Even with all the static, he could hear the reporter excitedly broadcasting yet another battle. He didn't want to hear about the war right now, but with his face all lathered, he heard anyway. The Battle of Midway had just ended. Japan had sent a large fleet to capture Midway Island at the westernmost tip of the Hawaiian chain, but fortunately the United States had cracked Japan's naval code and learned of its imminent invasion. It had gathered the ships that had survived Pearl Harbor and the Battle of the Coral Sea for an ambush on the Japanese.

Poor Lester. He would soon be in the middle of it all, and he felt bad for ignoring him so much, but it was too late now.

The newscaster was rapidly recounting the Japanese bombing raid. The outdated U.S. bombers had flown in low and launched torpedoes against the Japanese warships, but the Japanese guns downed most of the slow-moving planes. Greyson cringed at the thought.

He wiped his blade and shaved off the stubborn whiskers while the radio static popped erratically. Still he could hear the reporter describing how American dive bombers swooped in next, pounding the enemy aircraft carriers while their planes were refueling on deck. The Japanese lost several aircraft carriers and hundreds of planes and skilled pilots, and one U.S. aircraft carrier had been sunk and way over a hundred U.S. planes. But it was obviously a clear victory for the Allies, the first, in fact.

He was glad to hear that, but then anguish swept over him as the newscaster proceeded to explain how the aircraft carriers had become the most important weapon in the Pacific, crippling Japan's naval power during this most crucial battle. Cold chills raced up his arms. Lorna's husband was on one of those carriers. Crushing guilt washed over him, a drowning flood, and he sliced himself with the blade. Blood oozed down his chin in a thin, steady stream. He grabbed some toilet tissue, tore off a small piece and slapped it on the cut. It immediately turned a crimson red.

Why had he come down here anyway? He should have stayed where he belonged! But he wanted to see Lester before he left. He could never get away from it. All his friends were going or gone, fighting overseas somewhere, and he would be, too, if it wasn't for that blame—someone was banging on his door. He rinsed the suds off his face and hurried to it.

"Lorna!"

She stood there shamelessly, large tears streaming down her face.

"What're you doing here?"

"I…I came to say goodbye."

"I thought we did that yesterday."

She ducked her head.

"Lorna…Lorna…Lorna…."

She fell into his arms, and it was all he could do not to carry her off with him.

The train lurched away from the station, away from Virginia Beach, away from the girl who held his heart. Slowly it picked up speed and soon was racing up the long, steel tracks. He glanced around at the other passengers. They all seemed settled in for the trip, calmly reading newspapers or resting already with their eyes half closed. He wished he was one of them. Instead, he fought the raging turmoil within, the big hole that was expanding with every mile.

The gap widened, and Lorna watched the red caboose disappear into the hazy distance until all she could see was a tiny dot against the horizon. She gulped back the tears. He had to go—there was no other way, but the big, black train was draining every bit of life out of her as it sped away, every bit of pleasure, and she felt the tedious boredom pressing in again, but far worse was the enormous guilt that suddenly pushed down upon her. Now that he was gone, she stood on the boardwalk, feeling empty. She stared across the heaving swells of water, and the impact of the last two weeks hit her like a thousand smacking waves.

"Oh, God, what have I done?"

She stood there for a long time while the sunny skies disappeared behind a shroud of clouds. She stood there as they thickened and darkened and until raindrops began to fall gently upon the waters and the sand and upon her.

"I'm sorry, Hayden...I'm so sorry," she cried.

The long, hot summer slowed to a snail's pace as Lorna helped her mother with the housework and the small vegetable garden out back, tying up the prickly stalks of the prized tomato plants. She fed the piles of dirty clothing into the agitating washing machine and watched it do its thing. She even cleaned out the smothering attic, searching for anything to keep her mind occupied, to ward off the loneliness and the ever-present guilt that harassed her day after day.

"Why in the world do you want to go up in that hot attic, Lorna?"

"It needs cleaning out."

"I know that, but in the summertime?"

She even checked into getting involved with the war work that some of her friends were doing, but her folks squelched that idea immediately. They insisted she stay home and take care of Cory, and he was more irritable than usual, constantly fretting and crying.

"It's his teeth, Lorna! He's cutting teeth. I remember when you cut your'n. Nobody was more fussy than you."

She wished her mother wouldn't always compare him to her, for Pete's sake. He was his own little self, and he was the only thing that gave her any pleasure these days. She missed Hayden terribly, but that wasn't all. Her mind often traced back to the beach and to the young fisherman. But it was more like a dream now, a fairy tale somehow that was fading away more and more each day—not real anymore, and for that she was thankful.

CHAPTER THREE

Greyson Ralston chugged up the rural road in his second-hand pickup. He wished his folks would move in closer to town now that they were getting older. What was he going to do if one of them suddenly took ill way out here? But he knew that was out of the question. They would never leave. His sister had already broached the subject with them, and so had his brothers. The trees flanking the narrow two-lane road that skirted the base of the mountain were beginning to show signs of an early fall. Every now and then he spotted one actually half-turned, ahead of its time for no apparent reason. The road was as familiar as the back of his hand, every dip, every rut, and he knew what to expect around each and every curve. How many times had he pushed up these hills and sprinted down them in an all-fired hurry. He could hear his pa scolding him now. "Gonna get yourself killed one of these days!"

His folks had always been more protective of him, far more than the others. His sister said it was because he was the baby, but he knew better. It was his "sickness" as they called it, and they were always harping on him. "Do this, Greyson...don't do that...be careful, Greyson...watch out, Greyson!"

But now the roles were reversed, though it was obvious it hadn't dawned on them yet, especially his pa. It was more or less up to him to look out for them. Ever since Mildred moved to Richmond, the lot had fallen on him, lock, stock and barrel. Daughters seemed to automatically step up to the plate, but now she was gone, conveniently removed. William, the eldest of them all, was too busy with his own growing family. Of course, Jack would be helping. Jack was always more sensitive to other's needs, but he was gone, too. The old familiar hurt stabbed him again, and he wished with all his heart he could be overseas with Jack, fighting the Germans.

He could see the two-rut graveled drive up ahead now, narrow, parallel paths with small clumps of grass spiking up through the middle as it wound up to the small, weatherboard house. He would have to get more gravel before winter set in, that's for sure. The small house was pressed deep into the dark, leafy folds of spreading oaks and looked like it had grown there, too. There was a paltry plume of smoke rising up out of the chimney. For goodness sake! It was still summer, though it would be September in a few days. The truck bounced up the driveway, over some gullies and exposed rocks, and he looked for his pa to appear in the doorway any moment.

Sure enough, there he was, smoking his pipe and leaning against the doorframe, fidgeting with his left suspender. It was a picture already permanently etched in his mind, always the pipe, always the fidgeting.

"Hi, Pa!"

Mr. Ralston waved him on up and headed back inside, his stooped posture more apparent than usual. Greyson climbed out of the truck and followed after, pulling the door shut behind him. The blazing woodstove met him head on. Way too hot! His ma was scurrying about, obviously pleased to see him.

"Back already, son?" She patted his arm like he was five years old. "Thought you were taking a vacation."

"I was."

"Have a nice time?"

"Yes, ma'am."

Pa, refilling his pipe, watched him cynically.

"See the ocean?" she asked, clearing off the table.

"Yes, ma'am."

"Now that would be something to see," she chuckled. "Wouldn't it, Pa?"

He frowned. "I'd rather be right here, not where storms are always spewing up. Right here at the foot of the mountains, and you can count on them staying put!"

Greyson wondered if he was peeved at him for going, but he could be that way sometimes. "See you started up the stove, Pa." He wiped his forehead and peered out the kitchen window. "Need some wood cut up?"

"That'd be right nice of you, son. 'Course I can still chop a cord of wood good as ever."

Ma twisted around. "It's not the chopping that gets him. It's the carrying in. I told him I'd help, but you know how stubborn he is."

"Shucks. What you talking about? I can carry as much wood as any of the boys!"

Greyson pulled open the back door, glad for the bracing air, and headed for the woodpile. He dropped the first log on the chopping block and grabbed the old axe, the same one he had used as a youngster, the same one that had flown off the handle once and landed at Pa's feet. He checked it first, and then lifted it high into the air and slammed it down with a thud—a hard, decisive force, splitting the solid oak firmly in two. He grabbed the next log and split it just as determinedly. It was the first time he'd felt this good since he had returned home. He chopped and chopped at a fierce pace, without taking a break while his ma watched from the doorway.

"Look at that boy, Pa, would you. He's gonna kill himself."

Mr. Ralston leaned into the window. "Chopping like he's got a fire burning at his coattail!"

"What you reckon's wrong with him?"

"How do I know, Ma?"

"Didn't seem like himself when he got here. I knew something was wrong with him."

"Now, Ma, don't go getting yourself all riled up. He's a grown man now."

"Don't you reckon I know that, but he's not like William and Jack."

"If you want somebody to go to worrying about, you got Jack."

She wheeled around to the sink and commenced to scrubbing dishes quiet-like. Pa figured she was praying. She always prayed when Jack's name was mentioned. It had been hard on her ever since he left for the war. Jack was the gentle one, not wild and testy like William could be, nor worrisome like Greyson with his sickness. Jack had always been a comfort, soothing-like.

He flopped down in the wicker rocker pulled up close to the toasty stove and wondered if Greyson would take him up to the old place. It'd been nigh about six months since he'd been, he figured, right about springtime it was, and he had a hankering to go. Whenever the smell of chimney smoke started up, he was drawn to the mountain somehow. He couldn't explain it, but it worked like magic.

Greyson came back in, rubbing his hands together. "That's some hard oak."

"All oak's hard, son. What you think about riding up to the old place?"

He reached for the dishtowel to wipe his hands on and glanced around at his pa. "You sure you want to go today, Pa?"

"Day's good as any other, ain't it?"

He mentally tallied his to-do list that he had planned to accomplish. He really needed to change the oil in his truck. It was well overdue, plus he had hoped to wash it, too. Oh, well, what the heck.

They headed up the mountainside, his pa rattling on about the changes he noticed, and soon eased onto the smooth Skyline Drive, enjoying its picturesque views. His pa pressed into the window. Greyson wondered why it was so important for him to always come up here. One would think he wouldn't want to return to such unpleasant memories. It had been a long time since they left the mountain. Though he was only a kid when they were forced off, he would never forget it. His mind automatically switched to other thoughts. Lester was probably on a ship by now, but that was no more pleasing, depressing, in fact. He recalled him saying one night when they were working at Skyland that he never wanted to go to war. But he had changed his mind apparently, or circumstances had changed it for him. Only a year after they had served together in the Corps, things changed. The war changed it. It changed everything, including the rehabilitation of the Park that they were working on. It had halted instantly, come to a complete standstill. CCC camps began to shut down, one by one. And then there was Pearl Harbor!

He understood now that all the camps were gone, and it made him sad to think of it. He had heard, too, that the government was closing up all the facilities in the Park. They might as well, he thought, what with the gas and tire rationing. Nobody would be coming up here. He felt a bit guilty himself, but how could he not bring his pa.

"Lotta work there." Pa was pointing to the edging of rock walls lining the Drive, curving walls, layers of massive stones, miles and miles of them and quite pleasing to the eye.

"I know, Pa, but you have to admit they're better than what they used to be."

Pa looked around at him.

"You remember those long metal wires attached to heavy posts, the first guard rails? These rock walls are a sight better."

"A waste of money if you ask me." His father had never accepted the whole idea of the Skyline Drive. "Folks don't need to be spending good time just riding around in these mountains…ought to be busy making a living and taking care of family matters."

It was no use arguing. Greyson well knew that when his pa made up his mind about something, that was the end of it. They approached one of the side roads that dipped sharply off the Skyline Drive, graveled and hemmed in with masses of green mountain laurels. He loved to come up in the springtime when clusters of fragrant blooms turned them a soft pink. *Little pink teacups,* Rayna Rose used to exclaim every spring. That's what she thought they resembled. The truck bounced along with his pa leaning forward, anxiously looking for the place. It was even hard for him to find it, now so grown up with trees and brush and weeds.

"There she be!" Pa hollered out. The old chimney protruded out of tangled poison ivy vines.

Greyson braked. Mr. Ralston was fumbling with the door and pushing it open, climbing out before he could come to a complete stop.

"Hold on, Pa!"

But he was already out, his legs spread wide and his gray hair blowing wildly in the gusty wind. It was much windier than below.

"Need your hat?"

Paying no mind, he was shoving the scruffy brush aside and heading to the cabin. Greyson scooped it up off the seat anyway and followed after. He handed it to him, and he pressed it down over his ears, never looking up. He was pacing back and forth in front of the cabin.

"It used to be here," he was mumbling. "I saw it the last time…the last time we were up here…."

"What, Pa?"

"The front stoop…it used to be *right here*!"

He was staring down into a thick clump of jumbled brown weeds. Greyson came up beside him. There was only a crumbling pile of stone and a few chestnut logs lying there. A lump formed in his throat as a hazy memory filtered through—he and Rayna Rose leaning up against those stones, and it was so hot. It must have been July or August, but the stones were cool, he remembered, so cool to the touch, and Rayna Rose was having such fun making mud pies out of the wet, black dirt because it had rained the night before. He remembered fussing with her because he didn't want to make mud pies. He wanted to play soldiers. He loved to play soldiers. He swallowed hard. Memories of his twin sister always had a way of clouding his day.

"I reckon somebody's walked off with it."

"The front stoop?"

"T'was good chestnut wood…sho somebody would take it on away if he had a mind to."

"Why didn't you get it, Pa, if you wanted it? Why didn't you get it before?"

"We made a deal…me and them gov'ment folks. I don't go back on my word."

"You mean when you sold the place?"

His pa whipped around, a deep frown darkening his face. "I never said I sold it to them. They took it! You know they did!"

"But they paid you, Pa."

"Don't matter none."

"Well, at least we got a nicer place."

"I know that…still and all…it ain't the same."

Greyson knew how much the old place had meant to him, or at least he thought he did. The land had been in the Ralston family for several generations, and the cabin was built by his pa's father. He stared at the remains, what was left. The fierce mountain storms were taking their toll, and it was slowly falling in from the vicious winds and icy winters. Even the charred scars from the burning were barely visible now. He shivered at the thought and pushed off the memory.

At least the cool breeze felt good. He walked back to the truck and sat down on the running board. The old house had been nothing to brag about, that's for sure, but his pa wouldn't admit it, not in a thousand years. Mildred always complained that it was drafty and damp, but he didn't remember that. He only remembered good things like the pleasant smell of bread baking in the woodstove, and the pretty wild flowers waving in the meadow, and the fun he had when it snowed, barreling down the hillside back of the house in Ma's big wash basin. He especially remembered how he loved sleeping up in the loft, he and Rayna Rose. He stared up at the open window. She always wanted to sleep next to it so she could see the trees blowing, she said. He glanced up the hill to the cemetery. When they moved off the mountain, it was as if he had left a part of himself here, and he had.

His pa was still traipsing around and around the cabin with a big stick in his hand, poking at first one thing and then another. Greyson patiently watched him for a while, and then called out, "It's mighty windy up here, Pa. You ready to start back now?"

"I'm coming directly."

The boisterous wind whipped off his hat, sending his thin gray hair standing straight up. He stooped down for it, and then trudged up the hill to several gnarled apple trees, twisted and broken. He used to brag so much on his Milam apples, Greyson thought as he watched him, knowing where he was going. He watched him push on up the hill past what used to be the orchard, and stop in the middle of the tall, waving weeds. He knew he should follow, but instead he climbed back in the truck.

After awhile, they drove silently down the mountain.

CHAPTER FOUR

A cormorant was flying over the Back Bay, its outstretched wings reaching wide and glistening in the autumn sun. They always came with the cool weather. Abruptly it soared downward and skidded to a graceful landing as Lorna watched. It floated for a second, then dropped its head and long black neck into the water and disappeared beneath the placid Bay. She waited for it to come up. But all she could see was the sweeping expanse of water, as if there had never been a cormorant.

An old skiff tied up next to a leaning willow rocked lazily on the gentle Bay. It had been there for some time, and she didn't know who it belonged to. Suddenly she had the urge to untie it and row out, out to the big water. Or better still, she imagined herself like the mysterious cormorant deep below the placid waters. There would be no dilemma, no facing her parents, no ugly scandal and no guilt.

"Oh, God!" she cried out in a half-daze. What was she thinking?

But there seemed no way out, and the guilt was the worst part of all! Gulls screamed in the distance. She must get control of herself. She gazed out over the water and wiped her eyes. She searched for the cormorant, but still saw no sign of it. Her thoughts turned to Cory, and she chastised herself for such forbidden thoughts. He was her world! Suddenly the cormorant popped back up, angling its long virile neck. It looked her way and then disappeared beneath the waters again.

"Lorna!"

She jumped.

"We've been waiting for you." Her father stood there with his hands deep in his pockets. She pushed herself up from the ground.

"I'm sorry…."

"What're you doing way out here so long?"

"Just looking at the Bay."

"Well, you better come on. Your mother's in a tizzy, anxious to get dinner over. You know how she gets."

That night, Lorna twisted and turned in her bed. She stared at the crib beside her and Cory's small, sleeping form, and nightmare visions filled her head. She had to come to a decision!

A week later, she rode with her father up to Virginia Beach. His sedan sputtered and churned its way up the soggy, sandy road. The sweet gums were turning their multiple colors, and she stared at them while clutching the stamped letter in her pocket, her palm damp and sweaty. Her father needed to go into town to pick up some hardware and supplies for his latest project. He was planning on closing in the back porch, making it into a room that could be used in the winter also. The house seemed to grow smaller as Cory grew bigger. He was beginning to crawl now and pulling into everything. She had asked if she could come along, and her father thought she just wanted to get out of the house for a while.

"Could we stop at the post office, do you think, Dad?"

"Got something to mail?"

"Just a letter to an old friend." She hated lying to him.

The clerk glanced up as she handed the letter over to him. Imagining he knew its secret, her face flushed red, and she quickly left. After buying the supplies, they headed back home, but stopped off in Pungo. Her dad needed some tackle. She wondered if he was thinking of fishing more. She sat in the car and watched him walk into the store, but soon he was back, and they headed on. It had been raining off and on for several days, a drippy, fine rain, and the gullies lining the narrow roadway were flooded as usual and spilling over into the road. It was a messy lot.

"Nowhere for it to go," her father complained.

"What's that?"

"The water...nowhere for it to go."

"Oh."

"You feeling all right?"

"Yes, sir."

"Seem sort of preoccupied or something."

"I'm fine, just tired, Dad," she answered a bit irritably. He drove on quietly, rubbing his chin and thinking to himself—*temperamental, that's what she is, a might high-strung.* First she's happy, and then she's crying. How does a body know what to expect? It sure would have been easier had she been a boy like little Cory, but then concluded it was probably his fault. He knew he had spoiled her, being the only one, and she was such an angel as a child. How could he help it?

The posted letter shifted along with hundreds of others, passing from hand to hand, obliviously, out of the sunny sweep of Virginia Beach, away from the coast. It slowly made its way westward to the Eastern Front Range of the Appalachians called the Blue Ridge Mountains, and to the valley below it, the Shenandoah Valley.

Greyson pulled up to the mailbox. He was bushed. It had been a long day. He drew out the mail, absently sorting through it for anything for him, and suddenly caught his breath. He knew before he read the return address, and immediately he could feel his heart beginning to pace rapidly. Nervously, he parked his truck in front of the boarding house where he had a room that served as bedroom and living quarters. He dropped the rest of the mail in the hallway and closed his door behind him. A small folding table sat beside his bed, and he leaned on it, staring down at the envelope with trembling hands and trepidation.

Why was she writing now? It was over! They had agreed that it was the best thing, the only thing to do. It had been months since that unreal fantasy. Finally he ripped open the envelope and pulled out the letter written on white-lined tablet paper, and his face contorted.

"Oh, no...."

He sank onto the chair, twisting the letter back and forth in his hands, perspiration beading on his forehead. Stunned, he didn't know how long he sat there, but after awhile he got up and headed for the door and out to his truck. Numbly, he stuck the key in the ignition and drove off, not knowing where he was going. He just needed to be doing something.

Anything.

Without thinking he headed to the mountains, into its calming presence, into its solid strength. The higher he climbed, the better he felt. He remembered doing the same thing when he was a kid, after they had been pushed off the mountain, but then he was walking, not driving.

Whenever his pa had scolded him, or William had teased him unmercifully, he would head up the mountain, racing as fast as his little legs would carry him.

He pulled over to the side of the mountain road and shut off the engine. Maybe it would clear his head now. He climbed out and started up a familiar trail, listening to the pervading silence except for the occasional call of birds. Gradually his nerves calmed and the jittery feeling in his stomach quieted as he breathed in the cool, fresh air.

It wasn't the end of the world!

Chipmunks scurried up ahead of him, over fallen trees and beneath the packed leaves. A picture of his twin sister scrambling through the woods, her dark head bobbing through the brush in pursuit of one of the little creatures, flashed before him, and he wondered what she would look like now. He had often wondered that, yet a picture never quite formed in his mind. It would never materialize. She would always be that little girl with the dark, curly locks and smirking look on her pixy face whenever he crossed her. She was forever locked in the past.

Something stirred up ahead, something larger than a chipmunk, and he watched a doe move lightly out of the brush, gingerly stepping over, ever cautiously and followed by a shy, spotted fawn. She nibbled on the green leaves of a young striped maple, and the fawn followed after. He sat very still, knowing the slightest movement would chase them away, and slowly the penciled words on the white-lined tablet paper began to register with him. How could he have been so naïve?

So dumb?

But he knew why. He hated to admit it, but he knew why. There was no denying that she was lovely and willing, even welcoming, but he couldn't place all the blame there.

That wasn't fair. It was the timid, little fellow all over again, the faint-hearted one that was afraid of life, the sickly one, emerging again! Greyson Ralston, whom the girls liked but shied away from because he had…fits! It was him, and he was out to prove something, but what?

The doe and her fawn disappeared into the tangled underbrush, and he sighed.

He sat there for a long time. He didn't want to leave. He wanted to soak up the timeless peace of the mountains as long as he could, as if maybe it would sustain him for whatever lay ahead, and he didn't have a clue what that would be, but somehow he knew things would never be the same.

He stared up into the canopy of leaves now turning their individual colors. Soon they would transform the shady forest and then begin to fall, one by one. They would tumble down, more and more until the mountains would literally pulsate with them, floating and parachuting to the ground. He loved it. Rayna Rose had taught him to appreciate them years ago when they would lie on their backs with the brisk smell of autumn in the air. They would lie there staring up into the glowing color.

Clouds silently slid overhead, gradually darkening the forest. It was getting late, and he knew he should get up and head back down. He would in a minute.

The late September sun was unusually warm, easily fooling one into thinking it was still summer. Greyson had just arrived and having followed her instructions, was waiting at the same spot where he had first seen her. The ocean was relatively calm, and the beach was empty just like it had been that first time. Suppose she didn't show up? What would he do then? Surely he couldn't go to her house! He touched the letter in his pocket. It was brief. He had reread it over and over again, each time wondering if somehow it might not be true. For the last couple of weeks, he had walked around literally in a daze, but finally he realized he had to act, to do what she said.

Then he saw her, gliding over the sand dunes, sea oats waving about her, and the sunshine bouncing off her long, pale hair. He could hear the swish of her soft, yellow dress, and he braced himself for the encounter.

As she approached, a cluster of gulls rose screaming before her. And then she was standing before him, as lovely as ever. She bent over and pulled off her sandals. Awkwardly they sat down on the sand. Side by side, they stared at the endless waves lapping at the pebbled shore. They sat quietly, anxiously, all previous intimacy gone. The unborn child, though invisible, was clearly a wall between them.

He tried to think of what to say, but couldn't and instead watched her rub her bare feet in the sand.

She was just as uneasy and sat there watching the water come and go.

"I guess I was foolish," he finally stammered. "But I never thought…I never would have…."

"Me neither," she half whispered.

The gulls returned, wheeling overhead and crying raucously.

"I'm so sorry." His words sounded flat and empty even to himself, but she turned to him, realizing for the first time what a good person he really was.

"I just don't know what to think," he was saying. "I don't know what to do…what we *can* do."

She ducked her head.

"Your parents know?"

"Certainly not…at least not yet." She looked up. "…but I will have to tell them at some point, of course."

"Of course."

"Greyson…."

"Yes."

She looked into his eyes, and he caught a steely glint in them, something he had never seen before, and it frightened him.

"I've been thinking about it for weeks, day and night actually…and…."

He waited for her to finish, knowing instinctively that it wouldn't be what he wanted to hear.

"Hayden must never know…I can't imagine what he would do…and I'm afraid that somehow I could lose Cory…I can't let that happen!"

He was silent.

"You do understand…."

He nodded slowly.

"…and this baby…I don't actually feel like it's a baby yet." She jumped up, twirling in the sand, her yellow dress whirling about her. "See, I don't even look pregnant!"

He watched her as if he were watching a movie, objectively, in some way oddly removed, set apart from it all, but then he couldn't be. He was the villain, a scoundrel if ever there was one.

She stopped twirling. "But I am, of course." She flopped back down beside him. "There are ways, you know…."

He sat up straight.

"But I could never do that. I could never take a life! So I have decided that I will give it up."

"What?"

"Just what I said, I'll give the baby up…you must know I have to."

"But…to whom?"

"I don't know…not yet anyway. That's why I wrote you…I thought maybe…maybe you might know of some place up your way, some home for…you know what I mean. And it might be better that the place is far away from here. My folks will help me…I'm sure…when I tell them. They will find a way. The last thing they would want is for everyone to know about it!"

The world seemed to be closing in on Greyson. He stood up.

"Well?"

He stared at her.

"What do you think?"

"I…I don't know…it's just such a shock…I can't seem to think at all right now."

She turned back to the water's edge where sandpipers darted back and forth, following the waves as they washed in and out, probing for the minuscule crabs.

"Well, you have to, Greyson. I don't have that much time."

The first winter snow fell early in November, dusting the mountains and valleys below, and then it thickened, becoming a blanket of unspoiled white. Normally it would have melted by now, but the temperature had dropped suddenly, freezing it hard, and the white had turned a dirty, crusty brown on the roads. Greyson knew the Skyline Drive would be closed, so he took the long way around to his folks. He needed to check on them, make sure they had enough food and plenty of wood, but that wasn't all. His stomach was churning. He had skipped lunch, and that didn't help any. He figured his mother would have something good cooked up. One of his fondest memories was the sweet-smelling aromas that spilled out of her kitchen when he was a kid, and that tantalizing fragrance of yeast rising. He could never get enough of her biscuits, especially those hoecakes. He tried to savor the memory, to bask in its pleasure, but unwillingly his thoughts returned to Lorna and his dilemma.

Knock…knock…knock!

"Doggone it."

Another link had broken loose on the old set of chains. He would have to get out in the ice and cold and fix it when he got to his folks. He couldn't stand that repetitious pounding, and it would sure as shootin' bang a hole clean through if he didn't do something. He needed to invest in a new set anyway, another thing to add to his growing list, he thought irritably as he approached his folks.

The truck ground up the drive, and he noticed how lifeless the little house looked in the clutch of winter, cold and wet, stuck up in the frozen recesses of the skeletal trees. It had never been a pretty house, but now it actually looked grim. When he first saw it as a boy, however, he was pleased as punch. But it was novel then with the smell of spanking new wood, and it was built just for them. He had felt rather important for a while, like he was somebody. That is before he began to miss the old place, and that didn't take long. The new house came with only a trivial piece of land, nothing like the wide-open meadows and ridges and hollows of the mountains, and he quickly realized that he had been cheated. He pouted off and on for days, maybe weeks, he didn't rightly remember, but no one paid him any mind. They were preoccupied themselves, immersed in their own worlds, each trying to adjust to the new life forced upon them.

His ma seemed to bend with the changes first, busying herself with the house, but Pa was totally at a loss. He remembered him pacing inside and out, getting on everyone's nerves more often than not. He would start one thing and then forget what he was doing, and they would find him sitting out by the woodpile or down by the big oak tree. He would be staring off in the distance, and they would leave him that way. What else could they do?

William was next. He adapted rather easily, and it wasn't long before he seemed to actually be enjoying it, too, and that was not surprising. The close proximity to town and other young folks was certainly in keeping with his age, not to mention his spirit. He had always been the most willful and contrary of the lot. And much to his parents despair, he had taken a liking to whiskey, more than a liking actually. And he was able to fulfill those desires more easily once they moved, although it had never been difficult on the mountain, with all the corn liquor available. In fact, he had helped out with old man Diggers' still until Pa had found out and threatened him in no uncertain terms. Though moonshining was a fairly acceptable practice for the most part in the Blue Ridge, his pa didn't hold to it one iota. He had seen what it could do. Both his older brothers had succumbed to its power, stumbling in drunk night after night, scrapping with one another and chasing his poor ma to an early grave. And he certainly wasn't going to tolerate it in his house.

But once they moved, William could scoot into town and meet up with other like-minded young fellows, though it was still a good hike, several miles actually. He took Jack along occasionally, disappearing once their chores were done. Mildred fretted, suspecting what they were up to, and would always alert Ma. And this became more a worry for both her and Pa. At least on the mountain, Pa had understood the moonshiners and knew who ran which still, and he had them all sized up pretty well, not just for the quality of the corn liquor or apple brandy, but also for its sanitation, but once in the Valley, he felt totally lost.

Greyson climbed out of the truck, pushing the past from his mind, and gazed at the frosty mountains rising up behind the place, hazy and gray with ice. They were awesome, encased in winter's grip. The mountains always wore each and every season with the elegance of royalty, he thought as he stooped down under the truck to survey the damage. He struggled with the broken link as the biting cold seeped into his bones. Then stretching out on his back on the cold ground, he tugged and tugged on the chain and glanced up at the spiral of gray smoke from his pa's chimney. It was rising up a bit, then curling back downward—more was coming, that's for sure, either snow or freezing rain. He wondered again if Lorna had told her folks yet.

"That boy's gonna catch his death, Pa. Look at him out there lying on that cold, wet ground. What's he doing?"

Pa peered out the window. "Must be a broken chain."

"Why can't he just let the old chain be…fix her when it warms up?" She hustled back into the kitchen, shaking her head.

"You don't understand, Ma. He can't let that thing knock a hole plumb through his fender!"

"Better that than he have one of…one of his…."

"Ma!"

Greyson bounded through the door, bringing with him the winter's chill. "Got something I can wipe my hands on?"

"I reckon so." She grabbed a dishtowel. "Didn't know you were coming today."

"Get her fixed, son?" Pa asked.

"Nope. Had to come in to get warm."

"Well'sa, you can fix it once't you eat. You gonna stay for dinner?"

"Wouldn't miss it for the world." He wrenched out of his damp, wool coat. "By the way, what would I be missing?"

"Your ma's fixed up some of that ham your Uncle Sims brought up here the other day."

"Sounds good."

"That ain't all," Ma added. "Got some sweet potatoes baking yonder in the oven, almost ready."

"Thought that's what I smelled."

"And some more of them string beans I put up. You know how you love my string beans."

They sat down at the small square table covered with a bright cloth—one that Mrs. Ralston had stitched together herself, boasting yellow tulips and rows of purple hyacinths—it was protected with a piece of clear plastic. They bowed their heads, and Mr. Ralston asked grace. Then he looked up with his beady gray eyes that had a way of boring straight through you and finding out your inner thoughts before you were ready to reveal them. He smiled at Greyson. "Makes a body feel good to sit down to the table with his offspring. Yep, makes a body feel real good."

Greyson swallowed hard and picked up his fork.

They ate quietly, and then Mrs. Ralston pushed up from the table, accidentally pulling the clear plastic with her.

"Watch out, Ma!" Mr. Ralston bellowed out.

She slid it back just in the nick of time. "How about some lemon pie, son?" It sat warming on the woodstove, and she reached over for it. Greyson stared at the stained potholder she gripped, one of those colorful, handmade ones, not completely square by any means. Memories were rising and pushing for attention, he and Rayna Rose learning how to make them...and his ma patiently teaching them. He sat up abruptly.

"Ma...Pa...I came up here to talk to y'all about something...something very important."

His parents stared at him, catching the grave tone of his voice.

"Of course, I wanted to check on you, too, but there's something I need to tell you. I wish you'd sit down, Ma...if you don't mind."

She slid the lemon pie to the center of the table and eased back onto her chair. What in the world? Was his sickness worse? She certainly hoped not. He hadn't had a spell for some time now, at least that's what he said. Maybe he hadn't been telling the truth!

Greyson pushed his chair back, scraping it on the worn linoleum, and his parents waited. "It's about...well...when I went to Virginia Beach...I met someone...."

Ma clapped her hands. "I knew it...I knew it...didn't I tell you, Pa? Our boy's done gone and got himself a lady friend...."

"Ma, let the boy talk!"

He cleared his throat. "Well...that's partly right, Ma...."

She sneered at Pa.

"But that's not all."

They both leaned forward.

"I know this will come as a shock to you…I know you will have a hard time understanding it…understanding any of it for that matter, and I won't blame you either…."

"Son, how long you gonna go 'round the mulberry bush before you get it out?"

"Just let me finish, Pa…will you?"

The old man settled back and reached for his pipe. He pulled out his tobacco pouch and began packing it. He didn't understand young folks nowadays. They made a mountain out of a mole hill most of the time. His back had commenced to aching again, and he wished he could go sit by the fire and warm it. That always seemed to help a bit.

"Ma, I know you and Pa raised us all up…teaching us right from wrong," he continued, "and you did a good job of it, too, but sometimes things have a way of…well, sort of getting all turned around and mixed up like…."

Ma was frowning. She didn't like the sound of this. What could her boy have done? He'd always been such a good boy!

"Well, you ain't robbed a bank or nothing, have you?" Pa blurted out, rapping his pipe impatiently on the table.

Greyson sighed.

"Don't pay him no mind, son. You tell us what's happened."

He twisted in the cane chair. This was harder than he'd expected. The right words just wouldn't come, and he realized that there weren't any right words.

"Is it about this lady friend, son?" Ma asked, patting him on the hand.

"She's pregnant!"

She jerked back like he'd slapped her.

Silence followed—an awful tangible silence.

His pa stood up, laying his pipe aside. "And is this baby your'n?"

All he could do was nod his head.

Pa walked over to the window and stared up into the cloudy gray sky. "Well'sa, it ain't the best news in the world, that's for sure, but worse things done happened. Fact is, I never told it, but it happened to Uncle Frank. Nobody knows it but your ma and me. Was kept all hushed-up like, but once't they up and married, that was the end of it. You gonna marry her, of course?"

The look on Greyson's face was pure agony.

"Well, you are, ain't you?" his pa whirled around.

"I can't, Pa...."

"Who ever heard such fool stuff...why not?"

"...because...because she's already married."

Ma's hand flew to her mouth, and she stood up uncertainly, grabbing hold of the table.

"You all right, Ma?"

"Yes, son...yes...I think so anyway." And she sank back heavily onto the chair. His pa still stood by the window, his face ashen, unmoving, a picture snapped in time, and she figured she'd better take over. "Now, tell us the story, son. Tell us the whole story." She leaned toward him earnestly.

The day was fading into dusk when the story was finally finished, and the three of them sat somberly at the table, resolutely in fact. They sat there as shadows fell over the house. They sat there listening to the moan of the wind that had begun to embrace them, and to the faint bay of a hound howling off in the distance, and they sat there as twilight settled over the mountains, ushering in the night.

Then Greyson rose to leave.

"Son?"

He stared hopelessly at his mother.

"You know we'll help you any way we can."

"I know, Ma."

The door closed behind him, and they heard the truck start up. They listened to the broken chain knocking as he drove off.

"Didn't get it fixed," Pa said wearily.

"I don't reckon so. I wonder what in the world Mildred will have to say about all this."

"Don't matter none…a body can't give up his own flesh and blood!"

CHAPTER FIVE

There was panic in the Sandbridge household, and not because of Cory cutting more teeth, though he had been awfully fussy for days on end. His grandma rocked him back and forth, the chair beating a hard rhythm on the wooden floor, but her angry look was locked on Lorna, who shrank before her with downcast eyes.

Her father sat solemnly on the couch beside her. "Well, I don't think going on and on about it is gonna make it any better," he concluded. They had been sitting there for over an hour, held captive by the shocking predicament, not knowing what to think, much less what to do. They had voiced their dismay, their disappointment, and their confusion. They had blamed, cried, and accused and then shut up, only to start all over again but still had no answers.

"Well, somebody's gotta do something!" Mrs. Morgan pushed the rocker even harder, her heavy shoes banging the floor with each plunge.

"I don't see any other way but to do what Lorna says. We certainly can't keep it…and have Hayden show up from the war and find…he's got a new baby waiting at home!"

"Lorna, I just don't know how in the world you could've been so…."

"Now, Estelle, it's not doing anybody any good to keep harping on what she did wrong. She knows that better than anybody. We just have to figure out a way to make things right…somehow…someway."

Lorna gratefully lifted her tear-stained eyes. Her father seemed to have aged years since she broke the news. He looked at her desperately. "You suppose he…this Ralston fellow…might come up with a place? One of those adoption places?"

"He's looking into it, and he's going to get in touch with me as soon as he has some news."

"Hah!" her mother blurted out sarcastically. "You'll never hear from him!"

Lorna smarted. "Yes, I will, Mother. He's not that kind."

"*Not that kind!*" The rocking chair halted, and Cory commenced to crying again.

"Now, Estelle!" her dad pleaded, running his hand through his thinning hair, and looking anxiously from one to the other.

"What do you expect me to say?" her mother fired back, the rocking chair flying again. "You expect me to understand this…this outrageous mess she's put us all in? Well, I can't!"

Lorna began to sob softly.

"I can't understand how you could do this to us, Lorna! How could you?"

Her father stood up and reached for Cory. "Give him to me, Estelle. No use in upsetting the child, too. I'm going outside to see about the hens." He carried him through the kitchen and wearily pulled open the back door. Cory's crying ceased to a gentle whimper as the door closed behind them.

Her mother shook her head. "How can he be thinking about hens at a time like this?" But Lorna knew better; he just needed to get quiet, the way he always did when he was troubled, and he was more than troubled now.

That winter would stick in Lorna's head as the winter out of Hell itself. It was trying for them all, but for her it was pure torment. As her belly grew, so did her mother's rage, and so did her own guilt. It reached deep into her soul, bitter and painful. And when she first felt that tiny flutter within, she thought it was just too much to bear and cried herself to sleep that night and many nights thereafter. But all this she kept to herself for she knew it was her burden alone. She expected no pity, and she knew she deserved none.

When it was no longer possible to conceal the secret, she was shipped off to Norfolk—like her dad's catch of fish, she thought sarcastically. Her hiding place was a boxy stucco building with just two floors, but that was all that was needed. There were only four staying at the time. Two underage girls and another about her age, but she avoided them like the plague. She didn't want to talk. She wanted to be alone, and the days dragged by like syrup from an ice box. Besides, it was too risky to talk. She needed to maintain her privacy and her secret, but some days she would have given anything for a friend to confide in, to pour out her heart to. But though she didn't talk, she heard enough to know the other girls' predicaments. Two of them were giving their babies up for adoption, but one would be keeping hers under a cock-and-bull story. She was only sixteen, the family was moving, and it would be disclosed as her baby sister or brother. Her mother would be known as the child's mother. She felt sorry for them all, just like herself, but she was relieved that Greyson was at least handling her situation. She knew she could trust him.

The worst part was being separated from Cory. It was all she could do to tear herself away from him when her folks visited, which was only on the weekends, and his crying for her was pure anguish. But she had come to terms with it, and steeled herself to be strong, to get through it. Thanksgiving and Christmas were the hardest, only shells of the former gleeful activity. Her folks brought Cory on Christmas day, but just for a short while. A winter storm was brewing, and they were anxious to get back home. She watched him leave, toddling clumsily down the hallway, her dad holding onto his pudgy little hand, and the ready tears stung her eyes. She had missed his first step.

The New Year brought hope that it would soon all be over, but with it was a foreboding, a sense that it was only the beginning. Her folks always brought Hayden's letters, which were infrequent, but that was okay because she struggled to answer them anyway, to sound happy and lighthearted when her heart was breaking. Her letters were brief so that she wouldn't have to lie so much.

When the snows fell in February, deep and heavy, she heaved her own heavy self up off the twin bed and sighed. She was thankful to have a private room, but it only added to the bizarre life she was living—a dream, a far-away dream that couldn't possibly be true—a wretched nightmare.

Finally the March winds blew. They blew fiercely up the Atlantic coastline, whipping up foamy white suds and slapping them onto the beaches in a riotous fashion. The bubbly suds rolled across the hard, wet sand like tumbleweeds on a prairie, but the sun shone. It shone bright and lusty. Lorna was glad the snow had melted. It would make it easier to get down the long hospital steps, and she couldn't wait to get out, and away from its smell of antiseptics and strange medicinal odors. She wished she could be out there now with her hair blowing in the wind, and her lungs filling up with the moist, salty air. She had always loved the break of winter and imminent promise of spring.

She gazed out the long window and waited, glad to finally be alone. Her folks had just left. Her father had wanted to stay, but she insisted otherwise. It was something she must do alone. The Norfolk hospital was big and efficient, but she detested it and stared impatiently out the curtained window. She could easily see the parking lot below and wished he would hurry up. The small bundle lay on the bed, but she purposely avoided looking at it. She couldn't! She glanced back out the window.

Certainly there could be no problem, though she knew Virginia had become strangely quiet because of the new rationing. All along the eastern seaboard, from New England to Florida, pleasure driving had ceased, and if caught, the gasoline ration books would be confiscated from the drivers. Well, she need not worry—this certainly wasn't pleasure driving!

There he was.

She watched his pickup wind around the parking lot and cautiously back into an empty space. It was an old truck—certainly not as nice as Hayden's sedan. He got out and slammed the door shut, then stood staring up at the building. She stepped back. She didn't know why, but she didn't want him seeing her waiting.

The discharge papers were completed faster than expected, and they left the hospital. With a strange look on her face, Lorna carried the small bundle while he held tightly onto a bulky diaper bag as if it were his lifeline. He watched her as they descended the steps and headed for the truck. Her face was impenetrable, hard to read. Was it masked or was she really that heartless? He opened the door and helped her in. Once in, he noticed that she held the bundle tightly against her but wouldn't look at it. He walked around and climbed in the other side, placing the diaper bag on the floor between them, and wondered what all was in it. She didn't say, but instead waited for him to pull out, to carry out her instructions, and he maneuvered slowly out of the parking lot.

"Turn left," she directed automatically.

It had all been schemed out, and her parents were waiting for her at the disclosed spot. But her dad's obvious sadness bore down hard upon her, for he had always loved children, and when it turned out to be a girl he had unashamedly broken down in tears.

They wove through the sprawling urban city, silent at first until she began to recite a litany of instructions that he struggled to remember, most of it pertaining to the mysterious diaper bag. Soon they left the city and drove out into a rural area, finally ending up in a deserted spot that backed up against a body of still water, covered with a slimy, green film. He shut off the engine and looked at her, but she was staring straight ahead, expressionless. He climbed out, walked around, and opened her door. Without making eye contact, she slid out of the truck and handed him the bundle just as a black sedan eased up from the other side. He could see two people in it, her folks he assumed, but they did not get out. She had orchestrated it very well.

Strong winds whipped the pink blanket, and he pulled it tightly about the infant as Lorna walked away. Just before she reached the sedan, she stopped and turned as if she had second thoughts, but only momentarily. She glanced back one last time, and then ducked into the car.

Driving away from the coast, Greyson fought an avalanche of conflicting feelings and confusing thoughts. He tried to focus on the highway, glancing down every now and then to the seat beside him. Thick, dark hair escaped the pink folds of the blanket. She didn't resemble Lorna at all. She didn't even resemble him.

It was *Rayna Rose!*

As if things weren't already complicated enough! Tears flooded his eyes, blurring his vision. Just when he thought he had finally been able to put it all behind him, and forget the past that had haunted him since childhood, now this!

Tightening his grip on the steering wheel, he struggled to get control of himself. Surely he was experiencing some kind of panic attack or probably delayed exhaustion from everything. Needless to say, it was surreal. How could he be driving down this highway, leaving the coast behind, with a baby beside him? A newborn! Suddenly he heard a soft sucking sound, and the reality of the situation hit home. What was he going to do?

Well, first things first. He had to get home, back to the Shenandoah. He glanced down again. She would never know about the coast, the sprawling Tidewater area and the vast ocean. She would grow up in the mountains, just like he and his sister did.

He swiped his tears. "That's who you are...*little Rayna.*"

How could she be anything else? The infant stirred in her sleep, and he held his breath. Suppose she awoke and began crying. But she didn't, and his mind strayed back over the years, back to his twin sister as the highway swept homeward.

Her memory was never far from him and was every bit a part of the Blue Ridge, just as the steep ridges and deep hollows where they once played. At times it was as if they were still playing in those dense forests and on its wooded slopes. Though they were twins, they could not have been more different, he with his sandy hair and she with a head full of dark ringlets, inherited from the Ralston side. He had been wiry and delicate, but Rayna Rose was strong, not just in body but spirit, too. Tenacious, some said, tough as steel, Pa used to brag. But she was also impulsive, getting them into trouble more often than not. He was the cautious one, always guarded, even back then, but William called it something else.

"You're gonna be a sissy!" he chided him every chance he got.

"No, I'm not!" he would bawl, and his ma always came to his rescue. He could hear her now. "Leave him be, William," she would scold. But how he hated that word sissy!

Suddenly he realized that cars were passing him, more and more whizzing by, and he sped up. He must keep his mind on his driving, on the present, but it kept vacillating between the past and the future, the unknown future. Out of the blue a siren wailed, and he grabbed hold of the steering wheel with both hands. Tensely he glanced up into the rearview mirror and saw the flashing red light and the police car behind him. But it zoomed on past and up the highway, and he breathed a sigh of relief, realizing that he had actually felt guilty as if he were stealing the baby! Shaking his head, he chastised himself. You idiot, she's your baby! You have a right to take her away, to take her home. Nobody else wants her!

It was at that moment that the bond was sealed.

He relaxed and drove on for over an hour, and the winds increased, buffeting the pickup, and then the baby began to cry, a thin, frail cry at first. But it strengthened, growing louder with each outburst, and anxiously he looked for a place to pull over. Why was she crying? He spotted a church up ahead and pulled off the highway and into its vacant parking lot. It was a small, clapboard church, and he checked around for anyone in sight, thankful to find it empty. She was squalling now, and he was totally flustered, wondering what to do next. Suddenly he smelled it. Just what he had been dreading!

He slipped off the pink blanket and stared down at the tiny infant, so fragile, but her little arms were flailing fiercely, her eyes were wet and clinched tight and her face was crimson red from screaming. Timidly he eased her around so that he could better take off the soiled diaper. He wished his hands were smaller; they felt like the jolly green giant's. He wished she would stop crying. It made him terribly nervous, but awkwardly he removed the stinking diaper and dropped it to the floorboard. He began heaving. This was ridiculous! She was just a baby, for goodness sake, but the rank odor was almost causing him to vomit, and he struggled to get control of himself. Her screaming escalated as his trembling hands tried to gently wipe her little behind. He never knew babies came so small, and he felt awfully clumsy. He grabbed a clean diaper out of the bag and stretched it out on the seat. He folded it this way and that way, but no matter how he tried, it ended up looking like it would swallow her. Finally he gave up and slid it beneath her and grabbed one of the safety pins. He held it up. It looked enormous and frightfully dangerous. Terrified that he would stick her, he slowly and gently pinned it on. She stopped crying. He held his breath, and then relaxed a bit and assessed his work. It was so big and droopy that he knew if he lifted her up, it would fall right off, so he didn't.

Instead he tenderly smoothed her fine dark hair, but then she cried out again. Now what?

She must be hungry, he thought, and he reached into the diaper bag again, pulling out one of the ready-made bottles. He eased her closer to him, gently inserting the large nipple into her mouth. Immediately the crying ceased, and she sucked greedily. He sat there watching her with a growing sense of contentment slowly stealing over him, and if there had been any doubt before, it was gone now.

Lorna had told him to burp her after she ate. "Lay her over your shoulder or over your lap," she'd reminded him in the truck. He dreaded that part as he stared up at the white steeple piercing the dark-blue sky. What would the preacher think if he were to drive up? But nobody came, and as the winds thrashed the truck, he watched her drain the bottle. And then she closed her eyes.

"No, no…you musn't do that…you have to burp!"

He rolled her over his leg and began gently patting her back. He patted and patted, and wondered what would people say when he arrived back home with her? What would his brothers say? *His sister?*

He knew his folks would help in any way they could, but was it fair to them? They were getting on and worn out from their own burdens through the years, but he would need help, that's for sure. He had to work, now more than ever, and it was already decided that he would move back home. A loud burp suddenly exploded, and unexpectedly he jumped and then laughed at himself. Maybe it wasn't so hard after all.

Pulling back onto the highway, he hoped he would have enough milk to last until he reached home. There were two cans of evaporated milk and syrup in the bag with instructions of what to do, what to mix and how much, but he knew that would be a major undertaking and certainly hoped to be home before then. The foul odor of the dirty diaper lying on the floorboard began to saturate the truck. He must find a filling station and get rid of it soon, and he needed to fill up anyway. He glanced down. Obviously it wasn't bothering her any. She slept on peacefully as he drove past field after field, shadowed in the evening's declining sun. Houses appeared every now and then, spaced off to themselves, their warm yellow lights already shining out into the gathering dusk, and he wondered about the families inside, most likely sitting down for supper or perhaps preparing for tomorrow, happy families probably. And he wished he was able to change the past as he'd just changed her diaper, and he would never have gone to the coast! He certainly wouldn't have gone fishing that day. If only he had known. The baby stirred, and a pang of guilt washed over him.

The sky darkened. Stormy clouds were forming up ahead, rolling in, black and ominous, and he felt his chest tighten. He tried to push the familiar feeling aside before it took over. Remember, I'm in control! That's what the positive thinking book said, he reminded himself.

"I'm in control," he repeated over and over. "It's just a storm, after all."

But the clouds began to swirl and snake downward, listing over the highway, and he knew he was losing ground. A few raindrops started to fall, spattering the dusty windshield, then more and more until his wipers raced to compete with them. The winds increased rapidly and thunder roared, and the memories of his childhood chased him on. He tried to outrun them, but he knew it was inevitable.

Haunting Memories....

He was just a mountain boy, totally unaware that he was positioned to live through what would become one of the most notable periods in America's history—an era that would be studied and analyzed for decades to come. It would be poked and pried, rationalized and questioned by scholars and financial experts and politicians even into the next century.

Before the famed Great Depression, however, most of Greyson's memory was swathed in a hazy sort of film, one obscure event merging languidly into another through silky strands of vapor. The sharp, distinct images of recollection only emerged and actually crystallized in the summer before the crash. It was one of the last pleasant memories he had before things began to change.

He remembered even the fine details and how the summer shadows had lengthened, and the mountain ridges buzzed with excitement. Folks were all worked up over something called Hoover Day that was about to happen. It was to be held over in Madison, and everybody was talking about it, everybody, that is, except his pa.

Apparently the local chamber of commerce decided it would be a good idea to have a big bash and invite the President of the United States and the First Lady. Who ever heard of such a thing? But they wanted to show their appreciation for all that the president had done for them, like building the new school for the less fortunate, those who had no way of getting to a school because of where they lived so far back up in the mountains. It was because of such benevolent acts that many in the Shenandoah highly favored the president and his first lady.

Not only for their generosity, but the president had selected a place up on the Rapidan for his summer camp. Now that was something! Out of all the places he could have chosen anywhere in the vast United States, he had decided to build their summer home here in the Blue Ridge, and they were mighty proud of this. The news was out. It was the constant talk of the mountain folk, and the press was having a heyday with it, being just the sort of news they could sink their teeth into. Not only the mountain folk and the press, but it was becoming the talk of Virginia and spreading out across the nation. Imagine the President of the United States partying with a bunch of mountain folks!

"We going, Pa?" Greyson asked.

"Son, I wouldn't be caught dead at that highfalutin shindig!"

"Why, Pa?"

"'Cause I said so."

"But why, Pa? I wanna go."

"Ain't no place for me or you neither. You might as well get that notion out of your head!"

"Pa...."

"Ever since the president bought that place on the old Rapidan, we've had no peace at all. City folk, gov'ment folk and soldiers running all over the place."

William rallied to his kid brother's defense, "Aw, Pa, it's gonna be a nice time, they say."

"And what about them hogs?" Pa was riled up now, feeling like the whole family had gone nuts. "Whoever heard of bringing in truckloads of hogs just because of a few snakes?"

"Not just a few, Pa," William retorted. "When they started blasting those mountains, rattlesnakes came out in droves. I saw them myself."

"Well, no hogs are gonna get rid of them!"

"Can we go, Pa…can we go?" Greyson whined.

Pa just shook his head and walked off.

"They gonna have a picnic, too, Pa…lots of good food…Leonard said they will, and everybody's going…even Leonard." He trailed after his pa. It would be a terrible mistake if Greyson's friend got to go and he didn't. It would just give his friend one more thing to lord over him, and that he didn't need.

"Aw, you can go with me," William said.

Pa whipped around. "Who said you're going?"

"Won't be no harm, Pa. I'd like to see the president and the first lady, too. They say she's a mighty fine lady. Fact is, I've already seen her." He smiled smugly.

Ma's head jerked up. "William, boy, what're you talking about?"

"I did…I saw her riding way up on the ridge just last week—liked to knocked me over when I saw her there, looked like she was studying the trees."

"William, you're crazy!" Mildred spat out. "You know the president's wife wouldn't be out here riding in these mountains."

"It was her, looked just like her picture in the paper. Besides, nobody round here dresses like that!"

"Like what?" Ma and Mildred asked simultaneously.

"All fancy-like, must have cost a mint."

"The boy's most likely right, Ma," Pa stated, having calmed down a bit. "I hear tell she does a right smart riding in these here mountains, got a hankering for wildflowers and such. Don't make much sense to me, but that's what folks say."

"How come you didn't tell us you saw her?" Mildred challenged, still not convinced. "You never said a word."

"I forgot." He couldn't let on that he wasn't alone, that he had met the Shillings girl up there, and they had gotten some corn liquor from old Diggers and were having themselves a little party. But they were afraid that the first lady might have seen them. He blushed at the thought.

"Can I go, Pa…can I go with William?" Greyson persisted.

He glanced around at his oldest son, wondering if he could trust him to go off to such a shindig, and especially taking the child with him. "I don't know. Ask your ma, boy."

He grabbed hold of her apron. "Please, Ma…please?"

"Now, son…suppose you…well…you might have…."

"Aw, let him go, Ma," William snapped. "I'll take care of him."

"What about me?" Rayna Rose asked, coming back in from feeding the chickens and catching the tail end of the conversation.

"Absolutely not!" Pa retorted.

Hoover Day arrived on the seventeenth of August, with automobiles chugging onto the fairgrounds as early as eight o'clock in the morning, and they kept coming for over two hours. The crowd mushroomed, and families dragged out large picnic baskets, enough for themselves and more to spare. Some came from quite a ways and had been traveling for days, hoping to see the president and be a part of the gala event. Brunswick stew steamed in big, old wash pots, surrounded by thousands of tin cups and hundreds of loaves of bread, and people pressed in against one another for the best spots. It was going to be a day like none other!

William and Greyson pushed through the surging crowd close to ten o'clock. They had caught a ride with William's friend, Douglas, up in the hollow, but Douglas took off with his lady friend as soon as they got there.

"I knew we'd be late," Greyson complained, staring hard at the throngs of people. "We'll never see the president now!"

"Aw, quit fretting. See that big platform up there? You'll be able to see just like anybody else."

Greyson looked at the raised platform and the crowd clustered around it. He had never seen so many people in all his life and dressed in the spiffiest clothes, jackets, and ties and hats. The ladies mostly had on wide-brimmed hats, even some of the young girls. Everyone seemed in a jovial mood, and he began to relax. "I bet Jack's gonna be sorry he didn't come."

"Jack's mad at the president."

"Why?"

"He's mad at everybody, I think."

"Why?"

William shifted his sack from one arm to the other. "'Cause of the move."

"But you said we probably won't have to move."

He shrugged. "Who knows?"

"Aw, William, you done lied."

He poked him in the ribs. "Don't call me a liar, boy. Nobody knows what's gonna happen yet."

Greyson rubbed his side, growing angrier by the moment, and he had smelled liquor on his breath, too. He saw him and Douglas take a swig of it before they got here. They thought he wasn't looking, but he saw them. Maybe he ought to tell Ma when he got home, but then she would never let him go anywhere with him again, so he brushed it aside and hurried after. "You gonna give them the squirrels?"

William nodded and headed toward several ladies who were busy with preparations. He turned over the two squirrels, and they ambled off.

"You see all them big wash pots with squirrel stew?" Greyson asked.

"Not squirrel stew, knucklehead...Brunswick stew."

"Smells like squirrel stew to me." He looked up at William, who was smiling the silliest smile he'd ever seen. He followed his eyes to a fancy-looking young lady standing a few yards away, and she was smiling back.

"Why's she got an umbrella? Don't look like rain to me."

"Who?" William frowned down at him.

"That girl you're looking at."

"Who said I was looking at anybody...and that's a parasol...not an umbrella."

"Oh."

"What're you watching me for anyhow?"

"I ain't watching you...and it looks like an umbrella to me."

"Shows how much you know. Thought you'd know things with all that reading you and Rayna Rose been doing."

"Why couldn't Rayna Rose come too?"

"Because she's a girl."

Greyson wondered again why boys and girls were so different, or why they were treated so. All of a sudden he noticed a strange looking object hovering just above the treetops. "Look at that!"

William glanced up. "Well, I'll be!" They watched it slowly circle over the grounds while the crowd pointed, laughed, and clapped in astonishment.

"What is it?"

"A blimp!" William answered.

"An Army blimp," the gentleman next to them added.

"The president?" Greyson asked.

"The governor!"

"Who?" William could hardly hear midst all the clamor and excitement.

"Governor Harry F. Byrd," the man practically hollered.

Greyson was disappointed. He'd come to see the president, not any governor. The blimp descended gracefully and landed on the hillside behind the exhibition building while music played loudly from the bandstands.

"The Richmond Light Infantry Blues and the Monticello Guard!" their informer announced proudly. "That's why we're here." William was glad to be standing by someone who knew everything or at least thought he did. He figured the ones dressed in the colonial uniforms must be the Monticello Guard, but decided not to show his ignorance.

"We're from Richmond."

William nodded.

"Where're you from?"

"Not far from here."

Greyson wondered what Richmond was like. It must be an important place, he concluded. After the governor and his party had disembarked, the large blimp slowly rose and began to circle the grounds again, each time making a wider circle. Greyson watched until his neck hurt.

"Come on." William pulled him off from the crowd.

"Where we going?"

"Nowhere...just moving around some, that's all." But Greyson saw that he still had his eyes on the umbrella, or parasol, or whatever it was. He could see it bobbing up ahead of the crowd. William could really be boring sometimes, he decided, and wished again that Rayna Rose had come. They shuffled in and out of the packed crowd, with William nodding and speaking briefly with others while Greyson was bumped and jostled and feeling hungrier by the minute. He could actually hear his stomach growling midst all the racket and commotion, and he remembered that squirrel stew in the big wash pots.

"Can we eat now?"

"Not dinnertime yet...it's not even noon."

"It's almost. Look up there." Greyson stretched his neck backwards and winced at the blazing sun. "It's just about on top."

"Here he comes!"

The shout was taken up by the teeming crowd, and guns began firing, their loud blasts reverberating throughout the morning air.

Greyson grabbed hold of William. "What's that?"

"The president! What do you think?"

"Why do they need to shoot them guns?"

"It's the twenty-one gun salute...they always do that."

He pressed his hands over his ears and ducked his head. He hated the loud blasts, and so many, too! William glanced down and yanked his hands off.

"What'd you do that for?"

"You're acting like a sissy again."

"I am not!"

"There he is!"

"Where?" He perched on his tiptoes, but all he could see was a bunch of men all looking alike.

"Right there in the middle!" William pointed impatiently. "The one with the hat on."

He stared at two men with brown hats and black suits. It must be one of them, he thought, but decided not to ask William again. He was downright snappish today and Greyson figured it must be the corn liquor.

"And that's Mrs. Hoover right there beside him. I'd recognize her anywhere." A lady with a big black hat and a flowery black and gray crepe dress stood there smiling, and Greyson knew then which one was the president.

"Who's the other fellow with the brown hat?"

"The governor...the one who got off the blimp."

"Oh." Greyson nodded as the band loudly struck up "Hail to the Chief," and there was a great ovation. It was definitely a warm and showy welcome. The crowd was determined to demonstrate how grateful they were that the president and his wife were locating the retreat in their mountains. Greyson smiled, feeling all good inside. Now he could tell Rayna Rose that he had seen the president.

Afterwards they stood in line to get their stew, hoping it wouldn't run out before they got there. They were relieved when they saw the steam rising from the wash pot in front of them and smelled its tantalizing aroma.

"Somebody said there're fifty pots of it," a portly man boasted while shoving in front of them. William frowned.

"He broke in line!" Greyson cried.

William shook his head at him, realizing that the man happened to be with a lady already in line.

"It won't run out," the man responded sarcastically. He would prove to be right, but the five thousand tin cups did.

They were all used up well before the stew, and William and Greyson considered themselves doggone lucky to get one.

"What're they gonna do now?"

"Not my problem." William headed over toward the roped-off area, where the notable guests stood, in order to get a better look at the president and the first lady. Dodging lines of people moving in the same direction, he made his way up close, but the crowd thronged them. Still they were able to find an opening.

"Wow!" Greyson exclaimed, coming up behind him. The biggest ham he had ever laid eyes on sat on the president's table. "I bet that pig weighs every bit of fifty pounds!"

"S-h-h-h-h. Stop gawking!"

"What?"

"Stop acting like you're from the mountains or something!"

"But I am from the mountains."

"Well, you don't have to act so backward." William cuffed him on the shoulder, not hard but just enough to hurt his feelings. He fought his tears. He wasn't backward, and he wondered what was wrong with being from the mountains. William must be going through that peculiar stage his ma talked about. He sure wished he'd get over it, and he suddenly wished he had stayed home with Rayna Rose.

"You gonna finish your stew?" William asked, evidently feeling a bit contrite for his actions.

He nodded and lifted his tin cup, draining the last bit and then wiped his mouth on his sleeve. He jerked his head up quickly to see if William had noticed, but he was looking elsewhere.

When it came time for the president's speech, William pulled Greyson in as close as they could get.

"Both Mrs. Hoover and I feel greatly honored by the general reception you have extended us today. It is a welcome as one of your neighbors and it is as a neighbor that I participate with you."

"He's our neighbor?"

"No, knucklehead…s-h-h-h-h."

It was apparent that his address was falling on appreciative ears. The crowd was hushed, listening intently to every word.

"In the early years of our republic, Virginia was the home of presidents, and it would seem appropriate that with the changing years, the president should at least have a weekend camp in Virginia. There are other sound reasons why such a connection should be maintained between the presidents and Virginia.

"The fact is that those strong Virginians who selected the site for our national capital were apparently impervious to heat and humidity or at least they were unaware of how much pavements and modern buildings can contribute to raise the temperature. But Virginia herself now offers the antidote in the wonderful mountains which you have dedicated to a national park and the access to it that you have provided by your newly improved roads."

Did he say park? Greyson looked up at William, but was afraid to ask.

"…I have thought it appropriate to accept the hospitality of your citizens and your mountains for one or two days each week and thereby combine both relief and work without cost to either. And I have discovered that even the work of the government can be improved by leisurely discussions of its problems out under the trees where no bells or callers jar one's thoughts from the channels of urbanity.

"You have demonstrated yourselves good hosts and good neighbors with that fine courtesy for which Virginia is known to the whole nation…"

Greyson smiled. William didn't know everything. They were neighbors!

"...you have proved this sentiment of neighborliness by lending me a part of your park, by improving a road, by securing the fishing rights on a beautiful mountain stream and even providing me with fishing tackle. I, on my side, am glad to lend my services as a good neighbor to you by acting as a sort of signpost to the country of the fine reality of your proposed new national park."

"But..." Greyson's smile froze, then turned to a frown, and he tugged on William's shirt. "But...Pa said the Park will make us leave!"

"S-h-h-h-h," William silenced him, and he flopped down on the grass, wishing again that he had stayed home with Rayna Rose. He didn't think he liked this president anymore.

"In this case it is the excuse for return to the woods and streams with their retouch of the simpler life of the frontier from which every American springs. Moreover, I have learned that fishing has an important implication and even sounder foundation of such an excuse from the presidential point of view. I find that many presidents have joined the ranks of fishermen only after their inauguration as president, although I can claim over 45 years of apprenticeship—that is, in fishing, not in presidency."

William grinned. Anybody who liked to fish couldn't be all bad!

"I have discovered the reason why presidents take to fishing—the silent sport. Apparently the only opportunity for refreshment of one's soul and clarification of one's thoughts by solitude to presidents lies through fishing. As I have said in another place, it is generally realized and accepted that prayer is the most personal of all human relationships. On such occasions as that men and women are entitled to be alone and undisturbed."

Greyson pulled at the blades of grass and wondered if the president might also be a preacher.

"Next to prayer, fishing is the most personal relationship..."

Poking his finger into the soft earth, he slumped over on the grassy field. When would the president finish talking? He wished he was back home playing soldiers or climbing up the apple trees or even making mud pies with Rayna Rose. Anything was better than this!

"Moreover, it is a constant reminder of the democracy of life, of humility and of human frailty—for all men are equal before fishes. And it is desirable that the President of the United States should be periodically reminded of this fundamental fact—that the forces of nature discriminate for no man…"

That night William, keyed up from the exciting day, tried to relate much of the long speech to his folks, but once he mentioned the proposed Park, Pa wouldn't hear anymore and stormed out the door.

"Son, you know better than to bring that up."

"But Ma, we can't just stick our heads in the sand anymore. I didn't used to think it would happen…but after today…and hearing the president and all—"

"Still, it's best not to talk it up around your pa. You know how it riles him."

"Well, it riles me, too, but we've gotta be ready and know what to do when the time comes."

Rayna Rose lifted her head from her reader. "Ready for what?"

Ma shook her head at William, and he clammed up.

"Ready for what, Ma?"

"Don't pay no mind to him. Go on back to your reading, child." But her dark eyes had clouded over with that brooding look again, and she closed the book and climbed up into the loft.

Greyson's memory skipped to the fall and to the hard talk that followed that winter, scary talk actually. He remembered feeling afraid whenever they mentioned people jumping out of skyscraper windows, and men hopping boxcars on trains looking for work, and some actually falling off and under the trains. Sometimes he would have nightmares afterwards.

But mostly folks talked about hungry people standing in long lines to get soup and sadly shook their heads at such a thing. He tried to picture it all. He had always been able to picture things that grownups talked about, like catching big fish or chasing foxes out of the henhouse. He had even pictured the big black bear that William came home bragging about, the one he shot at but missed. He was good at picturing things in his mind, but it was hard for him to picture this new talk for he had never seen a skyscraper or a boxcar, but he could see a long line of people standing and waiting for a bowl of soup. All he had to do was remember William and him standing in that long line waiting for the squirrel stew…or Brunswick stew, whatever it was.

Though he only caught bits and pieces of what was going on in the country, still there was a sense of dread that had settled over the Ralston household. He knew they were having hard times too. That's what his ma said whenever he asked for a penny for a licorice stick. He knew they were having hard times when his pa came in fussing because there was no sale for his bark down in the Valley, and he especially knew it when his shoes got holes in them and no new ones turned up. Instead his ma cut up cardboard and fitted it into them, but the cardboard never stayed in place. He didn't have to walk far before it had worked its way up the sides and was sticking over the top. It was more than worrisome, and he would have to stop whatever he was doing or wherever he was going and take off his shoe to fix it.

But the tragic times that were plaguing the big cities didn't quite have the same effect on the Ralstons and all those hidden away in the aged Blue Ridge Mountains that rose up from Virginia's Shenandoah Valley. They were more fortunate, for they relied on rabbits and squirrels for dinner and corn and potatoes from their steep hillside gardens, something that couldn't be taken away from them, and they certainly didn't have any money in the banks to fret about.

Plus, times had always been hard for them.

They didn't know anything different. And though factories and stores and banks were closing up throughout the land, leaving millions jobless and penniless, the mountain people coped as always, concerned mostly with what the weather held for them, whether or not the snows would let up so they could get out to the chicken house or barn, and when the ice would finally melt. And when spring came, they wondered when the rains would come and nurture the newly sown seed, and on into summer, whether or not the winds would die down so that the corn stalks wouldn't be ripped to pieces. But most of all they were concerned about whether or not the government people would return.

They had been there more than once, with their sharpened pencils and clean tablets and their prying questions. They had been there just last Tuesday, and it was very troubling. They arrived early in the morning, announcing that they had to move off the mountain. Greyson's pa was livid.

"They don't know what they want…first they say move, then they come up here saying we can stay…now they say move again…what's a body supposed to do?"

"Don't go getting so upset, Pa. I don't think they know themselves what they aim to do." William was pulling his twelve-gauge single-barrel shotgun down off the wall. "Be back later, gonna do a little hunting." He slammed the door behind him and headed to the woods. He was confused himself, even after that nice speech that the president had made back in the summer. Things kept changing, and he could understand his pa's frustration. He was aggravated, too. But it wouldn't do any good, he thought, creeping stealthily through the still forest, looking for game. What was gonna happen was gonna happen, and he had a feeling it wouldn't be that much longer.

James Ralston watched his eldest son disappear into the woods and shook his head. "Nobody in this here house seems worried a'tall. Reckon we'll be sitting out on the creek bank before anybody pays any attention! Harris over in the hollow says it's bound to happen now…since they up and passed that gall-durned law!"

"What law, Pa?" Rayna Rose asked, with a noticeable quiver in her voice.

"That blasted Condemnation Law."

Ma frowned at him. "That's been awhile back now, Pa, and we're still here."

"Virginia don't have no right to condemn my land!"

Ma nudged him in the side as she edged around the table. "Gotta get these biscuits rolled out. Be dinnertime before you know it." She hadn't missed Rayna Rose's face drawn up in a dark, pinched fashion. The small child stood quietly in the doorway, taking in every word, and she knew about the government and laws. She had read about them and learned about them in school. People had to abide by laws once they were passed, everybody had to, her teacher said. If they didn't, they could get into big trouble and even be sent to jail!

"You know they gonna send us down off the mountain!" Pa continued, oblivious to them all. "We'll be stuck in some little coop, packed in like a bunch of hens…they don't give a hoot about us!"

Mildred shook her head as Rayna Rose stole out the door, across the roughhewn porch, with its uneven planks, down its two wide steps and past the washtub filled with her ma's wilting foxglove. She headed down the hillside by the springhouse, with its gurgling, cold water. She didn't see Greyson filling up a bucket, and she marched right past him on up the matted path, climbing the hill toward the now spent orchard, her head downcast as she slipped quickly up the worn path. Maybe her pa was wrong, though he did know most things…but not everything Greyson said…not like God or anything.

"Rayna Rose!" Greyson called out, noticing her scoot by. He dropped the bucket with a thud and took off chasing after her. "Rayna Rose!"

But she didn't turn around.

He flew up the path and caught hold of her. "What's wrong with you, silly gal?" he blurted out.

"Don't call me that!" She jerked away.

"Well…what's wrong with you then?"

"Nothing."

"Ain't so. You acting like you'd seen a haint!"

"Not scared of haints."

"You gonna tell me or not?"

"I don't wanna move."

He figured that was the problem. She always acted up whenever the gov'ment men came. But that was stupid, won't nothing they could do about it. He wondered if all girls acted like that, but he knew better. Mildred didn't carry on that way, and neither did the girls at school. What made Rayna Rose so stubborn and hard-headed and crazy-like sometimes? He sure didn't know.

"...and I'm not gonna either!"

"You'll have to if they make us."

Her dark eyes pierced him. "They'll have to catch me first, and none of them city folk can outrun me."

"Ain't none ever tried."

"They better not!" She slowed down, deep in thought as they reached the apple orchard with its stunted, twisted trees, now almost bare. It had been a meager crop this year, but still a few hung on. She reached up for one and bit into the hard, green apple and then plopped down under the tree with an audible sigh. The already fallen leaves, small, crisp and brown, formed a soft cushion beneath her, and Greyson sat down alongside her. A chilled wind was picking up, and he zipped up his jacket. He was just as concerned about moving off the mountain, but he tried not to think about it. That way he didn't worry, and his ma said that most things folks worry about have a way of never happening anyhow. And he didn't believe those gov'ment folk were ever gonna make them move. A loud gunshot reverberated in the distance.

"Reckon William's got something."

"Pa said we'll be sitting out on the creek bank when they move us off the mountain."

"They can't do that!"

"He said we might live in a chicken coop!"

"I don't think it's gonna happen anyhow. I been hearing talk of it since we was little."

"You really don't believe they're gonna make us move?"

"Nope."

She realized he didn't know anymore than she, but still his words were a comfort, and she said, "Wanna make mud pies?"

"Aw shucks, Rayna Rose. I don't wanna make mud pies. We did that yesterday and the day before that. Let's play soldiers."

She scrunched up her dark eyes.

"You never wanna play soldiers," he complained.

"Listen!" Her ear was cocked toward the woods.

"To what?"

"Just listen."

It sounded like someone or something was throwing sticks about. She jumped up and headed into the woods.

"What is it?"

"Sh-h-h-h." She motioned him on, and he followed after, though fearfully. They picked through the prickly underbrush and tangles of withered blackberry bushes, and then they heard a loud drumming.

"Aw, it's just an old peckerwood."

She pressed her finger to her lips as they came to a clearing, and she stood there smiling up at a tall, dead oak. A large woodpecker, the size of a crow, was perched high upon it, busily hammering and casting aside considerable pieces of bark that fell noisily to the hard ground.

"Sh-h-h-h!" She frowned at him. "And it's not a peckerwood, for goodness sake!"

"That's what Pa calls them."

"Well, it's a woodpecker, Greyson Ralston. You've got to learn how to talk right. And it's not just any woodpecker either."

"Well, what is it then?"

"A pileated woodpecker," she whispered. "My favorite."

"Why's it your favorite?"

"Can't you see?"

Greyson wrinkled his forehead and studied the large black and white bird.

"Just look at him. Looks like he has a tuxedo on…a black tuxedo."

"A what?"

She slapped her hands on her hips. "A coat that people wear sometimes…rich people."

How was he to know that?

Annoyed with his ignorance, she admonished, "Greyson, if you would read, you might know as much as I do."

"But I don't like to read."

"That's the problem. Now look at his bright red crest against the black and white. Ain't he pretty?"

"Thought you said we're not supposed to say ain't."

"See…you're learning."

"How do you know it's a he anyway?"

"All the pretty birds are."

The woodpecker flew off, and they headed out of the woods, hand in hand, with Greyson happy once more. No matter what was going on out in the world with the ugly Depression, or even the trouble on the mountain for that matter, when he and Rayna Rose were okay, all seemed right somehow.

Ma slid the pan of biscuits into the hot oven. "Now, Pa, you oughtn't to talk such bothersome stuff in front of the youngsters. You know how they fret about it."

He shook his head. She was a fine woman, but sometimes she did have a worrisome way. Didn't the Good Book say something about a nagging woman being like a continual dropping or something like that—a man had a right to talk in his own house!

The screen door slammed shut behind William, and he smugly held up a stringy rabbit by its long ears without a sign of buckshot.

Ma eyed it proudly. "You go ahead and skin it now, son, and I'll fry it up for supper tonight."

Mildred glanced at it disapprovingly while setting the table. "Looks downright puny if you ask me."

"Well, I didn't ask you, Miss high and mighty."

"Now you two hesh up that squabbling!"

"Where's Jack?" He stood there swinging the dead rabbit. "I shot him…let him skin him."

"Jack's not here. Don't you remember? He's gone over to Mr. Viar's to help him with his woodcutting."

"Where's Greyson then?"

"Sent him to fetch some water awhile back, that boy! Don't know what I'm gonna do with him. Call him when you go out. See what's taking him so long."

Mildred snickered. "If you think Greyson's gonna skin that rabbit, you have another thought coming! Just the sight of skinning makes him upchuck."

"Now, Mildred."

"Well, it does, Ma. You know it, too."

William charged out the door. "He's gotta learn sometime or another."

"Leave the boy alone now, William," Ma hollered after, glancing around at Mildred, who was rolling her eyes at the ceiling. They all thought she took up for him too much.

CHAPTER SIX

As the seasons passed, the troubling times only intensified with the deepening Depression. The unemployed passed four million, and idle men sat around on the sidewalks of big cities like Chicago and New York to small rural towns like Childersburg, Alabama, and Roanoke, Virginia. They sat around hopelessly, and President Hoover became the ready scapegoat. Though he appointed a Commission for Unemployment Relief, it didn't stop the criticism. Even the national cartoonists were having a heyday with their popular *Blame it on Hoover* cartoons, and those in the Valley of the Shenandoah and high up on the crests of the Blue Ridge also began to believe or at least wonder if it was not his fault. People were scared, discouraged and disillusioned, and they needed somebody to blame.

And then the skies dried up, refusing to send forth the needed rains. Days passed, weeks passed, months passed, and still no rain.

The whole country was thirsty, but the western states were hit the hardest as dust filled every crevice and every known area inside and out. It became a virtual dustbowl, the newspapers reported. *For Sale* signs were popping up all over Texas, Oklahoma, and Arkansas, but there were no buyers. There was no money. Livestock died, and beaten-down farmers loaded up their old cars and trucks with their meager belongings and disheartened families and hit the roads for California. Abandoned farms, inundated with dust, stretched out across the plains as these later-called Okies pushed on with a thread of hope and a dream. Hundreds and hundreds of miles they covered, leaving those behind who had to literally scratch out a living, selling eggs for ten cents a dozen—that is if they could find anyone to buy them.

It was a pitiful time in America's history.

Though Easterners didn't contend with the deadly dustbowls, they also watched the skies with wistful yearning and prayed for rain, but the rain didn't come. And though the Depression had not impacted the mountain folk like those in the cities, the drought was a different story. It baked the earth, cracking it all around them, sending squiggly lines running out in all directions, and ever widening by the day. It was one of the most severe droughts on record, scorching the crops and creating famine. The hungry livestock resorted to eating bark and twigs as the grass lay brown and parched. And then the forest fires erupted, sweeping the high ridges of the Blue Ridge, but the mountain folk's resilience kept them going.

Mr. Ralston pulled out the last of the cabbage buried in the hole underneath the back porch. Always a hardy lot with strong spirit, the Ralstons hunted more and made do just like the rest of the mountain folks. Even Greyson was sent out with William and Jack, hunting for squirrel and rabbit, or anything they could get, though he hated it and cringed at every shot.

"How come you ain't shot at anything?" William taunted while reloading his rifle.

"Ain't seen nothing."

The two older brothers exchanged knowing looks. "We sure could use some good rabbit stew," Jack said pointedly.

"Well, you ain't got nothing either," he snapped back. They returned empty-handed and met Ma's expectant eyes as she looked up from her knitting.

"Sorry, Ma, no luck today," William apologized, but Mildred couldn't hide her disappointment and stomped about the kitchen. She would even settle for another one of those stringy rabbits. "Guess it will be left-over stew again tonight," she fumed.

Ma frowned at her. "Well'sa, can't have luck every day, boys," she said. "But you're right, Mildred. We've still got some stew left over from yesterday. We'll add a little water to it, and it'll be just fine, that and some cornbread."

But Mildred wasn't listening. She had switched her thoughts to other things and was thinking about the picture that Adele had shown her at school, the one with the lady all dressed up and looking so smart. Her name was Garbo or something like that, and she had her hair parted down the middle, and wore a striking long dress with puffed-out sleeves. The fabric looked thick and beautiful, and her waist was so thin, especially compared to her shoulders that appeared rather broad. Adele said it was because the dress had shoulder pads, large shoulder pads, and she wondered if maybe one day she might be able to have a dress like that. If she had anything to do with it, she would, but she figured she'd have to move off the mountain first, maybe to the city. Nobody in the mountains dressed like that!

"What's gonna happen when we can't hunt anymore?" Jack asked all of a sudden.

"What're you talking about?" Pa demanded, coming in with a shriveled head of cabbage tucked in his hand.

William looked up. Now he'd done it! There wasn't any need to bring that up, besides it was just a rumor. Rumors were flying all over the mountains like buzzards—big, black rumors!

"Fellows over in Dark Hollow said they heard once the Park's finished, the gov'ment's gonna cut out hunting. Said we won't be able to kill squirrels or rabbits, won't be able to kill nary a thing!"

Pa stared at Jack, his face growing redder and redder. "Whoever heard such a fool idea? If they go and do that, they might as well chase us off the mountain!"

"Now, Pa," Ma tried to appease him. "...you know you can't believe everything you hear. Every week we hear something different. Now bring me that cabbage. I forgot all about it."

"Why don't they go someplace else?"

They all turned to Rayna Rose sitting quietly in the corner.

"Someplace where folks don't live!" she insisted, almost as heated as her pa.

"Because they want our mountains, little sister!" William replied.

"Why?"

"They want a park close to the city folks...you know, city folks from Washington, D.C. and Baltimore, and Richmond, places like that. I reckon there'll be millions of them coming up here, maybe even some from New York City!"

"Lord, have mercy!" Ma exclaimed, holding the cabbage over the basin and rinsing it with a dipper of water.

Greyson was halfway up the loft ladder. "I can see them now running all over these mountains," he cackled. "First time a bobcat creeps up on one of them, he'll be high-tailing it back home!"

They enjoyed a good laugh, even Rayna Rose. Greyson could always lift her spirits, but Pa just stared at them incredulously. Supper was rather subdued, everybody careful not to say the wrong thing again. It seemed he was on edge more and more these days. Afterwards, William and Jack followed him out to the woodpile where he commenced to stacking what he had chopped up earlier.

"Have you heard about the Hoover Highway?" William posed delicately as Mr. Ralston stacked the wood into a neat pile.

"I heard tell of it…but whoever heard of building a highway on top of these mountain ridges!"

"They say they're hiring farmers like us, Pa, to help build it—farmers with tools, picks and plows and such."

"You been drinking, boy?"

"Naw, Pa!"

A few logs tumbled down, setting off an avalanche. Pa swore under his breath, and then looked up to make sure Ma wasn't in hearing distance. Jack set about stacking the logs back up for him.

"But it's true, Pa, and I was thinking—"

"Thinking what?" It was more of a challenge than a question.

William stepped back, scuffing the wood chips that encircled the chopping block. "Well…that we could use the money…and I wouldn't mind the hard work. Like you always said, hard work ain't never hurt nobody!"

"Could I help build it, too, Pa?" Jack asked, intently placing the logs one atop the other.

"You ain't old enough!"

He whipped around and headed back to the house.

"But I am, Pa." William straightened up tall and erect.

Mr. Ralston just stared at him and went back to his stacking.

He wasn't about to give up this easy. "But Pa, it's not the new Park I'd be building…but the highway. And you yourself have fussed and fussed about these muddy, rutted roads. You know we could use some good roads up here. You can't argue that!"

"Do what you want, son." Though William could hear the despair in his voice, and it bothered him, it wasn't enough to discourage him from the likelihood of making some money, not to mention the excitement of doing something other than cutting up wood and hunting for scarce game.

By the end of the year, though, the news was grim. The Depression was worsening. *Closed* or *Out of Business* signs were posted throughout the land, and banks had failed left and right, taking with them millions in trusted deposits. Two hundred and fifty-six banks failed in just one month, the stark gray month of November. And then on the eleventh of December, the United States Bank went under with over two hundred million in people's hard-earned money. No one had believed it could happen! Who would have ever guessed it? The nation was shocked, and a haunting gloom hung over it like never before.

Christmas held no hope whatsoever, for who had money to indulge on the Christmas spirit? But ironically, it was that Christmas that Greyson would remember in all future Christmases. It was that Christmas that Rayna Rose showed him just how much she loved him.

They were asleep in the loft. William and Jack slept on one side, and he and Rayna Rose on the other. Mildred's bed was downstairs near their parents. Hers wasn't exactly a bed, but a makeshift contraption consisting of two benches cleverly slid together with a bulky straw mattress on top. However, she liked it well enough, particularly being able to be downstairs and closer to the fire. Outside, the wind was howling and whistling through the rocks and trees, and scraping the stiff, naked branches up against the cabin.

"What's that?" Greyson whispered.

Rayna Rose didn't move.

He shook her. "What's that noise?"

Her eyes fluttered open, and she squinted in the dark. "What noise?" She wasn't any too happy being aroused out of her sleep, especially by another one of his unfounded scares.

"Sounds like somebody or something scratching on the house!"

"Greyson—"

"Listen!"

She rolled over and peered out the window. "I think it must be Santa Claus."

Always the gullible one, his eyes bulged, and he slid beneath the covers.

"Come on." She was already up and pulling her clothes on over top of her long nightgown.

"What're you doing?"

"Going to see."

"You crazy!"

She yanked the covers off him. "Come on…let's go," she ordered in a muffled but commanding tone. "You woke me up, so get a move on!"

Reluctantly he followed, tugging on his shoes and coat. They crept softly down the ladder. All they needed was for the boys to hear them, and that would be the end of it. They tiptoed past Mildred's bed and shuffled through the kitchen. Rayna Rose gently pulled open the back door, shuddering at its noisy creak and carefully closed it behind them. She pressed her finger to her lips as they stepped out into the cold, dark night. The wind lashed at them, and Greyson edged in as close to her as possible, though he figured she had plumb lost her senses. He glanced around at the shadowy trees silhouetted in the slice of moon and weaving back and forth in the robust winds. He nudged up even closer as she marched boldly across the back yard.

"Quit bumping into me, silly!"

He backed off. Then a familiar howl sounded in the distance, and he grabbed hold of her coat sleeve. "Hear that?"

She shook him off.

"A wolf."

"Come on, scaredy cat."

"Where we going?"

Still not answering, she marched on across the yard and turned to gaze up at the housetop. Its weathered cedar shakes, now a silvery gray, glistened in the moonlight, and a few flapped in the strong winds, but that was all.

"He's gone," she sighed.

"How do you know it was him?"

"It's Christmas Eve. He always comes on Christmas Eve." She pointed to the roof. "See the long scratches up there?"

He strained to see, but the rooftop was full of scratches from the fierce winter ice storms. However, he never doubted his twin sister. She just seemed to know things better than he did, better than most people.

"He was here all right."

"You think he left something?"

She stood there smiling in the moonlight, her dark eyes mere shadows now, and then without a word fled back to the house. He was hard at her heels when something small and furry scurried in front of them. She bent over to catch it, and he sailed over top of her, slamming his head onto the frozen ground.

"Oh-h-h-h!" he moaned.

"Sh-h-h-h!"

"What the heck?" He rolled over and pushed himself up, rubbing the large rising knot.

"Now look what you did!"

"What did I do?" He started to cry.

"Hesh up, Greyson. You're gonna wake up the dead!"

He sniffed back his tears.

"And you scared that baby raccoon clear off, the one that's been hanging around here."

"I didn't mean to," he whimpered.

She glanced around but saw no sign of it. "Well come on, we better get back inside before they hear us."

They crept into the house, through the living room, and around to the spindly tree propped up in the corner, its strong cedar scent permeating the whole cabin. A shaft of moonlight fell through the window but not enough to see much, just the occasional glitter of the silver tinsel. Greyson dropped to his knees and groped around in the dark for something, anything, but he found nothing, only the galvanized bucket filled with dirt and stone.

"What are y'all up to?" Mildred's sharp eye was staring at them in the darkness. "Get back to bed before I call Ma!"

They scrambled up the ladder lickety-split, pulled off their coats and shoes and dove under the covers. They lay there silently for a bit, then Greyson couldn't help it, he began to snivel, a soft weeping sound. Instead of Rayna

Rose's usual scolding, she hugged him tight and patted his back.

"It's all right, Greyson, don't you worry none. I've got you something real special like. You'll see in the morning." She continued to pat his back, and his tears finally abated, and soon he was asleep.

Christmas morning was subdued as expected. Only a few, small, handmade gifts lay under the tree, nothing to get excited about until Rayna Rose presented Greyson with her surprise. He dug into the wrinkled newspaper.

"Rayna!" he cried out.

A shiny pocketknife gleamed in his hand. He had never seen anything so beautiful, and he jumped up and down, hugging her around the neck. She was grinning from ear to ear, but otherwise there was silence in the room.

"Rayna Rose, where'd you get that knife?" Pa finally demanded, carefully eyeing the coveted gift.

"Found it."

"Found it where?"

"Down by the creek bank…I washed it up real nice and clean like."

She was smiling proudly, and heads turned from one to another. It was obvious that the knife was brand new and could never have been down by any creek bank, that's for sure. Ma stood by anxiously wringing her hands, but Pa seemed downright baffled until suddenly he remembered that day taking her with him to the general store over in Elkton.

He stood up. "Rayna Rose, come with me."

She stared at him, dread filling her eyes. Mildred conveniently escaped to the kitchen while William and Jack uncomfortably watched the scene unfold, remembering their own particular times of chastisement.

"Get your coat first."

She slowly reached for it, casting piteous eyes in Greyson's direction. He looked from her to his pa but was afraid to say anything. There was a deliberate force in him that was not seen often, but they all knew its intent. She followed him on outside into the cold, frosty morning. Greyson ran to the window and saw them disappear behind the henhouse. He looked back at his ma, and then to his brothers.

"Do something!" he sobbed, but he knew they wouldn't. Then he heard her piercing cries coming from the back of the henhouse, and he sank to the floor with his hands over his ears, feeling every whip of the razor strap on his own back, and he hoped he never saw another Christmas.

The new Skyline Drive was on its way to becoming a reality the next year, and by late spring, William was sweat ing it out with the rest of the local crew. They toiled long and hard to create a road out of nothing, cutting down trees, pulling up stumps, scraping and grading a narrow and curving thread atop the crest of the rugged mountains. It was grueling labor but William enjoyed every minute of it. It was manly work, and not only this, he sensed that this road would be different! Never before had anyone tried to build a road, a real bona fide road up on top of Virginia's mountains. Why, you could look one way and see the Shenandoah Valley spread out for miles and miles, and then turn around and look the other way and set your eyes on the rolling Piedmont. And having a share in it made him feel special-like, even if it did end up being a part of the Park.

But he didn't talk much about that, especially at home, though he heard the men discussing it, and it was no secret that there were big plans up ahead. However, he wasn't about to agitate his pa anymore than he already was. Besides, most of the mountain men seemed to think that they would be allowed to stay on in the Park once it was created. That's why a number of them had gladly agreed to give right-of-ways through their land for the new road, but, of course, that wasn't the main reason. They were paid handsomely for it, as well, and who could turn money down in times like these?

"What good would it do to make us move anyhow?" the men asked one another over and over throughout the day. William asked himself the same question as he sweated in the broiling sun. Look how we're helping with the road building, he reasoned, and who knows what else we might be able to do along the way, even after the Park's established. The whole idea undoubtedly encouraged him.

"Watch out for that tree!"

He jumped out of the way just in time, and a large tulip poplar swooshed down within feet of him.

"You come nigh to getting yourself flattened out, boy!"

William felt his anger rise. It wasn't his fault that the proper warning wasn't given.

The weighty, robust farmer commenced to sawing off branches. "What's your name anyhow, young fellow?"

"William…William Ralston."

"One of the Ralston younguns, huh? I know your pa…known him for years, back when we were young, used to see him around. Ain't seen him in a coon's age, though, he doing all right?"

"Yes, sir," he answered, still rankling over the untimely episode.

"How come he ain't helping to build this here Skyline Drive?" Folks had begun calling it by its proper name only just recently, and they all agreed it was more fitting. Still there were those upset with the deepening Depression who insisted on calling it the Hoover Highway.

"He's not too taken with it and the whole idea of the Park."

"Just what I figured. Well, truth be known, I ain't either, but the money's good, and I might as well get it as somebody else...because it's gonna be built, you know. Yes sirree, you can bet your bottom dollar on it. Now that Hoover's got his place here and all, it's gonna be built!"

And William knew he was right.

Mr. Ralston was also breaking new ground. His usual field south of the cabin was plumb wore out, he complained, and he needed to let it lie fallow for a while, besides Ma expected to get some rain this year. She'd been praying real hard, she said, and she knew God was gonna answer. But it was going to take some work to get the side field ready, so full of rocks it was and even a few straggly trees.

"Now, Jack, hitch up ol' Max to the slide, will you, and Greyson, you get busy getting them rocks out of here. We got us a whole lotta work before we can get some corn planted."

"Can I help?" Rayna Rose cried out, quickly running after them.

"Nawsa, you gotta help your ma in the garden." He meant the patch beside the kitchen where the tomato plants grew along with some beans and potatoes and Ma's special herbs.

"But I wanna help with the rocks, Pa."

"They too heavy for you."

"I can pick up many as Greyson!"

"Rayna Rose, I done told you. Don't be so gall-durned hardheaded. Your ma needs your help in the garden."

She spun on her heels and headed back to the house. Greyson watched her go, wishing she'd been born a boy, too.

It was a long morning, a back-breaking morning for all, but still he took pleasure in following behind Jack. He had always admired his older brothers and hoped one day to be just like them. They were tall and strong and smart as tacks, his ma said. 'Course they didn't read all the time like Rayna Rose. He figured she'd be smarter than them all one day. He glanced down at her working in the garden. He had always felt closer to her than anybody. He reckoned it was because they were twins, and twins were supposed to be closer, folks said. And then, too, they had been born much later than the rest, on the tail end, his ma was famous for saying.

Before noon, they had most of the larger stones removed and piled up in a great mound around the big, old chestnut, one of the few still living. He enjoyed picking up the smaller ones and pitching them onto the pile, hearing their resounding clunks as they pounded the others.

"Greyson thinks he's a baseball player, Pa, instead of a farmer," Jack kidded. "Just look at him."

"Don't matter none just long as he gets them rocks out of my field."

"I'm not gonna be a farmer!"

Jack laughed. "'Course you're gonna be a farmer, boy. You gotta stay here and help Pa once we're gone."

"Why?"

"'Cause you're the youngest."

"So?"

"The youngest always stays."

"Why?"

"That's just the way it is, and you're the lucky one. You get the place after Pa dies."

He looked puzzled.

"Pa was the youngest in his family…that's why he got the place instead of Uncle Jonas and Uncle Sims. Right, Pa?"

He didn't answer. He was intent on clearing the side field.

"What about Mildred and Rayna Rose?"

"Oh, they'll get married off to somebody or another and move on to their husband's place. It's always done like that, right, Pa?"

The old man muttered something under his breath.

"Now William and me, we gotta get our own places."

Greyson became quiet, pondering this new revelation. He continued picking up the rocks and slinging them onto the growing pile, but he was staring around at the place differently now. He saw the Rhode Island Red chickens pecking around the cabin, and Rayna Rose and his ma hoeing in the garden next to it. Mildred was hanging something out on the clothesline as the mountain breezes whipped it back and forth. It looked to be Pa's long underwear that Ma was fussing at him to put away till next winter. He glanced at the buildings down the hillside where they kept Max and the cow, seeing them in a whole new light, and then behind to the hog pen that he and his pa had just recently nailed some new planks onto. They always kept two hogs for killing in the fall. He looked in the other direction where the cabbage field was and then up the hill to the apple orchard, his pa's pride and joy. He didn't particularly like the idea of being a farmer, he had never wanted to be a farmer, but he loved the place and he had to admit he couldn't imagine living anywhere else.

Rayna Rose stopped hoeing and stared at the guys out in the field. She watched Jack loading the big stones onto the slide, and she saw Pa deadening a tree, cutting through the bark all around the trunk. She hated to see him do that, she hated seeing any tree killed, but she understood it was necessary. The sun couldn't get to the corn if he didn't, and she knew Pa would cut it down later on for firewood anyway, something they had to have in the cold of winter. Greyson was still pitching stones, and she could hear their dull thuds. Why did she always have to do girl's work?

"Rayna Rose, what're you doing?"

"Resting."

Ma rubbed her back. "It's almost time for dinner, child. We'll rest then. Let's finish this here row." She commenced to scratching the hard soil, and Rayna followed after.

"I might as well be making them flowers!"

Ma looked up. "What flowers you talking about?"

"William said some kids are making paper flowers and selling them up on the new Skyline Drive...said people pay good money for them, too. I reckon it would be a mite easier than hoeing."

"I better not catch you doing such a thing! We don't need their money!"

"I didn't say I was gonna do it, Ma. I just said it would be a mite easier than hoeing."

"Well, maybe so, but hard work ain't never hurt nobody!"

Rayna figured she'd better change the subject. "Can we go merkel hunting after we finish?"

"Not today. Gotta finish here and then get dinner ready. Think of all them good beans we'll be eating soon and all through the cold winter, too. You know how much you love beans."

She also knew her ma was trying to encourage her to do more hoeing, but that didn't work. It just meant standing over the hot wood stove when she had to help with the puttin' up. She hated puttin' up all them jars, with sweat running down her neck, down her arms and just about everywhere, with her hair sticking to her head. Yuck, she hated that most of all. She'd much rather be outside doing men's work in the fresh air along with the birds and the trees and the wind and the sun. She kept looking over her shoulder at Greyson.

He picked up another rock and swung it forcefully to the pile.

Plop.

He glanced at her proudly, and she stuck her tongue out at him.

January brought excitement to those weary workers toiling on the new Skyline Drive, including William, though he wasn't personally involved with its cause. Yet any good news connected to the Drive was sufficient grounds for him to make merry. And this was definitely one of those occasions. There was going to be only one tunnel dug through the mountains, and this was not far from the Thornton Gap Entrance on the north end. For several months they had been drilling, blasting and clearing, carving through six hundred feet of solid granite. It was their greatest challenge yet. Secretly William wished he was one of those working inside the dark, damp tunnel, clearing away the loose boulders and stone. He wouldn't mind the bleak cold and back-breaking labor, but they still had him grading the slopes further south. That wasn't any picnic either, but he could walk back and forth to work. And word had it that he would be helping with the overlooks next. Oh well, at least he was able to closely follow the tunnel's progress, and they broke through to daylight that month. Quite appropriate, he figured, being that it was the New Year, and he rushed home to relay the thrilling news, but not before swinging by his usual stop-off to pick up a bottle of corn liquor on the way. He figured it called for a bit of celebration.

Awhile later, he burst through the door, bringing the frigid air with him, and singing high and off key, *"She'll be coming 'round the mountain…."*

Everyone was seated at the table and stopped eating at once.

"Well, she's through!"

Pa stared at him, his mouth full.

"Marys Rock Tunnel!" he exclaimed, grinning from ear to ear.

"They got through?" Pa was shocked.

Ma frowned at him for talking with his mouth so full, but he paid her no mind. He had never believed that they would do it, thought they were crazy to be digging through a mountain in the first place.

"Reckon nothing will stop them now!" Greyson said, glancing over at Rayna Rose.

William shook his head. "I didn't figure they'd make it this soon, but they've had three shifts working, about fifteen men on each shift, and somebody said the machinery's always going except on Sunday." Suddenly he felt a bit woozy and pulled out a chair at the empty place beside Mildred, and she immediately caught a whiff of his celebrating.

"Well, I'm glad they ain't working on Sunday," Ma said. "And I don't know that I'd be driving through that thing myself!"

"Ma, you don't drive," Greyson laughed.

"If I did, I wouldn't go in there."

"Aw, Ma. They know what they're doing," William scoffed, giving Mildred a frowning side glance. "They got all kinds of engineers working on that thing. They been studying and studying it, to make sure it comes out just right."

"Maybe so, but I ain't going through it!"

Jack chuckled to himself.

Pa wiped his mouth, looking rather puzzled. "I still don't know how they got through it."

"Dynamite, Pa."

"I reckon I know that."

"About a thousand pounds a day. Stick that dynamite in holes about twelve feet deep, and light it. Boom!" He clapped his hands and roared.

"I reckon that'll do it," Pa replied.

"Can we go see it?" Rayna Rose piped up.

Pa looked over at her like she'd lost her mind.

"But I've never seen dynamite."

"And you ain't gonna either."

"They wouldn't even let you get close, Rayna Rose. I've seen them do it," William boasted. "Makes a mighty big blast and smoke and dust like you never seen!"

"I'm sure it's a curiosity," Mildred commented, inching her chair away from him.

"A curiosity! Listen to her, Ma," William flared back. "I have you know, it's a miracle, that's what it is!"

"Now I wouldn't go that far, William," Ma argued. "We ain't talking about the Bible and Jesus, you know."

"Aw, Ma, you know what I mean."

Within a week, traffic was coursing through, even though the road was not officially open. Word was out what it was like—dark and damp and water dripping down into it. The ground above it was spongy from springs, and it could be quite slippery on those cold, wintry days for both driving and walking. Still some folks walked down from the Panorama to see the new marvel with its gigantic icicles hanging from the entrance on frigid days. This only proved Ma's point, but even so, it fast became one of the most popular sights along the Drive.

By autumn, there were scores of takers.

Jack bounded into the house one day, his face flushed red. "Pa, you're not gonna believe this!"

"What now?" He waited for Jack's tale to unravel, knowing the boy particularly relished anything exciting or even absurd at times. William was the realistic one, thick-headed as they come, but realistic still. Jack was a dreamer. He didn't know where he got it from, and to his dismay, it seemed like Greyson was cut out of the same mold.

"I just got back from the new road…cars are bumper to bumper up there. You've never seen anything like it!"

Ma looked up from the dough she was kneading. "You don't mean the Skyline Drive?"

"Yes, ma'am. It opened up today."

"Well, I'll be!"

"And like I said, Ma, vehicles are bumper to bumper up there!"

"Who would've thought it?"

But midst the deepening Depression, it was a definite ray of hope for Virginians and especially the local folk, well most of them anyway. If this could be accomplished, then maybe not all was lost. Maybe there was hope for the future. Maybe things were looking up and one day the awful Depression would be over.

"Never would have believed it!" Ma muttered, pressing the sticky dough into yet another ball.

"And it's not even paved yet," Jack added as Pa silently left the kitchen. "You hear me, Pa?"

"I heard you, boy." But he had disappeared into the back room.

"Somebody said they're gonna charge twenty-five cents a car to come up here to get on it."

Ma looked over her shoulder. "Whoever heard such… paying to drive on a road?"

"That's what they said."

Pa had slumped down on his bed, but he could still hear them talking. He knew they'd finished the road between Thornton Gap and Hawksbill. He kept up with its progress just like everybody else, though he didn't let on that he did. It wasn't something he liked to think about, let alone discuss. But he sure thought they would have paved it before they opened it up. Just couldn't wait, he figured.

As he sat there mulling over what the future held, just like Jack said, hordes of eager sightseers were flocking to see the man-made marvel. They drove slowly along the crest of the mountain, wide-eyed and amazed at what they saw—miles and miles of mountain ridges and steep drop-offs that swept down into picturesque valleys of the Shenandoah or the Piedmont, and the distant rolls of the Alleghenies, waves and waves of them stretched out, swelling up into the clouded, misty blue sky, subtly fusing with it, becoming one.

Incredible!

The pull-offs were jammed, and people were parking on the grass and anywhere else they could find a spot. Sometimes the men would stop and jump out in their pressed suits, starched white shirts and flashy bowties, the ladies close behind them, dressed in their Sunday frocks and steep high heels. They would cautiously peer out over the mountains and valleys, and maybe ask a question or two of the young CCC enrollee posted there to help, but mostly they were anxious to move on, to see more of the mountain crests. They were bowled over with this novel wonder and couldn't wait to get back to their respective homes to tell about it, and the more they saw, the more they had to tell.

The train of cars rolled along atop the mountains, past the chestnut ghost trees still standing idly by, now void of leaves and patiently awaiting their fate. It moved across the freshly smoothed-out dirt road, stretching past grazing cattle that lazily lifted their heads to stare at them and then returned to their eating, the only ones oblivious to such a sight, while timid deer or other mountain creatures stopped dead in their tracks.

The visitors stared unbelievably at the surrounding sights, but unknowingly, they were creating a spectacle themselves, a caravan of black metal bumping and heaving along, and belching off steam from the arduous climbs. Weaving through the mountains, the long train of cars was foreign to the otherwise natural and peaceful ambiance, creating a cold and stark contrast. At least the mountain folk thought so as they discreetly peered out their windows or watched the strange sight from their leaning porches.

Though piqued with curiosity, their expressions displayed that of fear or sometimes anger, but mostly sadness for they knew that the inevitable had come.

But Jack, for one, wasn't going to fret about it anymore, no matter what his pa said. Ever since he'd begun working up at the resort, he had a different perspective. Mildred said it had broadened his horizons. Maybe so, but he understood now that there was another whole world out there beyond these mountains—people who dressed differently and talked differently, people who had time to play—grownup people, even. Life wasn't all work from dawn to dusk, peeling and hauling tanbark down to Elkton, or chopping wood till your back nigh broke or trying to plow up a field that was infested with stubborn stones. He had come to the conclusion that he might like to live that way, too, but he wasn't about to divulge such sentiments, especially not in front of his folks. He had heard about the Skyland Resort ever since he was a kid, heard that it was a place for rich folks. He had to admit it sure seemed that way. It certainly wasn't a place for a mountain boy unless you worked there, but he was scheduled to work or rather privileged to work on Labor Day weekend.

It should be some affair, too, he gathered. They were to have another one of those big bonfires after dark, the ones you could see for miles and miles around, even down in the Valley. Though he had never seen one, he had heard tell of them. William had seen one, and he said it was something else. Before setting out, he dressed in his best clothes and slicked down his hair with water, plastering it down on both sides where it seemed to have a mind of its own, always sticking up like he'd just come in out of a wind storm.

Mildred said he needed some of that new hair cream, but who could afford such as that?

Though he had heard all the stories, he was totally unprepared for such a gala event. Not only was the bonfire tremendous, greater than anything he could ever have imagined, blazing high into the darkened night with fiery cinders ascending into the lofty trees, but the guests were all decked out in the most curious outfits. The women were in colorful get-ups with broad hats and gaudy beads and feathers and ribbons dangling all about them, and the men were in suits and ties or bowties, and some had on the most ridiculous-looking hats. He had never seen such a sight. Somebody told him it was a masquerade ball, and they were trying to outdo one another. Well, that may be, but it seemed sort of childish to him for grown folks to be acting in such a way, and he couldn't imagine what his pa would think. Everybody appeared to be having a swell time though, laughing and joking and dancing around, and he almost wished he could join in, but respectfully stayed in the background, watching and waiting on the tables.

He couldn't help but notice one young lady all dressed up in lavender ruffles from head to toe. She looked like a picture he'd seen in the Sears catalog, only prettier, and he was surprised when she glanced his way and smiled. He dropped his head and busied himself with his duties. She might be making fun of him for all he knew. They did that sometimes, he'd been told. But they didn't know how much the mountain folk made fun of them! With all their high-falutin airs and big schooling, they still don't understand us, he thought smugly to himself, wiping his hands on his apron. Most of the time we have it on them!

He couldn't help but remember old Tom, who lived not far from the resort. He was always putting one over on them, acting like he and his family were plum nelly destitute just so the guests would take pity and bestow all kinds of goodies on them. They racked up quite a booty that way. Of course, he would never do that. Folks oughta have more pride, but still and all, he couldn't help but be amused at how gullible some of these city folk were.

"Hello there!"

Startled, he knocked over a pitcherful of water that splashed over the white tablecloth, soaking everything in sight, including his own britches.

"I'm sorry," she giggled. "Did I surprise you?" It was her, and she was standing right in his face, smothered in a lavender cloud. He backed off in spite of himself.

"My name is Victoria." She smiled coyly.

"Mine's Jack," he uttered, furiously trying to clean up his mess.

"You work here?"

What did she think? He was a masquerader! He nodded.

"Isn't this a grand party?"

Nodding again, he began to feel like one of those jack-in-the-boxes.

"You know why everyone's so dreadfully happy."

"No, ma'am."

"You don't have to call me ma'am."

What about Pink Princess?

"Surely you know that the Shenandoah Park will soon be a reality!"

He glanced around as if his pa were standing over his shoulder.

Suddenly the band pitched high.

"I must be going now. It's almost time for the grand march." She whisked him lightly with her fan and slipped off as quickly as she had come, a blur of lavender vanishing into the teeming crowd, and he scurried back to the kitchen, but with lifted spirits and a renewed heart. She hadn't made fun of him at all. In fact, she acted as if she liked him, and feeling rather jovial, he whistled a tune under his breath.

But the country beyond Skyland was another story. It had deepened in its woes, sinking in the miry clay, yet the progress of the national park inched forward. Though congress had authorized the park back in 1926, numerous challenges had impeded its progress, pressing it down to almost a snail's pace. However frustrated and bewildered, the powers-that-be stubbornly forged ahead, boldly determined and persistent in their relentless endeavor to see it to fruition.

Virginia had condemned the land with its sweeping blanket Condemnation Law, but the federal government still was unable to accept it for the proposed Park—not until Virginia could hold claim to the properties, and this wasn't proving to be too easy. Though many residents moved off the mountain without resistance, there were others who stubbornly refused to go, holding onto their land with pride and might. They weren't going anywhere!

They didn't figure the government could take their land, and they held onto their trust in the Constitution, their trust in America, adamantly believing that in the end, they would prevail and be able to stay. A few actually sought help through the court system, stalling the whole process even longer and giving false hope to them all for days and months.

It was definitely a time of uncertainty, anxiety, and gloom for all the people on that stretch of the Blue Ridge Mountains.

CHAPTER SEVEN
(Back to 1942)

When Greyson first saw the mountains looming up ahead, it was dusk, and he shook off the memories of his childhood, so glad to be home. The prominent rounded peaks welcomed him and embraced him in their age-old, solid strength, but the soft, sucking sounds beside him belied any joy he usually experienced when he saw them. And he tried to imagine life ahead!

He couldn't begin to guess what his sister Mildred would have to say. Since she'd grown up and married Harry Etheridge, everything seemed to annoy her, not the least his folk's place. It was too small, too mountainous, and too obscure. Time and time again, she'd tried to persuade them to sell out and move closer to her, into a neat, modern apartment complex, but Pa wouldn't hear of it.

"I've been forced to move once, but that was the last time!" he argued.

He figured on staying where he was until he died—at least he could still see the mountains rising up sharply behind him. But Mildred hadn't given up. She was working on Ma now.

Greyson wondered if Mildred was as concerned for their welfare as she portrayed, or if she wasn't just plain embarrassed over their humble lifestyle. Appearance was paramount with Mildred, always had been, and he figured she must have suffered something terrible from the stigma of his spells, though she never said anything. But he recalled her humiliated looks whenever they occurred in public, though she was embarrassed by far less things. He well remembered that episode with William's daughter, Francine, when she penciled lines on the back of her naked legs to give the illusion of hosiery. She had used eyebrow makeup to do the job, and Mildred literally flipped out, forcing her to scrub off every hint then and there. "What in the world is becoming of this Ralston family?" she had fumed.

Oh well, he didn't care what Mildred had to say!

Darkness had gathered at the foot of the mountain when he pulled up in the driveway, the new gravel scrunching beneath his tires. He slid out and went around to the other side to lift out the pink bundle. The yellow porch light flicked on, lighting a path for him, and his parents stood at the window straining to see.

"Does he have her?" Ma asked anxiously.

"Got something in his arms."

"Oh, my!"

"Now don't go getting all google-eyed, acting like you ain't never seen one."

"Pa...you know this here baby's different. Why, it don't even have a mama!"

"She's got one, but—"

"S-h-h-h-h," she hushed as Greyson pushed open the door. He'd seen them watching.

Ma rushed to his side, eagerly peering into the blanket.

"She's still sleeping, Ma."

Mrs. Ralston's face spread into a sweeping grin. "Why look, Pa, she's got a head full of...full of thick, black hair just like…." And she collapsed on the couch with her head in her hands.

"You all right, Ma?"

She nodded as he brought the baby over to her. "That's why I named her…I hope you don't mind…but I named her Rayna."

The old woman reached up for the tiny infant and hugged her to her bosom as tears unashamedly rolled down her face. Pa stood by awkwardly, nervously fidgeting with his suspenders. He didn't say anything, but he thought plenty.

Spring rolled full-speed into summer and summer lazily into fall, and soon it faded into winter. And, behold, it was spring again! One after another, the seasons passed as time had since time began. Practically unnoticed, they passed as Greyson watched his baby grow. He watched her roll over, he watched her push up, and he proudly watched her take those first steps.

Ma was beside herself, happier than she'd been in ages, and the baby helped to take her mind off Jack. Not only that, but she felt the bloom of youth again, tending to the child's every need. As she rocked her back and forth on the front porch, she thought of how odd life could be. This baby who should have and could have turned their world topsy-turvy, upside down with pain and turmoil—instead had brought such peace and love into the home. It was difficult to imagine life without her now. Why, she herself had just been waiting to grow old and die when baby Rayna showed up, giving her a whole new lease on life!

The birds' songs were livelier now, the tree frogs' chirping and cicadas' drone more pronounced, musical to her ear, and the sunshine blazed brighter than ever before. She couldn't wait to get out of bed every morning to check in the new crib that Greyson had bought to see if that precious little thing was awake, to see those penetrating eyes staring up at her just like her own Rayna Rose. Sometimes she actually felt confused, like she was reliving her life all over again. It wasn't her granddaughter at all, but her daughter lying there in that crib staring up at her with those dark, luminous eyes.

But in reality, she knew better. She knew it was Greyson's baby, and she was determined to love and protect her. She also believed that God had especially showered her with this happiness in light of her undying sorrow. Even Pa seemed to have mellowed in her presence—not nearly as ill-tempered as before. He wouldn't dare pick her up at first, but Ma often found him standing over the crib, just staring down at her.

Ironically, this precious baby, this catalyst for renewed joy, also brought on another side of Greyson, a melancholy side. Though he loved her dearly, he was slowly slipping back behind that dark curtain again. Angry with himself, he fought it, knowing full well what it was like. He didn't want to go! He didn't want to lose himself among its heavy folds.

It had been a long time since he had sunk in depression, though signs had begun to surface with the advent of the war, the fact that he couldn't go, that he couldn't do his part. He recognized the distressing signals, for he had succumbed to its tentacles before as a young teenager, when he realized he was different. The preacher had tried to help him back then, explaining that everybody has some cross to bear, though his ma downplayed his epilepsy. She didn't want him to feel different, but he had cried like a baby, though he was thirteen years old at the time. Why couldn't he have been short or skinny or have a thyroid problem like Elmer Jones and be big and fat? Or maybe have to wear glasses like Maynard Eggleston and have his eyes pop out like frog eyes? Anything would be better than this silent phantom that pounced on him suddenly, throwing him mercilessly to the ground foaming at the mouth and making him the laughing stock of the mountain!

Anything!

But Pa had chastised him for feeling sorry for himself and made him get up and over it. A good thing, too, otherwise he would never have left home or gotten through school. But now he wondered what good it had done? It seemed that his life was destined for failure. He thought of his brother Jack's infrequent letters. Though he realized his life was in constant jeopardy, still his correspondence reeked of adventure and heroic purpose. And Lester was still over there, and even his old friend Leonard was serving in the Pacific now. That was definitely an ill pill to swallow.

He knew people looked at him curiously—why was such a strapping young man not overseas? He told himself he didn't care, but he did. And then there was the whole affair with the lovely Lorna, though he had to live with his own stupidity over that. And now he was a single parent! How was he going to raise Rayna? As she stumbled about, clumsily holding onto whatever she could grasp, he worried about her future when she got older. What kind of life would she have without a mother? He knew his folks wouldn't be around forever, then what?

The poor little thing—it wasn't fair to end up with only one parent, and the ever-present guilt racked his soul.

Just as he had predicted, Mildred was mortified when she learned of the child and apparently decided to dismiss her completely. So she was an illusion? he thought sarcastically. Was that her tactic? Perhaps she really believed the child didn't exist—she never acknowledged her when she visited, which wasn't very often. William accepted her well enough, chalking it up to his little brother's bad judgment, which, of course, was obviously true. Furthermore, William had his own scandalous behavior to live down, so he wasn't one for judging too harshly. Jack was spared the family scandal, and they figured he didn't need to know until he returned home.

So he forged ahead, burying himself in his work, though his job at the plant didn't help matters. Monotonous and eternally boring, it allowed his mind to wander randomly and explore anything it pleased, while his hands mechanically performed their expected tasks. But he didn't want to think! Especially about the war and the tender embraces of young couples tearfully parting, and the curious looks or blatant questions about why he was still around. And certainly he didn't want to think about Jack being over there and getting hurt or worse. Not only the war, he didn't want to think about Mildred's shunning of his baby girl either, and he particularly didn't want to think about the future, her starting school one day and other little girls asking questions about her mommy.

He knew they were talking, the neighbors, that is. They had talked about his spells, he had heard them, though his folks tried to conceal it, but that was when they lived up on the mountain, and mountain people always talked. What else did they have to do? They didn't mean any harm; talk was entertainment. Maybe it was a bit better down here in the Valley. Maybe. But he could handle it. He pulled his old shell around himself, and safely cocooned within its folds, ignored them all. He had learned how to deal with it.

But what about *her?* When the talk and looks would be directed toward her instead of him? If only he could shield her. The war and his sickness weren't nearly as troubling as this new worry. But for now, the child was a marvel to him, and to them all, especially how much she resembled her namesake with those dark locks and dark eyes that had a way of visibly clouding over whenever she was disturbed. She could also be just as willful and stubborn. It was at those times when the Ralston family felt that they were being shifted into reverse, the hands of the clock spinning backwards, back to another's stage, one that was perpetually filled with drama. For Rayna Rose had undoubtedly enhanced life on the mountain, and her ringing laughter still echoed in Greyson's ears. He could feel her energy even now, her vitality, though it had been stilled for years. He wondered if little Rayna would possibly display such qualities, such individuality. Already there were signs.

Before she was two years old, she had taken it upon herself to ramble off into the woods.

"Stay right here by the door while I make up the bed," her grandma had charged, "...play with your little doll."

No sooner had she turned her back, Rayna scooted outside, across the back yard on her wobbly legs and into the deep forest. Ma was frantic. Not knowing whether to follow after or call for Pa, who was out in the garden, she did both. Racing toward the woods, her apron flying in the breeze, she bellowed out, "Pa...Pa...come quick...the baby's gone...gone into the woods!"

Fortunately she didn't go far, but sat down on a patch of cushiony green moss to watch a raccoon scratching at the base of a dead poplar, and that's where they found her.

"Lord, have mercy, child!" Ma shooed the scoundrel off and plopped down beside her, her sagging breasts heaving up and down as she gulped in the cool, forest air. Pa scuttled up behind her, ready to scold but his anger melted when he saw her, and he simply grabbed her up in his arms and stomped back to the house.

"Come on, Ma." And she loped after.

It was just the beginning of many such escapades over the next year or so. Most of them they kept from Greyson, afraid he would think the child too much for them and possibly look for someone else, someone younger to care for her, and they couldn't bear the thought of that. But they also knew that Greyson had enough on his mind. They noticed how he was often preoccupied these days, and in that dark and strange world, a world they couldn't enter or comprehend and thus usually ignored, hoping it would go away. It was a mystery to them both. Never had they known anyone in the family to suffer from such problems, and they figured it had to be connected to his epilepsy, another mystery to be sure.

William was puzzled why his brother didn't date or even seem interested, such a handsome young fellow he was, but Greyson was determined to avoid any more heartaches, any more disasters. Besides, how could he explain his spells to anyone?

And how could he explain Rayna?

The bludgeoning, long war finally ended. There was Victory! The Nazis were defeated, and the Japanese surrendered. Prisoners of war were set free, rations were discontinued, and soldiers were discharged and returned home, and families were once more happily reunited. There was ecstatic singing and dancing in the streets, and prayers of praise going up all over the world, throughout America, and including the Valley of the Shenandoah.

Jack had come home, crowding into the small house. And at last Greyson's dark curtain lifted, allowing him to escape its despondency once again. He couldn't hear enough about his big brother's war escapades, though Jack was obviously reluctant to talk of them. Instead, he preferred to wallow on the floor with little Rayna, letting her crawl all over him. It seemed to ease the difficult transition back into the normalcy of life, and away from the memories of the war. Rebuffed more than once, Greyson finally quit asking and simply enjoyed his long-missed presence. They spent happy times together, taking lengthy walks, simply enjoying the outdoors and the season. But the house was far too small for them all, and Greyson wanted to move, to find a larger, more convenient place for him and Rayna, yet he was afraid to.

Suppose he had a spell?

She would be scared to death. She hadn't experienced that yet, and he dreaded the day, but he knew that he couldn't keep them from her forever. It was inevitable, and he felt trapped. So together, he and Jack added another room onto the backside of the house, but in no time Jack was talking of moving out himself, moving over to Charlottesville. An Army buddy there had been after him for some time to join him in a business venture, a small real estate firm, and he liked the idea. What's more, he planned to attend college on his GI Bill. Jack's tour of duty overseas had confirmed what he had been feeling ever since he had worked up at the Skyland Resort. He wanted to move on with his life, experience things outside the realm of what he had known, find out what was out there, and Charlottesville was growing every day, he understood. It seemed the very place, not too far away, but yet a whole new experience for him.

Six months later, he moved and found more than a new home and a place at the big university; he proposed to a girl named Marian. After a whirlwind romance, they were married. The wedding was relatively large, enormous in Pa's eyes, who thought it all foolishness to spend so much money on frivolous things, things you couldn't eat or wear on your back in the cold of winter.

Greyson was asked to be the best man, but he gently refused. What if he had a seizure? He couldn't run the risk of ruining their beautiful wedding. But it was at the wedding that he met Alma, a handsome young redhead, a second cousin to Jack's lovely bride. He was immediately taken with her striking hair and dancing hazel eyes, and without thinking, put aside his concerns. And she was drawn to raven-headed Rayna right away, which softened his heart instantly. Maybe, just maybe. They began courting, and his depression vanished. The exact opposite of his ever-cautious nature, she was a happy sort of girl, carefree, which was just what he needed. His folks and Jack liked her well enough, and William was obviously pleased, glad to see him finally interested in somebody.

Then it happened.

It was a beautiful summer day, a Saturday, and they were going on a picnic, he and Rayna and Alma. She had brought a basket with small wedges of chicken salad sandwiches, chips and slices of pound cake that she had made especially for the occasion. She also had a jug of sweet tea. It was the weekend before July the fourth, and they drove up to the Skyline Drive and over to Big Meadows, a large, treeless area packed with tiny wildflowers and low-lying blueberry bushes. Immediately Rayna was romping through the expansive meadow, chasing butterflies and trying her hardest to snare one. At three years old, she was quite energetic, inquisitive, and demonstrated an enormous interest in her surroundings. Greyson watched her fondly while he and Alma rested beneath a lone sapling that offered a slight bit of shade.

"It sure is big," she remarked, gazing all about.

"Not as big as what it used to be."

"How big was that?"

"About a thousand acres once, they say, but that was around the turn of the century. It was used for grazing back then, by the elk and bison, and then later on with cattle."

"Well, it still looks awfully big to me."

"It is, but the trees and shrubs have reclaimed some of it, though it's still pretty impressive…and it's been here a long, long time."

"How long?" she quizzed playfully. She had learned a good while back how to stroke the masculine ego. Let him think himself smarter and certainly superior, and then you have the upper hand. She smiled up at Greyson beneath her wide-brimmed hat that sheltered her carrot-colored mane, and he grinned and scratched his head.

"Nobody knows…but for hundreds of years, I'm sure."

"I declare!"

Rayna continued to tirelessly chase the elusive butterflies, and Alma pulled out a magazine from her bag and began to flip through it, though he found it odd that she could do so in the midst of such beauty. A bumblebee buzzed about, seeking its dinner, and the tranquil setting, fused with the heat of the day, created a hypnotic sense, a thought provoking mood. His eyes roamed the meadow, and out of the corridors of time he could hear those historic words coming from the president. They rang out loud and clear.

"...we are preserving the beauty and the wealth of the hills, and the mountains and the plains and the trees and the streams."

He searched for the spot, the precise place where he and William had been standing that day, but he couldn't find it. Still he would always remember the feelings that welled up within him. It was another Fourth of July. Actually it was the day before the fourth back in 1936. He would never forget it.

"We seek to pass on to our children a richer land—a stronger nation. I, therefore, dedicate Shenandoah National Park to this and succeeding generations of Americans for the recreation and for the re-creation which we shall find here."

He remembered President Roosevelt's exact pronunciations—*the recreation and the re-creation*—and the stir that they had caused. And when his booming voice concluded, a loud applause had wafted over the meadow, and he vividly recalled feeling torn, not knowing whether to clap or not. Then William had punched him, and he began to clap, though he felt like a traitor and was glad his pa wasn't there.

A sizeable bird soared overhead, its shadow sailing over them, a hawk maybe, and he studied it absently as he reminisced the past. Alma glanced up from her magazine.

"You're looking awfully grave."

"Just thinking."

"Oh?"

"Remembering when the Park was dedicated."

"Were you here?"

He nodded.

"So was I!"

"I didn't see you," he kidded, welcoming the lighter mood.

"Well, we were here all right...my parents and my sisters and me, and we were so excited. Well, all except my youngest sister, who was being a spoiled brat, but that's another story. It was a big deal, and I remember Skyline Drive being one way that day. Remember that?"

He shook his head.

"Well it was, one way south before the ceremony and one way north after it. I don't know why that stands out with me, but it does."

"I'd forgotten about it, but you're right, and they also had those tank wagons stationed along the Drive for gas and oil. They intrigued me."

"That's a male thing," she laughed.

Rayna's dark head was bobbing across the meadow, quite a ways off, and he called out for her. She turned immediately and waved to them, and then slowly headed back.

"Remember all those troopers moving the traffic?" Alma was stuffing her magazine down in her bag. "Fifty or more. I thought it was ridiculous to have so many."

"Well, they were there to protect the president, too."

"I guess so. It was a great day, wasn't it?"

Rayna was racing toward them. "Daddy, can we look for—"

Unconsciously, he cut her off, "Not until we eat."

"It's high noon, Daddy," Alma joked. "Why don't we eat now?"

"Yes, Daddy! Let's have the picnic!"

So they traipsed back over the meadow toward the car, taking the long way across. The sun was directly overhead by then, beating down mercilessly. The cool mountain breezes had mysteriously ceased, and the hot, dry grass scrunched beneath their feet. Alma pulled her magazine out again and vigorously fanned herself with it.

Rayna whined, "It's hot, Daddy, and I'm tired!"

He hoisted her up on his shoulders, and she squealed with delight as they marched across the wide open meadow, picking their way carefully through the squatted masses of blueberry bushes. He thought about how red they would turn come fall and wished it was fall now with its refreshing coolness.

"I didn't remember it being this far," Alma said.

Greyson led her on with Rayna swatting at the butterflies over his head in quick jerky movements. He was breathing hard and fast, and each step seemed more labored than the last. How much longer? He couldn't wait to get to the car and let Rayna down. It would feel so good to rest.

"I should have worn my other shoes," Alma complained, but her words seemed distant and vague to him, like they were floating from the other side of the meadow.

Rayna was clapping her hands and singing, "Picnic… picnic…picnic…."

It was all ringing in his ears with a loud buzzing, and suddenly he let out a sharp cry and dropped to the ground. Rayna toppled over him, and Alma screamed out.

"Daddy!" Rayna leaped up immediately.

Greyson was rigid and unconscious, and his skin was turning a bluish cast as he lay upon the wild grasses.

"Daddy!"

Alma stood frozen in her spot, a stricken look on her face. He was jerking uncontrollably, a stiff, strange and inhuman sight.

"Daddy's dead!" Rayna wailed, and she commenced to jumping up and down in a frenzied state just as he started to breathe again, heavy, irregular gulps of air while saliva ran down his neck.

Alma suddenly realized what was happening and yelled for help. A group of tourists were just coming onto the meadow, not terribly far away, and a young Ranger was leading them. He rushed toward them with the tourists in tow. They circled around, concerned but curious.

"Step back, folks!"

He cleared the space around him for air, immediately taking control of the situation, but Rayna still wailed hysterically, unable to be comforted.

The inevitable had happened.

And the following week Greyson couldn't get out of her sight. She had suddenly become his shield, his protector, scrutinizing his every move, watching and waiting, and though he understood completely, still it aggravated him. All his life, everyone had been protecting him, smothering him it seemed, and now even his baby daughter! All but Alma, that is. After the Big Meadows incident, she had decided such pathetic doings didn't fit into her plans and quietly disappeared off the scene. Greyson reverted back into his shell and stayed there throughout the summer and on into the fall and winter.

Then it was March, and the imminent approach of another spring slowly began to lift his spirits. Hints of its arrival were everywhere, in the treetops, subtly swathed in reddish hues, and furtively poking up through last year's damp, matted leaves. The new growth of wildflowers welcomed him, and in the air there was an obvious clarity and warm freshness. The bird songs were enchanting, and not only was it almost springtime, it was Rayna's birthday. She was turning four years old, much to everyone's joy, and they showered her with gifts and festivities. Ma baked a whopping chocolate cake, four huge layers, one for each year, a huge delight for her, and everyone showed up. Everyone, that is, except for Mildred and her family, who were far too busy to make it. Greyson surprised her with a small music box that she wound up over and over, and the high-pitched tune of "Don't Sit Under the Apple Tree" reverberated throughout the house day and night. It became a shrill, penetrating squeak, rattling his nerves whenever he was home, and he silently regretted his choice.

Then the dogwoods bloomed.

Frequent showers began to water the thirsty earth, and the forest behind the house dripped and dripped, and Ma watched her flowers bud and blossom. Every day she would snip a few and stick them in a Mason jar. They would sit there on the window sill, bathed in sunshine and brightening up the whole kitchen, until someone noticed that they had wilted, and she would take them back outside to nature and dump them at the edge of the yard, only to snip another bunch and repeat the whole process.

With the spring came Pa's restlessness and endless yearning to return to the mountain. He wanted to walk through his orchard again. He could picture the snowy profusion of white blossoms blanketing the slopes, frosting the ground, and delicately blowing through the fresh, spring air. He longed to turn up the rich, black soil for another garden and sow his seeds once more. He wanted to drink of the cold, clear water that gurgled from his spring. These yearnings never failed to put him in a bad mood. The family could count on it from year to year, and they sought to counteract by diverting his attention. As spring lengthened, William and Jack would visit more or sometimes take him out for the day.

Mildred showed up unexpectedly one Friday and took him and Ma home with her for a few days. They hoped the change would help, at least take his mind off the mountain place. The following day, Jack and Marian arrived and offered to take Rayna with them into town for the Saturday matinee. *Life with Father* was playing, starring the popular William Powell and Irene Dunne, and they were anxious to see it. The couple had become more and more interested in Rayna lately, perhaps because they craved a child so much themselves and were trying hard to start a family. They picked her up early that morning. Greyson was invited, too, but he opted to stay home, actually looking forward to some time alone.

"You ever been to a picture show?" Marian asked as they headed down the road with Rayna seated primly on the back seat, holding onto her shiny new pocketbook they had given her for her birthday. It matched the black patent leather shoes that stuck out in front of her.

She shook her head, and Jack noticed her looking back toward the house. "Don't worry about your dad. He's got things to do today."

She twirled around. "What things?"

"Oh...guys like to get off to themselves sometimes and do things...things we like." He was surprised at her unexpected fervor.

"Like what?"

"Well, you know...man things."

Her small forehead furrowed. "Did you know my daddy has fits?"

"Yes...but they aren't exactly called fits."

"I know. Grandma explained it all to me. They're epileptic seizures, but Grandpa said they're fits."

"Well, he can't help them, you know, and he hardly ever has one."

"He had one at Big Meadows."

Jack wondered where this conversation was going. "I know he did."

Marian tried changing the subject, "The show today is about a father, also, and I think you'll like it."

"I wonder if he has fits, too."

Marian frowned. "Probably not."

"My daddy's make him fall down and yucky stuff comes out of his mouth and—"

"Rayna," Jack interrupted. "You like ice cream?"

She nodded and glanced back out the window, but there was no sign of the house now. "How long will we be gone?"

"Not that long, and we'll get some ice cream on the way, too."

"I fell off my daddy when he had the fit."

"Well, we're certainly glad you didn't get hurt."

"And we never did have that picnic."

Greyson had welcomed their offer to take Rayna out to the matinee, very appreciative of their recent interest in her. He was also looking forward to time to finally rest. He knew that's what he needed, and that's what the doctor prescribed. But how could he? Working long hours, and when he wasn't, having to be both father and mother. It wasn't easy.

So why was he having second thoughts now? Even wishing he hadn't so readily agreed, but that was selfish, entirely selfish. Was he becoming narcissistic? God forbid! He went into his bedroom and pulled down the coverlet to lie down, trying to clear his tired mind of all the racing thoughts that constantly took control of it, thoughts of the past, thoughts of the present and thoughts of the troublesome future. Before he knew it, he was sound asleep. The sun climbed high, perched overhead and then began its timeless descent. It was afternoon before he awoke. He glanced toward the window, surprised that he had slept so long. The sun had a declining slant now, but he felt rested and better than he had in some time. He could hear the birds singing outside, and he got up.

He rambled about in the empty kitchen, fixing himself a bologna and mustard sandwich, and sat down at the table. He glanced around at his ma's cabinet with its different colored wood, a light, yellowish hue with reddish maple doors on top and bottom. The metal shelf was also that yellowish hue, though he could barely see it now, it was so filled with her mixing bowls and different cooking paraphernalia. Pa had managed to buy it for her when they moved into the new house, and she highly prized it. She said it set off the kitchen, and he had to admit she was right. Otherwise it would be rather bare. An exposed enamel sink jutted out from underneath the lone window, the ice box stood directly across the room from it, and a hefty wood stove filled the corner. But still, it was a sight better than the old kitchen on the mountain, although Pa would never admit it.

There was no pretty cabinet on the mountain or sink or ice box. Instead he remembered shelves nailed onto the wall for Ma's dishes, and he could barely tiptoe to reach them. They were in the step-down pantry, and he used to jump up and down the lone step over and over. It was a fun thing for him to do, especially when he couldn't go outside. He remembered the large bucket that sat on a lower shelf below the dishes, and the gourd dipper, and usually there was water sloshed out around it. And he certainly remembered all those trips out to the springhouse. He had hated being sent out to fetch water, but now the ill-effects of the daily chore had faded, and the refreshing gurgle of the cold water was a pleasant memory. The coolness of the rustic little springhouse on a hot summer day was a satisfying reminiscence to dwell on, and he sat there immersed in such far away thoughts.

Somehow memory had a way of reinventing itself over time, diminishing the unpleasant, tangible aspects and wrapping itself in a rosy, feel-good sort of aura. Thus his memory of the old place had dimmed with the years, shrouded in haze, losing all former rough edges, and now it was permanently flavored with yeasty aromas and sweet scents of the apple orchard in bloom and the smell of tomatoes dangling from acid vines on hot summer days. Maybe he was becoming nostalgic like his pa. Perhaps it was an age thing, but he wasn't old, certainly not that old!

Suddenly he felt rather alone. He finished his sandwich, cleared off the table, and then paced throughout the small house, his good mood slowly dissipating. He was feeling quite uneasy, but a golden glow was spilling in through the windows, and a warm inviting sun was pulling him outside. He decided to take a drive.

Automatically he headed up the mountain and figured he was becoming more like his pa, for sure. He knew he probably shouldn't be driving, but he had to get out of the house, and there wasn't that much traffic on Skyline Drive. Besides, the doctor had assured him that this increased dosage would do the trick, and he didn't have anything to worry about. He certainly hoped so, more for Rayna than for himself. It was undoubtedly the most powerful medicine he had prescribed thus far, and it certainly seemed to be working. He gazed up into the clear blue sky and watched a hawk sweeping low. He had never liked hawks, the vicious predators always seeking small, innocent prey. It vanished over the treetops just as he saw the sign up ahead.

A familiar calm embraced him as he pulled onto the Drive and glanced around at the spring trees hedging up against it, bearing their new crop of leaves. He inhaled the freshness of the mountains and drove on, conscious of how its peace pervaded his very soul, soothing it more than any prescribed drug. He noticed the Allegheny goatsbeard growing in bunches. He had always liked it and decided it really did resemble a goat's beard. He wound around the curves, up and down the slopes, the sun's warmth seeping deliciously through the windows, and the ever-present memories returned.

It was the season he remembered most. Springtime. The season made for the senses. Warm evenings with the sun dropping behind the mountains, leaving a vivid outline etched on the horizon. He could still see it, and he could almost hear the tree frogs, with their incessant song, and the cicadas. He could hear the spring rains pounding the small cabin into the long nights, and smell the morning after with its pungent, earthy fragrance. He could taste the blackberries. And he could almost feel the energy that boiled over in his veins, that youthful vigor bursting forth when he scrambled outside into the early morning to face another day, another aimless day on the mountain filled with a boy's dreams.

Every mile, every ridge, every curve in the road conjured up the past out of time's bleary shadows, bold and clear, just like it was yesterday. He wallowed in it, happily hunkered down in its cozy warmth. He was a boy again, and he and Rayna Rose were perched comfortably up in one of Pa's apple trees. It was in full bloom, a cloud of pinkish white shrouded them, and honeybees danced about. They were singing a silly old tune that Uncle Sims had taught them—but suddenly the picture changed, and he was plunged into that painful abyss. His thoughts whirled back to that spring day that he couldn't escape. The government men had come the week before, telling them that they *would* have to move off the mountain, but Pa wouldn't believe them. And then the mail came and the notice.

Notice to Vacate.

They were all there, the whole family, Ma and Pa and William and Mildred and Jack and him and Rayna Rose. They all read it, even he and Rayna Rose. He could still see it clearly in his mind, all typed out neat and business-like and signed by the Chairman of the State Commission. They had stood there in silence, absorbing the awful gravity of the situation. He remembered reading it over and over again, trying to understand how something so small, just a piece of paper, could send them off the mountain, and then Rayna Rose bolted out the door.

"Let her go...she'll be all right," Pa said, his voice displaying tired resignation. "She'll just have to get used to it like the rest of us...ain't gonna be easy for none of us, that's for sure." He pushed on past them and out the back door, with his head hung low and his spirit broken.

"Gonna be the hardest on him," Ma said, worriedly. "Pa's hardly ever been off the mountain except down to Elkton, ain't never cared nothing about the Valley and the towns and such, nothing about anything but this here place."

He remembered jumping up abruptly and taking off after Rayna Rose.

Ma had called him back, "Greyson, don't you go and run yourself and get all hot...you hear...you'll have a spell!"

He vividly recalled his anger at hearing those words, and even angrier at hearing William's sarcastic response.

"Let him go, Ma. Y'all pamper that kid too much, gonna make a sissy out of him...already have if you ask me."

"I ain't no sissy!" he had yelled back over his shoulder, tears stinging his eyes.

The memory took on life, and suddenly he was bounding up the worn path all over again. The sun was piercing the treetops, scaling the ridges and splashing a quilted patchwork on the ground, but he was focused ahead, straining for a glimpse of Rayna Rose, but he couldn't see her anywhere. He figured she had run up the path. She usually did when she got angry or upset. He wondered why she always got so gall-darned upset. He didn't like it anymore than she did that they had to move off the mountain, but what could they do? Won't no need in acting like this! He was panting hard as he tore through the ripening orchard and over the weedy field. Then he caught a glimpse of her red dress disappearing into the forest.

"Rayna Rose!"

She kept on running.

She's about as hardheaded as they come, he thought angrily, dodging the rocks in the path. Must be that Aunt Belle again! Ma said she took after her, but she'd been dead for years, long before he and Rayna Rose were ever born, but Ma said she was just like her.

He was tired of running after her all the time but suppose he didn't. Something might happen. He knew there were bobcats in the deep woods and even mountain lions sometimes. Folks had seen them. With that in mind, he ran all the harder. He recognized the trail she'd chosen. It was one they'd explored only a few weeks ago, but gosh, he hoped she wouldn't go all the way! He was feeling awfully short of breath.

But Rayna Rose had one thing in mind—to run away. That would teach them—teach them all—especially them old gov'ment folks. They'd never catch her and make her move. Nope, she won't gonna move for nobody! This was her home!

She knew Greyson was chasing her, but she could outrun him any day, besides somebody had to do something, and he sure wouldn't. He was just too darn nice! She sailed through the forest, ducking under tree branches poking left and right, determination driving her on. She forged straight through the tangled blackberry bushes, briars ripping her dress and tearing at her arms, but she never slowed down. If they couldn't find her, then they couldn't move. They'd have to stay. Maybe they'd all change their minds. Grownups had a way of changing their minds anyway. Look how many times they had already. Huffing and puffing, she raced on, not caring where, beggar's lice clinging to her torn dress.

Greyson slowed to rest and noticed the forest growing darker. He glanced up to the sky. How quickly it had changed. Now a leaden gray with heavy clouds moving in, blowing in from the west, they were already blocking the sun.

"Rayna…Rayna Rose…."

She heard him calling and glanced back; she could see him now, but barely. She also noticed the forest growing dark and the wind kicking up. A storm must be brewing, she thought, and she didn't like storms, but Greyson was especially afraid of them. He would be plenty mad if they got caught out in one, too. She started to turn back but remembered the gov'ment men and kept on running. The darkened clouds were now swirling in an ominous fashion, casting threatening shadows over the woods. Still she ran on.

The wind increased, twisting and bending the tender saplings and flipping their leaves over to their sallow undersides. All of a sudden thunder reverberated throughout the forest, and Greyson cringed. Doggone Aunt Belle! She must be like her, and she was thick-headed just like Pa said, too. But she was gonna catch it when he caught up with her!

The rain began to fall, scattered drops at first, pelting the leaves overhead, and then big, splashy globs slapping at his face. It increased steadily, beating its incessant drum upon millions of leaves around him, creating an imaginary setting. At any other time he would have been tempted to hunker down and listen, to discover what it was like down close to the earth with all the tiny insects beneath the leaves, the secrets of nature, but not with the thunder and lightning, no way! And certainly not with Rayna Rose racing to who knows where. He wished he had his sweater, and, even more, he wished Rayna Rose would get some sense in her head! She might be smarter than him, but she sure didn't act like it.

The rain was pouring now, falling in solid sheets, making it difficult for him to see, but he pushed on anyway with his head down, terrified of the lightning that was zigzagging across the darkening sky. Leaves were ripping off and sailing throughout the woods, and claps of thunder wrapped the entire forest in a sinister embrace.

"Rayna Rose!"

He couldn't see her. Slipping and sliding on the soggy, wet ground with sudden rivulets streaming across the path, he swiped at his eyes with his sleeve and struggled to stay on his feet. Then he saw her up ahead.

"Stop, Rayna Rose…stop!"

Was she deaf? He didn't know whether she was deliberately ignoring him or whether she couldn't hear because of the wind and rain and thunder.

"Stop, Rayna Rose…you crazy?"

Then he remembered the tree, the old, fallen chestnut they had discovered the last time they had ventured this way. It was massive and completely hulled out on the inside, probably from some wild creature—who knows what—but they had climbed up in it, pretending to hide from the world. It must be just up ahead. He strained to see through the solid wall of rain that was drenching him from head to foot. If they could make it, they might have some shelter. A tremendous crack of thunder blasted throughout the forest, seemingly shaking its very foundation.

"Rayna Rose…run to the tree…the fallen chestnut," he screamed out. "Run for cover!"

He could barely see now, but he caught a glimpse of her red dress, and it looked like she was slowing down, and then it disappeared!

"Rayna Rose!"

Struggling frantically against the onslaught of wind and rain, he finally caught up. She had fallen and was lying in a pool of water, a forced stream that had emerged from the mountainside, over brush and rocks, pushing its way downhill. She was fighting to get up but kept falling back into the muddy water. He grabbed hold of her and pulled her drenched body up and half carried her toward the old chestnut. He could see it just ahead as lightning lit up the forest.

It was almost dark now, more like twilight than daytime except for the incessant streaks of lightning. Panting harder and harder, he pulled her on. They were within a few feet of it when he collapsed, and the two of them fell to the sodden earth. Instantly, Rayna Rose realized what had happened, and it brought her up with a start.

His body was stiffened and jerking uncontrollably and looking frightful in the lightning flashes, and she was afraid to touch him. Afterwards he lay very still, stretched out in the soaking rain, his eyes closed. She began to pull him toward the chestnut. Though he was thin, he was taller than she, and it was difficult to maneuver him.

"I'm sorry, Greyson," she cried as she pushed and rolled him up into the round, gaping hole. She tried to squeeze in too, but he was like lead and there just wasn't room for them both. "I didn't mean to hurt you," she pleaded, hovering over the tree and rubbing his matted hair. The downpour of rain beat upon her and mingled with her flood of tears. She waited for him to come to. He always came to, but the wind turned cooler and then colder, and still he slept.

He never got his chance to scold her, he thought miserably, or to tell her he was sorry, sorry for what happened. If only he hadn't had that seizure!

When he came to, the storm had abated, all was still except for the dripping trees, but it was a good while before he was able to drag himself back home, even with her help. They had stumbled out of the soggy wet woods, down the slippery mountainside, soaked and exhausted, and met William and Jack halfway coming after them. It was the first time they weren't lectured. Instead, the boys picked them up and carried them the rest of the way. The following day she took ill, and each day she fared worse.

He remembered sitting out on the porch steps, anxiously waiting for the first sign of the doctor. William had gone down to Elkton to fetch him. He remembered Ma calling to him over and over from the house, "Any sign of them yet?" She never left Rayna Rose's bedside.

"No, ma'am," he answered every time.

"Keep on watching and let me know when you see them coming."

He had strained and strained to see out over last year's wasted cornfield. It was a cloudless sky, and the sun was shining brightly and bouncing off the tin roof of the chicken house, almost too brightly for him to see anything at all. But the image of him sitting there, drawn and hunched over, with his hands cupped over his eyes, was forever etched in his mind. Why couldn't it have been a sunny day when she ran off instead of stormy? Then she wouldn't have caught a cold, and she wouldn't have gotten sick!

He remembered how grateful he was when he finally spotted something in the distance and saw that it was William and the doctor.

"Here they come, Ma! I see them coming!"

Mildred was waiting at the door as the wagon pulled up the mountainside. Wearily the doctor, short and rotund, climbed down and headed for the porch, his unruly beard, peppered black and white, rested lightly on his chest.

"How you doing there, son?"

The old doctor had patted him on the head and walked inside, his black satchel bumping up against the door. He smelled of mothballs as he passed by, and it had lingered with him over the years, a sickening, haunting smell. Mildred welcomed him in, pulling him towards the bedroom, and William followed after. But he had waited outside, still hunched on the steps, unable to go in.

A sudden blast thrust him back to reality, an earsplitting car horn. It had come up unexpectedly behind him, and he realized how slow he was driving. He pulled over to the side of the road, and it sped by impatiently. Teenagers stared out at him, angrily shaking their fists.

What was he doing?

Why was he rehashing old times anyway; why was he doing that? It only took him down the same dark path, and he didn't want to go there again. He had come up here to enjoy himself. He pushed the past back into its place, to a place he had hollowed out for it, a place in the recesses of his soul, a deep, secret place like the big, old, fallen chestnut. He had created it years ago, conveniently so, a place to keep her memory, tender and painful.

He glanced around.

Unknowingly, he had stopped right beside the dirt road that led down to the Mission—the little Episcopal Mission down in the hollow—and it was a happy remembrance. It was called the Upper Pocosin Mission, the one they had attended as kids, and suddenly he had an overwhelming urge to see it again. Mildred and William used to go to meetings there from time to time. Meetings that were specifically for the young people, and sometimes Jack went, too. On rare occasions they would let him and Rayna Rose tag along, but grudgingly, and only when Ma had insisted on it.

He edged the car more over onto the grass and climbed out, and then started walking down the rough, dirt road, sandwiched beneath poplars, oaks, hickorys and others, tall and straight. It was a pleasing road that led on for about a mile. Blackberry thickets abounded, holding long-ago memories, and his twin sister's image floated among them, but still he pressed on, deeper and deeper into the tranquil forest. It silently closed in behind him as he descended, the lush undergrowth embracing him in its calming foliage. It was almost like he had stepped into a time machine that transported him back to boyhood, and he was following behind Mildred on the way to the Mission.

"Quit idling, Greyson, and get on up here. We're gonna be late for the service!"

Vaguely, he remembered her chastising, and then it all flashed back vividly, perhaps because it was one of the few things that they had to do outside of their daily routine. He remembered sitting around with the older kids as they laughed and teased one another. It was a carefree mood as such get-togethers are at that age, whether it be a picnic, a ballgame or a church meeting. They were testing the waters, dipping their toes in and balancing the bridge between childhood and the puzzling adult world. He remembered singing hymns with them, spirited hymns, and trying to keep in tune. He had never been one to carry a tune, and Mildred would frown down at him one minute and then giggle the next. In fact, he recalled a lot of giggling on those occasions, and usually he didn't know what they were giggling about, but he giggled along with them anyway. It made him feel good.

He smiled at the pleasant memory while making his way down the narrow road, cautiously stepping over occasional fallen trees and crunching through decaying leaves, and dodging mushy places where spring rains had washed and settled. Those times at the Mission were welcomed interludes in the midst of what was often doom and gloom on the mountain, for they were the days preceding the move. He found himself growing more anxious to see it again, though he didn't remember it being this far, but, then, it had been a long time. Birds flashed over his head, flitting from one tree to another, and he couldn't help but wonder what it would have been like to remain on the mountain.

Suppose there had never been a Park?

Would there still be hundreds of people living on the mountain? Would the Mission still be open with young people filling its doors with giggles? Would he still be living here? He recalled that day years ago when he and Pa and Jack were clearing the field, and he was throwing rocks onto the pile. That was when Jack told him the place would be his when he grew up.

But that was foolish thinking. What good did it do? He glanced around at the vacant forest, but only vacant of people, he thought. Its serenity was deceiving, for life was evident all around him, thriving life, pulsating life. He could hear the subtle but constant rustle beneath the dead leaves, tiny creatures hidden from sight. And the woods were popping with fresh, green growth, and tiny, colorful wildflowers poking up through layers of decaying remnants. He gazed up at a towering, grapevine-wrapped poplar swaying in the mountain breeze. It would be loaded with grapes come fall. It used to frustrate him when he was small because he couldn't reach them. Mostly they hung onto the upper limbs. Suddenly he caught a glimpse of something up ahead; the sun was splashing it a burnished gold.

It was the old Mission, folded into the bosom of the forest and sheltered by a thick canopy of lofty trees. A wave of nostalgia washed over him as he turned right and stepped out into a patch of dazzling sunlight.

There was a hush in the woods as he walked up to it and reached out to touch its mossy walls. He stood there and wondered why he couldn't remember a single sermon—most likely because his mind had been anywhere but in the Mission. Taking slow and measured steps, he trudged around it, stopping every few feet to examine the damp, cracked stones.

He sat down on its crumbling steps to let the old memories have their way. The silence was penetrating. The sun was slowly sinking behind the rim of trees, casting its fiery glow through them, setting the forest afire. He thought about his siblings, William and Jack and Mildred, but especially his twin sister, and his maddening illness. He thought about the dreadful move, his time in the CCCs, and then his ill-fated trip to the coast. He sat there trying to make sense of it all, grappling for some underlying thread that was meant to weave it all together into a beautiful pattern, some lovely work of art. He had read about people's lives being that way, but all he could see was chaos, a twisted mess, loose threads of mistakes and blunders dangling in obvious disorder. He could see no work of art, and then he heard it.

'Be still, and know that I am God.'

Jerking around, he half expected to see somebody, but there was no one—only the old Mission bathed in the setting sun and the slight movement of tree branches rubbing up against it.

Still the words echoed in his head.

They reached out to him as fingers from the past. And he remembered. How could he have forgotten? The preacher had quoted those words years ago when he was just a young boy here with his older sister and brothers. It had caused a stir within him back then, one that he had set out to prove. A thoughtful and too often analytical boy, he had wondered if he were to be perfectly still, would God come down to him like He had done with Moses on that mountain? Time and time again he had attempted to find out—in the cornfield and out in the apple orchard, but he especially remembered that day when he had tried it high up on the mountain, thinking that was the place!

He had lain there perfectly still on his back gazing up through the leafy trees into the clear sky. He must have lain there for over an hour, without moving, hardly breathing…and waiting. But after awhile he had given up and trod back down, figuring God was too busy for a mere boy in the Blue Ridge. And once they were forced to move off the mountain, he decided the preacher's God really didn't care about mountain folk anyhow, for if He did, why didn't He stop them gov'ment men?

It was a poignant memory as he sat fixed on the old Mission walls. The words kept hammering in his head, but not just his head. Something else was going on, something far deeper. He looked up into the soaring trees, and on past them to patches of blue sky, feeling like a boy all over again. Why did those words come back to him now after all these years?

"I AM STILL, GOD!" he shouted into the forest.

There was silence…but a tangible silence…a knowing silence.

Tears slid down his face, and it was as if all his life had taken place for this very moment—this capsule of truth, and he was ready.

He was ready to surrender.

And he slid off the stone steps and down on his knees while the sun dropped behind the mountains.

CHAPTER EIGHT

Lorna stared out the window. The myrtle trees were twisting in the cold wind, and she was glad they didn't lose their leaves like most things. Everything looked stark in the grip of winter; that's what she hated most. It was almost Christmas; soon 1947 would come to a close. It had been over two and a half years since the war ended, but still she could see that it hadn't totally ended for Hayden, who was often lost in thought—private thoughts that he wouldn't share or couldn't share, she didn't know which. But she didn't press him anymore. At first, she had encouraged him to talk, but to no avail. What little she knew of his hard times he had mentioned briefly upon returning, before he pushed them into his own private alcoves. He wasn't the same Hayden that had left her. It was no secret that he had barely escaped drowning when the ship he was on sank. She couldn't imagine such horror. To be on a ship as it listed beneath the deep sea, to fight for your life midst the freezing water, no wonder he was changed. However, when she saw that distant look cloud his face, she was overwhelmed with guilt, and her imagination took on all sorts of shapes and turns. And when his pensive eyes rested on her, she imagined that somehow, someway, he knew. But that was crazy!

Cory was taking his daily nap, and she was listening to the radio as she cleaned out the ice box, sopping up the cold water from the melted block. The popular tune fit her mood, a bit wistful and a bit sad.

How are things in Glocca Morra?
Is that little brook still leaping there?
Does it still run down to Donny cove?
Through Killybegs, Kilkerry and Kildare?

She absently hummed along with it. She had always loved the Irish melodies, just like Christmas carols and Christmas, but she could hardly wait till spring when the yellow-rump warblers would return. They would fill the myrtle trees with song, their bright yellow streaking the waxy green foliage as they darted in and out of its thick, new growth. Spring always lifted her spirits. She could get outside in the warm sun and dig her fingers into the soft earth and plant marigolds and zinnias, or just sit idly down by the Bay. Being cooped up in the house all day was definitely depressing, and Virginia winters could be so sunless, dreary and colorless, downright gray!

"Lorna dear, would you please turn that thing down… it's getting on my nerves."

She glared at her mother. She did have it down! Everything got on her nerves lately. She wondered when she was going home. It had been almost two weeks now. Ever since they had moved into the place, her mother found one excuse or another for these extra long visits. She couldn't blame her, though. It was a haven, with its sweeping lawn winding down to the Back Bay, its rippling waters surging first one way and then the other, depending on the ever-changing winds. Though they had always lived near the Bay, it was not like this. Theirs had been a winding, grown-up path with absolutely no view from the house. Hayden loved this place and had sunk all of their meager savings into the modest two-story farm house that sat languidly on three acres bordering it.

She switched off the radio. Her dad didn't seem to mind her mother's long absences either. No wonder. Ironically, Hayden enjoyed her company and so did Cory, who was developing into an engaging five-year-old, who could talk your head off, especially if he had your undivided attention, and if he didn't he would persist until he did.

"I didn't say turn it off, dear…just down."

"Well, I'm going out for a walk anyway…besides, isn't it time for your *Groucho Marx* program?"

"Oh my goodness!" Her mother shot upward. "I almost forgot…get your coat, dear. It's cold out there!"

Lorna jerked it off the wooden coat stand and closed the door behind her. She marched briskly down the long, narrow driveway bordered by water-filled gullies, still somewhat crystallized from last week's freeze. She glanced up at the dead tree nearby with the messy osprey nest, pieces of it missing now, blown away, and she remembered the brown and white osprey that sat on it last spring and the babies that appeared in early summer. She wondered if it would return this spring. Maybe. She had heard that they did. It must be nice to migrate, she thought, to spend the summers in one place and the winters in another. You'd never get bored that way, not that she was bored. How could she be with little Cory? It's just that she had been feeling sort of down in the dumps ever since her surgery. The hysterectomy had been necessary, the doctor insisted, and grudgingly she had agreed. It had been months now, but still she felt adrift, cheerless, and unable to shake it.

Hayden had taken it in stride. He was satisfied with his son, and it wasn't like she was going to get pregnant again anyway. They had tried and tried ever since the war ended.

It wasn't meant to be, she figured, looking up into the leaden sky. Of course, she was happy with Cory, but still she had hoped.

The winter winds caught the myrtle trees along the driveway, wrenching them back and forth, and she remembered another such day—and the little bundle with a dark head. She would probably be a beautiful child by now, and one day a lovely young woman. A lump formed in her throat. She would never know.

Unless?

She pushed the forbidden thought from her mind and walked on. She walked further than usual, and when she started back up the long driveway, she noticed the same empty osprey nest. She looked up into the sky and shivered. It was turning colder.

Cory was up from his nap when she returned, and she flopped down on the floor with him and played checkers for the next hour. Then Hayden dashed in, coughing and brushing off his coat. "It's snowing!"

Cory flew to the window, and she was right behind him. Sure enough, large, fluffy snowflakes were floating all about. A picture straight out of a Norman Rockwell painting, complete with the leaning garage that Hayden had intended to hoist up and straighten out, but hadn't gotten around to yet. Now it only added to the wistful ambiance softened by the snow's early dusting. Lorna leaned into the window. It would qualify for a cover of *The Saturday Evening Post,* she thought proudly.

"Mama, look!" Cory was jumping up and down and pointing to the sky.

"Is it really snowing?" her mother asked, more a complaint than a question. She had never liked snow.

"Sure is," Hayden replied.

"I thought it felt like it when I was walking." Lorna watched her husband vigorously warming his hands by the hot stove. "But your cold sounds worse, dear."

He shrugged off her concern, "I don't think it's going to stick though." He hoisted Cory up on his shoulders, lifting him up to the ceiling. "The flakes are way too big. Don't you think, son?"

"No, Daddy, I want it to stick!"

Lorna wished he wouldn't fret him so.

"I know you do, but what about the picture show?" he asked, dropping him gently to the floor. "If it snows too much we can't go."

Lorna hastened to the pantry. "I almost forgot!" She pulled out the ironing board and grabbed the iron. "I need to press my dress…Maureen O'Hara is starring in it, too, and she is so good…remember her, Mother?"

"I remember." She raised her eyebrows as Lorna went to get her dress.

"Don't get your hopes up too much," Hayden called after, wondering now if he should have said anything at all. "I really don't think it will stick, but we'll have to wait and see what happens."

"Well, I'm getting ready anyway." She was back with her dress, spreading it over the ironing board. She filled the bottle with water and began sprinkling it on the blue and white flowery dress, and then licked her finger and stuck it on the hot iron.

"You reckon she's on that blacklist?"

"Who, Mother?"

"Maureen O'Hara."

"Oh, Mother!"

"Well, she could be, you know."

"Mother, it's a beautiful new Christmas story called—"

"I know...*Miracle on 34th Street.* I heard about it already, but there are hundreds of those Communists," she prattled on insistently, "writers, directors and actors, all supposed to be sympathizers. That's what they say, and I sure wouldn't go to see anybody who's a Communist or the likes of them...and you never know about such things!"

Hayden caught Lorna's eye and shook his head. More often than not, he found himself the mediator. "You think maybe we could have some of your snow ice cream if it does stick, Mother?"

"Yeah, Grandma!" Cory grabbed hold of her and wrapped his arms around her knees in urgent pleas. She smiled down at him indulgently, forgetting all about the actors and writers and Communist sympathizers. "Well, I don't see why not, since it's not the first snow." They had had a couple of other light snows already, though none that really stuck, but they knew they were well overdue.

"I didn't think they counted," Hayden kidded.

Lorna eyed Cory's beaming face as she slid the iron back and forth. "I think we'd better count them," she laughed nervously, so pleased to be going out. Seldom did they go anyplace. Hayden was definitely a homebody. Usually she had to urge, nag or almost beg to get him to entertain an evening out. She finished pressing her dress and hung it up on a hanger, and then went to the window again.

The snow was still falling.

Two long, frigid weeks passed, and then Christmas Eve. Cory was ecstatic. Bubbling over for weeks now, his childish enthusiasm had at last boiled over to the others, especially his mom and grandparents. It was impossible for it not to. That was the magic of Christmas, Lorna thought, as they drove up the foggy road. It had a way of changing the scenery, brightly coloring it, not just the tree and lights and gifts, but also the hearts of people, young and old alike. It presented an opportunity for adults and even the aged to slip back into their former lives, and relive those happy days, those childhood memories, through their children and grandchildren or any other youngsters that happened to be about. Lorna loved watching Cory's face light up and seeing him so thrilled with everything. She only wished Hayden could get a little of the spirit, but he was as dry as ever.

"I hope they'll be ready," he muttered, pulling into the drive.

"They'll be ready," she snapped, applying lipstick with her little compact mirror, and smacking her lips together. She glanced at Cory in the back seat. "Don't take your stocking cap off, Cory. You'll catch cold."

He yanked it back down over his ears. "But I can't hear nothing!"

"Anything…son, you can't hear anything," Hayden corrected.

"But I wanna hear!"

The front door opened, and her parents shuffled out.

"Watch out for that ice!" Hayden hollered out the window, and her father grabbed hold of her mother's arm just in time. Teetering over the slippery drive, he gripped the door handle and pulled it open.

"Whew! It's freezing out here." He pushed and tugged to get her mother in. He clambered in behind her, and Cory hopped over on his lap. "But it sure feels good in here."

The heater was going full blast. "Hayden warmed the car up ahead of time," Lorna explained.

"And we appreciate it, too." Her mother leaned forward and patted him on the shoulder. He backed slowly out of the drive and turned down the narrow road closely bordered with frozen water-filled gullies. They passed by scrub pines mournfully bent to the ground, and by drooping, icy cedars arching artfully over barbed wire fences. They passed by brown marshlands encrusted with ice, and finally on past Tabernacle United Methodist Church, noticing warm yellow lights in the windows and a few vehicles pulled up close.

"Looks like they've started already," Lorna commented.

"I knew we'd be late," Hayden grumbled again. "You know Nimmo's always on time."

"Don't fret. We won't be the only ones," his mother-in-law chided, rubbing Cory's knee. "We've got plenty of time."

"Will we be back before Santa comes?" Cory asked worriedly, lightening the mood.

"I hope so," Hayden said, puffing on his Camel. "I hope so." He glanced up in the mirror and saw his son's furrowed brow.

"Of course we will," Lorna added swiftly, "...and you better drive with both hands, Hayden." She didn't like him smoking while driving anyway. "These roads might be slippery, too."

"I'm all right, dear."

They passed by the Lotus Garden Pond. "Look at those poor shriveled up lotuses," Lorna remarked. "They look so...so—"

"So ugly!"

"Oh, Mother."

"Well, they do."

Why did her mother always see the worst in things? She stifled a comeback and said, "But they'll be beautiful this summer. You can bet on that." She could see their lovely, soft, yellow blooms opening up, covering the entire pond. It was something looked forward to by everyone and had ever since the first colonists landed nearby at Cape Henry. They had quickly discovered the native wild flower growing in the water gardens and being tended by the Indians. Lorna had always been charmed by the story and, as a child, she used to imagine the Indians in full regalia, with bright colorful paint and feathers, carefully maneuvering through the still waters to pluck the coveted seeds.

The sedan bumped along, crunching through the icy, rutted road, and it seemed like they would never get there. In fact, her father had even mentioned the idea of switching to Tabernacle, which would certainly be more convenient, but her mother wouldn't hear of it. A mangy fox shot across the road in front of them, and Hayden swerved to miss it.

"Should have hit the blasted thing!"

"Hayden!" Lorna was embarrassed at his behavior on the way to church.

He frowned at her. "Well, I should have."

Cory jumped up from the back seat. "What was it?"

"Just a fox, dear," his grandma replied.

"Well, they are a nuisance, that's for sure," her father spoke up in his reassuring tone.

They rounded the curve and saw the beautiful, old church sitting in the fork of the road, shining starkly white in the gathering dusk, manifesting an aura of purity, one of holiness, and thus it should, Lorna thought to herself. Several members were filing in the open doors, and its warm glow fused out into the settling fog. The soft mist turned lightly gold, adding to the magical spirit of Christmas Eve.

"See, I told you so," her mother crowed. "We're not the only ones."

Hayden pulled up close, and they all climbed out and headed for the church, arm in arm, to keep from falling. Lorna held tightly to Cory's hand as he fussed with his stocking cap. They entered the small sanctuary and crowded into their usual pew. Candles flickered against the darkness, casting shadows about the plastered walls and ceiling, and Cory happily yanked off his cap. His static-filled hair shot out in all directions, and Lorna tried to smooth it down while he stared curiously up at the shadows. She smiled and remembered doing the same thing when she was a child.

"Mama, can we go up to the balcony?"

"No, dear."

"But I wanna see the holes."

"Sh-h-h-h." She pressed her fingers to her lips, and he frowned up at her. Ever since his granddad had shown him the places in the floor where the slaves had been chained, he was intrigued with the whole idea. She didn't like him filling his little mind with such unsettling thoughts, but he admired the boy's inquisitive wits, he said often, and he didn't see any harm in it. Of course, she had to admit that the old church certainly held a lot of history, having begun way back in 1791. It was well known that it had been used during the Civil War for housing the union troops and also as a federal hospital. But she figured Cory had a lot of years ahead to learn about such things, he was just a baby yet. She handed him a small piece of paper to scribble on.

The pews filled up, and she glanced around at the congregation. Most of them she knew, but not all of them. There were always new faces, strange faces on Christmas

Eve and Easter, especially Easter. She smiled back at the familiar faces that were looking at her, and suddenly her imagination took flight, and she felt as if everyone was staring at her and wondering about her. She felt as if they all knew her secret, every last one of them.

Look at her sitting up front like she's somebody! But we know, we know what she did—handed her baby over like a sack of potatoes!

Involuntarily she dropped her head and studied the back of the pew in front of her as Hayden pulled Cory over on his lap and took away the paper. He didn't believe in coddling him. Her parents were shifting left and right, trying to get comfortable. It was that same old feeling for Lorna, that feeling of remorse that usually harassed her whenever she entered the old church. She felt herself tighten up and her face growing hotter and hotter. She knew she would feel better once the service got underway. She always did, and she glanced up, relieved to see the preacher moving toward the pulpit.

Soon the Christmas carols began, and she relaxed, finding it more comfortable singing the familiar choruses along with the congregation just as she had all those years before. She knew she was being silly, thinking such ridiculous things, yet she couldn't seem to stop herself. It wasn't the people—it was her. It was her guilty conscience.

As she blended in with the familiar singing, the years also tended to blend together into one solid mass, and she was a little golden-haired girl again with pink barrettes stuck in her hair, anxious to get home for Santa, just like Cory. The preacher bowed his head, and her thoughts returned to the service as they all joined in prayer.

Our Father, which art in heaven
Hallowed be thy name.
Thy kingdom come.

Thy will be done in earth, as it is in heaven.
Give us this day our daily bread.
And forgive us our debts,

She clenched her hands.

As we forgive our debtors.
And lead us not into temptation,
But deliver us from evil:
For thine is the kingdom, and the power, and the glory, for ever.
Amen.

The preacher then opened his big, black Bible and proceeded to read the Christmas story, the story she had heard so many times, always the same and always moving, but tonight Lorna was deep in thought. How could God forgive her for what she had done?

How?

His monotone voice droned on, but she only half heard the familiar story. Instead her thoughts, hardened and painful, drifted to the Shenandoah.

CHAPTER NINE

Greyson sat hunched over his studies. He must finish his paper. The house was quiet, the stillness of those lonely hours stretching past midnight, with only the ticking of the clock punctuating its otherwise silence. His folks had been asleep for hours, and so had Rayna. He held his head—it was pounding. Too much studying, he supposed. "Burning the candle at both ends," his ma warned frequently. Working and studying and traveling back and forth, no wonder. He just hoped all the long hours wouldn't bring on another seizure. There had been only one since he began his schooling, though he knew the lack of rest could precipitate another at any time. In fact, that was probably the cause of the last one, but what else could he do? He was determined to finish, determined to become a minister.

The wind howled outside, and the eaves of the house creaked and shuddered. He leaned back in the chair and thought of his momentous decision and how shocked his parents were when he first told them. He had a way of doing that, he thought to himself. Though speechless at his totally unexpected announcement, they were pleased. And he was happy to see this satisfaction splayed over their otherwise stunned faces. Still it took some time to register.

"You know what you're saying, boy?" his pa had finally blurted out, and Ma gave him a scathing look.

She prodded more gently, "You done thought this thing all through, son?"

But Pa didn't give him a chance to answer. "We've never had no preacher in the Ralston family!"

"But maybe he's got the call, Pa."

He just stared at her.

"And it'd be right nice to have a man of the cloth in the family," she added, standing there firmly before him. "And when you get the call, Pa, there ain't no two ways about it!"

"But what about Rayna?" he argued, glancing out the window. She was swinging in the tree swing he had made for her, her feet equal with her head as she soared high into the air.

"What about her?" Greyson repeated, not a little chagrined at the unnecessary question. "You know I'll take care of Rayna like I always have. I just won't have as much time…time for play."

The old man turned to his wife for support, and she shifted uncomfortably in her chair. "Don't you fret none about that now, son," she said. "We'll help you. We gonna always look after our girl no matter what."

He slid his chair up close to the table, closer to the light. Though his parents had quickly come to terms with his plans, expressing complete confidence in him, and he was glad of that, still at times he wondered himself if he would make it. Was it possible? It was all very tiring and stressful, and what if his condition did worsen? Then what? But the new medicine apparently seemed to be working. It was supposed to be stronger—supposed to do the job. Perhaps it was a miracle drug, an answer to prayer for sure, but that remained to be seen. However, he would not let the seizures stop him! He pulled out a yellowed card from his pocket.

'If any man will come after me, let him deny himself, and take up his cross daily and follow me.'

He really didn't need to read it now. He had it memorized, stored away forever, but that little dog-eared card had become a stabilizing influence for him, a crutch whenever his faith faltered. The story behind it was rather puzzling, however, especially the timing. It had been given to him shortly after his fated visit to the Mission down in the hollow.

He was sitting in a little park in Luray when an elderly man approached him. It was a cool day for spring, but the old gentleman was dressed in unusually heavy woolen garb with a worn top hat, and he had a long, bristly beard, completely gray. His hand rested on a smart metal cane with the likeness of an eagle skillfully etched into it, but it was his eyes that stood out above all the rest. They didn't appear old at all, but pools of steel blue, bright and lively, and they seemed to reach into his very soul. For some time they had talked, and it was as if he had known the old man forever. Soon he was sharing his experience down in the hollow with him, and how he was seeking God's purpose for his life, but he never mentioned his epilepsy. It was still something he couldn't bring himself to disclose. When the old gentleman rose to leave, leaning heavily on his cane, he shook his hand firmly, wished him well and handed him the little 3x5 card with a Scripture verse typed onto it. He couldn't wait to get home and look it up, and when he did, he felt that the strange encounter was anything but accidental.

He smoothed out its frayed edges and stuck it back in his pocket. It always propped him up whenever he wavered, or wondered if he was putting too much on his folks or neglecting Rayna with all his work and studies. But he never once questioned his purpose. It was settled deep within—God wanted him to preach, of that one thing he was sure.

Rayna tugged her starched white dress down over her head, detesting the crinkly material and frowned at herself in the mirror. She looked like one of them silly fairies in her bedtime storybook! She hated dresses. Why couldn't she wear britches like her daddy?

"You look so pretty, child!" her grandmother exclaimed, bustling into her room. "You need some help with them buttons?"

She was twisting and squirming, trying to do it herself. Her grandmother stood there watching and thinking that she had never known one so determined. "Here, let me help you."

Reluctantly she gave in, and her grandma quickly buttoned up the dress. "I've got some oatmeal ready. We've gotta hurry, though...don't wanna be late for church."

"Grandma, when Daddy gets to be a preacher, do we still have to go to church?"

"Well, of course, child. We always have to go to church."

"But he can preach to us here."

Trying to hide her amusement, she grabbed hold of her hand. "Preachers have to preach at churches, Miss Rayna, and I figure we'll be spending right smart time in one. Now, come on here." And she marched her out to breakfast.

After Greyson finished his schooling, he was fortunate to be temporarily assigned to an old Methodist church over in the town of Luray. The regular minister had become sick but hoped to return. However, after a few months, it was apparent this was not to be the case. Though Greyson certainly didn't wish him ill, he couldn't help but feel blessed that things were working out for him, more smoothly than he had ever expected, and soon he was installed as the new pastor. His ma seldom missed a service, pressing Pa to go along with them to Luray every Sunday morning. Though grumbling all the way, he was secretly proud to walk into that fine edifice, with the stained glass windows and especially proud to see his own flesh and blood standing up there preaching to folks.

Who would've thought it?

Though he complained that it made him feel all funny-like inside, especially when he looked his way, there was no denying he was pleased with his youngest son. And it was some compensation for the fact that he was not farming high up on the mountain, for it had secretly been his dream to see that boy take over the place one day, though he had never once mentioned it to him. He had always known both William and Jack would be all right, they were strong and healthy, even if Jack was somewhat of a dreamer and William liked his whiskey a little too much.

But Greyson, he was a whole different matter. He had always believed that the mountain would be best for him, close to nature, away from the hustle and bustle of life. He had a sensitive soul, and with his sickness, well, it would have just been better. But that was water over the dam, he thought to himself. No use mulling over it now.

Rayna had immediately accepted her dad's new role and now seemed to fancy the whole idea. She was so proud of him and never complained about the long services. And that was a surprise to them all. She was most contented sitting between her grandparents, warmly sandwiched in the middle, while she dreamily listened to her daddy's soothing voice that generally put her to sleep about halfway through the service. Pa enjoyed it too, for she usually laid her head over on him instead of Ma's lap. He just wished that the others would come more often. It was only right. Occasionally, William or Jack did show up, but not Mildred, though he could tell that Greyson looked for her every Sunday, thinking she might surprise him one day. Of course, it was a long trip.

Mildred still lived in Richmond and was quite absorbed with her own family. Pa knew all about it, because every now and then she would come and pick them up, he and Ma, and haul them off to the big city; that's what she called it, and she was right. Ma was always ready at the drop of a hat, but he didn't give a scrap about it. And Mildred could be so bossy, but Ma made excuses for her whenever he said anything at all, so mostly he just let it slide.

However on Palm Sunday, she showed up. They all showed up, William and his family, and Jack and his wife, all shuffling in and cramming into two whole pews. Ma was ecstatic and so was Rayna. She loved her cousins, though they were a bit older, and she didn't see that much of them, yet they all fussed over her whenever they did come. But Mildred came alone and seated herself stiffly beside her mother, while curiously watching her baby brother enter and take his place behind the pulpit. She couldn't quite register seeing him clad in a black robe! She kept remembering him dirty and barefooted, making mud pies with Rayna Rose. She remembered dragging them both down to the spring to wash up for dinner, resenting the fact that it always fell on her to watch after them. She could still hear him hollering at the top of his lungs as she splashed the cold water on him. Gosh, it had been years since she'd thought about that, and it brought back vivid memories of the mountain place.

She wondered about the old spring. Surely it would still be there—that cold rushing water that tasted so good on hot summer days, but was achingly cold in the frigid winter and caused her teeth to chatter. And the berries—she remembered those tiny blueberries, her favorite, crunchy and sweet, yet tangy, and also the juicy blackberries that stained her hands purple. And her pa's cabbage patch, they grew bigger up there for some reason. And the apples, the tastiest apples she had ever bitten into. She wondered if any of the old apple trees still stood, but she didn't want to go back to see. No way. Perhaps it was the lonely cemetery up the hill, or more likely the upsetting memories, but she never wanted to see it again.

Two young lads marched somberly up the aisle to light the tall candles on either side of the pulpit as the organ pipes filled the sanctuary with deep, resonant sounds. The lads gingerly stepped up to them. One lit immediately but the other was obviously temperamental, and the young boy stood there striking it again and again. Mildred felt bad for him, knowing he must be totally embarrassed. She understood how little things like that would mortify a young teenager. She thought of her own children and wished they had come with her, but neither Edward nor Elaine were the least bit interested in Palm Sunday or their uncle's church.

With the stubborn candle finally lit, the young lads looked at one another, turned and slowly descended the few steps, retracing their measured pace back down the aisle. Watching them, Mildred felt somewhat ill at ease herself, perhaps because it had been awhile since she had entered a church door. She glanced down the pew to Greyson's child sitting contentedly and scribbling on a piece of paper, and she felt a stab of jealousy. Why did he have to name her Rayna? Why hadn't she thought to name

Elaine that instead? No, it had to be Greyson's little illegitimate child! She thought that Ma would have defied such a thing. But Ma was blind to everything when it came to that child! How it rankled her. Neither she nor Pa had ever shown such interest in Edward or Elaine. Of course, they didn't see as much of them, never had the chance to really bond with them, but she couldn't help it if she lived so far away. She glanced at her again, unable to deny the striking resemblance. And though she knew that to be the reason for the name, it still irked her. And wouldn't you just know it, she was growing up to be so—so downright pretty! It made her sick to her stomach!

"Let us pray," the deacon was saying as the young lads exited through the back doors. She bowed her head and listened to the long-winded fellow. When at last he concluded, she checked her watch. This was going to be a lengthy affair, no doubt about it, and she looked up to see her ma's eyes upon her, smiling sweetly. Saddled with guilt, she honed in on the hymn as they all stood together to sing. Afterwards, the black-robed preacher arose and walked up to the pulpit.

"Would you please turn in your Bibles to the book of John, chapter eighteen and verse thirty-seven," he instructed, and a sea of pages fluttered about her. She would forget to bring a Bible! She imagined her ma's eyes on her for sure now, but she focused on Greyson as he proceeded to read in a gentle, fluid voice.

"*Pilate therefore said unto him, Art thou a king then? Jesus answered, Thou sayest that I am a King. To this end was I born, and for this cause came I into the world, that I should bear witness unto the truth. Every one that is of the truth heareth my voice.*"

He stopped reading and locked his gaze on the small congregation as if waiting for something. Was he looking at her? All of a sudden it wasn't her baby brother's voice ringing in her ears.

He dove into his sermon with a decided fervor, "The key phrase today in this scripture is *bear witness*. We all know that Jesus left Heaven and came down to earth to make a way for us sinners—a way to Heaven. When he yielded to the cross and suffered and died there, taking our sins upon His shoulders, he was fulfilling God's supreme purpose for the Incarnation. This, of course, is general knowledge, amazing knowledge, but general knowledge all the same among Christians today. But I have come to see that there was even more in this marvelous Incarnation."

Mildred wondered where he was going with this.

"I hope that most of you are students of the Word, not just the New Testament but also the Old Testament, for that is where we see and hear God the Father throughout its ancient pages. That is where we witness His omniscience, His omnipresence, and His omnipotence…His magnificent might. Passages such as found in Exodus when He was talking to Moses.

> *But He (God) said, 'You cannot see My face; for no man shall see Me, and live.'*
>
> *And the Lord said, 'Here is a place by Me, and you shall stand on the rock.*
>
> *'So it shall be, while My glory passes by, that I will put you in the cleft of the rock, and will cover you with My hand while I pass by.*
>
> *'Then I will take away My hand, and you shall see My back; but My face shall not be seen.'*

The congregation was silent, and Greyson waited for the intended effect. "When I read this some years ago," he finally said in his soft-spoken but commanding voice, "I was suddenly made aware of the fact that we serve an awesome God. One that is too awesome even for us to see, much less understand."

His eyes rested long on the ceiling.

And then he continued, "In this passage, God is about to give Moses the second set of Ten Commandments up on the mountain. You may recall that out of anger, Moses had thrown down the first set and broken them upon coming down off the mountain and seeing all the people dancing and worshiping the molten calf that they had made from their golden earrings.

"Folks, the great God of the universe is too exalted and too holy for mankind to see! That is why He had to put Moses in a cleft of the rock, a protective place and cover him with His hand when He passed over. Think about it—such an intimate, personal, loving act.

"It gives us a glimpse of God's tender side.

"But it is His omnipotence, His power that is revealed mostly in the Old Testament. When God came down on the mountain, the Scriptures say: *'And mount Sinai was altogether on a smoke, because the Lord descended upon it in fire: and the smoke thereof ascended as the smoke of a furnace, and the whole mount quaked greatly.'* "

A few parishioners shook their heads.

"Many of you probably heard the thunderstorm the other night, around midnight, that terrible earth-shattering storm."

A host of hands flew up.

"According to the Scriptures, that is the sound of God's voice. Thunder! Second Samuel says, *'The Lord thundered from heaven, and the most High uttered his voice.'*

"And, then, in the blessed Psalms, David tells us:

In my distress I called upon the Lord, and cried unto my God: He heard my voice out of His temple, and my cry came before Him, even into His ears.

Then the earth shook and trembled; the foundations also of the hills moved and were shaken, because He was wroth.

There went up a smoke out of His nostrils, and fire out of His mouth devoured: coals were kindled by it.

He bowed the heavens also, and came down: and darkness was under His feet.

And He rode upon a cherub, and did fly: yea, He did fly upon the wings of the wind.

He made darkness His secret place; His pavilion round about Him were dark waters and thick clouds of the skies.

At the brightness that was before Him His thick clouds passed, hail stones and coals of fire.

The Lord also thundered in the heavens, and the Highest gave His voice; hail stones and coals of fire.

Yea, He sent out His arrows, and scattered them; and He shot out lightnings, and discomfited them.

"Lightning and smoke and coals of fire and a voice that sounds like thunder… frightening I must say." Heads were nodding.

"I've read such passages on this Palm Sunday to bring to our minds that we serve an amazing God, and we should fear Him in an act of holy reverence.

"I am afraid there is an absence of holy reverence today."

His voice rose slightly as he quoted from the Book of Leviticus. "*Sanctify yourselves therefore, and be ye holy: for I am the Lord your God.*"

A hush fell over the congregation.

"Folks, this is His charge to us all. We are to fear God. To fear Him and to love Him at the same time is the crux of the matter, a distinct paradox. Now this seems like a contradiction, doesn't it?

"But why is it so hard? Didn't you fear your daddy when he picked up the razor strap or your mother with the switch? But at the same time, you loved him or her.

"I believe that God realized that mankind had a difficult time seeing Him as a loving God because of His very nature, His power, His awesomeness...and that's why He sent Jesus down to *live* among us...to touch us...to love us...to heal us...to teach us...and ultimately to forgive us.

"Jesus, *'Who is the image of the invisible God.'*

"Yes, the Incarnation enabled us to understand the *heart* of God.

"Jesus bore witness to the truth...to God. He was able in His human form to connect to us, to show us the love of God."

He paused.

"His very name, *Immanuel*, means God with us.

"What a marvelous thing—the Incarnation. Otherwise, we would never have been able to grasp it, to understand God. Of course, I don't mean this literally. None of us can ever really understand God, but because of Jesus, we at least have a better understanding of Him.

"And here we are at this most blessed time in the church's calendar, Passion Week...and soon Easter. It is not just a time to dress up and come to church, a time to celebrate with new frocks and new hats and colored eggs for the children. It is a time to contemplate, to meditate, and to ponder the mysteries of God...the glorious Incarnation and the death, burial and resurrection of our Lord."

He paused again.

"And I conclude with what I quoted in the beginning, *'Every one that is of the truth heareth my voice.'*

"Are we hearing His voice?"

Mildred shifted in the pew and glanced down at Rayna asleep on her pa's lap, and she tasted the bile in her throat.

Soon the distance between the church and home was wearing on Greyson, not to mention his faithful parish, and after much consideration, he made the difficult decision to move into Luray, into the vacant parsonage that had long been offered to him. He needed to be there for the people, though it was a tough decision to be sure, and a heartbreaking one for his folks. However, they understood, and deep down they were happy about it because he seemed so satisfied, content for the first time in his life. They still enjoyed Rayna most every weekend, but she was growing up. She was growing like a weed, her grandma proudly pointed out, and quite self-sufficient, of this they were not surprised. And because of it, Greyson knew she would be okay.

As it turned out, she was more than okay. She made herself at home in the old parsonage, relishing its former but secret life. She wondered if past spirits possibly lurked in its dark interior, its shadowy corners, and behind its dated, walnut paneling or in the dank cellar below, which she had yet to investigate. Her imagination soared with it all, including its stark furnishings that also fascinated her, particularly the shiny, upright secretary that daily wooed her to sit down and write out her letters. She would indiscriminately pull out the fine, little drawers and question what used to be there. Perhaps some mysterious records or long-lost love letters.

Who had sat there before her? Most likely another dark-robed preacher, but that was far too dull. She preferred to let her mind develop all sorts of characters, maybe another young girl, one that perhaps had no mother, like her. What was it her daddy always said—possible but not probable? Her daddy preferred to live in the real world, but she was different. She would much rather let her thoughts wander and see where they might lead her. It was an interesting pastime, and her most favorite, after all. At times, she even pretended that she was the one who had lived there previously and, through her vivid imagination, discovered many secrets, like the dark stairwell.

She also enjoyed the steep stairs and wide, polished banister that led up to her small bedroom nestled in a snug alcove. It was absolutely novel to her, and her room magically looked out over the town, fusing her with an inordinate sense of dominion. She became the queen of the village, no less. Not the Luray village, of course, but one far more fascinating like those she read about in her library books. Indeed, the parsonage lent itself unreservedly to the young girl's creative and sometimes absurd musings.

But as a whole, it was a fresh challenge for her, a sweet experiment, one might say, and she pestered her dad to spruce it up with a little paint, not too much to alter its inherent aura, but just a little perhaps in the dreary kitchen. She liked a cheery kitchen like that of her grandma's, and she begged for a ruffled curtain to hang at its window over the sink, and possibly lace curtains on some of the other windows, especially hers. And a few pictures here and there to add a bit of color. Greyson was most compliant with such requests, and pleased with her overwhelming acceptance of the move.

As the months and seasons added up, blending into years, her independent spirit only swelled, and she easily accepted her role as lady of the house. More than acceptance, she rallied to the test. Mature beyond her years, she enjoyed it for the most part, and the parishioners adored her in return, for she was an enchanting and precocious child, adding a spark of youthful energy to the otherwise dull parsonage that hadn't seen a child within its walls for decades. And though she missed her grandparents, there was a certain grown-up aspect to living in Luray, just the two of them. She doted on her dad, and she had no aversion to school either. But she enjoyed being a Girl Scout most of all—or rather a Brownie—and couldn't wait until she was old enough to be promoted, to shed the dull, brown uniform for the coveted green. She regarded her membership seriously, as she did most things, never missing a meeting and striving to complete each and every listed requirement.

It was a warm, summer day, and she was attending her troop's main event of the season. She was allowed to go camping overnight with them now. It happened to be a rather remote place down by the river and shaded by scaling old sycamores, with large leaves that rustled in the slight breeze. They were sitting around the campfire roasting marshmallows for their s'mores. She was on her second one already, and chocolate oozed down her chin. She casually wiped it off with her sleeve while staring up at the pasty white trees.

"Oh, Rayna!"

She looked up at Emma Witherspoon rolling her eyes at her twin sister Eugenia, who had turned up her nose.

"Look at your sleeve!" the well-groomed child pointed out, and Rayna noticed a long, dark smear across it. Taken aback by the sudden unexpected reproach, she was speechless as the two girls giggled with their heads together. She stared at them and then rose and walked over to the riverbank.

The Shenandoah was lazily cutting its way through the Valley, and she dropped down beside it. She wouldn't let those silly girls bother her, and she watched the river push its way over and around the large, smooth rocks. She thought about what her grandpa had said, something about water being one of the most powerful energies. There were rapids up ahead in the distance, not big ones like the rapids in her geography book, but smaller ones. She studied how they swirled around and over the stones and thought of the many waterfalls up in the mountains and how they gushed down over fallen trees and whatever else was in their path. She loved to watch them and hear their constant roar. Sometimes her dad took her on hikes, and they followed the path of the mountain streams to the mighty waterfalls. She knew the tumbling water flowed into the mountain streams that ran down off the mountains and into rivers like this one, and Grandpa said the rivers flowed into the mighty Atlantic. Maybe one day she would be able to see it, the mighty Atlantic, that is. She couldn't imagine so much water that you couldn't see across it, but her dad said it was so. He had seen it once. She tossed a pebble into the river and watched its circles widen and widen before the current swept it away. Mrs. Shilling, the troop leader, watched her.

"Why don't you go fetch that little Ralston girl, Mrs. Turner?" she said finally. "She's way over there sitting all by herself."

Mrs. Turner followed her gaze. "But she likes it that way, I think. Rayna Ralston is a loner, you know, probably because she's grown up in that gloomy, old parsonage with nobody but the preacher."

"She has grandparents, I understand. But growing up with only adults does tend to make one somewhat a loner, always fading into the surroundings instead of joining in with other children."

"Sometimes I think she'd rather spend her time with the rocks and trees than with them. Just look at her!" Mrs. Turner whispered.

A pine twig caught Rayna's attention as it floated downstream, and she found herself daydreaming again, though her grandma frowned on such, saying she needed to keep her mind on what was going on instead of some fairy tale in her head, but she didn't think about fairy tales. She had never cared one grain for fairy tales. Instead she preferred to invent her own, and she saw herself floating down the Shenandoah past the fields and pastures with cows grazing beneath the white sycamores that hung out over it, and on out between the hazy, blue mountains, further and further until she reached the distant ocean.

The sun danced on the coursing waters, and it literally sparkled, but suddenly a shadow appeared. She looked up to see a great bird swooping low and then off toward the mountains, its outstretched wings sweeping up and down, then straight out as it rode the wind, and she felt herself soaring with it. It was a delightful sensation, light as a feather. She jumped as Mrs. Turner's hand touched her shoulder.

"Come on back with us, Rayna." Reluctantly, she got up.

Greyson hoped that his baby girl was having a good time on her excursion. He chuckled to himself as he drove down the country road to visit old Mrs. Lindsey. Baby girl—why he couldn't believe she had turned eight years old! He wondered if he had been too busy with his ministerial duties to realize how fast she had grown, or did all children grow up that fast? His thoughts traveled back to his own childhood, funny how it seemed to drag along with him. He used to question if he would ever grow up, especially when they lived up on the mountain. He could see himself sitting out on the porch steps on an early summer morning much like this one, and its fragrances still lingered with him. Fresh morning scents of wet grass and wild flowers beaded with the night's dew, and his ma's Rose of Sharon that grew up against the porch, the one she prized and scolded him for pinching off its blooms.

He remembered watching the sun pop up over the mountain, a searing ball of fire, with seemingly long fingers stretching out over the cornfield in warm pink colors, painting it a soft pastel and slowly burning off the heavy mist.

He pushed on down the dusty road, basking in such thoughts and hoped that Mrs. Lindsey was feeling better this week. The old lady was having a time of it with her rheumatoid arthritis, but in spite of her crippled hands and swollen feet, she was a faithful parishioner, and she never complained. He was blessed with a number of faithful parishioners just like her. Black-eyed Susans had shot up along the roadside, just like the ones that used to bloom next to his pa's shed. They were his ma's favorite, and he remembered them gently waving in the mountain breezes, and the butterflies alighting on them. He must have sat out on that porch a lot on summer mornings because all these intricate details stuck vividly in his memory. Those aimless mornings, perhaps it was the welcoming anticipation of each new day that wouldn't leave him. That comfortable, lazy feeling as if time stood still, and he could do whatever his little heart desired. His only care being the question of what to do, whether to go down to the creek and fetch some minnows or whether to climb up the apple trees, or maybe get Rayna Rose to hike with him out to the ridge where they could see forever, but there was no hurry to make up his mind.

No, there was never any hurry on the mountain. He drove on down the road with that thought in mind.

CHAPTER TEN

Someone once said the only thing in life that you can count on not to change is change. A disconcerting phrase to be sure, but its valid meaning is proven in each and every life as it inevitably declines. And the Ralston household was no different. It was suddenly and significantly changed during the fall of Rayna's eighth year. Without any warning, it was forever altered.

She pushed the porch swing back and forth, her eyes clenched and her long, dark lashes wet on her cheeks. The funeral service man came out to remove the flower arrangement beside the front door and smiled sympathetically at her, but she turned away. She didn't want him to see her cry, and he stepped down off the porch, got in his vehicle and drove off. Besides, she wasn't going to shed anymore tears—it didn't do any good. It wouldn't bring her grandma back! She glanced around the side of the house to the clothesline with the zigzagged pins still clasped to it, and she halfway expected to see her stretching to hang up the wet laundry. The door opened again, and Greyson looked at her.

"Ready, Rayna?"

She nodded and pushed off the swing. "Grandpa coming?"

"He's getting his jacket."

She started for the car, and Greyson sadly watched her. Pa would be spending a few weeks with them in the parsonage. He hoped it would help him. He was already lost without Ma. They had been married for over fifty years, and she had always been the glue that held the family together.

His pa shuffled out at last, looking about absently as if he needed to do something, but he didn't know what.

"I'll lock up, Pa." Greyson pulled the door shut behind him and turned the key in the lock, his own thoughts buzzing about in his head, but he must be strong for them both.

Rayna was already waiting in the back seat, and Pa climbed in up front, without looking at her. He seemed to be in a daze. Greyson got in and started up the road. He noticed Rayna had rolled her window down and was staring back at the place, but she was thinking of something else. She was remembering the wood thrush that flew into the house, into the kitchen when Grandpa left the screen door wide open, waiting for her, and she was lagging behind. It was about a month ago, and she was peeved at him because he wouldn't let her climb to the top of the big chestnut oak out beyond the woodpile. He thought she would fall, but she had never fallen out of a tree. Now his words came back to her loud and clear. "Get that bird out of here!"

She had run around clapping her hands and shooing the bird from corner to corner until finally it flew back out the door. And she demanded, "Why'd you get so mad over a little bird, Grandpa?"

"Just an old superstition," he had answered.

"What superstition?"

"If a bird gets in a house, somebody's gonna die, but we don't believe in such things."

She wondered now if he did.

Greyson kept glancing up into the rearview mirror. She looked so small and helpless. His ma was the only mother she had ever known, the only feminine influence in her life, the only one to understand those things he didn't and couldn't. Who would she turn to now? And when she grew older, when such things took on alarming proportions? It was a troubling thought, but he knew children were resilient, especially Rayna. He would need to spend more time with her, that's for sure, and with his pa, as well. His small parish would understand. He knew they would embrace them. They were a wonderful congregation, compassionate almost to a fault. In fact, he felt that they had helped him more than he helped them, in every way, even with his epilepsy. After a few months of his installation, he had opened up and disclosed his secret, though he hadn't had any seizures for over two years. Obviously the medicine was working, but it was only fair to be up front. He certainly didn't want to fall over at the pulpit one Sunday morning!

But his mother's death had come as a shock. She had hardly been sick a day in her life. She had gone peacefully in her sleep, and for that he was glad, and also thankful that Rayna wasn't sleeping with her as she often did. Pa had found her the next morning.

He wanted him to preach the funeral, but he simply couldn't. Instead he had read a portion of the Scriptures, and they buried her on the mountain next to Rayna Rose.

As he drove toward Luray, there was a noticeable silence. Both Pa and Rayna seemed lost in their thoughts, and he didn't want to disturb them. Besides, he didn't know what to say. About halfway there, Pa spoke up in his matter-of-fact way, "Your ma had a fine funeral…as fine a funeral as anybody'd want."

"Yes, sir," he responded softly. "She did that."

Rayna said nothing, and Pa reverted back to his silence. All that could be heard was the rush of the wind through the open windows, and Greyson's mind unwillingly returned to the funeral and the cemetery. Instead of the past fading into the distance, it seemed to be reopening with each new grave. But it was his twin sister's that still haunted him, and seeing her sunken grave amidst the weeds yesterday didn't help any. His mind traced back to that day she ran away, to that fateful storm that had so unexpectedly erupted. Two weeks after, she had died. Taking her last breath, she had simply slid out of this world and into another. Peaceful like, but standing there in the drizzling rain as they lowered her small casket into the ground, he had felt like someone or something had sliced him in two.

What did they say about twins?

The whole household was devastated. How could Rayna Rose be gone? She had been sick, for sure, but she had been sick before. The doctor said it was pneumonia, brought on by getting so wet and chilled. Ma was beside herself, wailing day and night, but Pa had grieved quietly, walking through the rustling cornfield and apple orchard hour after hour. The rest of them, William, Mildred, and Jack, moved about the house sorrowfully, alternately crying and trying to console their parents. So caught up in their own grief, none of them noticed him crouching silently out on the steps, never shedding a tear. He couldn't. He didn't feel he had a right.

After that, the day Rayna Rose was buried, he couldn't sleep by himself. He tried for he didn't want to be called a sissy, but the nightmares came. They always came, slipping up on him, and subtly lulling him into their enticing hazy vistas—muted rose-colored mornings or amber sunsets or sometimes warm, fair impressions akin to a Monet painting. But then it would suddenly change with dark mountains looming and a raging storm. The wind and rain and lightning and thunder bearing down on his sleeping form, and he would see it—the gaping hole. It was always the same, and it was always waiting. But it was more than a hole. It was alive, palpable as it waited. However, the vagueness of a dream that prevents its possessor from distinguishing exact details never allowed him to determine who it was waiting for—whether for Rayna Rose or for him. He would wake up trembling and in a cold sweat, with his heart beating wildly. So Mildred took to climbing up in the loft with him, and he was surprised that his brothers didn't tease him like they usually did.

That dreadful summer eventually passed between stifled sobs and strained silences as the Ralston household dealt with their enormous grief, each one separately, each one in his or her own way. Then it was autumn, but not even the vivid mountain colors could lift the heavy cloud that had settled over the cabin, dark and weighty. It bore down upon them as the chores were done, as the meals were fixed and then eaten in silence, as the clothes were scrubbed and the fields were plowed. It bore down in a mind-numbing, hope-crushing way while all around them the colors deepened, and the leaves began to fall, scattered at first and then more and more until the mountain turned brown and wintry.

That's when Greyson first heard it. The thin, familiar voice, *"Make mud pies with me, please…."*

It was when he was looking out the window one night. Everyone else was apparently asleep. After that, he had heard it several more times. It seemed to whine in the trees when darkness fell, but he didn't tell anyone.

Shortly after, around the middle of November, the preacher came to visit. "I know it's hard on you folks," he rasped in his low, aging voice. "…but we have to move on."

Then Mildred commenced to dropping that same phrase every now and then, and finally he heard his pa repeat it. *Move on.* The words seemed to roll off their lips in his presence particularly, though no one ever looked directly at him; yet he felt that they were somehow measuring his response. He wondered if they were moving on, his folks and brothers and sister. He wasn't sure, but it looked like maybe they were, and he gave it considerable thought as the autumn drew to a close.

"I'm gonna sleep alone tonight."

Mildred backed off the ladder and looked up at him with surprise, though pleased with this unexpected announcement. Ma had stopped dead in her tracks and was staring at him. Pa's pipe was suspended in midair, his nightly ritual of packing it and placing it in the oval holder halted. But they each quickly recovered and purposely returned to what they were doing, and he climbed on up the ladder. He was glad that his brothers were not home yet, and he undressed and pulled on his heavy nightshirt in the dark. Surprising them all, he was asleep before his brothers ever showed up. They were admonished to keep quiet as they jostled up the ladder in the darkness, muttering in muffled tones. They peeped in and saw his small hump underneath the covers. Shoving across to the other room and throwing off their clothes, they tumbled in bed themselves, and the house finally fell silent.

But then the winds picked up, becoming a blowy night like so many in the Blue Ridge. And Greyson's eyelids flew open. Everything was black except for the barely diffused light spilling in from the small window over his bed, and he shivered beneath the heavy covers. Though frightened, he was drawn toward it like a magnet, the window that is, and he rolled over to it, pulling the covers with him. Would he hear it again? It was almost a moonless night, yet he could see clearly the skeletal trees, the shadowy oaks, swaying in the strong winds. He looked up into the dark sky. It was stippled with twinkling stars, a host of teeny dots against the blackness. He was glad to see them. Maybe the sun would be shining tomorrow. Maybe it wouldn't rain. The steady roar of the wind was actually comforting until he remembered his pa's words.

"These winds gonna blow us off the mountain...won't be no need for them gov'ment folks to move us then!"

He thrust the disturbing thought away and stared out into the distance. He could see the ebony outline of the far-off mountains. No wonder Rayna Rose always claimed this side of the bed. His eyes began to blur, and he blinked back the tears.

"*Move on...move on*," he whispered to himself.

The winds shook the oak branches, and the few stubborn leaves that had refused to fall were now twisting and flapping, struggling to hold on. Every now and then one would rip off and go sailing past his window, through the dark night. He glanced up again and noticed hazy, white clouds moving in. Eddying and churning. Maybe it was gonna rain. They drifted between him and the stars, blocking out their sparkle, and somehow added a cold eeriness to the night.

The steady, low rush of the wind seemed to hold the mountain in its grasp, and it gradually wrapped its hypnotic force around him. His eyes were becoming heavy. Where did Rayna Rose say it came from?

The wind?

Something about *treasures,* she had read it in the Bible. She had taken to reading the big, black Book just before—he wiped his eyes—and Ma had been so proud of her. She said Rayna Rose had an inquiring mind. Sometimes she would read it to him even.

'...and bringeth forth the wind out of His treasures.'

That's it!

He remembered. But where are His treasures? He leaned into the window, pressing his head against its damp, frosty pane, staring first one way and then the other, and up into the hazy clouds. A lone star poked out from behind them, twinkling as they shifted about. He wondered if Rayna Rose had found them, the treasures, that is. He hoped so.

A branch scraped the window, and he scooted back under the covers. Finally he slept, and the usual nightmares didn't come. Instead, there was only the steady roar of the wind, increasing and expanding, a soothing, comforting sound, and in his sleep the strong winds lifted up the small cabin, gently carrying it down off the mountain...down, down, down.

Greyson approached the town of Luray, the childhood memories fading away. After that night, he never heard her voice again, but he remembered it was a turning point for him. That night and those words, and he quoted them silently, *'He maketh lightnings with rain, and bringeth forth the wind out of His treasures'*. The long ago night eased his pain somewhat, and he looked over at his pa. He had dozed off. He glanced up in the mirror, so had Rayna.

He certainly hoped his pa would be able to make it without Ma, but it was hard to imagine. He was so dependent on her, they all were. In fact, there seemed to be an enormous fissure in the Ralston family now. Another crack that would never mend, but time would do its job. He had learned that. It would slowly close but never all the way. The fracture would always remain partly open.

Pa straightened up in his seat as they entered the small town. "We here?"

"Yes, sir."

He looked all around.

"The town's growing, Pa. I'll take you sightseeing later on."

The old man grunted.

Greyson didn't want him to continue living in the home by himself, but he knew it would be an uphill battle when he tried to move him away. He cringed at the thought of facing that dogged, stubborn streak of his. Well, he had a few weeks yet, and then he would cross that bridge. Right now, they all needed time, time for healing. His ma had been the stabilizing influence in his life all these years, and he was having just as difficult a time accepting the fact that she was gone.

Before a week was up, however, Pa had become fidgety, and Greyson knew it wouldn't be long before he would be anxious for home. He tried to keep him busy, driving him and Rayna around town to keep their minds off the past. He took them out for a cone of cream now and then, and over to the drugstore just to walk up and down the narrow, packed aisles. Sometimes they would find a trinket or a piece of candy, or some other little distraction. Every so often he rode them out further, down to the small town of Stanley even, just for a change of scenery. Once, he took them with him over to Charlottesville for a wedding he had to perform, thinking this would certainly be a nice diversion.

"I don't care much for all this, son," his pa finally voiced one day. "I know it's your home and all, but cars everywhere, people running here and yonder...kind of makes me feel like a frog in a henhouse. I don't know where to hop."

Rayna giggled. "You don't need to hop, Grandpa!"

"Rayna's right, Pa. Just sit back and relax. I'm going to take you somewhere today that I think you'll like." The old man doubted that.

"I know, Daddy!" Still giggling over her grandpa's unique choice of words, she winked at her dad in the rear-view mirror.

"You think so?" It was one of her favorite places, and he figured Pa might enjoy it, as well. They soon pulled up in front of a grand stone tower, and Greyson shut off the engine.

"Well...what in tarnation is it?"

"The Singing Tower, Grandpa!"

"H-m-m-m-ph."

"Come on, Rayna."

But she was already out and yanking open Pa's door. She grabbed hold of his hand. "It has forty-seven bells, Grandpa!"

"You don't say." He stared up at the imposing tower that was quiet now.

"Sometimes we come here..." Rayna was pulling him around it, "...and there's a man up there." She pointed way up to a small window. "And he's playing music with bells, pretty music, right, Daddy?"

The old man studied the tower for a moment, and then went to sit down on one of the benches with his eyes upon the ground. Greyson wished the bells were playing now.

That night after the busy day, Pa retired early. Rayna sat out on the parsonage porch with her sweater wrapped around her to knock the chill. She was rocking back and forth in the big rocker that creaked rhythmically. She had complained that the parsonage needed a swing like her grandma's, and Greyson wondered if that would be possible. He would bring it up at the next meeting, he thought to himself, and sat down on the steps in front of her. Her former gaiety was gone. "You're mighty quiet tonight, Princess." It had become his pet name for her.

She nodded.

"Have a good time today?"

Again she nodded, and he decided to wait until she was ready to talk. It was dusk, a cool evening with a slight hint of rain. A lone figure appeared, walking down the street. You could hear the hollow sound of his heels against the stone. It was Mr. Worsham out for his evening stroll. He paused momentarily and tipped his hat.

"Evening, Reverend. Evening, Miss Rayna."

"Good evening to you, Mr. Worsham," Greyson returned the courtesy, but Rayna was silent as if she hadn't even heard him. The old man passed on down the street and out of sight, his cane clicking against the pavement.

"You okay, Princess?"

She looked over at him intensely. "Daddy...Grandma's in heaven, right?"

"Yes...you know your grandma was a believer."

"Then she should be with the other Rayna."

He shifted uncomfortably on the steps. "That's right."

"Well then, I know she's happy...and she won't ever look sad again...for every time she talked about her, she looked sad."

Greyson stared up into the darkening sky.

CHAPTER ELEVEN

Autumn faded, and a cold winter set in, filled with arctic temperatures and enough precipitation to bring the sleet down throughout December, January, and February. It sheathed the Virginia mountains along with its valleys and even the coastal marshlands into an icy world, intricately encased. But it also brought down the electric wires, and Virginians hunkered down to face its nasty onslaught, at least knowing it wouldn't last forever. They piled up stacks of firewood, large pyramids on the back porches, and set the stoves a blazing. They lugged out the smelly oil lamps and candles for light, and pulled on their woolens and long johns, huddling close to the fires to discuss the woes of the world. At least it was a means of distraction from the frigid winter, particularly the worrying situation in Korea. They weren't ready for that! It was too soon. They were just settling down to getting their lives back together, and now this.

It had begun during the summer, when troops from Communist-ruled North Korea invaded South Korea, but that was all so far away. But so was Germany and Japan. They couldn't make the same mistake twice!

However, now there was the newly created United Nations. Maybe it would prevent another war. Responsibly, the much admired entity took on its role and called the invasion a violation of international peace and demanded that the Communists withdraw. The public was greatly relieved to hear this, happy to hear it, but it didn't happen. Thus the embryonic United Nations asked its members to give military aid to South Korea, and sixteen countries responded, sending troops. Forty-one sent military equipment and supplies, but still over 90 percent of all the troops, equipment and supplies sent over were from the United States, and thus another war commenced into bloody combat, another war for Americans to deal with.

"Why is it we have to always send our boys over?" Lorna's mother grumbled. "I thought this United Nations thing would make a difference. You'd think some of the others would step up to the plate!" She had been bitter about it for days.

"Well, now, Estelle," her father responded patiently, looking up from his cozy spot on the couch. "It's just that we're a big country, and we've been blessed so. You know that." He glanced over at Hayden, who was behind the newspaper. He didn't look up.

Her father realized it was a volatile situation for sure. China was fighting on the side of North Korea, and the Soviet Union was giving military equipment to them. Both President Truman and the United Nations had tried to halt the Communist advances, but to no avail. Though the president had ordered ground troops into action way back in the summer, and the Allied forces had begun fighting the North Koreans the first of July, still war had not been officially declared.

But it was war!

Everybody knew that. Most of all, the families that had seen their young men board ships and sail out to the unknown, wondering if they would ever see them again. Now it was winter and another year, and people gloomily braced themselves for a dreaded repeat of the past.

"Well, the general certainly made a mess of things!" Lorna's mother persisted, settling herself heavily on the opposite end of the couch. President Truman had named General Douglas MacArthur Commander in Chief of the United Nations Command, which had authority over all the Allies.

Her father looked anxiously from her to Hayden, but either he was deep in some article or he simply didn't want to talk about the war, and if he had to guess, it would be the latter.

"Did you hear me?"

"I heard you, Estelle," he responded. "Just wait. He'll take care of it like he always has."

"How can you say that?"

"Look what he did last September—that amphibious landing at Inchon!" He was getting a bit irritated with her now and couldn't help bringing up the successful landing. He was more than ready to praise the general's surprise move that had turned the tide of the war in the Allies' favor. It was something he had applauded often, and he knew that she knew it, too. Seoul, the capital of South Korea, was captured afterwards and taken away from the Communists, who had held it, and then the Allies were able to move north.

"Well!" she snapped. "I don't know about that." It aggravated her that he held the general in such high regard. But just about everybody did—in fact, everybody but her.

"That took some doing you have to admit..." he continued, now on a roll. "...because those tides can vary more than thirty feet at times!"

"That might be...but he sure blundered when he misjudged the Chinese!"

He couldn't argue that. MacArthur and his sources of information had seriously underestimated the size of the

Chinese army. China had warned against further advances, but the general, hoping to end the war before winter, had ordered the Allies to press on, and they did. The U.S. and Chinese troops clashed at the end of October, and bloody fighting ensued until the first of November when the Chinese withdrew. More than three hundred thousand Chinese troops had crossed into North Korea in the fall.

Lorna's father couldn't understand how the general had been so mistaken. However, MacArthur believed that the Allied forces outnumbered the Chinese, and he had ordered another advance by the end of November. Hopes of a quick war soon vanished. China sent a huge force against this advance, forcing a historic retreat. The Communists had attacked Seoul on New Year's Eve and occupied the city again, but the Allies had dug in, inflicting heavy losses on them, and now were moving north again.

"You'd think he would know better!" she kept on. "Didn't he learn anything from the last war?"

At that, Hayden rose and left the room. They looked at one another, and her father stood up angrily. "Don't reckon he wants to hear all that!"

"I don't guess any of us do, but it's here whether we want it or not." She found herself alone in the room and was glad of it. She bent over and began picking up the scattered newspaper.

"Men...they sure are a messy lot."

At last the bitter wintry weather ended. Lorna stared out the front door with relief, but more than relief, she was excited. The coastal winter had subsided, the crystallized ice in the tidal flats and road ditches had melted, and the salt marshes had begun to sprout new growth. The warblers were back and scores of songbirds were about, flitting in the wax myrtles and singing their hearts out. And the laughing gulls could be heard screaming over the nearby sandy beaches, their unique cries lifting the spirits of young and old alike. Even the mallards waddled conspicuously along the Bay shores, and the killdeer amused the unsuspecting with their clever tricks. An unexpected spring buoyancy welled up within Lorna. Not the usual vigor and oomph brought on by the coveted season, but far more, one of spirited anticipation.

She was going to Shenandoah!

"But why do you need to go all the way up there?" her mother demanded in her usual domineering way.

"Just a get-away, Mother…to see the area and the caverns; you've heard about them, and to do a little shopping, you know."

"There's plenty of shopping up at Virginia Beach, don't you think?"

"Certainly, Mother, but still I could use a change, and Hayden's all for it, too. He understands that I've never been away from here, and now's my chance. He thinks it will do me good."

Her mother rather suspected as much. She knew she had been pretty glum lately, and certainly Hayden had noticed. Maybe it would be a good thing.

"If you mind keeping Cory, Mother, just say so."

"Of course I don't mind keeping Cory. I just don't understand why you want to go way up there! How many girls did you say are going?"

Lorna gritted her teeth. Would she ever grow up in her mother's eyes? "It will be six of us all together, but only five coming back. Angelina will be staying with her aunt awhile longer."

"She must have a grand house to put you all up."

"Maybe so."

"And you're going up to the mountains, too, you said?"

"That's what Angelina has planned."

"Bet it's cold up in those mountains."

She shrugged her shoulders and opened the door.

"Better take some warm clothes with you!"

"Angelina, you sure your Aunt Wilma's ready for us?" Mrs. Crossly asked, settling herself for the long ride.

They cackled like a bunch of school girls, and Mrs. Crossly frowned at them. Opal Crossly was the same age as the rest of them, but she preferred being addressed formally. Why, they didn't know. Lorna wondered if it didn't make her feel a bit superior. Of course, she was in a way, with her blue blood lineage that she proudly mentioned whenever possible, but she didn't need to be stuck in the past, for goodness sakes. This is the fifties! Lorna regarded the varied group with amusement as she drove up Pacific Avenue. She had offered to drive as soon as the question came up, and was pleased that no one else wanted to.

Angelina commenced to entertaining them with her unique talent, which always broke them up. She had a real knack for mimicking, and this time it was her aging aunt who was the victim, though it was all in jest for she really did care for her aunt. It was a happy group setting out that morning, excited and eager for a little diversion. For the most part, they were all young mothers, young homemakers, earnestly in need of a break from their mundane, never-ending schedules, not to mention the chaos and hectic environment that often ensued in trying to raise and discipline the little ones. So this was a true get-away, just the thing to restore their sanity.

A misty haze hung over the old resort city, not yet burnt off by the emerging sun that drew thousands to its beaches each and every year and had since the 1800s. But it was quiet as they drove through, too early for the bustling crowd. Most of the group had watched the city grow and were still watching. It was changing, though. Some of the changes were good, some not so good. Beach erosion was now a problem with the frequent nor'easters and the violent sea beating mercilessly upon it.

"The sea looks calm today," Lane pointed to the great expanse of blue beyond the boardwalk.

"Did you hear what they're going to do?" Diane asked.

The response was negative.

"They're going to dredge sand out of Rudee Inlet to pump back up here."

"Well, they need to do something," Angelina said. "If they don't, we won't have any oceanfront before you know it."

"Yeah, I can remember when we had a lot more."

Both Lane and Angelina agreed.

"But how're they going to dredge it all the way up from Rudee Inlet?" Faye asked, frowning.

"With a pipeline, somebody said, must be a really long one."

Lane suddenly pointed up to a soaring, red-brick building that was being built between Pacific and Atlantic Avenues. It was going to be the tallest apartment building in Virginia, sixteen stories high.

"The Mayflower," Mrs. Crossly announced from the back seat. "That's what they're going to call it…certainly not a very fitting name."

"Why do you say that?" Lane asked.

"Well, it would be more appropriate to be called the Godspeed or Discovery or the Susan Constant, don't you think?"

"I get your point, but how many people do you think know the names of those ships anyway?"

"I, for one, being from the great state of Massachusetts—we hold claim to the Mayflower."

"Ah...Mrs. Crossley...you were how old when you moved to Virginia?"

She glared at Faye. "Just a youngster, you know that."

"Maybe three?"

"There abouts."

"Uh-huh, that's what I thought." She rolled her eyes and tilted her head upward at the rising new building. "I can't imagine living up so high."

"They'll have some view, though." Diane stretched over Angelina for a better look. "Still, I don't like it. Takes away from the whole scheme of things if you ask me."

"Just doesn't look beachy," Faye added. It was shaping up that way, to stand out like a sore thumb, towering over the small, modest cottages and completely changing the overall appearance of the old southern beach.

Lorna's mind had left the idle conversation and conveniently slipped out of the Oldsmobile barreling up Pacific Avenue. Her thoughts returned to her secret plan. If only she could get off by herself, just for a few hours. She realized she was hoping for next to the impossible, but what did she have to lose? She had to start somewhere!

Faye leaned forward and tapped her on the shoulder. "Lorna, lady, what's with you? You've been quiet as a mouse ever since we left."

"Just keeping my mind on my driving."

"That's a good thing," Mrs. Crossly declared.

Lorna wondered again for the umpteenth time if she could possibly be lucky enough to find him. A place called *Elkton* couldn't be but so big, and he had even called it a hole in the wall, she vaguely remembered. Not to be disrespectful, but he was jokingly comparing it to Virginia Beach. But suppose he doesn't know where she is, she thought suddenly. Could that be possible? She had heard about it. Someone giving up a child for adoption and then losing all contact, never again to find him or her, but she couldn't think about that now. She must be optimistic. He would know—he must know.

After leaving the beach behind and all familiar facets of it, the group became quiet with the monotonous ride up the long highway, and Diane and Angelina, sitting up front, even fell asleep, their heads rolling with the curves. Those in the back seat conversed in soft, muted tones, and Lorna was left to reflect on her own situation, her growing discontent and impatience lately. She knew she shouldn't feel this way. She had a nice home, a hard-working husband and, of course, her precious Cory, but still she couldn't shake the restless feeling. It was all wrapped up in her past, and she couldn't unravel its obvious stronghold, though she needed to get beyond it. But it was ever before her, hanging there dark and unresolved. That was the most disheartening of all. If only she could find out something, like she was growing up in a lovely place or a cheery home somewhere. Then maybe she would have more peace. Maybe she could let it go, if she knew that she was happy. The orange *Gulf* sign glared up ahead, bold and welcoming, and she slowed down to turn in.

"Great!" the trio in back piped up. She pulled into the filling station, and they began tumbling out and heading for the small, rusty sign declaring *Ladies Restroom.* Diane and Angelina woke up and heaved themselves out, as well, though still half asleep and stumbling after. The attendant bent down to her window.

"Fill'er up?"

"Yes, please."

He was just finishing his long strokes across the windshield when they returned with Cokes and snacks, joking and laughing, and cramming back into the Oldsmobile. "I bought you some, too, Lorna." Angelina poked a bag of salted peanuts her way. "But I'll hold your Coke for you."

They were visibly tired when they finally reached the Valley, all except for Lorna. She was much too keyed up. She studied the small town of Luray, but there wasn't a whole lot to see. What had she expected? That she didn't know, but soon she hoped to investigate, that is after they returned from their stint in the mountains. Unfortunately, that was the first thing on the agenda, but at least it was only for one night. She felt herself growing more and more impatient by the moment. Why did they have to go up there anyway?

When she finally stretched out beside Mrs. Crossly in the not-too-comfortable double bed, trying to get her head situated in the huge, plastic rollers, she questioned her plan. Suppose she couldn't find him? Suppose he had moved away? People nowadays moved around more than they used to. God forbid! Suppose he had died? She would never find out what happened to her!

Becoming completely unnerved, she realized she was bone tired and tried to settle down just as Mrs. Crossly bellowed out! She was snoring—a dreadful rising and falling racket. Why did she volunteer to sleep with her? Of all people! She could hear Angelina's stifled giggle over in the next bed and knew she and Diane were deriving great pleasure from it. She liked Angelina best of the whole lot in spite of her endless teasing. Ever since they met at the Cub Scouts meeting, they had become fast friends. Not only because Cory and her son Wylie were best buddies, but because they seemed to have a fair amount in common, as well. However, she had to admit none of this was the real reason for their continued friendship. Not on her part, anyway. It was primarily based on the fact that Angelina visited this quaint little town from time to time, and once she had mentioned Shenandoah, that was it. Her intentions were set. It was only a matter of executing the plan, but that took time, over half a year to be exact. She puffed up her pillow and snuggled underneath the soft covers, which did a tolerable job of muffling the maddening snoring, and soon she fell asleep.

"I never saw such beauty!" Diane exclaimed the next day.

They had driven up to the mountains after visiting with Aunt Wilma. Now they were in the Shenandoah National Park, sitting in the rustic dining room at the Skyland Resort and overlooking an amazing view. Though it was much cooler than on the coast, it was actually a rather warm day for spring and absolutely breathtaking. Lorna leaned into the large window. It was so different, different from anything she had imagined. She scanned the treetops that scaled the mountain ridges, and searched the wide-open distant vistas, the freshly plowed fields down below, and the tiny farms so far away.

Where was she?

"Lorna, you look like you're in another world again," Lane said, and she jerked away from the window.

Angelina smiled sweetly. "Well, what do y'all think?"

"Charming…simply charming," Mrs. Crossly stated. "Unpretentious and quite lovely."

"All of the above and more," Diane agreed whole-heartedly. "But are you speaking of the resort or the mountains?"

"Both."

"Well, I have to confess that the mountains do give me a closed-in feeling," Faye admitted rather sheepishly. "I've never felt this way before."

"Really?"

She looked at Angelina apologetically.

"I've heard others say that, but I've always enjoyed visiting the area and Aunt Wilma, of course. After living all my life in the flat tidal land, it's interesting to come up here to explore the mountains. However, Uncle Thurstan, Aunt Wilma's husband, may have agreed with you. He passed away a few years ago, but he never cared too much for the mountains." She chuckled. "He always said that the land looked all rolled up like a blanket and needed to be stretched out."

"Well, I'm glad you brought us up here."

"Thanks, Lane…thought it would be a great way to kick off our little vacation. So what will we order, ladies?" They pored over the menus.

"Fried chicken," Diane answered first. "This mountain air has worked up an appetite for me."

"You haven't done anything yet," Angelina kidded.

Mrs. Crossly folded her napkin discreetly across her lap. "Think I'll try the trout."

"You haven't had enough fish already?" Diane challenged.

"Not mountain trout."

"I'm going for the country ham myself," Faye added. Lorna agreed with her, and Angelina concurred that it was an excellent choice.

"So what are we doing today?" Lane asked.

Angelina closed her menu and leaned back in her chair. "Well, we have lots of choices. There're many trails, but one of my favorites is the hike down to Dark Hollow Falls. It follows a mountain stream all the way. Or we could go over to Big Meadows and just stroll around the meadow, always a pleasant thing to do. Or we could climb a mountain." She waved her hand toward the window. "There're plenty to choose from, or we could just drive across the Skyline Drive north or south—anything would be nice on a day like this. We can't lose."

"Let's not climb any mountains," Mrs. Crossly snapped, "don't think I'm quite up to that today." All morning she had been nagging about a backache that she insisted came from the inferior bed she was subjected to.

"What about a walk then," Lane suggested. "I'd love to see more of the beautiful Drive, but I think we need some fresh air."

"Not just a walk, Lane. We need some exercise," Faye added. "Need to get our hearts beating fast. What about that Falls you liked so well?"

"Great pick."

"You sure we're up to it?" Mrs. Crossly looked a bit worried.

"Ah, it's a piece of cake."

The lively group set out, descending the popular trail, down, down, down, beneath the leafy forest, and it enfolded them in its outstretched arms. The gurgling mountain stream pleasantly accompanied them.

"I see why they call it what they do," Lorna commented. "The sun seems actually shut out." It was definitely a dark, shady trail, and the murmuring waters seemed to muffle out the rest of the world, creating a calm, muted setting.

"But it's invigorating!" Diane exclaimed. The creek bed was almost overflowing from the accumulated spring rains over the past few weeks, and the murmur rose as they descended.

"What did you say?" Mrs. Crossly asked.

"It's invigorating," she repeated loudly.

"Yes...well, I must agree...bracing and quite challenging to one not so used to such a drop in elevation." She picked her way cautiously down the path behind the rest of them. It was her way to live more on the edge of life rather than in the mainstream, obviously afraid too much would perhaps be detrimental to her well-being.

Diane reached back and grabbed hold of her hand. "Come on, lady."

"Very well," she stepped up her momentum in spite of her misgivings. "But one must remember that every step we take down, we most certainly will have to climb back up."

They trudged down together, passing mountain laurel thickets on their left, though not yet blooming, still pleasing to the eye, then a wood of humongous hemlocks with dark-green needles and dense, pyramid-shaped crowns. Lorna noticed other hemlocks piercing the sky on both sides of the stream. Many of the trees lining the trail had their roots exposed from the heavy rains and flooding they had endured through the years, but still they grew taller, reaching for the sky. Bright green ferns nodded in the breeze, climbing up banks of moss, and fragile bluets dotted them by the thousands.

The downward path was rock-strewn with slippery pebbles they had to watch out for. At times the accompanying stream offered sheer pools of water, naturally dammed up, with speckled brook trout circling in them, and they had to stop and examine them.

"I suppose there were Indians here at one time, and they probably fished for these very trout," Lane said.

"Hope not the same ones," Diane kidded.

"But you're absolutely right, Lane," Angelina replied. "The Monacans and the Manahoacs were here before anybody else."

Soon the trail's descent grew steeper, and the hypnotic hum of water was drowned out by something louder. It was the falls up ahead.

"You're almost there!" encouraged an older couple strenuously pushing themselves up the incline with the aid of improvised canes. They were dressed in matching khaki trousers and bright red shirts, and their sweaty faces were flushed almost as red.

"See what I told you!" Mrs. Crossly muttered when they were out of earshot. "A piece of cake, huh?"

But even she was in awe when they reached the bottom of the falls. The swift water, leaping over the massive stone cliffs and ricocheting off one ledge to another, was tumbling forcefully down the sheer rock precipice. The deafening roar all but drowned out their trivial conversations.

"Splendid!" she exclaimed, "a work of art!"

The others smiled at one another and found seats on the large boulders to stare up at the magnificent sight.

The following morning, the sun rose clear and bright over the mountains. Only a few lazy clouds floated between it and the Valley stretching below, casting subtle shadows over the cultivated fields and over the ribbon of river that snaked through it, the beautiful Shenandoah.

Lorna stood gazing out the window of their rustic cabin. Skyland was a lovely place, and any other time she wouldn't want to leave. But there was an urgency burning in her soul. She couldn't wait to get back down to the Valley and on with her impending task. She had to admit, though, that she had enjoyed it, even piling into the cramped quarters, all six of them, and she had slept better, to boot. Mrs. Crossly had wisely requested a rollaway cot, obviously not happy with sharing a bed. Diane made up a comfortable pallet on the floor, also preferring to bed down alone. That left her to sleep with Angelina, and Lane and Faye shared the other bed, which made it all the better. And after a restful night, she was wide awake when the sun first popped over the mountains, sending long golden streamers into their room.

They breakfasted again in the pleasing restaurant, and Lorna bought a few items for Cory, Hayden, and her folks in the gift shop. Then they were on their way, pushing back across the sunlit road. But Lorna's mind was far ahead, already off the mountain and down in the Valley. She had convincingly begged off for the day, using her unexpected time of the month as an excuse. Perfect timing, she didn't even have to lie, only embellish it somewhat.

"Gee, that's a bummer!" Angelina consoled.

Guilt-ridden, she turned away from her friend. "It's okay. I'm just happy being here, but I think maybe I'll take a walk later on if I feel better."

"Whatever you say," Angelina added sympathetically. "You just do what you feel like doing, dear. We'll use Auntie's car. I think she intends to go with us anyway."

"Good thing she wasn't with us yesterday," Mrs. Crossly muttered under her breath.

"Looks like you survived!"

She glared at Diane, who loved to agitate her.

Aunt Wilma's generous, two-story house didn't quite fit her mother's description. Set back among sizeable oaks with lilacs embracing it on both sides, it was more homey than grand, and the decor was simply old and comfy. Aunt Wilma couldn't have been more charming, and she was undoubtedly delighted to have them all as her guests and couldn't wait to show them around. That was all the more reason Lorna experienced a twinge of remorse as they drove off. She didn't like deceiving them, but how else could she get away? She waited until they were out of sight, and then struck out herself.

Stopping a few blocks down the street, she studied the crinkled map and then headed south to Elkton, happy to find that it wasn't all that far, though she would have to pass through a couple of other small towns on the way. Normally she would have enjoyed the sweeping vistas of the legendary Valley, but her mind was too absorbed. With every mile, her anxiety increased, and all she could see was that little pink bundle! And that was simply ludicrous after all these years, but it was ever before her, just like the day she walked out of the hospital.

Soon she passed through the town of Stanley and was out of it before she knew it, then on through miles of more pleasant rural countryside. The next one was the actual town of Shenandoah—much smaller than she expected. She wondered what it would be like to live out here in the Valley, in one of these tiny towns sandwiched in-between the mountains. Maybe not much different from Sandbridge, she concluded, driving on.

What would she say to him if she did find him, after all these years and so much time? She practiced out loud, but the awkward-sounding speech made her more nervous. At last she entered the small town of Elkton and steered up one street, then down another, trying to decide where to stop. Subsequently she chanced upon a small post office. She pulled up in front and got out. She climbed the few steps and opened the door. The postmaster was alone. She was glad of that. He lifted his head halfway and glanced at her beneath his green visor, which cast an eerie, greenish glow over his otherwise pale face.

"May I help you, ma'am?" Though his customary question raised her spirits a notch, she still struggled for the right words.

"Yes, sir…I hope so anyway," she stammered. "I'm looking for someone who lives here in Elkton…someone by the name of Greyson Ralston."

"You mean Reverend Ralston?"

"No, sir." She shook her head. "This person would be about my age…tall…sandy hair…nice looking."

"Yes, ma'am. That's him…Reverend Ralston."

Lorna just stared at him.

He went back to sorting his letters. "But he doesn't live here anymore…did as a boy…lived out yonder at the foot of the mountains with his folks, nice people the Ralstons, but he left way back, moved over to Luray. You'll have to drive over there, Miss."

"To Luray…."

"Yes, ma'am," he repeated. "To the Methodist church, that's where you might find him."

Taken aback, she just stood there, puzzled and trying to absorb it all.

He looked up. "You know how to get there?"

She nodded incredulously, not about to tell him that's where she'd come from. She thanked him and stumbled out of the post office and down the steps.

A preacher!

It didn't register. Greyson a reverend—somehow that didn't fit the image that she had carried with her all these years. A businessman maybe, or possibly a hard-working machine operator, or perhaps even an artist or writer with his keen sensitivity, but a preacher! Never! Maybe she was getting ahead of herself. Maybe it wasn't the same person. No, it probably wasn't, but still she had to follow the lead. What else could she do? Her mind raced on, surely this would be some wild goose chase, and yet it didn't seem possible that there would be two Greyson Ralstons in this tiny town. That was highly unlikely. She wished she had thought to ask about his family or if he was even married, but the shock had erased all logic from her mind.

She retraced her drive, totally confused now and more flustered than ever, back up the narrow road, by the wide open fields, again oblivious to their unique beauty. She passed through the little towns as before but still couldn't believe that he could be in the same town where she was staying. Talk about coincidences! She vaguely remembered passing a Methodist church earlier. But no—there must be some mistake.

Back in Luray, it wasn't hard at all to find the church, but she drove by it several times before getting the courage to stop. This is ridiculous! She silently scolded herself, why did you come in the first place? Finally she pulled up and sat there staring at it, her resolve quickly dwindling. She was losing faith in her own usually aggressive manner, but she hadn't come all this way to give up now! Her heart was pounding as she pushed herself out of the Oldsmobile and walked up to the church. She started as a man of the cloth suddenly opened the door and headed directly toward her.

"Good morning, ma'am. May I be of assistance?"

She breathed a sigh of relief. The elderly minister's smile was warm and genuine, and she suddenly wanted to pour out all her troubles, all her secrets to him. "Good morning to you, Reverend." She glanced around. "I…I'm looking for Reverend Ralston."

"Oh, I'm sorry, ma'am. You just missed him. He and Rayna have gone out for the day. You know, they have so little time together."

He *must* be married, she thought, backing off. Of course, he would be, but for some reason this bit of news caused a stir within her.

"They'll be here later on this evening if you wish to check back then. They'll be over in the parsonage." He nodded in its direction. "Wish to leave a message?"

"No…no!" She promptly shook her head. "That's all right. I'll check back later…maybe tomorrow."

She hurried to the car, hopped in and shot out of the driveway. Now what? She would just have to wait. On edge, she headed back to Aunt Wilma's, already figuring out how she would beg off more time without raising any eyebrows. She could tell that Lane for one was already wondering.

However, the task didn't prove any too difficult. Aunt Wilma had instantly become a favorite among the ladies, and when she offered to escort them to the caverns the next day, they readily agreed. That was just the thing. The Luray Caverns happened to be the largest and most popular caverns in the east, and the group was looking forward to seeing them. Angelina had described them the best she could, but it was impossible to do them justice with mere words, she said. So they were all eager to explore them, and Lorna hated that she would miss out, but it was her only chance, and she turned the opportunity down to her friends' dismay.

"You feeling that bad?" Diane challenged.

She nodded. "I hope you don't mind, but I think I'll pass."

"Leave her alone," Angelina said. "I know how it feels. When I'm having my period, I don't feel like doing anything at all."

"What a pity," Faye said as Lorna walked out of the kitchen.

"She's acting awfully strange," Lane declared as they left for the caverns.

Faye nodded to this and turned to Angelina, "You think she'll feel up to dinner tonight?"

"I certainly hope so, before it's time for y'all to leave. It would be a crying shame if she doesn't."

Lorna headed to the Methodist church again, more anxious this time for she knew he might be there. Suppose it was Greyson? Though she had rehearsed for weeks, her mind was suddenly a vacuum. Would she become tongue-tied, as her mother liked to say? She glanced up to the leaden sky and wished the sun would shine. Instead, it was a dismal gray with a hint of rain. It seemed to reflect her mood.

She pulled up in the exact spot as yesterday and glanced over at the parsonage, a two-story house out of the same dark red-brick as the church. She hadn't paid much attention before, but she supposed it pretty well fit the description of a parsonage. Though it should appear welcoming, it was anything but, rather intimidating, in fact. Summoning all the courage she could muster, she got out and walked toward it, her legs feeling awfully shaky. The stone porch was slippery with dew as she stepped up on it, and she knocked quickly before she lost her nerve. But it seemed like eons as she stood there. Surely someone was home. Her courage began to dissolve, but then the door opened.

Greyson stood before her.

No, it wasn't Greyson, but a preacher in a long, black robe, which lent him a certain holy air, quite disconcerting. She stared at him completely astounded. His sandy hair was prematurely graying, and he had a slight beard, and obviously carried more weight, not too much, but certainly more. Only the deep, thoughtful eyes were the same as she remembered, and they penetrated her now. All this flashed in seconds as they stood there in stony silence—neither knowing what to say. Then his demeanor changed abruptly, and his face darkened. He stepped out on the porch with her. Wasn't he even going to ask her in?

"Why are you here?" His voice carried no warmth, though there was a tremor that she failed to hear.

"I…I had to come…"

Before she could finish, Rayna pulled open the door. "Daddy…" She looked from Greyson to her, and suddenly Lorna's knees went weak. She could only stare at the raven-haired child.

"Go back inside, Rayna!" He spoke sternly. "You don't need to be out here in the air."

The child flashed a radiant smile up at him and popped back inside, closing the door behind her.

His face flushed. "She's just getting over a little virus," he explained awkwardly, and Lorna nodded as if in a trance. But the normal statement lent a measure of reality to the surreal meeting,

"Is it…is it her?"

He didn't answer.

And she wondered why she had asked, she didn't need to.

"Rayna is my daughter." His answer was flat and conclusive.

She stared at him.

At last the reverend standing before her filtered through, and he motioned her toward a chair. She was grateful, for she felt like she might collapse at any moment. She dropped onto the cushioned rocker, and he sat down across from her, still and tense, his black-clad shoulders firm and erect, but she could feel his eyes fixed on her.

"Rayna…is that her name?"

"She's named after my twin sister."

"It's a…lovely name."

"Why are you here?" he repeated.

She couldn't think of an answer. Why was she here? Her mind was baffled, doing strange things, racing and darting incoherently. What crazy mania had driven her to such? What was the point? She could feel her heart beating wildly as if it might jump clean out of her body. What good could possibly come of it?

He was glaring at her, a cold, icy stare. "What do you want?"

She looked down at the stone porch. "I…I have what I came for," her voice trembled.

"Are you surprised?"

"Yes…and no. I guess I should have known."

He was silent.

She looked up. "She is beautiful."

He nodded.

"Is she…is she a good little girl?"

"A very good girl."

"Is she happy?"

"What do you think?"

"Of course...of course she would be."

Guilt washed over him for being so brusque, so cruel, but yet he couldn't help it. Fear was gripping his very soul, an unknowing, unexplainable fear.

"And does she...I mean...does she know?"

"That you are dead."

The cold statement pierced the warm spring air and hung between them.

He shifted in his chair.

"I see." She stared at the closed door.

He felt worse than a heel, yet he was compelled to show her that all was well, that things must not be upset.

She stood up, and so did he.

"Thank you, Reverend Ralston." She wasn't being sarcastic. There was total sincerity in her voice. "Thank you...for everything." And she walked off the porch and down the steps. He started to call her back, to ease the visible pain etched on her pretty face, but he couldn't. The words wouldn't come.

He watched her get in the car and back down the drive, but he couldn't see the tears that blurred her vision. She wanted so to know more, to know every detail of the child's life, to look into those dark eyes and into her little heart, but she couldn't. It would be too much.

The ride back to the coast was just as jolly as the trip up—that is for all except Lorna. The hole in her heart was still there, but now it pulsated with life. Now the empty frame had a picture in it—a lovely picture of a raven-haired child. She stared at the long road stretching up ahead.

"You okay, Lorna?" Lane asked suspiciously. There was definitely something going on, but what on earth?

She nodded without turning her head, afraid to speak, afraid that her voice would betray her.

Deciding it best to change the subject, Lane added, "Well, we certainly appreciate you driving us."

Again she nodded.

"It's been a great trip!" Diane exclaimed from the back, oblivious to the one-sided discourse up front. "Just look at all this beauty we're enjoying, too. *The Eden of the United States.*"

"I never heard that one before," challenged Mrs. Crossly.

"Then you don't know your history, dear," refusing to let her friend's negativism squash her happiness.

Mrs. Crossly shot her an irritated look.

"Those are the words of our very own Thomas Jefferson, my lady. You never heard that?"

"No, ma'am. I haven't."

"Well, it's how he referred to the Shenandoah Valley and its surrounding mountains. That's why he built his home and the university…in Charlottesville."

"Leave it to Diane to study up on the history…who but her?" Faye kidded, playing the role of peacemaker. "And speaking of history, what about General MacArthur? Can you believe that President Truman fired him?"

"He didn't fire him!" Lane corrected.

"I beg your pardon, but I read it in Aunt Wilma's paper and meant to tell y'all, but I forgot."

"I read it, too, but you don't fire generals, Faye. He was removed from command."

"Same difference."

"Now that's an intelligent statement," Mrs. Crossly commented.

"I can't imagine what my father's going to say about it," Faye said, and Lorna wondered, too, what her dad would think.

"Well, he wanted to bomb bases in China to end the war. I can't blame the president," Faye continued. "We would have a Third World War if the general had his way."

"Oh, I don't think so," Lane disagreed, her tone rather stilted. Like Lorna's father, she and her family were avid supporters of the general, and it would prove to be arguably a bone of contention for days to come.

With all the chitchat, the ride home did seem shorter, and it was a bit more comfortable since there were only five of them this time. The afternoon had been clear and sunny when they started out, but then the sky had clouded up, and soon a light drizzle had set in, just enough to harass the wipers. They had been on the road for over an hour, and the Oldsmobile was moving along at a clipped pace, along with a steady stream of other vehicles, all thinly stretching the speed limit. But Lorna was in a hurry. She couldn't wait to get back home, to see her Cory, hopefully before he went to bed. Suddenly she spotted a flashing red light ahead and eased off the accelerator along with everybody else. A state police car was pulled over to the side of the highway, and the trooper was walking up to a small, white sedan, with the dreaded notebook in his hand. Lorna noticed a young girl, probably in her early twenties, sitting very still behind the wheel, and waiting. The stream of cars passed on by, each one relieved it wasn't them, Lorna included.

"Better slow down," Mrs. Crossly's voice warned from the back seat.

"I have. Hayden says I have a heavy foot." She knew he would be awfully upset if she got a ticket. Hayden always drove within the speed limit, and she bet Mrs. Crossly did, too.

"Well, you're not by yourself," Diane piped up, "and I paid for it last November."

"You got a ticket?"

She leaned over Faye to Mrs. Crossly. "Yes, ma'am, I did, but I was the scapegoat. There was a whole line of cars with me, and I was the only one pulled over."

"The scapegoat," Lane chuckled.

"Well, I was, and I told him so, too."

"You did?"

"Not exactly in those words, but I asked him why I was the only one he pulled over."

"What did he say?"

"He was a smart little cop, you know the kind, probably just out of police school…a know-it-all! They think they're it sometimes."

"Well, what did he say?"

"He said, 'When you go fishing, do you catch all the fish?' "

The roar of laughter erupted as the Oldsmobile sped on up the highway, and Lorna was glad for her friends, glad that she had had this time with them even though it was overshadowed with the sadness of her meeting.

Her mind flashed back to it, and once again she was standing there on those stone steps of the parsonage, reliving it all over, every minute detail, the look of surprise on Greyson's face and then how it changed, clouded over. She tried to put herself in his shoes, and wondered how he must have felt after all these years—to have her suddenly show up on his doorstep. Did he think that she had come to take her away? God forbid! Yet, there was plainly an element of fear in his eyes.

But it was *her* face that remained with her—such radiance, and such obvious love for her daddy. It was a deeply painful moment to remember, yet at the same time a tender moment. It warmed her heart to remember the child's fleeting look. And she well knew that she would relive this trip over and over in the days to come, and the years to come, and probably rehash and analyze it until there was not a shred left to dissect. She already knew it was that look that would surface, skim to the top, that look that would perhaps bring her peace when the guilt grew too much. And her name—she had always felt bad that she hadn't named her, couldn't bring herself to, and instead had simply listed 'girl' on the birth certificate. It had helped to make it unreal somehow.

Rayna.

It stuck in her throat, a beautiful name! She wanted to shout it from the housetops. She wanted to tell everybody, especially her friends racing up the highway with her. She needed to tell somebody! She wanted to pronounce it slowly and clearly, let its syllables roll smoothly off her lips, but she couldn't. She hadn't even said it aloud yet. She would though. Once she was alone, maybe down by the Bay. She would tell it to the seagulls and the red-winged blackbirds and the old osprey up on its messy nest if it came back this year. Yes, she would tell it to all of them.

The Oldsmobile sailed on down the highway but staying well within the speed limit now. Finally the flat, tidal lands were stretching out ahead, silhouetted in the twilight, reaching all the way to the ocean. It was late when they arrived home. She crept into Cory's bedroom, though he had been asleep for a while. She leaned over the bed and smoothed his tousled hair from his damp forehead, and placed a teary kiss on his cheek, but he didn't stir.

CHAPTER TWELVE

Greyson packed up the tent, the bedding and all the paraphernalia while Rayna bounced around on top of it, in and out of the truck and back and forth to the house, a bundle of energy and excitement, impossible to contain. The weekend was thrust upon him before he was ready. It was supposed to be a nice one, and he dreaded the thought of spoiling it. He tied the bundles in the back of the truck, securing them with a long bungee cord. Again he thought about the surprise visit, and it brought on another flood of anxiety. It had been crushing down upon him ever since. He knew he had to tell Rayna the truth, but he had always hoped to wait until she was a little older, when she might be able to handle it better, but he didn't think it could wait now. Somehow, someway he had to tell her. Not that he had lied to her for she had never talked about her mother. For some reason, she just assumed that she was dead. At times he had wondered if maybe Ma or Pa had secretly told her that, for she never asked. And she seemed content with just the three of them. They were all she ever needed, but since Ma had died, he wondered if she felt the same.

And suppose Lorna came back?

Just the thought made his heart stand still. No, he must be the one to tell her. He had promised to take her camping again and decided maybe that would be the best time, the peace and quiet of the forest. They always seemed closer there, and so here he was packing up. But was there ever a good time to tell a child that her mother didn't want her?

At least the forecast was good, sunny and warm even in the mountains, and he was glad for that. He was also glad that his pa had decided to return home last week, making the trip possible. However, knowing he was alone didn't help matters particularly. It only added more worry to his already taxed mind. But then he was reminded of the Scriptures. Worry was the opposite of faith. He had just preached on that very topic recently. And one cannot please God without faith! Did all preachers struggle with such shortcomings? The Apostle Paul certainly did. That's why he liked him so; he could easily identify with him.

'For what I am doing, I do not understand. For what I will to do, that I do not practice; but what I hate, that I do.'

He was right there in the boat with him, paddling along with his own shortcomings, but it was the guilt of the past that plagued him most. He knew that God had forgiven him, but would Rayna? How could a child at the tender age of nine comprehend such a complex mess? Undoubtedly he had to soften it somehow, certainly not focus on the details, but even so, how would she deal with it?

"You ready, Daddy?" She hopped up in the back of the truck again, moving things around, trying to help.

"Almost."

"I can't wait!" She sprang up and down impatiently, her dark locks bouncing, falling into her eyes. She had on her faded jeans and her favorite pull-over sweater, the colorful one he had given her for Christmas. She called it her Joseph sweater. They locked up the parsonage, taped a note on the door, and then left.

They drove up to the Park and when they pulled into the campground, the sun had just sunk below the mountains, leaving a rosy-streaked sky. They pitched the tent and searched for firewood, and then went for their accustomed hike. They hadn't gone very far when they came upon a Ranger, who was also busy gathering fallen sticks and dead wood.

"Hello, young lady," he smiled at her and Greyson.

"You gonna have a campfire, too?" she asked.

"Matter of fact, I'll be having a big one. Why don't you folks come on over and join us. I might be telling some ghost tales."

"Thank you, sir," Greyson responded, but he knew as he said it that Rayna wouldn't go. She wasn't too enthralled with ghost stories, and he couldn't blame her. The last time she heard one, she couldn't sleep for nights and had to crawl in bed with him.

But as they walked away, she wasn't thinking about ghost stories. Instead she was remembering another Park Ranger and that day at Big Meadows when she was quite little. She had not witnessed another one of his seizures since then, but the memory stuck with her, vivid and scary. Though they didn't talk about it, it was never far from either of their minds. And Rayna thought if they didn't mention it, maybe it would never happen again.

So she forgot about it, and skipped off through the leafy forest. "That's what I'm gonna be when I grow up."

Greyson quickened his pace to keep up with her. "A Park Ranger?"

She nodded vigorously and jumped up high to grab hold of a dangling grapevine twisted around a tall, straight poplar.

"Well, I don't think they have girls as Park Rangers."

"Why not?"

He couldn't answer that. It was not something he had ever given much thought to one way or the other.

"Why not?" she persisted, swinging out on the vine in wide, jerky circles.

"I'm not sure, Princess."

"Well, I'm gonna be one." She dropped the vine and scuffed off through the packed leaves, with that determined air he had become accustomed to. He chuckled to himself, but only imagined what Pa would have to say about it.

After supper, they cuddled up by the campfire, and Greyson was searching for the right words to start his dreaded talk.

"Daddy?"

"Yes?"

"Are these mountains haunted?"

"Haunted? Why do you ask?"

She sat up. "Grandpa says they are."

He laughed softly, trying to lighten the mood. "You know how Grandpa is."

"He said they're haunted by the mountain people who used to live up here."

"I think he just means that they loved these mountains so…that their spirit is still here."

"Is your spirit here, Daddy?"

The poignant question caught him off guard. "Well… maybe so."

"But spirits are ghosts, and I don't like ghosts!"

"There aren't any ghosts here, Princess. Don't you worry about that."

He hugged her, and she snuggled up closer, and he remembered how he and Rayna Rose used to be afraid of ghosts, but they called them haints back then. He let his mind trail off to those long-ago days, and before he knew it, he realized Rayna had fallen asleep. He sighed and looked up at the moon that had climbed high above the trees, and myriad stars were blinking against the inky-black sky. It was too late now.

He gently lifted her and placed her inside the tent. He had missed his chance. After romping through the woods, gathering firewood and chasing squirrels up the trees, he should have known this would happen. But he was frustrated. He had envisioned a tender moment with her on his lap, a special time to tell her about her mother. Now he would have to wait till tomorrow, and it wouldn't be the same in the morning.

He sat back down and stabbed at the campfire with a large stick, shifting the logs about, stirring it up, and watching the cinders leap into the air. He wouldn't tell Rayna, but he believed his pa was right about the haunting spirits. As if in a trance, he stared at the flames that lapped hungrily at him and reached higher and higher into the darkened sky. Then it all flashed back—the raging fire, his mother's cries and that horrible sick feeling down in his gut. It happened about six months after they were forced off the mountain, and his folks had decided to drive back up, to visit his twin sister's grave, for one thing. The mountain place was like a giant magnet for his pa anyway, though he and his ma had gone with him that particular day. She had a bouquet of foxglove for the grave. She always took flowers.

He remembered how he enjoyed the ride back up the mountain, bouncing along in the piece of truck his pa had purchased for mere pennies once they moved, but he loved it, both the truck and the ride. He recalled his heightened anticipation of seeing the old cabin again and especially his room upstairs. He missed it. There was no loft in the new house or an upstairs even, though it was certainly far nicer. It was the middle of summer, a hot day, but he remembered it getting cooler and cooler as they climbed up the mountain.

He kept poking the fire, the memories gripping him now, determined not to let go. Suddenly a log burnt through and caved into the ashes sending up a shower of sparks and huge puffs of smoke that enveloped him. Coughing, he whipped around to face the dark forest. It was the smoke they had seen first that day, and he distinctly remembered its ominous dark swirl curling up from the old cabin. His pa had come to a screeching halt and jumped out, racing toward it. And he and Ma had followed hard on his heels.

The cabin was on fire, and there were two young men standing there beside it, watching.

"What in tarnation?" Pa yelled out, running up to them with raised fists. He remembered being afraid that they would hurt his pa. He had never seen him act so. The young men looked surprised, too.

"Just doing our job, mister," one of them answered. "We're supposed to burn it down."

They looked like young lads, not old as Jack even, but he recognized their uniforms. They were CCC boys. Not the same ones that had helped them move off the mountain with those big trucks, but different ones. He liked the CCC boys and couldn't understand why they were burning down the cabin. Pa knew, but it didn't make any difference to him. He knew their mission. They were responsible for turning the land back to its natural state, removing all the fences, and wiping out the gardens and orchards, and taking apart or burning all signs of previous life. But he didn't care if it was their job. All he could see was the old cabin on fire.

The young men stood there looking nervously from one to the other. They were obviously taken aback, not expecting this turn of events, though it was one of the jobs they hated most. There had been more than one occasion where residents or others had slipped back into vacated cabins, creating more trouble for the Park Service, and by burning them down, it made it impossible for that to happen. That's why they were there. It was a mammoth job to clear such a vast area, thousands of acres, and a complicated mission to be sure, but it was also a heart-wrenching job at times.

"We're sorry, mister...but this was our orders...you know."

His pa had dropped his hands to his sides and stood there helplessly, staring at the flames, but his ma kept wailing, louder and louder. It was just too much for her after all that had happened. He remembered shaking and not being able to stop as he watched the flames lapping at the front porch and the front door and reaching up to the eaves. He remembered watching the small upstairs window, the one in the loft, and he remembered the nauseating feeling down in his gut as he clung to his ma's skirt. But then the thunder rang out, and they all looked up to a suddenly darkened sky. Rain began to fall, hard and relentlessly. The CCC boys jumped back in their truck and sped off, but he and his folks just stood there in the rain. He could almost feel its penetrating chill again, pounding him and soaking him from his head to his bare feet, but he couldn't move—he was hypnotized by the dying flames.

The rains finally won out, and the fire died down to smoldering embers. By then they had backed beneath the leafy canopy of the chestnut oak that he had played under so often. Though wet and blackened, the cabin still stood with only part of the porch and the lean-to gone. His mother stopped crying and went back to the truck for the foxglove.

Greyson once again smelled that sickening stench of burnt chestnut logs mixed with the rain. It came back to him full force as he poked at the campfire. It had lingered with him throughout the years along with the doctor's mothballs. What our senses carry with them and evoke at a moment's notice, he thought. Life can be hard. He would talk to Rayna in the morning.

CHAPTER THIRTEEN

Almost a year had passed since the surprise visit, and Greyson finally let his guard down, comfortable again in his daily routine. He didn't think that she would return. There was something in her manner, in her eyes that day, something final. Besides, how could she? She had her own life and family back home on the coast. He still couldn't believe that he had not even asked about the young lad. He would be about a year older than Rayna now. But at the time, he was in such shock he could only think of one thing, and that was Rayna.

The television was blaring downstairs. She was watching one of those noisy westerns again, and he knew his pa would be fuming when he came in from his gardening, for he hated those shows. He went to the top of the steps.

"Rayna, could you please turn that down a little?"

The volume dropped a few notches. Talk about generation gaps, he thought, returning to his work. It was hard being caught in the middle of a crotchety old man at times and a wisp of a girl, bottled up with high energy, who wanted to be surrounded by racket of any kind. He stepped back into his bedroom, which also served as his study, and stared at the stack of open books sprawled out on his desk. He was in the middle of a sermon but hadn't been able to pull it together all week. He didn't know why, but it was stuck in his mind, budding, blossoming and ripening, yet it wouldn't emerge. It was like a block wall obstructing it, and it just wouldn't materialize.

Sinking down at the large oak desk, wedged in between the two small dormer windows, he felt the warmth of the sun as it spilled in over his paper, clear, pristine rays after last night's rain. He stared at the mess of notes and scribbling cluttering the desk, and his mind seemed just as cluttered. He glanced out the window to his right, into the dazzling sunlight. Maybe it would clear his fuzzy thoughts, but then he saw his pa shuffling across the lawn in that sagging, old, gray vest. He wished he could throw it away, but his pa wouldn't hear of it. It was all he could do to get it off him once in awhile to wash. Otherwise it smelled of damp wool and stale smoke, and even after a wash, the determined, old smells still lingered, but he insisted on wearing it. He could be awfully stubborn at times.

He watched him reach down to pick up something, but he couldn't tell what it was. He couldn't see anything on the lawn and wondered what he was picking up. He stood up for a better look. There appeared to be something in his hand, obviously something quite small.

Now he was moseying over to the peony garden at the edge of the back yard. It was bordered by a low, mossy wall that had been there for about as long as the house, he figured. The peony garden was one of Rayna's favorite things about the parsonage. Every spring she waited anxiously for them to bud and open up their enormous lush heads, displaying their pristine white petals splashed with a hint of scarlet. He had to admit he loved them just as much, but they had never been particularly interesting to his pa, and he watched him now curiously standing over it. Usually he relished the wildflower garden they planted the first year he had come to live with them, and each year he patiently dropped more and more seeds into it. But it was on the other side of the house, bordering the slate walkway that curved around to the church.

The old man sat down on the rock wall and opened up his hand. Greyson leaned into the window and could barely see squiggly little worms dropping onto the garden. He smiled to himself. His pa would do that. He would feel that those fishing worms would be happier in the rich, black dirt of the peony garden instead of the prickly, mowed lawn. He didn't like the feel of the manicured lawn and grumbled about it often enough. Greyson knew that he missed his home, but there was nothing he could do about that. He couldn't stay alone now.

Even more troubling was the fact that he seemed to be homesick for the mountain place these days. That's what he talked about over and over, and this bothered him. Of course, his pa had always missed the place, but he didn't dwell on it, and he had finally adjusted after the move, as well as could be expected, that is. Greyson realized however, as people aged, they often reverted back to the past, back to their childhood, back to what they deemed the good old days. He studied his pa's bent over frame, far more fragile these days.

He sat back down at the desk and began reading his last thoughts and then balled up the paper and tossed it into the trashcan beside him. He pulled out a clean sheet and stared blankly at it, but the only thing ringing in his head was the wretched gunshots still blasting downstairs and even louder now. He knew she would sneak it back up. She figured he was lost in his studies, and he should be.

But he smiled to himself.

In spite of her hard-headedness, she was the joy of his life, and he couldn't believe how fast she was growing up, and how well. He stretched back in his chair and studied the sunrays piercing the treetops, trying not to feel too prideful. But he couldn't help but be proud of how she was turning out so far. He thought again of how easily she had accepted the truth about her mother, and how she didn't question his wrongdoing. She had quickly dismissed it. He had been told that young children were often that way, but Rayna was a complex child. He wasn't about to believe that she didn't ponder it all in the solitude of her room. He could see her doing that, but yet he had not witnessed any signs.

He heard the screen door slam shut, and suddenly the gunshots ceased. Though his pa's complaining didn't sit well with Rayna and bugged her more often than not, she was always sensitive to him. She loved her grandpa. Then he heard her soft but deliberate patter coming up the steps.

"Daddy, here's your paper." She crossed the room with the rolled-up newspaper. "Grandpa brought it in."

"Thanks, Princess."

"I'm gonna work on my leaf project now."

"Need any help?"

"Grandpa's gonna help me." And she scooted out the room and down the stairs. The leaf project was another one of her Brownie assignments, and she was clearly taking it seriously. It wouldn't be long before she would be promoted up to the Girl Scouts, and he knew she was counting on that.

He pulled the rubber band off the newspaper and scanned the headlines. *Ike Promises to go to Korea if Elected.* He liked Ike and hoped he would be elected. He seemed like a kind man but also rather dignified. Certainly that derived from such a successful and victorious background, one that even his opponents couldn't deny. Adlai Stevenson undoubtedly exhibited a strong sense of wit and intellectual prowess, but Greyson had lost faith in the Democratic Party. He believed they were to blame for the government taking more control over people's lives, and that he didn't want. William accused them of allowing Communists to obtain government posts. He wouldn't go that far, but he certainly had more trust in Eisenhower. The man exuded integrity. But he and William didn't discuss such things around Pa. He didn't want anything to do with politics—period! Ever since Roosevelt sold them out, he argued, he wanted no part of future presidents or the government. And it was true that, initially, when the Shenandoah National Park was begun, President Hoover had no plans to move the mountain people off the land, but when Roosevelt took over, all that changed. However, Greyson couldn't put all the blame on the president. He knew there were many people in power that wielded considerable influence.

The screen door slammed again, and he glanced out the window. The two of them were walking hand in hand across the lawn, talking excitedly. He watched them head over toward a poplar, and Rayna reached up to pull off a large green leaf. She shook off the drops of water, and they studied it in deep concentration. Then she flipped open the cigar box Pa had given her and placed it inside. Pa didn't smoke cigars anymore or even his pipe now. He used to do both, but then tapered off to the pipe. Now he had quit that. He didn't know why, but he had a hunch it had something to do with living in the parsonage. He watched them head around the side of the house and out of sight.

His sermon lay waiting, and he got up and closed the door. It was Friday, and Sunday would be here all too soon. He knew he had any number of old sermons that he could fall back on, and his flock wouldn't mind. Probably half of them wouldn't even remember it, but that was not the way he did things. Not the way God wanted him to do things, he figured. If he wanted his people to feel the hand of God afresh, then he needed to feel it himself!

"But Grandpa, I want a whole lot of different leaves in my book," Rayna complained, looking around at the limited possibilities.

"Well'sa, you ain't gonna find them here."

"Maybe Daddy will take us up to the mountains."

"Naw…he's too busy working on his sermon, and we ain't to disturb him neither." He sat down on the small concrete bench beneath the aging willow tree that graced the side yard and pulled out a large, white handkerchief from his back pocket. The day was growing rather warm, and he proceeded to wipe his brow.

Rayna slid in beside him. "Why don't you take off your vest, Grandpa?"

"I'm all right."

She gazed up at the wispy branches gently dangling and swaying above them, thinking to herself that if she could wait until Monday, maybe then her daddy would take her. She knew he often liked to rest on Mondays, and sometimes he liked taking a ride. She decided that's exactly what she would do.

"Grandpa?"

"Uh-huh."

"Did you ever collect leaves when you were a kid?"

He rubbed his stubby whiskers, the lines of his face firmly etched, and thought for a moment. "I don't recollect doing so, 'course that's been a long time ago when I was a boy, but I sure did enjoy climbing trees, all kinds of trees.

Oaks, poplars, maples, hickories, and cucumber magnolias, but my favorite was the chestnut, and there was a pile of them, too."

"I know. Daddy told me about them."

"We looked forward to them chestnuts every year."

"What'd you do with them? Eat them?"

"'Course we ate them, but we sold them, too, got a right smart piece of money for them. And we needed the money. Shucks! Times was hard on the mountain."

"Then how come Daddy says you always want to go back?"

He shot her a funny look, and she figured she had said the wrong thing.

"Rayna, child, you know I ain't learned like your daddy, and I can't put things nice like he can, but alls I can say is there was a feeling up there on the mountain, a special-like feeling. It's hard to explain."

She watched him lean over and stuff his handkerchief back in his pocket.

"When the sun shone down on them ridges, I felt all snug inside just like I figured them big old rocks did when they were baked hot as—" He caught himself and looked over at her as if he'd forgotten she was there.

She smiled at him.

"And when the winds blew, and it seemed like they blew most of the time, well'sa, I felt like I could withstand them winds just like the old mountain, no matter how hard they blew. I reckon somehow I growed up feeling like me and the mountain were the same, you know. It was a part of me, and I was a part of it."

"But the house you lived in, it was a little bitty place." She had seen the decaying cabin more than once and always wondered how they could all fit into it.

He chuckled. "It won't no big thing, that's for sure, but we made out just fine. Yes, ma'am, we made out just fine, and your grandma, she loved it, too."

The mention of her grandma tended to dampen the pretty day just a bit, but she was determined not to let it. "Grandma grew up on the mountain, too, didn't she?"

"'Course she did, right over the ridge from me, in the next hollow."

"Were y'all playmates then?"

"Naw, I never set eyes on her 'til she was right about thirteen or fourteen, I reckon." He stretched his legs out in the sun, seemingly taking his time with this pleasant memory, and Rayna waited patiently. She was used to his deliberate pauses, figuring it took more time for old folks.

"I had a hankering for blackberries one summer day and went picking, a day much like this one, and I happened to look up and here she come, riding up on an old piece of a mare. It looked like it done seen better days, for sure. You could see its ribs sticking out, but she was riding it proud-like, just like it was some stallion in a fancy show." He chuckled again. "Yeah, your grandma was some lady!"

Rayna tried to picture this, but all she could see was her gray-headed grandma's backside hanging out the laundry. It simply wouldn't translate into the image he was describing, and she decided to change the subject. She didn't want him getting all misty-eyed like he did sometimes, so she interjected, "Daddy said he loved the mountain, too."

"He sure did. That boy, he was a natural for the mountain, except he had a tendency to get skeered sometimes. Both he and Rayna Rose was always talking about haints back then, but there won't no haints up there."

She watched his face cloud over.

"…and he oughta be up there right now." His voice rose with a quiver. "He would be the rightful owner. The place woulda been his, you know."

Rayna looked at him questioningly. "You mean the mountain place would have been Daddy's?"

"Yes, ma'am."

"And he would be a farmer?"

"I reckon so."

"And I would be living up on the mountain, too?"

He hesitated, but only for a second. "Yes, ma'am."

"Hm-m-m-ph."

The old man glanced over at the church. "'Course I don't know what he woulda done about this preacher business." And neither did Rayna.

Soon it was autumn, and the gray days of November set in. Cold winds blew in slight tufts of snow that swirled around Luray's chimneys, with clouds of smoke rising up and then curling back downward. Pa paced throughout the house, at least the first floor. He never climbed the stairs for his arthritis was bothering him more and more these days. There was no need for him to go upstairs anyway, he said. There were only two rooms up there; one was Rayna's bedroom, the other was Greyson's. His was on the main floor, and it was a good thing, too. Already he could feel the cold air seeping beneath the window sills. Winter was the hardest on him, imprisoning him within its walls, and not allowing him to get outside to his vegetable garden or just to mosey around the church grounds. And trapped inside, he became more and more irritable.

Greyson sat in his chair, reading the newspaper and glad that his pa was napping. The house was unusually quiet, and he scanned the political news. Eisenhower had won the election and would soon become the new president. It was a pretty good victory, too, thirty-three million to twenty-seven million. He read all the viewpoints, both positive and negative, but he especially took note of the incoming president's words.

"*Our government makes no sense unless it is founded in a deeply felt religious faith and I don't care what it is.*"

He mulled over the statement and agreed with the first part, at least. He had never put much stock in denominations, although certainly he was fond of the Methodists, but he well knew that all denominations were man-made. But *faith*—now that was a different matter—*faith* in the Lord, the Creator of it all.

"Daddy!" Rayna bounced into the room, interrupting his theological ponderings.

He closed the paper and looked up at her.

"I know what I want for Christmas!"

"Oh, you do, do you?"

"Yes." She was dancing a jig in the middle of the living room floor, whirling around like a spinning top.

"And what would that be?"

"A chipmunk!"

"A what?"

"You know, one of those little furry animals with stripes down its back, a chipmunk, Daddy."

"Now Rayna, chipmunks are wild creatures. They're not for pets." He had been halfway expecting this, with all the hints she had been dropping left and right in the past week. He figured she was gearing up for a kitten or a puppy maybe, and he was prepared for that. But a chipmunk?

Her head drooped, and she resorted to the familiar pout that always melted him and usually ended in her favor.

"Besides, you can't buy a chipmunk," he explained gently, glad to have a logical argument.

"But I know where we can get one!" she responded, instantly switching back to her previous merry mood.

Now it was coming together, and he waited for her explanation. She had edged up close and was looking up at him with those luminous dark eyes. "There's one in our back yard, Daddy; he lives out next to the peony garden, next to the old wall. I've seen it."

He smiled. So had he. "It's time for the encyclopedia, Princess."

She threw him that saucy look of hers, twirled around and crossed the room to the bookcase that consumed one whole wall.

"The letter 'C' if you don't mind."

"I know!" she snapped back and plucked the encyclopedia out of the neat row of matching, dark green volumes. She brought it to him, though crossly, aware of his intentions. He flipped to the appropriate page and slid over, patting the spot beside him. She wedged in with an audible sigh as he pointed to a picture. It was a diagram of a chipmunk's underground burrow, intricately sketched, showing two different tunnels leading to a large, round nest, and there was a chipmunk sitting squarely in the middle of the nest munching on something.

"Did you know that they have homes like this?"

She squirmed. "I thought maybe so."

"Would you like to live in a burrow like this?"

She wrinkled her nose at him.

"But the chipmunk loves it, because it's the way God made him."

"I know that, Daddy," she responded rather sharply, knowing where he was going with it.

"Well, maybe the chipmunk wouldn't be happy living in a house like ours without any long tunnels."

She knew he had her, and she also knew he was probably right. She slumped back in the chair, and he wrapped his arm about her. "But, you know, kittens seem to adapt quite well to houses."

She sprang to her feet. "Could I have a kitten, Daddy?"

"We'll just have to wait and see what old Santa thinks."

She gave him a hug and disappeared upstairs. Once more he pondered the mysteries of life, remembering how his twin sister had also loved chipmunks. Would the parallel ever end? And then again, did he really want it to?

President Eisenhower was inaugurated as the thirty-fourth President of the United States in January and pledged to seek peace. The hellish Korean War, or Conflict as some still chose to reference it, was yet raging overseas, but on the fifth day of March, Soviet Premier Joseph Stalin died. Then the Soviet leaders suddenly began talking of the need to settle the disputes peacefully, and they accepted the United Nations' prior proposal to exchange thousands of sick and wounded prisoners.

So the truce talks were going on, and now it was springtime, and there was noticeable hope in the faces of Americans, young and old alike. They were optimistic, they were eager, and they were impatient. There had been too many wars and far too much killing for way too long. They were ready for peace.

Rayna sat quietly out on the front porch. She was in her own world, oblivious to such issues. She stroked Mr. Ike, her tabby tomcat, which was rapidly shedding its cuddly, kitten cuteness. Now it exhibited its natural innate traits, not the least of which was its hunting skills that annoyed her to no end. It seemed bent on displaying the results of this prized skill, notably depositing it on their front porch, dead and mangled, directly where one had to either step over it or on it. And though she was a tomboy through and through, she was repulsed by the sight of death, and more times than not had to scramble for her dad to remedy the troublesome situation.

Her eyes rested on the newly green poplar leaves and the unfurled daffodils planted by the front sidewalk that seemed to be smiling up at the morning sun. She smiled, too, listening to Mr. Ike's soothing purr. It was a comforting sound, but she decided to check on the peonies, to see how they were doing, if they were budding yet.

She slowed the swing and rolled gently out of it, leaving the sleeping cat, and crept off the porch. Skirting around the side of the house to the back yard, she noticed Mr. Tomlin's station wagon pulled up to the church. The one with the faded wood along the sides, and she remembered that there was a deacons' meeting this morning, and her daddy would be tied up until lunchtime.

Shucks!

Oh well, maybe they would come to a decision today. That would make her daddy happy. She certainly hoped so, for they had been talking about that sign long enough. The one out front that gave the information of the services. They had been studying the possibility of changing it. It needed a new coat of paint, but some thought it needed revising, to be more embracing perhaps, others liked it the way it was. She didn't see anything wrong with it anyhow and wondered why grownups had to spend so much time trying to see eye to eye on things that didn't mean a hill of beans.

A covey of mourning doves lifted off the back lawn and fluttered into the treetops as she marched across the freshly mowed grass. The stone wall was still wet from the night's dew, but she sat down on it anyway, enjoying the damp, earthy fragrance mixed with the freshly-mowed grass. She examined the peonies, which had a long way to go yet. Plenty green, but she couldn't find a single bud. She rubbed the velvety moss spreading alongside the wall, mingling with the dense ivy, and listened to the low cooing of the doves.

"Rayna, I'll be next door…a deacons' meeting…check on Grandpa, would you?"

"Okay," she replied and watched her daddy step briskly across the lawn to the church but decided to wait on Grandpa. He was probably snoring away anyhow. She didn't know how he could sleep so much. She continued to watch the doves. A couple had dropped to the ground in search of food, and every now and then studied her with their small, black eyes.

All at once, she caught a quick movement to her left. It was the chipmunk hole, and her eyes grew larger. A teeny chipmunk, a new baby apparently, was sticking its head out. She sat very still, hardly breathing, not wanting to frighten the little guy, but it didn't seem to notice her at all and inched up higher. She could tell it wanted to come out but didn't quite have the nerve or whatever chipmunks have. And then it slipped back into the hole and out of sight as its mama scampered across the yard and disappeared in it, too. She jumped up and peeked down into the small round opening but could see nothing.

He was back! Or more likely a she, and now with a baby and possibly even more! Who knows? She couldn't wait to tell her daddy and had an urge to rush into the church office, but thought better of it. All the familiar automobiles were now lining up outside, trailing off from Mr. Tomlin's, even Mr. Heerspink's. He had been quite ill lately and sorely missed at the last couple of meetings. He was one of her favorites. They were lining up and down the street since they couldn't all fit in the driveway. She went back to sit on the wall and wait for another possible appearance, deciding to keep it a secret. She liked secrets.

Greyson seated himself among the group of sedate, older men, sipping his coffee and feeling more and more intimidated by the moment. He didn't know why he always felt this way. He was the minister, for goodness sake! Yet, the deacons' meetings never failed to generate these feelings of inadequateness in him. Perhaps it was the fact that most of them had white heads and had been here long before him, but he was also well aware that several of them were inclined to think themselves actually in charge of the church, owners if you would. And then there was the ever-present awareness that most of them held claim to more degrees or more talent than he had ever hoped to attain, and this knowledge bestowed even more lacking feelings upon him. But wasn't that the truth of the matter? He was lacking! Who was he that God would choose to use, to speak through? Who was he, except for the wonderful grace of God?

"Reverend Ralston, what do you think?" Mr. Heerspink asked, bringing him suddenly out of his brooding thoughts, and he looked up questioningly.

"I'm sorry."

"What do you think of the words *'All Invited'*?"

"Certainly, Claude, we want to invite all…everybody, of course."

"Everybody?" Mr. Tomlin questioned.

"What's your concern, Herbert?" Mr. Brown asked pointedly, tapping his pencil on the table.

"Well, Lawrence, you know what that could do?"

"It could open up a can of worms!" Mr. Bradley declared, agreeing with Mr. Tomlin. "That's what it could do."

The others glared at him as if he had just brought down the gavel with such contentious words.

"I believe you have a valid point, Arthur," Malcolm Friedman alleged, "a very valid point."

"Maybe we should just leave it be, the welcome part, that is," Mr. Brown conceded.

Greyson studied the group of deacons, solid citizens like most deacons in any church, well-meaning men, hard-working men, though most now were retired. He knew they meant well but wondered how long they were going to rehash this thing. It was becoming quite tedious.

Rayna looked up as her grandpa stepped across the lawn, leaning heavily upon his new wooden cane and wearing his gray vest. She figured her daddy would be provoked. He had specifically asked him this morning to take it off for the laundry today, but she knew her grandpa. He did what he wanted to do. She saw him glancing back and forth from her to the house.

"Looking for Daddy?"

"Where the dickens is he?"

"At a deacons' meeting."

He snorted his disapproval. "What're you doing?"

"Watching for chipmunks."

"They back?"

She nodded, forgetting her secret. "They hibernate in the winter, Grandpa, and come back in the springtime." She wondered how he could be so old and yet not know such things. "And did you know that chipmunks can carry up to nine acorns in their mouth at one time?"

"Really?"

"That's what the encyclopedia said."

He edged up beside her and peered down the hole. "They down there?"

"Yes, sir." She wasn't going to tell him about the little one though. That one she would keep secret.

"Hm-m-m-ph." He swung his cane out poking at the hole.

She sprang in front of it. "No, Grandpa! You can't do that!"

"Ain't nothing but chipmunks."

She flashed him one of her dark looks, her face drawn up and her hands planted firmly on her slight hips, and for a moment, time melted away. It was his little Rayna Rose up on the mountain. Slightly unnerved, he shifted over to the wall and dropped down upon it, noticing how the ivy was taking over, and grateful that there was always something in life to divert one's attention. He would have to get out his clippers, maybe this afternoon. It would give him something to do.

Rayna saw how he looked and immediately felt remorseful. "There's a baby down there, Grandpa."

He looked up, rather chastised.

"A little baby chipmunk."

He stared at the silent hole. "You see it?"

She nodded.

"Better watch out…Mr. Ike's gonna get him."

"Grandpa!" She stomped off.

"Where you going?"

"Inside." She stalked across the lawn and into the house. The old man sat there, wondering what he had done now. Seemed like folks were forever jumping up and running off or giving him strange or puzzling looks, and for what, he couldn't figure out. He stared at the hole and then pushed up from the wall.

"Ain't nothing but a bunch of chipmunks anyhow," he muttered to himself.

It was only a week later that Greyson pulled up in the driveway and saw Rayna sitting on the front steps with her head in her hands. He leaped out and ran up to her. "What's wrong, Princess?"

She lifted her tear-stained face, and a new rush of tears gushed out. He cradled her in his arms, rocking her back and forth. "What is it, Rayna?"

"Mr. Ike…."

Fearful, he glanced around for the yellow cat, but didn't see it anywhere.

"What about Mr. Ike?"

She buried her head in his chest. "He killed my chipmunk!" And she cried all the harder.

Grandpa appeared on the porch, shaking his head. "I told her so…I told her it was gonna happen."

Greyson shot him a stern look, and he shuffled back inside.

"I don't want him…I don't want Mr. Ike anymore!" she cried out.

"Now…now…." He continued to rock her in his arms, letting the sobs subside and the hurt slowly ebb. "I know you feel that way, Princess…but Mr. Ike isn't to blame."

"Yes, he is!"

"Poor old Mr. Ike was just doing what he was made to do. Remember our conversation?"

She nodded, but still refused to forgive him and began to cry all over again.

"Rayna, Rayna, Rayna…."

"And now it won't have a mommy!"

"What're you talking about?"

"The baby chipmunk…it won't have a mommy."

"There's a baby chipmunk?"

She nodded, her head still pressed into his chest.

"You never told me that."

"It was my secret, but I had to tell Grandpa because he was gonna hurt it."

"I don't think he would do that."

Her head jerked up. "He was poking the hole with his cane!"

"Well, you know Grandpa sees things a little differently sometimes."

"What's she gonna do now…the baby chipmunk?"

He felt the sadness in her words. Why had she referred to the baby chipmunk as a female? "Well, we will have to keep an eye out for her, I suppose."

"Grandpa buried her mommy."

"That was nice of him, don't you think?"

She nodded. "He buried her on the other side of the peony garden…I told him to."

"Sounds like a good place to me."

"I know she won't be able to smell the peonies when they bloom, but I thought she would like being there."

"I understand."

CHAPTER FOURTEEN

The war had ended. It had been two years since the armistice agreement was signed, and Korea was behind them. The country was finally at peace, in the midst of a passive and calming period, in fact, and people were focusing on more pleasant things for a change. Buying homes, buying automobiles and washing machines and television sets and anything and everything they had yearned for in the past and couldn't get. They were pushing up and out, and also moving about, traveling more. At last, after the Depression and wars, they were experiencing the American dream. Plus there was a relatively new phenomenon, a happy trend called the vacation.

Previously, that had pretty much been for the privileged few. It was unheard of for most, but more and more families were enjoying them now, in the blissful fifties. They could finally afford to buy automobiles and the gas to run them. They could actually save up enough money to go, not everybody, but many could. And now they had new interstates, thanks to Eisenhower, and motels were popping up all along them, their winking signs enticing them in. And families were sailing down the sunny four-lane stretches in search of new places and new pleasures. They were particularly flooding onto the beaches, and Virginia Beach was a favorite on the list of those living on the eastern side of the nation. Its plentiful sun, sea and sand beckoned, and its long boardwalk was a must to experience. It was fast growing more and more popular, with lots to offer those looking for fun and entertainment.

Lorna was working as a part-time sales clerk in one of its shops up on Atlantic Avenue and benefiting from the lively activity. She relished the overall prevailing happy mood of the beach, and had settled into a comfortable routine, staying quite busy. That with Cory's on-the-go schedule kept her racing in circles most of the time. He was either caught up in softball or basketball or whatever other ball-playing sport he could get into, but she didn't mind. Only her mother complained, nagging her regularly about it all, especially the job. She was dead set against women working outside of the home, especially when they had children. It just wasn't done, but Lorna had found that staying occupied was her best ally. Not that she was unhappy, but it helped to keep the past in the past.

After the Shenandoah trip, she found herself consumed with thoughts of the sweet little girl in the doorway. That precious face, outlined by those thick, dark curls, was ever before her. It nearly drove her crazy for a while, until one Sunday morning some months later. They happened to have a visiting minister at Nimmo, and she was convinced he was sent from God just for her!

He was preaching on forgiveness and how Christ died for the sins of all mankind. She had heard it all before and certainly had a good head-knowledge of it, but for some reason, those riveting words hit hard and heavy that autumn morning. They reached down into her heart, illuminating her sin and deep need as never before. They stirred a desire within her, a desire to settle up with God once and for all. By the end of the week, she made her way across the sprawling lawn, down to the Bay, to sit by its calming waters. It was a surprisingly mild day for the first day of November, and the sun shone intensely. The waters sparkled with glittering diamonds that danced over its glassy surface, and a subtle, warm breeze caressed her. She watched a leaf fall from time to time from the almost bare trees draping the banks. She watched them cartwheel to the water and skim its placid surface, riding along to destinations unknown, and she thought again of the sermon.

'Come unto me, all ye that labour and are heavy laden, and I will give you rest.'

How she needed rest. Rest from her troubling thoughts, rest from the nagging memories, rest from the ever-present pictures of the little raven-headed girl, and, most of all, rest from the guilt. Somehow sitting there by the water in the warmth of the sun, she felt God's presence even stronger than in the church pew, and the words tugged at her heart.

"I do come, Lord..." she whispered, and looking up into the cloudless sky, a brilliant blue, she relinquished her stubborn will to His.

"...please forgive me!"

Birds fluttered in the treetops.

"I know I'm not worthy, but give me the rest that You promised."

And though the past was ever before Lorna Blackenstaff, never once leaving her side, it wasn't a dark encumbrance anymore. No longer was it a weight hanging from her slender shoulders. And she finally came to terms with the shock of that distressing meeting, and actually discovered a certain source of pleasure in knowing that they were together, Greyson and Rayna, the two of them, living happily up there in the Shenandoah. And if ever she was prone to doubt it, all she had to do was remember the look on the child's face, that fleeting moment.

And with it, she found new hope. Hope to see her again one day.

Afterwards, she was able to relax and give Cory her undivided attention, and they grew even closer, though she realized this was partly due to the fact that Hayden never seemed to have time for him. Sadly, she watched them growing further apart with the years, and she had to fight the bitterness that welled up in her. Couldn't he see that the boy needed him? In spite of the way he acted, he needed him. However, the more Hayden rejected him, the more Cory seemed bent on annoying him. It was a vicious circle, spinning out of control. She struggled vainly to bring them together until it became painfully obvious to both of them, and they resented her intervention more than the awkward relationship itself. What could she do?

Hayden found his consolation in his work. Now with the good times, an emphasis on growth, achievement and not just ample but additional material assets, insurance was a viable profession, a needed accommodation to protect it all. People were buying it like crazy. His business was booming, and he had opened up another office over in Norfolk, which required even more of his precious time, leaving little or none for Cory, even if he had the mind to spend it with him. But it didn't seem to bother him. He was caught up in the web of success, an edifying but deceiving fantasy, yet it gave him a sense of accomplishment, one that parenting had failed to do thus far.

Likewise, Cory had found his solace elsewhere—in his music. Lorna wondered if he would have become so enthralled with it were it not for his father's lack of attention. But then she was probably paranoid, or at least naive. He was coming of age during a radical time, a unique era, for sure. The novel and electrifying music was shaking up the country from the east to the west. How could he not fall into it? It was a soothing balm for his disquieted soul. She remembered her own teenage days, the restlessness, the yearning for something different from the ordinary, and the boredom of it all, and then the war. She quietly pushed the thoughts aside, but she understood her boy and wanted better for him.

"Where's your mother, Cory?" his grandmother asked as he dashed through the door.

"Haven't seen her." He headed to the pantry. "Cool!"

She stared after him. "What'd you say?"

"Cool," he repeated, grabbing a box of graham crackers off the shelf. "I'm hungry as a bear." Slipping the box beneath his arm, he reached for the bottle of milk from the refrigerator and poured a glass full, brimming over the top. He sat down to devour his crackers, soaking them first in the cold, thick milk, each time with a slosh onto the table. His grandmother stood by, watching, shaking her head. She couldn't believe what a big strapping boy he'd become, tall as his dad and almost as big at just fourteen years old. When would he stop growing? But what bothered her most was how he was changing. Wearing that ridiculous hair style—flat top or whatever it was called—and using silly words like cool when he didn't mean cool at all, and instead of walking like a person was supposed to walk, he just sort of swaggered now. And the music! She had warned Lorna and Hayden that they'd better do something before it was too late! She leaned into the kitchen window. She should be home by now.

"You sure you didn't see your mother when you came up the drive?"

"Nope."

"Cory!"

"No, ma'am."

"Well, I suppose she'll be here soon."

He finished his snack, escaped to his bedroom and suddenly the loud, rhythmic music was blaring through the closed door.

Well, you can knock me down,
Step in my face,
Slander my name
All over the place,

"Cory!"

She was not going to listen to this heathen music another minute, if it could be called music! And she'd seen that disgusting guy on television, wiggling and grinding like nothing she'd ever witnessed before.

Do anything that you want to do, but uh-uh,
Honey, lay off of my…

She banged on his door.

"Ma'am?"

"Cut that thing down!"

"Oh, Grandma…"

"What is this world coming to?" she muttered and turned back to the cupboards with a vengeance, yanking out pots and pans and banging them left and right. "Those crazy rock and roll nuts!"

She grabbed hold of her cleaning rags and vented loudly, "What a mess! Lorna never has time to clean out her own cabinets. If she didn't have to go up there and wait on all those loony, harebrained tourists, she would!"

She plopped herself on the floor and stretched up underneath the kitchen sink to begin her project. She wished Lorna would come to her senses and quit that foolish job anyhow. She didn't need to work! Hayden made a good salary. She couldn't figure her out. As if that was anything new! Why, just when she thought she was done with church, turned bitter against it, she up and commenced to teaching Sunday school. Lord have mercy! Who would have ever thought it? Her Lorna? No doubt about it, she was full of surprises. She vigorously scrubbed down the shelving paper lining the cupboard beneath the sink, the Pine-Sol about to asphyxiate her, but still she relished its fresh, clean smell. It seemed to clear her mind, and she sure needed that.

The front door opened with a straight shot to the kitchen, and all Lorna could see was her mother's backside.

"What are you doing, Mother?"

"What does it look like?" her voice echoed from beneath the pipes.

"You don't have to come here and clean up." She dumped her things on the end table, tired and certainly not up to a confrontation. In fact, she had been working real hard lately on improving their relationship. "I wish you wouldn't do that, Mother," she expressed more gently, though it annoyed her to no end that she was always finding things wrong with her place.

Mrs. Morgan kept right on scrubbing.

"I was going to get to that soon as baseball season ends, and we're not so busy running back and forth. I was actually going to change that shelving paper." She realized suddenly that she was half yelling, competing with the blaring music coming from Cory's bedroom. Though he had turned the volume down, the vibrant sounds still reverberated loud and clear.

Nine, ten, eleven o'clock, twelve o'clock, rock
We're gonna rock around the clock tonight

Her mother poked her head out from under the sink shaking a yellow-gloved finger at the closed door. "Just listen to that racket!" The raucous beat was bouncing off the other side.

Lorna tried to be calm.

"Sounds more like a nightclub than my grandson's bedroom. What're you going to do about it?" she demanded, pushing a strand of damp hair out of her eyes.

"All the teenagers listen to it, Mother."

She shook her head incredulously.

"It's really not as bad as it sounds. It's just silly words. Ridiculous concoctions that make you laugh if you listen to them."

"I think not!"

Lorna suppressed a smile. The suggestion was bizarre to her, as well.

Her mother heaved herself up stiffly, bracing her fleshy arms on the counter, and stared at her daughter. Lorna had on one of those new sack dresses that hid her nice figure. Her thick hair was swept up in a puffy pompadour, which made her look older and more sophisticated, though she still looked way too young for a son big as Cory. But Lorna always took pride in her looks, and she had to admit, she was certainly an attractive lady, even if she was her daughter. If only she had the sense to go with it!

Lorna sank down onto a chair. "I had to work late today...a lot of inventory to put up for the season."

"I wondered where you were. Cory didn't even know where you were. Lorna, don't you think it would be nice if—"

"Please, Mother, not that again. I'm awfully tired."

"Mom!" Cory dashed out of his room all of a sudden. "Guess what, Mom?"

"What, dear?"

"Franklin had on a pair of those plaid Bermudas today after school. I couldn't believe it, but they really looked cool on him. Remember you wanted me to buy a pair last week?"

"And you thought they were too sissy with that cute little buckle stuck on the back."

"Mom, don't say cute, and besides, I didn't know all the guys would be wearing them!"

"All the guys?"

"Well, if Franklin wears them, everybody will before you know it. Just like the guitar."

She knew what was coming.

"Y'all decided yet?"

She glanced at her mother, who was taking in every word. Oh, well, she'd find out sooner or later. "Your father and I discussed it last night, and he's okay with it, I guess."

He shot into the air with a gusty whoop, and hopped over the recliner to give her a bear hug. "Mom, you're the best. I can't wait to tell Franklin." Before she could respond, he had dashed back to his room.

"What in the world was that all about? Pray tell me."

"Cory's going to join a little band."

"A band!"

"Some guys at school are putting one together."

"What for?"

"Just for fun, Mother. Lots of kids are doing it."

"I didn't even know he could play!"

"Well, he's learning. Hayden bought him a guitar, and he's been practicing day and night. Listen, you can hear him now."

"I've been hearing it, mind you, ever since he came home, but I didn't know he was playing, too. I'm surprised at Hayden. Music has never been his thing. When did all this come about?"

She wasn't going into all the details and pleadings that it took just to get him to agree, though her mother would, no doubt, love to hear it. She never failed to side with Hayden, another thing that exasperated her. And why was she even having this conversation?

But Mrs. Morgan was standing there waiting for an answer.

"Hayden knows he loves music, Mother. He might not really like the whole idea, but he understands it's important to Cory." She couldn't believe she was saying that and questioned her own motive. Did she feel compelled to support Cory that much? "Besides, he's learning more and more every day by playing along with his records, and I for one think he has a pretty good ear for music."

"H-m-m-m-ph. Don't know what's going to be next." She stooped down to put the pots and pans back in, and pushed up into the cupboard again.

Cory cracked his door. "What's for supper, Mom?" He saw his grandma stuck up in the cabinet and burst out laughing. "I'm gonna take your picture, Grandma!"

She whacked her head trying to squeeze out.

"Cory, behave yourself," Lorna scolded, struggling to contain her own laughter. "He's just kidding, Mother." But Mrs. Morgan emerged with a dark scowl on her face, not seeing the humor at all.

"Sorry, Grandma," he apologized, grinning mischievously.

"You ought to be ashamed of yourself treating your grandma this way!" she scolded, pushing herself up from the floor.

"I said I'm sorry," he repeated good-naturedly while edging the door closed between them so she couldn't see his smile.

Lorna intervened. "How about spaghetti?" She hated it when her mother harped on him, just like she did her when she was young.

"Sounds good. You staying, Grandma?"

"Your grandpa should be picking me up anytime." She was still rubbing her head.

"Sorry again, Grandma." He popped out, deposited a quick kiss on her cheek and darted back to his bedroom.

"That boy has you wrapped around his little finger, Lorna."

CHAPTER FIFTEEN

Rayna gazed at herself in the mirror. Her thick, dark mane fell to her shoulders, and she piled it all up on her head, twisting and knotting it with one hand, and turning to the right and left, admiring the effect. She preened and postured, striking a bold pose. She was partially pleased with the image of emerging maturity. For thirteen, she wasn't all bad, at least better than Glenda Basten. Glenda was the most popular girl in class, but she had a big nose and straight hair, a mousy brown color.

She loosened her locks, letting them cascade down again. Her daddy said she was the prettiest of them all, but he hadn't even seen all the girls. She studied her slight figure. Well, maybe she didn't have all the curves and the big boobs that some had, but she was coming along. Besides, she didn't really want them too big—that was disgusting! She glanced at the clock on the wall. She'd better hurry. She couldn't be late again, and then she cringed, remembering what day it was!

"Do I have to, Daddy?" she griped as she sat down to breakfast.

"Of course you have to, Rayna." He poured the orange juice into the three small glasses.

"Where's Grandpa?"

"Sleeping in, I guess. Should be here soon. He wasn't feeling his best last night, remember?" His pa seemed to be feeling poorly more often these days, but he had to remember that he was getting on in age, and it was to be expected.

"I hate shots!"

"It's only a little shot."

"But you know I hate shots, Daddy...you know that!"

"Would you rather get polio?"

"Now, Daddy, that's not fair." She began to pout.

"No, but it's reality. You know what happened to the little Jennings boy." He was referring to the young lad who lived over in the Valley and had contracted polio about six months prior, and now he was paralyzed waist down. It had shaken up the entire community.

The toast popped up with a bang, browner than usual, but he grabbed it anyway and began spreading butter on the two slices, thinking of the child he had seen in the hospital in Charlottesville. He hadn't been able to get her off his mind. She was Herbert Tomlin's niece, and Herbert had requested that he visit her and the family. Herbert was one of his faithful deacons, and he couldn't turn him down. Furthermore, he wanted to try to help them through the horrible crisis if he could, but he had felt practically helpless, totally unprepared for such a terrible fate. And now the picture was indelibly stamped in his mind—the large metal tank and the little girl, only fourteen years old, just a year older than Rayna, lying there in that thing with only her head stuck out. He remembered the attached pump that kept her alive by changing the pressure of the air as needed. It was a frightening image, and they didn't know when she would be able to come out of it. Her muscles and breathing organs were paralyzed, and she could stay alive only by remaining in that monstrous tank. And the thing that bothered him the most was that her mother couldn't even hold her or hug her. He could see her now—the poor lady standing there fighting back the tears, with a look of despair plastered across her tired face. Though he preached faith, and he wholeheartedly believed in it, he wondered if he would have enough if polio attacked his precious Rayna.

"Are we still going camping?" She was picking at her cornflakes and sloshing the milk around with her spoon.

He passed the toast to her. "Of course, the shot doesn't affect that." He sat down across from her and sipped his coffee, pushing the thoughts of the Charlottesville child away the best he could. "Your things ready?"

She nodded, stubbornly refusing to exhibit much emotion. She was still peeved about the whole shot thing, but secretly she couldn't wait to go camping. So often her daddy was pulled away from her by a parishioner or some urgent need, but when they went camping, she had him all to herself. Maybe she was being selfish; Grandpa said she was, but she didn't care. If she had to share him with a church full of folks always complaining about some ache or some problem, why, then, she figured she had a right to be selfish.

Late that evening they pulled into Mathews Arm Campground, the northernmost on the Skyline Drive, and the closest one to them. They generally preferred going south down to Big Meadows or Lewis Mountain, but it was dusk already, and the night was quickly coming on. They hurriedly unloaded the wood, the gear and all the unnecessary stuff Rayna had piled in. This always amused Greyson. She acted like they were going for a week instead of a night, but he figured it was a girl thing. He had learned over the years to accept such matters and not to question them. That way, things ran smoother, and he would do almost anything to avoid her emotional outbreaks. He knew that was a girl thing, too. They pitched the tent, Rayna working quickly and efficiently beside him. She drove in the last stakes and then rubbed her arm.

"Sore?"

"Some, but I'm glad it's over."

He smiled. "So am I."

He was surprised at her low tolerance for shots and pain, especially being so tough in other ways, not to mention strong-willed and independent to a fault at times. Again he silently thanked God that she hadn't inherited his epilepsy. He would willingly live with its inherent power over him as long as she didn't have it.

Supper was roasted wieners, and the juicy, tantalizing aroma caused Rayna to hurriedly slap the mustard and slaw on the buns. Greyson waved a pan of baked beans over the flames. Hastily, she tore open a bag of chips and shook them onto the paper plates, and soon they settled down in front of the blazing fire. The flickering flames danced between them as they leisurely savored their meal. After cleaning up, they returned to the fire, pulling their chairs in closer.

The gathering night fell quietly over the forest. Greyson stretched out comfortably while Rayna dodged the dark, curling smoke that always seemed to follow her no matter where she sat. Its curling puffs chased her from side to side. Still she prized the whole scene, and even the smoke's burning sensation in her eyes couldn't dampen it. Moonlight was spilling over the campground, falling between the tall, skinny trees. The stars were shining, too, appearing vaguely at first against the darkening sky, then more and more as the sky blackened, and now it was crowded with them. A solid wall of night creatures drummed in the background, a familiar, soothing sound.

"This is the part I love most," she said.

"The cicadas?"

"And…."

"Tree frogs?"

"And…."

"The moonlight?"

"And…."

"The campfire?"

"And…."

"Me and you?"

"Bingo!"

It was their game, the one they had played for years and years and never tired of. In fact, it seemed to take on a deeper meaning as Rayna grew older. Ironically, the sillier it sounded as the years passed, the more poignant it was. Then out of the darkness and the enshrouding forest came the melancholy sound of a nearby owl.

"And owls?" Greyson teased.

She giggled. "Remember how I used to be scared of them?"

"I remember…and I used to cuddle you when you were scared, too."

"I was a big baby."

He grinned at her.

"I know…I know…I still am sometimes."

"That's okay, Princess." In fact, he liked her being that way. It kept her close to him, he thought, as he leaned over to stoke the fire, wishing they could stay here forever, wishing that things would never change, and that he could capture this moment like a photograph and hold it forever.

"Wonder what Grandpa's doing?" she asked.

"Who knows, probably asleep by now."

"I bet he's homesick."

"Think so?"

"You know he doesn't like Richmond!"

"Well, he'll be back next week." He knew she was right. Pa never really enjoyed his visits with Mildred, and he could understand why. She had just grown bossier over the years, but still it gave them a break, and he certainly appreciated her taking him from time to time. William and Jack seldom took him anywhere, but then they had such busy families and wives that evidently demanded a good deal of attention. That he wouldn't know about, and maybe it wasn't such a bad thing after all.

"I know why he doesn't like Richmond."

"Why?"

"It's too big. Grandpa thinks Luray is big. You know what he must think of Richmond!"

He chuckled, and they fell silent again.

The cicadas' drum expanded all around them, and the dark forest lulled them into its secretive, woodsy magic that nightfall inevitably brings to the Blue Ridge. The flames died down to smoldering embers, and they felt as one with the mountains and all its creatures. Greyson let himself ease into its waiting embrace, feeling the tensions of the week slowly evaporate into the dark forest, but then a flashlight beamed toward them, darting one way and then another. It shot up into the trees and circled around. Apparently someone was putting up a tent.

He stirred up the fire again and stretched his feet in closer, enjoying the tingling sensation spreading up his legs, and making him quite drowsy. He wondered what he would do if he didn't have these times to recuperate, to get away from the rigors of the ministry. Though he loved it, sometimes the rigidity of it all bore down on him, especially the last few weeks, with all the sickness and the Heerspink child's wedding and then poor old Mrs. Tomlin's funeral, and the meetings. Why did they have to have so many meetings? Nothing ever seemed to get done without first a series of meetings, and long ones at that, never a short one. He wondered if they had meetings back when the church first began in Antioch. Somehow he couldn't picture Peter and the apostles sitting around discussing what color they would paint the vestibule or trim the eaves or what date to hold the annual revival. Of course, they didn't have vestibules and eaves and such things to concern themselves with then, and revivals weren't planned, they just happened.

"Daddy?"

"Uh-huh?"

"Remember it was up here when you first told me about my mother?"

He drew in his feet.

The sound of the cicadas' drum increased in the silence, and he hoped she wouldn't go there. His sense of complacency vanished. Instead she became very quiet, which was even worse, and finally he had to say something.

"Everything okay with you, honey?"

He saw her nod in the darkness.

"I just sometimes wonder about her…you know. Don't get me wrong, I don't want to see her or anything. I figure if she ever wants to see me, she knows where I am."

The knife sliced through his gut, and he sat up. Maybe this was the time to tell her about the visit. He always knew he would someday, but before he could gather the courage, she had jumped up and was scooting around the fire.

"What do you think of my hair?"

"Your hair?"

"Yes, Daddy. Do you think it would look good short?"

"Well…I don't know." He was puzzled. "I like it the way it is."

"I knew you would say that, but some of the girls at school are getting short haircuts, and sometimes I think I want one, too. But then I am afraid. Suppose I wouldn't like it? And it would all be gone!"

"As I said, I like your hair just the way it is." He knew the moment had passed, and he was glad.

The decade of the fifties was a gentle interlude, a welcomed pause in time, a Biblical Elim for Americans, sandwiched between brawling wars and hostility, the ever-clashing of aggressive nations. But after the soldiers returned from Korea, it took on a whole new persona. Though it was not without some measure of apprehension, the worrisome concern of the cold war primarily, it was just that. Cold. It never heated up to guns, blood and bodies. The years of the fifties just rolled along lazily, carrying its occupants with it, comfortable and happy. It was a good time to be alive, and those fortunate souls embraced it and rollicked in its favors.

One day it would be looked back upon wistfully, viewed through rosy glasses, but they didn't know it then. They were a part of it, the hustle and bustle and daily delights. They were the oblivious players creating the legendary decade and not concerned with the uncertain future. So it is with human beings, never realizing how blessed we are until time has had its way, until the sifting sands have flowed down through the fated hourglass. And then we look back with yearning, with nostalgic fondness, and with a longing to return.

But all things must pass, and this contented decade was no exception. It was already 1957, and the country was on the precipitous brink of another war, though it was certainly not aware of it. It was not something that initially stirred a great deal of attention, that being the way with most wars in their embryonic stages. It slithered in subtly and grew without most knowing what was happening. Besides, it was not anything Americans wanted to entertain in their happy lives. They had no desire to return to such a troublesome thing. And, of course, the war babies and post-war children had no memory of the struggles of the past, the gross and appalling combat. Therefore, the constant barrage of possible intrusions printed in their *Weekly Reader* and *Current Events* had no significant impact on them. The flashy headlines rolled over their heads like warm summer currents. The words held no fear. However, the talk of bomb shelters and Communist plans did arouse a certain degree of uneasiness, and when they were asked to hide under desks during the required drills, it struck an even more dissonant cord, but only temporarily.

This was the fifties.

Life went on as usual in the Blackenstaff household, as well. Cory, growing taller and maturing rapidly, was even more caught up in the rhythmic heyday of the times. The birth of rock and roll had taken a strong hold and was growing at an alarming rate, and music had become an integral part of his life. It relieved the boredom and eased the growing pains. He regularly followed the lives of the popular musicians—Buddy Holly, Chuck Berry, the Everly Brothers and Fats Domino, and Elvis, of course. And then with the New Year came an even more radical musician that hit the charts with a smashing success. Jerry Lee Lewis woke up the dozing grandmas with his dancing piano. His unique theatrical style captured an audience far and wide, and when he sprang to his feet, pounding the keys, young audiences everywhere went wild as his nimble feet boogied to the riotous rhythm.

Cory was right along with them. Mesmerized, and now he wanted to play the piano! Convincing his parents to buy one wasn't nearly as hard as he anticipated. Not as hard as the guitar, for they had visions of great pianists in their heads, especially Hayden. Images of Paderewski, Beethoven, Ellington and Gershwin floated before him, but when Cory pounded out…

Well I said come over baby we got chicken in the
Barn hoose barn what barn my barn

Hayden Blackenstaff was mortified.

We ain't fake it
Whole lot of shakin' goin' on

He couldn't understand this gangly youngster living under the same roof. They had grown further apart, and it baffled him. Lorna watched with sadness, but she understood. The two were simply too different, stretched to opposite ends of the psychological pole, more and more taut as the years progressed, with no slack allowed. Hayden was a severe man, living by his own code of ethics, which didn't hold for much sentiment or emotion, and certainly not for the disturbing craze taking hold of young people across the nation. But Cory was more like her, and she could tell that this exasperated his dad considerably.

Lately Hayden had taken to watching the news, following its daily reporting of what was happening overseas, and this took her by surprise. Why the change? He had never once wanted to talk about anything even remotely related to war. But maybe enough time had passed now. It was a new era, and perhaps he had been able to come to terms with his own war at last, to view it more objectively, though she would never know. Hayden didn't talk to her about things like that. He talked about what brand of milk to buy, or whether or not they might want to whitewash the garage again, or he talked about how the sedan seemed to be making a funny clicking sound and they might need to take it into the shop. He mentioned the pros and cons of political candidates occasionally, their particular quirks, or the increase in taxes and the changing positions of the parties. But Hayden didn't talk about feelings, neither his nor hers.

As he sat watching the news, he expected Cory to be as interested, but he wasn't. The thought of war repulsed the boy's sensitive nature, fine-tuned as it was. He would never fight! Instead, he distanced himself from any mention of it and immersed himself in a sport that Hayden deemed a complete waste of time.

Surfing!

But Cory loved it, though it was just catching on at Sandbridge. Of course it had been a part of the Atlantic shores since shortly after the turn of the century, somewhere around 1918, but it hadn't gained much attention, only a modest bit during the thirties when the newly styled surfboards appeared. They were hollow and lighter, much longer than the old boards and could be paddled faster, making it a lot easier to catch the vast Atlantic waves. Still the east coast lagged far behind the west, and surfing would not catch on in a big way until a few years later with the fiberglass boards. But there were those like Cory who religiously followed the emerging trend of California surfers. After seeing them on television, he decided to try it, too. Besides, rock music and surfing just naturally went together, he explained to his parents, like salt and pepper, like bread and butter. And always agile, he quickly proved to be a natural, spending as much time as possible out on the sunny shores. Sometimes Lorna accompanied him. She loved the beach, but mainly she wanted to support him in whatever was important to him.

The waves were particularly rough one Saturday morning the end of July, but he insisted on surfing anyway. High waves were what he wanted. They were calling for a nor'easter, and Lorna figured that was why. She held her breath every time he disappeared beneath the tumultuous waves and slowly exhaled when he was inevitably swept up again, a bit of human flesh riding the heaving waves, a mere speck on the moving, liquid landscape.

The winds were driving, spraying her periodically, and she tasted its salty mist. It whipped her shawl and blew her hair in a stinging fashion against her cheeks, but still it was warm, though not the usual for July. She watched a couple of gulls circle, swoop down in front of her, and just as quickly soar off again, fighting the strong gusts. A ghost crab caught her attention as it popped out of its hole, its two whopping, black eyes staring directly at her. It disappeared and then emerged again. She knew it would dash back in when someone happened by. But they used to frighten her when she was small, especially at night when they were feeding and racing all over the sand. She remembered jumping into her daddy's arms lest she step on one, and he would carry her across the moonlit beach.

She sat very still, watching the crab. Suddenly it darted sideways in front of her, practically grazing her toes. She smiled and glanced up lest Cory think she wasn't watching. Three young girls in skimpy bathing suits were approaching, strolling self-consciously down the beach, their long hair blowing in the wind.

Cory topped a wave and spied them, and the young lasses took notice, as well. She watched the familiar scene play out before her. They looked to be about his age, maybe a bit younger. The petite blond punched the sandy-haired one, who was more than fully endowed for her age, and their capricious giggles floated off into the salty winds, though the one that captured Lorna's attention was the smaller one with dark locks bouncing off her shoulders. She was unable to take her eyes from her, and watched her stroll on down the sandy beach out of sight.

"Mom!" Cory was running toward her with his surfboard in hand. "You missed it, Mom!"

"I'm sorry, son."

"And it was my best one yet!"

"I just took my eyes off—"

"Ah, it's okay. I'm getting better, a lot better. Don't you think?"

"Yes. Like they say, practice makes perfect."

"I wish Dad could see."

"Well, you know how busy he is."

"Mom, don't make excuses for him."

"Well...."

"Well, he's not interested. You know that. He's never interested in what I'm doing!"

What could she say?

"All he wants to talk about is insurance. You know he wants me to go into the business with him one day. He as much as said so just last week—and that will never happen!"

She knew it would be the last thing on his list. "Have you any thoughts about what you *would* like to do?"

He shrugged. "I don't know, Mom. You know I love music, but Dad would have a conniption if he thought I was serious about it."

"Well, you have plenty of time to decide."

He plopped down beside her and stretched out on the sand, facing up to the sun with his eyes closed.

"Here, you can have part of my towel." She slid over for him to get off the sand.

"I'm okay, Mom."

"Enjoying the summer?"

"I guess. Wish I could've gotten that lifeguard job though."

She knew he was disappointed, and so was she. He would have made a good one, too. He had always been an excellent swimmer, and the bummer was that his best friend Andy had gotten the job instead.

"Or at least one like Brent Sweitzer got."

"Which is?"

"Working in a theater."

She knew Hayden would certainly have balked at that. "Well, you don't have that much summer left."

"I know, but he gets to see all the movies for free, and all I ever do is cut grass!"

Though Hayden insisted he was probably making more money cutting grass than Brent was in the theater, still Cory yearned for what he called a real job. Lorna looked at his tanned body lying there in the sun. It was filling out more and more each week it seemed, strong and muscular. Her boy was becoming a man, she thought rather poignantly, as the wind sandblasted the two of them. Suddenly he shot up, grabbed his surfboard and raced back to the water. She understood his desire for a real job, for more independence. And though she wouldn't have it any other way, still it frightened her, for she realized that one day it would take him away from her.

And the plenty of time she had so casually mentioned to him, she knew was just an illusion. It was vanishing before her very eyes. Not in a flash. No, it was far more subtle than that, silently creeping away as she busied herself on all the minute details that so conveniently crammed the days, while she focused on each and every goal that crowded out what was really important. It is the eternal thief, she concluded.

She stared out at the restless ocean and the young fellow riding its waves.

CHAPTER SIXTEEN

Three years later, Cory Blackenstaff was standing in a group of anxious seniors, dreading the coveted walk down the aisle. He stood there with mixed emotions churning within and butterflies twirling in his stomach. Nervously, he stared at the audience, at the back of their heads, and he thought of his dad's curt remark.

"*Aren't you happy, son?*"

Certainly he was glad to be graduating, but with it came decisions, and decisions he wasn't prepared for. He still didn't know what he wanted to do with his life, and his dad was getting impatient. Though he loved his music, in reality, he knew he would never be another Jerry Lee Lewis or Ricky Nelson, or anything even close. He was mediocre at best, but he had come to terms with that. Everybody couldn't be gifted in music. It's just that he didn't know what he wanted to do. His mom was pushing college, and he was strongly considering it. Though he wasn't the best academic, he figured he could get through, and he realized it was becoming more and more essential. But his dad was driving harder for him to join in "the business." It was doing very well. In fact, it seemed to be the greatest pleasure of his life these days, but it was absolutely the last thing Cory wanted to do. Even if it wasn't insurance, he couldn't imagine working with his dad for the rest of his life. What a thought! He glanced around at the others and wondered how many of them knew what they wanted. Was he the only screwball walking down the aisle?

Lorna watched the curtain wave and billow out from the bustling around behind it. She knew it must be time, and then a soft strain of music started up in preparation for the imminent event, and a cornucopia of emotions gripped her—anticipation, happiness, gloom and uncertainty. She glanced over at Hayden. He was checking his watch.

She wished her dad could be here. Just six months prior, he had passed away with a sudden stroke, and she fought the anguish and grief again. Her dad had always been in her corner, no matter what. She just wished that she hadn't caused him so much worry, but she had given him Cory. And he had been so proud of him, too.

She pulled herself together and glanced over at her mother. She was sitting up rigid and erect on the other side of Hayden, anxiously watching the closed curtains, and Lorna felt a stab of guilt. Though they had never been close, just like Hayden and Cory, still she was her mother. If only things could have been different between them, more casual, certainly more loving. But she wondered about her mother's health now, losing all that weight recently, though she wouldn't go to a doctor. Losing her father had unquestionably brought life more in perspective. It was so temporal.

"The Graduation Song" suddenly filled the auditorium, nostalgic and moving, a definite sense of triumph, yet mixed with sadness, and they all stood in unison.

A lump formed in Lorna's throat as they turned to watch the excited students file down the aisle, one by one, and she strained to see Cory. Finally he was walking past them with his tassel swinging recklessly from side to side. He had a wide grin plastered on his handsome face, and out of the blue she remembered him running beside her up the sunny beach, trying to catch the gulls that circled overhead. He was about five years old and so clumsy at that point that he had toppled over headfirst. Surprised, he had looked up, covered in sand, but with that same grin on his face. She had laughed aloud and so did he. The lump in her throat grew larger, and she remembered reading all those bedtime stories and how drowsy they had made her, and all the little league games, sitting on those hard benches in the hot sun and sometimes in the cold, drizzling rain. She remembered the long, peaceful walks by the Bay when he got older, and their awkward grown-up talks and how embarrassed they both had been.

The seniors sat down up front, and she pressed over Hayden to see better, but she could barely see him, and she brushed the tears from her eyes.

That night she and Hayden sat quietly across from one another. Cory was gone to the big graduation party. He wouldn't be in until late. Quite late she was sure, more likely early morning. They had dropped off her mother on the way home. She was worn out. Hayden was hunkered down in his favorite chair, reading some insurance journal that had just come in the mail, but she couldn't settle down enough to read. After such a momentous occasion, how could she read?

The house was terribly still.

She puffed up the couch pillows and cleared her throat, hoping Hayden would notice, but he kept on reading. A sudden sadness sank deep in her soul. She could see the years stretching out ahead, quiet years without Cory, lonely years. She rose and went into the kitchen to tidy up. Things had been left a mess with all the commotion before they left for the school. She began to clear the table and filled the sink with hot, sudsy water, chastising herself for feeling so gloomy, so sorry for herself—that's what she was doing. Her mother had reminded her more often than not that it was her weakness—feeling sorry for herself—at least one of them. Hayden had been a good husband, he still was. And though he and Cory weren't as close as she would have liked, overall he had been a good father, and he was a good provider. No one could question that. He had worked hard for them, day and night sometimes, and she knew he would always take care of her.

She stared out the kitchen window into the darkening sky and gathering clouds. They glided overhead, their white outlines edged by the full moon, but somehow they only added to her melancholy mood. Next year, there would be another graduation, one that she would not attend, and she began to wash the few dishes and stack them into the plastic drainer.

A light evening breeze fanned the parsonage porch as Rayna studied the detailed information that she had received from the Park Service. She pushed the swing slowly but steadily back and forth, feeling absolutely great. School was out, and she had the whole summer ahead of her. She hoped to do some volunteer work up in the Park and couldn't wait. Some of her friends had paying jobs already, but she was glad her dad had encouraged her plans. Being that it was her last summer before graduation, he wanted her to enjoy it. Unconsciously she fingered the large school ring dangling on a chain from her neck. A wad of gauzy tape was wrapped around it to make it fit her small finger, but still it slipped off occasionally. And now the gauze was smudged and dirty, but she figured it was safer this way. She was going steady with Kent Walker, who had just graduated and would be starting college in the fall. Her dad wasn't too keen on it, but he didn't nag her about it. He was good about things like that. Some kids' folks nagged them about everything.

She lay the paper down beside her and stared at her dad's church next door. Of course, she knew it wasn't really his church—it was God's church. He had been reminding her of that ever since they moved here years ago. The setting sun was igniting its stained windows, and each and every depiction was intricately lit up, and she could see Jesus in one, standing at the door, ready to knock. It was her favorite scene and always had been. She remembered as a kid asking her dad whose door it was, and he had answered, "It's the door to your heart."

His response had puzzled her then, and she wondered how her heart could have a door. She smiled at the memory. It was like one of those parables that Jesus was always telling, and sometimes she had a hard time understanding them, too. But a couple of years later she finally grasped its depth. Her dad was reading from the book of Revelation one night during their evening devotions, and she was snuggled beneath his arm when suddenly those poignant words made sense to her.

'Behold, I stand at the door, and knock: if any man hear my voice, and open the door, I will come in to him, and will sup with him, and he with me.'

And she had done just that. She had opened the door to her heart and asked Him in. The sun dipped behind the church, and she watched the shadows fall over it. Her dad would be late tonight. He had a meeting in Charlottesville, and she knew he would be tired when he got home. He always was after those long meetings.

She got up to fix supper. She would keep his warm for him. The kitchen, too, had lost its golden glow that she always enjoyed in the late afternoon, and she flipped on the light switch. Soon she was mixing the hamburger and onions and bread for the meatloaf. She would make enough for Grandpa, too. He would be back tomorrow and glad of it. She wondered how much longer he would accept Aunt Mildred's invitations. But still she was his daughter, and she could tell he felt an obligation to go. Family is family, she reasoned, and again thought of what Kent had asked her yesterday.

"*Where is your mother?*"

The unexpected question had stunned her, and she answered abruptly, "I don't know." And she was right, she didn't know, not exactly.

He just stared at her.

"I don't know...and I don't care," she added emphatically.

"Okay by me," he had replied, though obviously annoyed.

She knew she was being insensitive, but yet she couldn't help it. She had felt violated as if he had lifted up her skirt or something. She was not going to confide in him the family secret! And what made him ask so brazenly? He knew from the beginning it was only her and her dad and her grandpa. Did he think himself a part of that special union already? Shouldn't he wait until she was ready to disclose the matter herself?

The subject hadn't come up again, but she wondered when it would, and she wondered what he really thought. Before, it never mattered a great deal, the question of her mother. Of course, she thought about her from time to time. Who wouldn't? But her life had been so full and happy with her dad and grandparents that it was never an issue, and she didn't want Kent to make it one either. She reached for the lettuce and tomatoes in the refrigerator bin, and pulled out her grandma's old cutting board that was dark and stained with memories, and began rapidly dicing the tomatoes, still irritated with the whole affair.

Oh well, she sighed, concentrating on the salad, I'll think about more pleasant things, like one more year of school. I can hardly believe it! And then college—she was looking forward to it. She wasn't quite sure what path she wanted to take, not just yet anyway, other than the fact that it must somehow involve working with nature. That part was settled. She couldn't imagine spending her life in an office or teaching school or being stuck in one of those cold, sterile hospitals as a nurse. That's why she had decided to major in botany. She sliced the slippery onion, blinking back the ready tears, and reached over to flip on the radio. The volume was blaring from yesterday, and the catchy tune immediately assailed her.

Poison iv-y-y-y-y, poison iv-y-y-y-y
Late at night while you're sleepin' poison ivy comes a'creepin
Arou-ou-ou-ou-ou-ound

She crooned along with it, swaying back and forth. It reminded her of a couple of years ago while hiking in the Park when she had come in contact with it and was covered from head to toe in no time flat. Her skin immediately felt itchy all over again.

"Poison iv-y-y-y-y, poison iv-y-y-y-....."

She grated the Swiss cheese onto the crisp, wet lettuce, anticipating her dad's delight in such a superb salad, but then his troubling words were there again. Why couldn't they have female Park Rangers? She had always felt a deep affinity to the Park as far back as she could remember, and she knew, of course, that a lot of it stemmed from the fact that she and her dad had been camping up there and hiking its many trails since she was just a youngster, but now she believed there was even more.

Her very being was tied to it.

She wondered if her dad felt the same as she tossed the salad with the large spatula. She knew her grandpa did. He had never recovered from the move, and the older he got, the more he talked about it. But she liked to hear his far-fetched stories at times. They were always interesting and quite colorful. Suddenly she was anxious to see him. He had been gone longer this go-round. Of course, it had certainly made things easier for her and her dad, a lot quieter and smoother. Though she hated to admit it, he was becoming more stubborn and fractious, but she understood. Old folks became that way sometimes, senile, her dad said, something about hardening of the arteries. She remembered how testy he had been with Kent just a couple of weeks ago. They were sitting out on the porch, swinging side by side and holding hands—that's all—when out of the blue, Grandpa bellowed out, "Look here, son...you barking up the wrong tree...Rayna ain't even blossomed out yet!"

"Grandpa!" she had cried out, completely embarrassed, but Kent had already dropped her hand and was sitting there stunned, his face in near panic. And she couldn't help laughing. The moment was priceless.

"Reckon I fixed his wagon," Grandpa had mumbled as he shuffled back into the house. But Kent didn't see the humor at all and under his breath called him a foolish old man, to which she took absolute exception. In fact, she seemed to be taking exception to a number of things lately that Kent said or did, but all her friends envied her and his overall gorgeous looks. So she just let it pass and was surprised how soon September rolled around again. Greyson was pleased, too—happy to see him conveniently whisked off to college, the prestigious Virginia Tech. And though it was often said that absence makes the heart grow fonder, he sensed her growing further and further away from the boy, and he was secretly glad.

Rayna's last year of school seemed to fly by. Perhaps it was the abrupt culmination of twelve long years suddenly finding itself quite used up, spent, and anxious to end. But soon it was behind her, over and done with, the dreaded exams, and all the tearful goodbyes, and the graduation revelry. Not to mention the long-awaited file down the aisle. And she was glad. Graduation was good, and it had its moments, but she had dreaded it in some ways. Formal events were something she had always shied away from, when all her friends would have two parents attending. It was only then that she felt a bit different, but so what?

Life was moving on.

Kent returned for the summer, but not the same Kent, and the change was not at all to her liking. She couldn't quite put her finger on it, but he seemed more distant to her and her dad, and especially her grandpa. Whenever the old man paced into the room, muttering his indistinct thoughts, Kent's brow wrinkled, and he made any excuse possible to escape. He had actually voiced a few offhand and bordering offensive remarks, though subtle to be sure, about her dad's devout profession. This bothered her more than anything. Obviously proud of his newly-acquired academic status, he readily offered his often distorted opinions to any who would listen, and it was beginning to grate on her nerves. Day by day, she was losing respect for him and not enjoying his company as before, but her friends were still so in awe of him that she questioned her own reasoning. Maybe she was being unfair, she thought, as she fingered the ring around her neck, and thus the relationship teetered on through another summer.

Then it was her time, a time that Greyson had dreaded for years, though he knew it was inevitable. He had always known it would be that way, he had suffered no delusions, but to what extent, he had not foreseen. Its magnitude was hardly foreseeable. When she left for college in the fall, he was utterly lost, at odds with himself and the world. However, in this case, the norm wasn't true. The reality was worse than the dread.

Life without Rayna!

Autumn even lost its magic. The colors held no joy for him, and the crisp vitality of the season that usually sparked something within, something that had lain dormant throughout the hot summer months, had lost its power. He dragged the old leaf rake through the pile of crunchy, brittle leaves, mounding them up in neat little piles. Then he raked the little piles into three big piles, stopping periodically to pluck out the leaves trapped between the rake's metal prongs. He stared up at the tall poplars towering over the church. They were bare now, no fluttering green or orange and ivory tulips. He was glad. Better that than have them hang on into the winter like those of his neighbor's stubborn oaks. He would have to fight the freezing elements then to get them up.

The late afternoon sun was unusually warm, and he had been at it for some time now. He stopped to rest, leaning heavily on the rake, and wiped his sweaty brow. His neighbor up the street, Mrs. Shilling, found him that way.

"Reverend Ralston!" she squealed out, tripping promptly over to him.

"Good afternoon, Mrs. Shilling."

"Why don't you wait for Jim to do that?"

"Jim's ailing a bit, I understand." He went back to raking.

Jim was the handyman for the church and usually took care of such jobs, but Greyson felt a need to be busy. His sermon lay on his desk half done, but he needed to be outside today, working with his hands, not sequestered beneath the sloping eaves of his bedroom study. He needed to feel the hot sun on his back and the cool, breezy wind in his face. There was something healing about it, being outside and close to the earth when the mind was disquieted and anxious.

He smiled up at Mrs. Shilling. "Besides, I need the exercise." She doubted that. Along with most of his parishioners, she was always a bit concerned for his health, ever since he so unbelievably took them into his confidence when he first arrived. As a protective sentry, they had pulled in the wagons and collectively and lovingly rallied around him, gently admonishing him to rest whenever he seemed unduly fatigued. But they had learned to offer their particular advice quite discreetly, for their beloved pastor was noticeably private when it came to such matters.

"Well, it is a nice day for exercise, Reverend. I have to agree with you. That's why I'm taking a bit of a stroll myself. How's our Rayna doing?"

He stabbed at a few willful leaves blowing off from his pile. "Seems all settled in. Thank you for asking."

But she felt the wound in his words. "What's the name of that college again?"

"Sweet Briar."

"I can't ever remember names. You know me, Reverend. And it's an all-girls' school, too, I believe."

"Yes, ma'am."

She was thinking to herself that this was a good thing. Young folks nowadays needed extra protection, especially the reverend's daughter. She was a sweet little thing, but had a mind of her own, and always had been a mite too independent for her own good.

Greyson's back was beginning to feel tired as he dragged the piled-up leaves out from under the nandinas that flanked the old foundation, but he wasn't about to rub it, lest she pounce on him to stop for sure.

"Well, it is in Virginia," she remarked encouragingly, thinking that the poor preacher certainly looked down in the mouth.

"Yes, ma'am." The school was not so far away, actually. It was located in the Piedmont of Virginia, not terribly far from Charlottesville, about fifty miles south. He was glad that she had chosen it rather than one much further away, but it might as well be in California as far as he was concerned. He yanked the leaves off the rake again, its metal prongs zinging back and forth.

"Well, I'll see you on Sunday, Reverend."

"Yes, ma'am, enjoy your stroll."

He raked for another hour or so, physically caught up in the leafy mission, and then pulled out the big, black bags, but his mind was on that school ring still hanging around Rayna's neck. She had it on when she left, but he could see the writing on the wall. It wouldn't be there long.

He bent over to stuff the leaves into the first bag, and the moldy dust immediately launched a coughing spell. He stopped to rest again. What surprised him most was why she still clung to it at all, not just the ring but the problematic relationship. It wasn't as if she needed security, not his self-sufficient Rayna. He saw his pa standing on the parsonage porch and thought for a minute that he might walk over to the church, but then he turned and went back inside. He thought he would never live to see the day that his pa would rather be inside than out in the sunshine, but he had changed. And he was growing weaker and more demanding. It took all of his energy and patience some days to deal with him, but what else could he do?

He glanced up into the sunny sky, and though his back ached, he was glad he had decided to rake the yard. He didn't feel so dead on the inside now. How could he with all this pulsating energy around him? The Shenandoah, like the elusive butterfly, was shedding its cocoon. It was in its transformation mode, and who could deny its drama? The painted mountains in the background had thinned, and there was an ever-thickening carpet of russet, gold, and crimson on the ground. In spite of himself, he began to feel better. Besides, he had so much to be thankful for. Rayna was happy, and he hadn't had any seizures in years now. The new medicine was a miracle drug in itself.

Or was it?

He propped the bulging bag up against a leafless poplar and walked around to the front of the church and pulled open the heavy door, welcoming its familiar creak. He stepped inside the hushed interior. It was so cool. Immediately he was besieged with the smell of old pine and the lingering scent of Sunday's chrysanthemums. He sat down, enjoying its familiar comfort. Only the earthy tang of moldy leaves that he had brought in with him invaded its space.

"Thank you, Lord...thank you for everything and especially for no more seizures!"

He looked up the aisle, recently waxed, and to the cross in the center, and a peace flooded his soul. He loved to come into the sanctuary when it was empty, but he knew it wasn't empty. In fact, it was then that he sensed His presence more than ever. He wondered about that as he sat on the back pew, for it was here that he felt most comfortable, after all.

It was here that God could minister to him.

He sat there for a long time, his head bowed, and he prayed. He prayed for his small flock, and he prayed for his father, for the patience to handle him. He especially lifted Rayna up for His tender mercies. Then he raised his head to soak up the quiet peace, and his eyes rested on the first pew where she had always sat as a child, from the very first day, staring up at him with those luminous, trusting eyes.

But she was starting out on her own now, so young and full of dreams, and that was the way it should be. He wondered what it held in store for her. Suddenly his own youth, for some reason, came back to him, and he remembered his decision to join the CCCs. His pa had balked, didn't like it one bit, but it had been a good decision in the end. The valuable lessons he had learned while there had remained with him throughout life. He thought about his old friend Lester. It had been awhile since he had thought of him. He wondered whatever happened to him. They had been such buddies back then, but had drifted apart over the years. Their paths had taken different turns. The last he had heard, he was involved in some horse-racing venture, and had married and divorced already. He was living up north, he couldn't remember where.

Lester had been a good friend. It's funny, he mused, how two people could bond so and depend on one another for just about everything, then go their separate ways, never to see one another again or rarely think of each other.

He recalled the many nights they had lain on their narrow bunks in the dark and watched the moon climb up over the mountains and talked of their private plans for the future. They were usually either too tired or too keyed up to sleep. Hopeful youngsters they were. That was when they were assigned to the Skyland Camp for the rehabilitation work, tearing off the old bark from the cabins that had originally been put on them and replacing it with chestnut siding. Most of the rehabilitation work had already been done, all but the residing, and that was their job. He had taken it painfully serious, too much to Lester's amusement, but then Lester viewed life through a different lens. His attitude was far more flippant, cynical to a point, and dangerously so at times. More often than not, he had had to pull him away from Luray and back to camp after their festive weekends, and sometimes to intervene on his behalf to keep him out of trouble. Lester liked to challenge authority, to push the envelope, but he had wanted no part of it, which was the only thing that ever created a rift between them. However, on the job, Lester was super, stronger than most, certainly stronger than he was, and he had a mind for carpentry. Much to his credit, he could put up more siding in a day than all of them.

Instinctively, he rubbed his hands together, remembering the rough bark. He had worn blisters for days. But though it was hard work, he didn't mind it. The camaraderie and sense of achievement that he had shared there at Skyland made up for it. Especially the feeling of belonging—something he had never had at school. But the CCC guys were like one big family. They had worked together, slept together, and played together. He heard a car approaching. It slowed down but kept on going.

He was glad. He didn't want company. He just wanted to sit quietly and watch the light filtering through the stained glass, watch it fade into the coming evening. He would finish bagging leaves tomorrow.

CHAPTER SEVENTEEN

In the winter of 1962, there was much ado about heavenly things, not heavenly as in spiritual, but heavenly as in atmospheric. It was on everyone's lips, for during the cold month of February the first American orbited the earth. It caused a good deal of excitement and not a little concern over what this might set off. Astronaut John Glenn's picture was plastered all over the newspapers, and millions of people everywhere were glued to their television sets when the Atlas rocket carried the spacecraft up into the sky. *Friendship 7* lifted off from Cape Canaveral in Florida and circled the earth three times. The historic flight lasted almost five hours.

Most people were happy to see it, some were ecstatic even, glad that America was not lagging behind the Soviet Union in the race for space now, but still there were those who questioned and feared its outcome.

"Got no business up there!" Pa blasted.

"Well, Pa, we don't have any choice, you know," Greyson responded patiently. "We can't let the Russians get control of space. Who knows what that would mean?"

"If the good Lord wanted us up there, by golly, I reckon He would've put us up there in the first place!"

Greyson knew there was no use arguing with him, and he certainly didn't feel like it. He figured he was coming down with a cold. He often did in March. He reached for the sliced ham in the refrigerator, wrapped in aluminum foil, and commenced to preparing supper, grateful for left-overs. But the old man wasn't through.

"Besides, I gotta feeling this is gonna upset things."

"What things, Pa?"

"You know what I mean...the balance of things, like the weather and such. You just watch. Man oughta keep his feet on the ground, got no business stirring up things!"

That night after Pa retired, though it was still relatively early, Greyson kicked off his shoes to relax, and Mr. Ike jumped up in his lap. He had grown rather rotund and heavy in his old age, and all he seemed to do now was lie around. Greyson stroked his furry neck, and the tabby nuzzled down, gently kneading his pants leg and purring softly.

The winter sky had darkened quickly, and he stared out the window into its inky blackness. He understood his pa's concern about the astronaut. Moving from a primitive mountain life to seeing a man flying into space—this was too much too soon for him, and he would never understand or accept it. Why, he was still having a hard time with television, calling it the devil's contraption and snapping it off whenever he could. At least Rayna didn't have to contend with that now. The sky suddenly lit up as a full moon shot out from under heavy, hanging clouds, and Greyson watched its powerful effect, intricately outlining the dark clouds, etching a stunning picture, a masterpiece painted in the heavens.

He sighed and picked up the paper to finish reading, though it disturbed him a great deal to read about the on-going controversy. How could they take prayer out of schools? But it did seem likely that it could possibly happen, and it sent cold chills racing up his spine.

What did God think about that?

He was glad that Rayna had finished already. Whoever would have thought it?

Mr. Ike reached up with one paw and lightly swiped at the paper, displaying a bit of his old mischief, and Greyson held it up higher. He finished reading and dropped it down beside his chair. His pa's uneven snoring was rising and falling in the other room. Winter was hard on him, not being able to get outside, though he seemed to have lost interest last fall. Maybe he would perk up come spring. He certainly hoped so. He used to walk around the church and check on the flowers and shrubs when he first moved in. He would clip off any dead branch or pull a stringy weed—accepted it as his job, more or less. All in all, Pa had adapted to the changes better than he expected. Maybe more resigned than adapted, still he hadn't complained a great deal. And when he did, Greyson figured he had a right. Jerked off the windswept ridges of the mountains with its innate freedoms and wide-open spaces and shoved down to a small parcel in the lowlands, and now reduced to a garden patch beneath the parsonage window. What could you expect?

Lorna arose early. She had a big day ahead, even if it was the first day of Lent. Somehow she always felt that she should be doing something different on this day, something more spiritual, something Holy, anything but working. But of course, she had her job and all those boxes to put up. And she knew she could do her penitence wherever she was, and in case she forget to humble herself and seek His presence, she had given up her most favorite thing of all.

Dr. Peppers! Just the thought made her crave one already. She could hear its fizz, see its foam and practically taste its cold, zesty pep. No more 10, 2 and 4 for her. She wondered what Hayden was giving up. He hadn't said, but they hadn't had much time to talk either. He was away at some insurance convention way up in Delaware. She flipped on the radio, as she had a habit of doing in the mornings, to hear the news while she dressed.

The local weatherman was announcing what she already knew, that the day would be blustery and rainy. The wind was gusting hard now. She could hear it rattling the old shutters, reminding her to check on the new ones that she had finally convinced Hayden to buy. She must also remember to grab an umbrella. She knew she would be working late today, but that was okay, she didn't mind. What did they call it? *Buy-In*? It had come with her recent promotion to manager, but she had to admit she felt more ownership now and didn't mind the long hours nearly as much as before. Besides, they were expecting a busy season, and she had a lot of ordering to do, plus cleaning out the storage room to make room for the new inventory. She had been trying to get to that for some time, and it was going to take awhile. She brushed her hair and pinned it up with those cute little combs that had just come in with the last shipment. Then she remembered the paint samples for Cory's room. She couldn't forget to pick them up. He would be so surprised when he came home.

The thought of Lent and Easter and everything about the season suddenly embraced her. She had always loved it, even when she was a child, even when she was a selfish teenager. Its profound meaning had forever fascinated her. The deep, unfathomable but abiding truth that inevitably drew one's attention, even if he or she sought to ignore it, like she had done for so many years. A loud banging interrupted her thoughts, and she peered out the upstairs window to see the garbage cans skidding down the driveway.

She squirmed into her sweater dress, delicately so, without messing up her hair, and hurried downstairs. She fixed her cereal, popped in a one-a-day vitamin and poured a small glass of orange juice. She gulped it down. Ugh! Hayden always chastised her for drinking Dr. Peppers for breakfast, but she figured it was her only vice, and everybody had a right to at least one. And she didn't smoke or drink—so there! She hurriedly ate and washed up the few dishes, and then pulled on her Chesterfield, wrapping the woolen shawl tightly about her neck.

But when she stepped outside, she wished she had dressed warmer. The winds cut straight through her. She heaved the door shut and headed into its potent force. Wow, blustery all right! The garbage cans had blown way out in the yard and were rollicking around. Well, they would just have to wait. She grabbed hold of the car door, and it literally flew open, bashing against its hinges.

The wind gusts were unusually intense as she drove, but she held tightly onto the steering wheel, reminding herself that the coastal winds were often very strong. It was all part of its natural character.

She drove up to Virginia Beach, the thought of Cory's spring break flashing through her mind, filling her heart with anticipation and excitement. Though he wasn't that far away—he was at college in Ashland, a small place just outside of Richmond—she still didn't get to see him that much. And she lived for his visits back home and spent days and days in preparation.

But he was coming, and she was delighted that he would be attending church with them, both on Palm Sunday and

Easter. He used to love Palm Sunday when he was a boy, she thought nostalgically, particularly when he got to wave the palms in the procession. She smiled at the tender memory. Though now he had a way of finding more excuses than ever to miss church, he had finally agreed to come with her, and she would hold him to it. She approached Rudee Inlet and stared at the ocean's surging waves, white and foamy. She switched on the radio. It was still only saying "windy," but something told her this was going to be more than windy.

When she arrived at the store, her new clerk, Carl Griggs, met her at the door. Carl was a young fellow about twenty-one and overly conscientious, but that was a good thing usually. His wide forehead was furrowed, and he couldn't talk fast enough. "Mrs. Blackenstaff…I'm so glad you're here…have you heard—"

"Carl, how many times have I asked you to call me Lorna?" She hated to be addressed as Mrs. Blackenstaff. It sounded so stiff and old! It sounded like her mother-in-law, who had been dead for years. She pushed on past him, throwing off her shawl, and he followed behind her, wringing his hands.

"Okay, Carl, what is it?"

He blushed and started over, "I'm sorry, ma'am…but have you heard about the flooding?" Before she could respond, he raced on, "They say the Bay's flooded into Lynnhaven Inlet and clear across Shore Drive…can you believe it? And I'm afraid from the looks of these waves, we're gonna be flooded soon—"

"Who says?" she demanded. "Where did you hear all that?"

"From my cousin…Jim Linkhorn…who lives up near Lynnhaven…he called me just before you got here…what do you think we should do?" His voice was quivering, and the radio was blaring something in the background. They both stopped to listen.

"*...higher than average tides and winds,*" the reporter concluded.

"See what I mean?"

She pulled off her coat.

"I'm worried about my mother, Mrs. Blacken...Lorna, and I think I might better get back home to check on her...."

Of all days, when she had so much to do, but what could she say? She knew his elderly mother lived close to the water.

"Yes...yes...go ahead, Carl. I'll be all right."

She could tell he was in no mood for inventory or anything else, for that matter. He was visibly agitated. She started to ask him to at least pull out the heavy boxes from the storage room, but he was already gone and racing up the street. The door was blown wide open, creating havoc with her fanciful, hanging chimes that were wildly banging around, clanging and piercing her ears. She seized it and jerked it shut, wondering why some people got so alarmed every time there was a storm, just higher than average tides and winds? I guess if you haven't lived here all your life, she thought more kindly, knowing Carl and his mother had only moved in a year or so back, maybe so. But then she knew Carl to be the worrying type, frustratingly so at times. More than a little frustrated herself, she pushed open the door to the storage room to tackle the inventory and sighed.

This was going to be a bigger job than she expected, she thought irritably as she tugged on the heavy boxes. Well, at least with the storm, she probably wouldn't have any interruptions. She could hear the wind pounding the building as she methodically went through the boxes, deciding what to keep and what not, but her mind kept escaping the storage room and seeking more interesting things, like what she was going to bake for Easter. Or what she was going to wear to church on Palm Sunday, or whether or not to take Cory's curtains down and buy him new ones to go with the new paint. More than once, she had to recount due to her wandering mind, but stubbornly and diligently she worked on for some time, almost forgetting about the storm, except for the rain beating hard on the roof. What else was going to happen? Life was full of problems, she thought, all the racial trouble going on, and the fear of the Russians, and President Kennedy advising everyone, prudent families, he said, to have bomb shelters. Hayden wouldn't hear of it, of course, and then Ernest Hemingway committing suicide—what a shock! Why, you'd think he had everything. Though he was awarded the Nobel Prize for Literature, he had never been her favorite author, but suicide? She remembered struggling through *For Whom the Bell Tolls,* and the whole book being about blowing up one bridge, and then there was all that bloody bull-fighting in *The Sun Also Rises*. Granted, he was a gifted author, but his subject matter simply didn't appeal to her. The only one she really enjoyed was *The Old Man and the Sea,* probably because it was about the sea, or more likely because it was so short.

Suddenly the weird sound of wind rushing through the old eaves broke into her musings, and she decided to check outside.

"Oh my!"

Water was pouring across Atlantic Avenue.

"This is definitely more than a storm!"

She looked back at the mound of boxes. Something strange was going on, and she recalled Hayden's warning after the last storm. He would be irate if she stayed on and got caught out in another one.

"Doggone it!"

She might as well close up shop, though she hated to, knowing it would put her even further behind. Disgruntled, she shoved the boxes out of the aisle, but did take the time to scribble the last column of figures into her new notebook, and grab up a few invoices she had begun the previous day. Maybe she could at least mail them at the post office on the way home. She crammed the rest of the paperwork back in the drawer, locked up the store and headed out.

The brutal wind met her head on, far more vicious than before, and she had to struggle against it to reach her car. She scrambled in and drove south, feeling like Carl Griggs. Waves were bouncing over the boardwalk and already parts of the street were flooded. She saw an automobile stalled in the high water, and she thrust the car into second gear and drove slowly through the swirling waters as the radio blared out reports of a bad storm with exceptionally high tides.

"I should say so!" she muttered as the windshield wipers flew back and forth.

It must be a nor'easter, she decided, and a bad one at that, but she hadn't heard anything at all about one coming! The water was now crossing Atlantic Avenue and out onto Pacific Avenue. She kept glancing to her left, unable to take her eyes off the angry, choppy ocean, turned the color of lead. It rolled and tumbled and spewed forth its foamy white suds. She saw it crash over the formidable statue of the Norwegian Lady in a furious fashion as she stood defiantly facing it. It was another nor'easter that had caused the noble lady's doom, or rather the doom of the ship she rode upon. It had broken up in one of these storms, taking its victims with it. The thought didn't ease her fears any, and she wished Hayden was home.

The winds rocked her automobile, and she wondered if he had heard anything about a bad storm, but he hadn't called. Forget the post office, she thought anxiously, just make it home. She crawled slowly and doggedly through the high water and back to Sandbridge, her fears increasing with every mile. Could it be a hurricane? Of course, she well knew that some nor'easters were every bit as violent, even if they didn't hold the notorious name. Nor'easters always played havoc with the narrow strip of land. That was its purpose—a buffer!

The rains were pouring now, and the swirling, angry waters rose, and more than once, she thought her car was going to stall in it, or be blown clear off the road by the raging winds, but finally she made it home. She was never so glad to see their long driveway, though it was now streams of muddy water, and she pulled up next to the garage. Pummeled by the windy force, she dashed madly for the house. The phone was ringing as she yanked open the door, and she left a path across the hardwood floor. It was Hayden, and she could hear the relief in his voice.

"There's a bad storm..." he was saying. "I've been trying to reach you!"

"I know...I know..."

"You want me to come home?" She knew he didn't want to leave her alone, but she didn't want to be a wimp either; besides, this convention was important to him.

"No, no...that's foolishness!" she said, staring down at the puddle of water encircling her feet. "You know I'm okay being alone, and I'm safe here. Don't worry."

He hung up saying he would call later.

What they didn't know was that this nor'easter pounding the Mid-Atlantic coast was unlike anything most people could recall. The last big storm of its size was way back in 1933. Normally nor'easters hit and left fairly quickly, that was their saving grace, but not this time. A mysterious and unusual mixture of three pressure areas was behind it, combined with atmospheric conditions of the spring equinox, which typically cause very high tides. Though Lorna was not particularly afraid of storms—she had grown up with them—this one seemed unusually creepy. The winds had magnified themselves and were gripping the old house, seemingly shaking its very foundation.

The phone rang again.

She grabbed it, hoping to hear Hayden's voice on the other end saying that he was on the way home.

"Mom…that you…you okay?"

"I'm fine, Cory…don't worry…."

The line went dead.

Disappointed, she dropped the receiver. Though she knew Cory would be worried senseless, there was nothing she could do about it. She didn't know that he had already hopped in his car and was headed home, with the radio blaring out the news that frightened him even more. He knew his dad was gone, and he didn't even heed the speed limits, flying eastward with only one thought in mind, his mom.

The power had gone off shortly after the phone went dead, and all she could do was wait for the storm to abate. She waited and waited—still it held. She picked up a book to read to take her mind off it. For a while, it did, but then everything darkened, and night came early. She paced back and forth from one room to another, carrying a flashlight and staring out the rain-washed windows, hardly able to see anything at all through the solid sheets. She tried to decide whether or not to prepare for bed but was afraid to change into her pajamas in case she had to suddenly leave. Then she heard a weird sound as if the house were twisting and pulling apart, and figured her imagination was amplifying every sound, as usual.

She grabbed the phone, still dead, and slammed it back down again. Why hadn't she told Hayden to come home? Forget the stupid insurance convention! Anything was better than this, being alone in this—whatever it was! Her nerves were beginning to unravel, and her mouth felt unusually dry. She fumbled her way to the refrigerator, though she knew she shouldn't, and then was chastised. No friendly Pepper-Upper! Oh well, she pushed the door shut, realizing she shouldn't have opened it in the first place. Anybody knew not to open a refrigerator once the power went off. She crossed over to the sink for some water. She hated water!

Groping back to the living room, she could feel the damp cold seeping into the house and grabbed an afghan. She snuggled down into the corner of the sofa and listened to the storm's fury. Ash Wednesday, she thought, the first day of Lent.

Imagine that!

She recalled another Ash Wednesday when she was but a child. She must have been about ten years old, and she had gone with her parents to a church service, but she couldn't remember which church. It wasn't her church. Her father had been invited by his boss, the one that gave them the washing machine later on, and they had all gone, she and her father and mother. She remembered her mother fussing all the way there. She didn't want to go to somebody else's church, though she felt she couldn't say no because it was his boss man. But what stood out most in the long ago memory was the ashes—ashes that the pastor blessed and then used to mark a cross on the people's foreheads. Not hers, because she refused to go forward—nobody was putting ashes on her face! Later her father had explained to her the sacred meaning—how the ashes came from the palms that they had burned, the palms from the previous Palm Sunday, and she had felt bad then because she liked palms. She even remembered the pastor's words.

"...for dust thou art, and unto dust shalt thou return."

It was all very reverent and mystical, and she wished she was at that church right now! Oh, to be surrounded by devout worshippers and a saintly pastor, instead of being here all alone. She would be happy to have him mark her with ashes. In fact, she had often thought that she would like that now, and maybe one Easter she would find a church that had ashes. Suddenly she felt ashamed of herself, getting so nervous and scared.

She wasn't alone!

She hunkered down in the soft folds of the afghan as the storm raged on and prayed for safety, not only for herself but for anybody who might be caught out in it, though she couldn't imagine such a thing. The pounding sounds of the wind and the rain and its monotonous drone ironically made her drowsy, and she had just dozed off when a deafening crash exploded above, bringing her suddenly to her feet.

What was that?

She stood there trembling. Whatever it was, she knew it had hit the house, and she grabbed her light, flashing it out into the hallway and up the stairs. She saw nothing.

She stumbled toward the stairway and gripped the banister. Though terrified of what she might find, she headed up the steps. What was that roaring sound?

Cold, blowing rain met her at the top of the stairs. It was coming from Cory's open door. She flashed the light, and to her horror saw that a tree had crashed into his room!

It was the big live oak that had shaded that side of the house for so many years. Twisted branches and shiny, wet leaves and shattered glass were strewn everywhere. Wind and rain were blowing wildly through a gaping hole, opening up the window to twice its size. The tree branches covered Cory's bed, and she stood there feeling totally helpless. What could she do? In spite of herself, she began to cry and scrambled through the wet branches and dark, curled leaves, pulling vainly at them. The flashlight's beam jerked crazily about in the eerie darkness, and she could see his blue striped curtains blowing straight out, twisting into knots, like nautical sails caught out on a stormy sea, and she thought crazily that he would surely need some new ones now. His high school pennant suddenly ripped off the wall and went flying out into the hallway, and she cried all the harder. Everything was getting soaked, everything would be ruined! Realizing she would not be able to stop the torrent of rain pouring in, she frantically began grabbing at stuff as it blew across the room.

She must save Cory's things!

She yanked at the quilt but couldn't free it from the heavy branches. It was his favorite quilt, too. All she could think of was that it was the one she had made for him years ago when she had taken that quilting class with her mother, and she had hated that class. She had hated every minute of it, mostly because she couldn't do it to her mother's satisfaction. But stubbornly she had finished it and been so proud. Now it would be ruined! She tugged fiercely, but the wet branches poked back, scratching and cutting her arms. She felt like a mad woman in a war against a tree.

But she must do something! Twisting between them, she wrenched harder, but it was no use. She struggled to free herself and banged her head with the flashlight. The tree branches were just too heavy. She flashed the light rapidly and began grabbing at first one thing and then another and was able to get a number of things out of his room, racing back and forth, though some of them were already soaked, and then slammed the door shut. She slumped down on the top step, swiping her wet matted hair and stared at the closed door. Water was seeping beneath it.

She pointed the light down the steps at his belongings lying in disarray where she had tossed them. She would have to move them downstairs as soon as she could muster the energy, but she was tired, so very tired. She thought of the new carpet they had just installed on the steps and wondered how she could be thinking of such at a time like this. Even if the house stood, she could only guess what would be the outcome after all this water. She could still hear it blowing into the room behind the closed door. Surely it would stop soon!

She dragged herself up, and then picked up the wet things one by one, clumsily carrying them downstairs, trying to hold onto them and the flashlight and the banister at the same time. The new carpet squished beneath her bare feet, cold and soggy, and she thought of how Hayden didn't want to spend the money for it in the first place. She pushed the things high up into a closet, cramming them onto a top shelf as if that would matter if the worst came. But she couldn't think about that! If only she could make it until morning, surely it would dissipate by then. She went to the window again, but could see nothing except darkness and sank back onto the sofa, hugging the afghan about her. And out of pure exhaustion, she fell into a fitful sleep as the wind roared outside.

It was a sleep fraught with fragments of her life, sketchy fragments, she and her daddy fishing together down by the fish camps, the sandcastles being washed into the sea, and then she was marching down the aisle on Palm Sunday at Nimmo, waving long branches high above her head, and loudly singing "Hosanna." Then the dream wasn't just visual anymore. She was older and could actually feel the restlessness and boredom, feel it the way dreams work themselves into one's inner being. She tossed and turned beneath the afghan as the rains beat down, and the dream turned sad, so very sad, a sadness that reached deep into her soul, and there was water everywhere for she was on a ship, a very old, creaking ship that was riding tumultuous waves in a frightful storm. Its sails were blowing straight out, and she was struggling to hold onto the wet, slippery railing. She was afraid, so afraid. It was a fear that consumed her entire body, every minute cell, but it was not for herself. There was something else. She was struggling to see what it was through the fog and rain and the salty mist that was stinging her eyes, and then she saw it! It was lying at the foot of a statue—a statue poised out over the front of the ship's bow defiantly. The statue looked like a woman, but no, it was wooden, but it appeared to be real, to breathe as the foamy water sprayed over it. It was focused on the high waves it was forging through, trying to protect what lay at its feet, something small, a bundle swathed in pink. But waves, humongous waves, were crashing over the sides of the ship.

She sat up in a cold sweat!

Clutching the afghan about her, she stared all around, still caught in the throes of the wretched dream. Slowly it began to recede into the darkness and release its ghastly hold. She glanced up at the window. A bit of gray was filtering through. It was morning but still the storm held on. She could hear the wind and rain, and for a moment she was suspended between the dream and reality. She jumped up, stepping into cold water. It was icy cold, and the house was almost as cold. Though she could see that it was only an inch or two standing, still it unnerved her. She sloshed over to the window and saw nothing but water, water everywhere, in the yard, in the road and more up in the low-hanging clouds.

She didn't know it, but the nor'easter had stalled and was pounding the coastline, playing havoc with vulnerable homes, hotels, and businesses everywhere, stretching up the coastline. The flooding rain, high winds, and tidal surges were not just in Virginia, but reaching up from Cape Hatteras all the way to New York, even inland, dumping large quantities of snow for several hundred miles. As far south as Alabama, the land was caught in blizzard-like conditions, but the seaboard was receiving the brunt of it.

The storm whipped not only North Carolina's outer banks, but also Virginia's, flooding out its ocean and washing away its sand dunes, flattening them up and down the coastline, and opening up free passage for the angry sea. Raging storm water flooded ashore, splintering beach cottages as if they were toys. Fortunately, most owners were either gone or had evacuated in time because the roads were soon under water, and some were washed away.

The powerful waves even broke up the nice concrete boardwalk and seawall at Virginia Beach, and the new Chesapeake Bay Bridge Tunnel that was under construction received a ruthless blow. "The Big D," a prized and important piece of custom-built equipment, was also destroyed, but it didn't stop there. The high waves bombarded Ocean City, Maryland, and Rehoboth Beach in Delaware, reaching over forty feet high. The steel pier in Atlantic City was partly ripped up, and Long Beach was cut through in a number of places. The battered coast was distressing, but more devastating was the human cost. Over forty fatalities would ultimately be listed, and another thousand injured one way or another.

Lorna stared out the window and wondered why no one had come. Where was Hayden? Where was everybody? She had no idea of the extent of the devastating winter storm that had held the coast captive for three whole days and through five high tides, but she rode it out alone. Hayden never made it home, for he was caught up in it, as well, on the coast of Delaware. Cory couldn't get through either until the storm let up, and when he finally reached the house and saw the big live oak lying on it, he froze.

Lorna was standing at the window, and she saw him staring up at the house and then racing toward it, and her heart took a leap. The door banged open.

"Mom!"

They clung to each other for a long time.

He was able to reach his dad at last to let him know they were okay, and he got his dazed mother over to a friend's house. She had survived the damp and bitter cold by staying on the sofa wrapped up in her afghan and a heap of blankets, but her peace of mind would take awhile to restore. With the help of some rescuers, they were able to cut the tree off the house and board up the hole temporarily. Otherwise the house was fine, only a good cleaning was needed. Water still saturated the carpet and stood in the floor, but most had flowed downstairs where several inches backed up into the kitchen and pantry. Cory mopped up as best he could for the time being, and then met his dad at Virginia Beach to help with the clean up, for that would take some time.

Atlantic Avenue was essentially a waterway for days. Canoes and kayaks rowed back and forth. Army duck amphibious vehicles transported children out to waiting school buses, and bulldozers rolled in to cut trenches to allow water to return to the ocean. Pumps and drain lines were set up to remove the remaining water.

But it was the little beach at Sandbridge that saddened Lorna most of all. As they approached its slimy, waterlogged, sandy road, she stared unbelievably. All of its small cottages were flattened, about fifty in total. And though she knew it would be rebuilt in time, still the wicked nor'easter had stolen her childhood memories. It would never be the same.

Greyson sat in front of his television watching the news in the aftermath of the storm. He looked out at the snow-encrusted trees and wondered. The terrific nor'easter had dropped nearly two feet of snow on the Shenandoah Valley, and up in the Blue Ridge Mountains, in Big Meadows particularly, there was close to four feet. A beautiful finale for the end of winter, he concluded, but knew that others were suffering from the storm's surprise assault. Many others in fact, up and down the coastline, and his thoughts unwillingly wandered back to that warm summer of forty-two. He pushed it out of his mind and began to pray for the victims of the storm, but his prayer was interrupted.

"Told you so!"

He sat up abruptly. "Told me what, Pa?"

"Didn't I tell you them rockets shooting off into space was gonna stir things up?" He paced back and forth between him and the television set.

"Pa, I don't think—"

"That's the trouble with you young folks—you don't think!" He marched over to the window. "Now whoever seen such a snow coming from a storm all the way down on the ocean?"

"A lot of people, Pa, have died—"

"I know that!"

"We need to pray for their families and—"

"I know that, too, but we need to stop sending them men up in space. They got no business up there!" And he stomped out of the room.

Greyson sighed and got up to switch off the television. He picked up Rayna's letter lying on top of it. He would reread it again. It was full of enthusiasm and always lifted his spirits. He could hear the cheerful lilt in her voice as she rattled on about school and her studies and about her roommate's imaginative decorating with all sorts of weird paraphernalia. She had adjusted easily to college life, and it wouldn't be that long before she finished her first year, and for that he was glad. So why did he feel so at odds? He supposed it was that empty-nest thing they talked about, and his pa's mounting challenges, and perhaps the inevitable changing world.

He didn't like change, but who did?

CHAPTER EIGHTEEN

Rayna read the enchanting words of John Muir. They rolled over her like a warm, sudsy bath as she sank down into the hefty, overstuffed chair that was wedged tightly between the two beds in her dorm room. She basked in his charming but realistic images and hoped Norma wouldn't be back for a while. Not that she didn't like her roommate, she did. But the comfy chair belonged to Norma, and so did all the other unnecessary accessories scattered about the room. She was always carting something else in. Norma was from Amherst County where Sweet Briar College was located; that's why she got to attend the private school at a whopping discount. It had been established that way, and any student from the county qualified. She didn't resent Norma's advantage, but secretly wished she could have gotten one, too. It was hard for her dad with his modest preacher's salary, but he insisted on her coming once he saw the place, not to mention it was an all-girls' school. She knew he wasn't fond of Kent and hoped she would eventually sever the thorny relationship and concentrate totally on her studies. Who knows, maybe she would.

She had been sold on the school, too, as soon as they drove up its long, narrow drive that wound through a pleasing deciduous forest that eventually deposited them at an old boxwood circle. It had been planted in the nineteenth century by the founder's father, someone named Elijah Fletcher. And when she got a whiff of that heavy boxwood scent, it clinched her decision. She decided right then and there that it was the place for her.

The secluded college rested in the midst of over three thousand acres of beautiful, wooded, rolling hills, and boasted of two lakes and miles and miles of winding trails, which certainly weighted her tilted scales. It had been founded back in 1901 by Elijah's daughter, Indiana Fletcher Williams.

Now that was an interesting name, she thought to herself, taking a break from her reading and glancing out the window into the dark night. She would liked to have been named Indiana herself, or even Maryland or Missouri, she chuckled. But whoever heard such? The only state she had ever heard used as a name was Virginia. And though she didn't particularly have anything against being named Virginia, it was so staid, so settled. The others definitely evoked more adventure, especially Indiana, and she wondered about her again. Indiana had founded the college in memory of her daughter Daisy, who had died quite young. That's what they had been told, and intrigued by such stories, Rayna draped her leg comfortably over the chair's wide arm, pondering the young girl's death. And she realized that if it hadn't been for that, she might not be sitting here at all. There might not have been a Sweet Briar College. Perhaps she would be in some other state. Who knows?

But the college had enticed her from the start. Any school named for a plant had to be good in her opinion. She wasn't familiar with the sweet briar and had immediately looked it up in her encyclopedia and found that it was a lovely wild rose. The initial information they had received explained that the college grounds used to be a large plantation with slaves and all, and that the plantation had also been called Sweet Briar. She reined in her wandering mind and focused it back on John Muir.

'*...the rocks, the air, everything speaking with audible voice or silent; joyful, wonderful, enchanting, banishing weariness and sense of time. No longing for anything now or hereafter as we go home into the mountain's heart....*'

"*The...mountain's heart*," she repeated pensively.

Such engaging words, and they conjured up passionate emotions, her own deep love for the mountains—but also a powerful longing, a profound homesickness, and it draped over her like a wet blanket.

She looked out the window again, seeing what she hadn't seen before when her mind was fiddling with names. The wind was blowing steadily outside, and naked treetops were twisting back and forth, rattling in its vigorous grip. She could see them in the moon's thin light, and she thought about her dad. What would he be doing right now? Probably sitting in his favorite chair, reading the paper, or perhaps he was thinking about her. She knew he missed her terribly, she could tell, and that's why she couldn't let on how homesick she was. She had to be delicate, careful to fill her letters with happy news to buoy his spirit.

She wished she could go home this weekend. Naturally, that was out of the question, too much cramming for all those tests next week. But Norma would be gone, and that much was good. She had a serious boyfriend already and found every excuse to get off campus. At least that would leave the place to her, and she should be able to get in a lot of studying. Norma was one of those chatty people, easily distracted, and didn't know when to shut up.

'*...the level sunbeams are touching the fir-tops, every leaf shining with dew....*'

Footsteps were traipsing down the hallway, the click, click of sharp heels, but they continued on past her door.

'...many mossy emerald bogs, meadows, and gardens in rocky hollows to wade and saunter through—and what fine plants they give me, what joyful streams I have to cross....'

She stopped reading.

She could see those rocky hollows up in the mountains, covered with moss. She loved moss, its smooth velvety touch. She remembered all the wonderful camping trips with her dad, and hiking, just the two of them, and wading across those tingling, cold streams, hopping over the slippery rocks. She could see them laughing and racing across the warm, sunny meadows with hands clasped, him leaning down to hold hers while butterflies danced about them. Why did one have to grow up?

Of course, she enjoyed being with him now, but it wasn't the same. And they didn't have the time these days, what with Grandpa always there and demanding attention. And then there was Kent. She sighed. What was she going to do about Kent? Why couldn't she make up her mind? Just when she was ready to call it off, he would up and do something really sweet that would totally confuse her. She heard more footsteps. This time she recognized them.

Norma burst into the room, and Rayna jerked her leg off the chair.

"Oh, silly, you don't have to do that!" She flung her coat down on the bed. "And you don't have to get up either. You studying?"

"Not now."

"Well, you'll never believe this!" The tall, thin girl was shaking her short-cropped head something furious.

Here it comes, thought Rayna, and she resigned herself to a long night. She watched her pulling off her boots.

Norma did quite a bit of riding and even kept a horse at the stables.

"Believe what?"

"*I heard it!*"

"What?"

"I heard her scream!"

Rayna knew she had to be talking about Daisy.

"…and it was really, really eerie…like something you never heard before!"

Rayna just stared at her.

"Well, I did…I swear…excuse me…but I promise you I did!" Ever since she found out that her father was a minister, she treated her a bit differently, like she was a fragile piece of glass or something.

"Norma—"

"I know, I know. You don't believe in ghosts or anything, but I tell you what… she's out there!"

"Where?"

"In the graveyard…I just got back from it."

Rayna had heard stories of the meetings with Daisy more than once since she arrived on the beautiful campus—incidents involving the impish spirit of the long-ago child, Indiana's child, that had lived here before her life was snuffed out. She had listened to the tales about a broken music box that still played on occasion, and strange laughter erupting in the halls of the old, Gothic buildings from time to time, and she had also heard about the screams, but she wasn't going to feed Norma's already heightened imagination.

"I thought you were at the library," she countered.

"I was, but Wanda Reynolds and Eloise Freeman talked me into slipping up there."

Rayna shook her head. She was talking about Monument Hill where Daisy and her family were buried, and it was a definite point of interest. She had seen it from a distance when she hiked out to the stables, but had purposely avoided it, particularly since Norma was so caught up in the heat of the strange legend or whatever it was.

But Norma squatted down in front of her anyway, dropping her voice to an exaggerated whisper, "It was dark and windy up on the hill." Her pupils were dilated to enormous proportions, turning her brown eyes black as she switched into her theatrical mode.

Rayna was amused.

"And we could see the statue all lit up in the moonlight, but we stood there for about half an hour before we heard it...I didn't really expect to hear it...you know, because we've been there several times before and never heard it." She hesitated for a second. "But all of a sudden there was this high-pitched scream...it sent chills clear up my spine, and we flew out of there lickety-split! We didn't stop until we got back!" She jumped up and flopped down on her bed, obviously keyed up.

"So you've heard the screaming statue," she tried not to sound too cynical.

"I knew you wouldn't believe me."

"I didn't say I didn't believe you...it just sounds highly suspicious, that's all."

"That's why you need to go with me next time!"

"I don't know—"

"Oh, come on."

"I'm surprised you're going back. You who believes in ghosts, aren't you scared?"

She sat up straight. "I was tonight. But now that I'm able to analyze it—no, I'm not scared. She's been screaming for years, they say."

Rayna smiled.

Norma ignored her. "Besides, I'd heard about her way before coming here. Uncle Joe told us about her years ago. He used to do maintenance work here. Lots of people have heard her, but I don't believe there's any harm in her. I believe she hangs around because this was her home...and maybe she misses it."

"Why does she scream then?"

Norma frowned at her.

Rayna slipped the bookmark back in her book.

"Muir again?"

She nodded.

"I don't believe you! All that woods stuff would bore me stiff."

They had been down this road before, and Rayna knew there was no use defending him. She would never understand. Norma was a smart girl, not in the literary sense, but she had lots of common sense and was a whiz when it came to figures, which was certainly not her forte.

"What you need is a little excitement, girl." Norma jumped back off the bed. "Will you go with me next time?"

"Maybe."

"Maybe, maybe, maybe, that's all you ever say. Well, some others are going again Friday night. I'm going, too, and I hope you will. We're going later this time, and maybe we'll hear or see more."

"Better not go too late. You don't want to get on the Dean's bad list." The Dean held absolute power and everyone knew it, especially Norma.

"Don't worry. He's not all that bad. It's his duty, you know, to keep us girls safe...and pure. Our chastity must be preserved!"

Rayna didn't appreciate her off-hand way.

But Norma laughed at her scowl and began pulling down her covers and undressing. "I never heard a scream like that…I hope I don't dream about it!"

Rayna turned down her own bed. The last time they discussed the famed ghost, she didn't get to sleep until after midnight, and she didn't want a repeat. Apparently it had been an exhausting night for Norma for she was asleep before Rayna changed into her pajamas. She tiptoed around the room, dimming the lights and preparing for bed, and then sank back into the chair to finish reading.

'The snow on the high mountains is melting fast, and the streams are singing bank-full, swaying softly through the level meadows and bogs, quivering with sun-spangles, swirling in pot-holes, resting in deep pools, leaping, shouting in wild exulting energy over rough boulder dams, joyful, beautiful in all their forms….'

"Wow!" she whispered.

Muir sure could paint a picture with words, and it stirred something within her. Wonder if she could write? Certainly not with such eloquence as Muir, but perhaps she could write about the Blue Ridge…and the Park…and its people. The thought excited her, and already images were floating about in her head. But then there was her dream of becoming a Park Ranger. What about that? Could she do both? Perhaps. She would take more botany courses. Certainly that would help in both areas, and they offered a number of them in the biology curriculum. That's what she enjoyed anyway. She was excited and full of anticipation as she continued to read.

'When we try to pick out anything by itself, we find that it is bound fast by a thousand invisible cords that cannot be broken to everything in the universe. I fancy I hear a heart beating in every crystal, in every grain of sand and see a wise plan in the making and

shaping and placing of every one of them. All seems to be dancing in time to divine music…'

She laid the book down and switched off the lamp.

Divine music!

The poetic words swam in her head as she climbed into bed and lay staring up at the dark ceiling. Norma was breathing hard in a sound sleep, and she was glad. It made her feel alone, and she liked it. It was one of the things she missed. There was never any privacy. Once Norma found out that she had grown up in a parsonage, she was constantly bombarding her with questions, ridiculous questions. Did y'all pray all the time? Read the Bible all the time? What was it like? Did you have to go with the preacher to all those funerals? Where did you keep the wine, you know the wine for communion? Did you sneak any? Do preachers really know everybody's business? All the juicy gossip, that is? Rayna had never thought of her life in those terms, certainly not intriguing, but evidently Norma did. Between that and the screaming statue, there was hardly ever any peace in their small dorm room, so she had taken to walking the grounds whenever she had an hour or so between classes, and she cherished those quiet times. She had done more of it in the fall when the trees were all scarlet and burnished gold. She would trudge through the crisp, fallen leaves, pretending that she was home, but now it was so cold. The wind was biting, and she hadn't gotten out as much, and when she did, she didn't stay very long. But maybe she would take a hike tomorrow.

Divine music!

It sounded like something her dad would say, something he would drop from the pulpit on a Sunday morning, or more likely when the two of them would be walking in the woods, perhaps in the still of winter, sensing its mood. He often quoted such poetic words, but not from Muir. His were usually from Solomon or David, and they were even more poignant and more beautiful. And she felt guilty. She must start reading her Bible more.

The next day was cold. A raw one for the end of March, but the sun was shining openly when Rayna finished up her first class. She had over two hours to herself since her English class had been canceled due to a death in her teacher's family. She rushed back to her dorm room, hoping to find it empty. Norma should still be in class. She pushed open the door and hurriedly changed clothes, dressing in her warmest tights and jeans. She pulled on two sweaters and her hiking shoes, those that her dad had given her just before she left. He knew she would be hiking after seeing the sprawling, woody campus. She tugged her heaviest jacket on over all that and wrapped a warm scarf around her neck, but she left her head bare. She detested hats or caps. Her dad said she must think all those dark curls would keep her warm. Lastly, she pulled on her leather gloves, stretching them tightly onto her small hands, and set out.

The air was bitter as she marched briskly outside, away from the red-brick buildings, away from the academic lectures, away from the constant drone of scholarly professors, and headed for the woods, to one of her favorite trails. She was all alone. No other takers today. The sharp wind buffeted her, and the wintry air held a definite hint of snow. It was exhilarating, just what she needed, and she hoped it would come, the snow that is, and lots of it.

The sandy road leading off to the woods brought her up to the old sycamore tree, leafless now, its scaly bark glistening white in the wintry glare, and she wondered how many students had passed by it. She had to stop and run her gloved hand over its peeling trunk, and she thought of Muir again. He would do that. She felt a kinship to him. He would understand her, not like Norma or most of the others. Or rather she would understand him. They would definitely get on. They were both Scottish, why not? Her grandma always bragged that she was Scottish, not just Scottish, but Scotch-Irish. She felt a tender moment of sadness. It had been awhile since she had thought of her grandma. She wished she could sit down and talk with her again. She would be more apt to listen now. I wonder what she would think of me here at college, she mused, drawing her scarf tighter and bracing against the wind.

She marched on, the stress of cramming for tests and juggling schedules falling off like scales, sliding onto the sandy road and close bordering brown turf. She could be herself now, no need to be sociable, and she took off running out toward the familiar trail and through the dense forest.

She could run forever!

Faster and faster, she raced, up and down the bumpy hills, through the scattered leaves and over fallen branches and exposed roots. She ran on and on until she was practically out of breath, and suddenly fell up against a tree, completely exhausted. She leaned back to look up at the tall poplar shooting up into the sky, straight as an arrow. It was not alone. All the lofty trees were jealously vying for the sun's thin rays as they reached high, soaring to the blue heavens. Only the pines had any canopy at all, and the bitter winds rocked them back and forth, their green needles bunched, stiff and top-heavy. She watched them sway ever so gently, creaking and sighing, and she was glad she had come.

A pervading stillness reigned with only an occasional rustling in the dead leaves, but she saw no movement, no signs of life. She sat down on a fallen log and listened to the subtle sounds of winter, inhaling the fine, cold air.

On the way back, she decided to veer off and take a shortcut through the woods to the new sanctuary, just established a few years prior, and she thought it odd to be called a sanctuary. But on the other hand, it seemed entirely appropriate.

She paced herself to a slow trot for it was a ways from her usual trails, and she couldn't exactly call it a shortcut. She finally entered the old forest and marveled at the huge white oaks that some said were over a hundred years old, maybe pushing two hundred. Who knows for sure? She studied their expansive trunks, finding it hard to imagine, and wished that they could talk, both them and the old sycamore. They would probably divulge a host of secrets. She smiled to herself. She had heard about the girls caught smoking in these woods and getting expelled for it. What else would they tell? When she finally returned to the dorm to change her clothes, Norma was there.

"Where have you been?"

"Hiking."

"On a day like today?"

"It was great."

"You've been reading too much Muir if you ask me."

It was only a week afterward that Norma came in very late, pushing the rules again. Rayna was already in bed, but she wasn't asleep, and watched her quietly slipping out of her clothes. She felt it her duty, as a friend, to warn her.

"Norma?"

"Thought you were asleep."

"I couldn't."

"You're worse than my mother!" She switched on the lamp, throwing a shaft of yellow light over her flushed face.

"I'm sorry...but I hate to see you get in trouble."

"Well, you don't have to worry about that!" Her resolute tone raised Rayna's suspicions.

"What do you mean?"

She flopped down on her bed. "We did it!"

"We?" She figured she meant Wanda and Eloise. "You went to the monument again?"

"No, silly. Derek and me...we got married tonight."

Rayna sat straight up. "You did what?"

"We got married."

She scrambled out of bed, throwing on her robe. She had one arm in and one out when Norma's hand shot out in front of her. The small wedding band glistened in the lamp's golden glow.

"But why...I mean why so suddenly...and so secretly?"

"Because we wanted to...and it's the only way. You know my parents wouldn't hear of it."

Rayna's mind was trying to sort out the inevitable outcome. Now what, not only for Norma, but for her? "Does this mean...will they—"

"Dismiss me?"

She was glad she had said it instead of her.

"Probably, but that's okay. It's all in the plan." She vaulted off the bed and gave her a whopping hug. "You're the only thing I'll miss here anyway. You know I never liked the whole studying scene. I'll leave that for you." She released her and dropped down into the chair, patting its broad arm. "Might just leave old comfy here for you, too."

Rayna stood there, not knowing what to say.

The dogwoods were blooming on the campus, their fragile white flowers lacing its dark forest. It was the end of April, and Rayna anxiously finished her paper, stacking it neatly together. It was a feat not easily accomplished. She enjoyed writing, but it had to be her way or no way at all, not dictated by others with such restricted boundaries. And thinking of boundaries, she couldn't wait to get outside. She could hear the birds calling. Her new roommate, a tiny thing called Leisel, was stretched out on her bed napping again. She did a lot of that, and Rayna wondered if she was well. She didn't want to ask her though, afraid of insulting her. Maybe she was born with a sluggish metabolism, or maybe she was just plain lazy.

"I'm going for a walk, Leisel."

She nodded, half opening her eyes.

Rayna shrugged and closed the door softly behind her. She sure missed Norma. One would think that she would be glad for the peace and quiet left by her sudden departure, but she surprised herself. Apparently she had become accustomed to her senseless chatter, and she had to admit that she was the closest she had ever come to a sibling. There was a tangible emptiness until Leisel showed up, but she couldn't fill it. She didn't measure up to Norma Campbell's yardstick, nor would any others.

She stood outside the dorm, breathing in the fresh spring air. She had finally decided to visit the cemetery. She figured she owed that much to Norma. Students lounged beneath the spreading, shady trees, some with books thrown open on their laps, others sitting or stretched out on the grassy slopes talking excitedly. Obviously, she wasn't the only one with spring fever.

She strode across the lawn, between the buildings until she came to the dirt road leading out to the stables and was soon loping down it, passing by the old sycamore again. Its new crop of leaves rustled nosily in the spring breeze, and she suppressed a desire to stop. Another time, she told herself and passed on by, the warm sun beating down on her back. She sprinted by the old barns on her right, used for storing hay or whatever, and thoughts of Daisy popped into her mind again. What would it have been like to grow up on a sprawling plantation, she mused, with so much activity all around, and especially so much land, with all these rolling hills.

The narrow, country road left the barns and sunny meadows, winding discreetly into the sheltered woods, curving up and down them and around steep, clay banks. It was dappled with splashes of sunshine now and then. The road was closely cropped with crowding trees, and she noticed a puff of white disappearing into the underbrush, a frightened rabbit she figured. Birds fluttered in the treetops, and the mournful sound of a dove revived childhood pleasures in the parsonage yard. She may not have had a plantation, but she certainly had a happy home, and she couldn't wait to get back. Her dad was already making plans for her return. She looked up ahead. The road veered off and led up to Monument Hill. She wondered why people always picked hilltops for their graveyards.

When she crested the hill, she was surprised at the arresting view below and the college buildings set off in the distance. They looked serene now, not noisy and bustling with female students, but her eyes were drawn upward instead to the towering statue of a maiden in a flowing robe of stone. She was hovering over the sunken graves, and a sense of timelessness embraced her, a sense of eternity.

It wasn't a large cemetery, but it was obviously well planned out and had been cared for over the years. An aging stone wall several feet high encircled it, and she walked slowly around it, unable to take her eyes off the soaring statue. The maiden's pedestal was huge, and it drew one's attention straight up into the swirling, white clouds as she pointed up to the heavens. Rayna felt dizzy staring up into the moving haze and caught hold of the wall. It was cool and damp to the touch, and she continued on around its circular expanse to a gate that led inside.

It was a peaked, black, wrought iron gate, just the kind you would expect, and it creaked when she pushed it open. She stepped into the cemetery, welcomed by the scent of aged boxwoods and arborvitaes. Maybe it was the fact that she was all alone except for those departed souls, or maybe it was the wistful setting high upon the hill, or maybe it was the awesome statue of the maiden towering above her, but she was most definitely drawn into its spiritual aura. Not mystical, like Norma had described, with screaming ghosts, instead there was a deep, abiding presence, and her tread was light as she stepped between the gravestones.

There was a second large monument, though not as tall as the fair maiden's. It was inscribed to Elijah Fletcher, and she recognized the tombs of Indiana and her husband, the parents of young Daisy. Her eyes then rested on a small flat stone between them, and she read. *Dedicated In Love—To the Sweet Remembrance Of Dear Daisy.*

She stared back up at the statue and the large cross clutched in the maiden's left hand. Her dad would certainly like it. She would bring him up here when he came after her. She glanced around one last time to take in everything before leaving and noticed an old fir tree growing into the stone wall like it wanted to get out. She rubbed its long, soft needles. It was different from any fir she was used to, and she wasn't sure what it was.

Closing the gate behind her, its metallic lock thudded on the quiet hilltop. She started to go but instead sat down on the stone steps, unwilling to leave just yet, and she wondered again about life and death. It had hung over her through the years, popping up rather frequently. Like Norma said, it was probably because of all those funerals she had witnessed. Maybe so. She looked back through the gate, thinking of those souls that had once lived and breathed just like her, once ran and worked and played like her, and she realized that one day it would be her turn.

She stood up, shook off the somber mood, and headed back.

CHAPTER NINETEEN
(1966 – Four years later)

Cory sat very still watching his mother take each labored breath. It had been two long weeks since the wreck, and each time his hopes were raised, they were dashed again. She had never come out of the coma. He knew it was touch and go from the start, but the doctors kept giving him hope. And then last Saturday, she had taken a turn for the worse. They had all but given up. Still he waited for a sign, a twitching eyelid, a flinching finger. Maybe, just maybe, she would recover. It wasn't out of the realm of possibilities. Far stranger things had happened in the medical world. A nurse entered to check her vitals, straightened the bed and smiled at him. She was a new one.

"Haven't seen you before."

"I'm new on this floor. I'm Maggie. If there's anything I can do for you—"

"Thank you, but I'm fine."

She smiled at him again, this time with obvious empathy and then left.

"*I'm fine*," he repeated to himself. What a stupid thing to say! He was anything but fine. His life lay in the balance, depending on what happened within these cold, sterile walls!

He sighed, but what else could he say? No use burdening her with his problems. She probably had enough of her own, and how nurses coped with such dismal circumstances day after day was beyond him anyway. It would be the last place he would want to spend eight hours a day. He crossed to the window and glanced at the trees with their tender green leaves. Soon they would be lush, shading the sidewalks with their quilted patterns. He thought of Sandbridge and wished he were there, wished that he could turn the clock back and that his mother was up and well like before. The laughing gulls would be returning for the summer as well as the fishermen and the surfers. He could almost feel the force of the powerful waves beneath him, surging, pulling, and the salty water washing over him, and he thought of that summer a few years back, after the Ash Wednesday storm. It was when surfing really took off in Sandbridge, and he had practically lived on a surfboard. The happy music of the Beach Boys played in his head again. And suddenly he remembered the turquoise transistor radio his mom had given him, and he was afraid it would melt in the hot sun. So she had propped it up beneath a towel with stalks from sea oats, making a tent out of the towel so that the hot sun wouldn't damage it.

She couldn't die!

She was too young…and he would be all alone. It was a strange feeling. His dad was gone and his grandparents, too. He had lost them all. His grandma was the last, finally succumbing to the lung cancer after a long battle. Heart attacks and cancer one could expect or at least understand, but a senseless wreck!

Again those last moments played out in his mind as they had done hundreds of times. And he tried to make some sense out of it, wondering if he could have done something to prevent it, but it had happened so fast. He had only turned his head for a second. Surely he had done that many times before—people did it all the time. Why did that big hay truck have to pull out? He pushed the painful picture away and sat back down beside his mother.

She was all he had…except…he replayed her last words over again and then thrust them off. It was too much, just too much to absorb all at once. He watched her small, still form barely holding onto life, and he let the tears come.

Lorna Blackenstaff died two days later.

Cory took care of the necessary details, having her body sent back to Sandbridge and contacting all the right people, renting a car and driving back alone, meeting with the funeral home representatives, picking out the casket, the burial clothes and flowers, and writing the obituary. He did it all mechanically as if it were someone else within his skin. He did it without emotion, for if he let down the battlefront, who would do it? He had to be strong. He had to hold up. There would be time to grieve later, plenty of time. And he knew how to suppress his emotions. He had learned that in the Marines. Wasn't that ironic? His training was helping him get through her death, and she had so hated him joining up. They had discussed it long into the nights, arguing at times. It was all tied up somehow to another war, and he had had a hard time understanding, trying to connect the dots, but now he did.

The funeral was held in the lovely old Nimmo Church, where fragrant flowers graced the small sanctuary, early spring flowers, jonquils, daffodils and forsythia. For that he was glad, she had loved the springtime, especially the flowers, and he made sure that her closed casket was draped with a profusion of them. Soft and brilliant yellows contrasted in abundance and sprayed the silver casket that rested before him, but he couldn't look at it. Instead he stared up at the preacher, focusing on his words, grasping for something to hold onto.

Friends and neighbors attended and afterwards offered their condolences with a kind hug or a trembling handshake. Their blurry eyes gawked at him as they awkwardly mumbled words of sympathy. Words that washed over him without meaning while he stood stoically in his neatly-creased, blue dress uniform as a good soldier should, holding back the tears. Mom would be proud of me, he thought, as the last visitor squeezed his hand, and they filed out to the cemetery.

He could hear the long trill of a killdeer nearby as they gathered around the gaping hole for the final words. The lofty trees above them fluttered in the gentle coastal breezes, and he remembered running through this very cemetery as a kid, his mom chasing behind him playfully. Oh, how it hurt!

The preacher cleared his throat as the parishioners and guests crowded in, and his low, baritone voice began to recite those familiar words, words he had heard in church, but never ever expected to hear this way.

> *Let not your heart be troubled: ye believe in God, believe also in me.*
>
> *In my Father's house are many mansions: if it were not so, I would have told you. I go to prepare a place for you.*
>
> *And if I go and prepare a place for you, I will come again, and receive you unto myself; that where I am, there ye may be also.*
>
> *And whither I go ye know, and the way ye know.*
>
> *Thomas saith unto him, Lord, we know not whither thou goest; and how can we know the way?*
>
> *Jesus saith unto him, I am the way, the truth, and the life: no man cometh unto the Father, but by me.*

With bowed heads, they listened as birds sang in the tall, overhanging trees, and then the preacher prayed. He prayed a long and beautiful prayer, but the words wafted over Cory, and then it was all over. He had given his sweet mama the best funeral he knew how. The people began to scatter, filtering out over the grassy grounds, the green turfs of new growth, between the irregular tombstones, somberly filing out one by one until there was no one left but him and the preacher, who came over and hooked his arm about him. "You all right, son?"

He nodded, unable to speak.

"Want me to come by the house?"

He shook his head. "I'm okay, sir," he managed to utter. The preacher patted him on the back and walked away, and Cory felt more alone than he ever imagined possible. He stared up at the prominent steeple and wished he had come with her that last Sunday. If only.

The preacher's dark-colored sedan soon backed out of the drive, the sunlight bouncing off its hood, and he glanced back at the young soldier still standing there beside the grave, his white hat clasped in front of him.

Three weeks later Private First Class Cory Blackenstaff reported for duty and soon after was on his way to Vietnam. The train rolled out of Virginia, rumbling westward, its metal wheels scraping and screeching against the long, straight rails. It picked up speed, rolling and humming monotonously. Soon it was dashing away from the east, leaving behind the crowd of cities and towns, and the droning hum and clatter synchronized its own musical harmony that calmed Cory's frenzied mind. Hour after hour, he stared out the window, seeing the trees zip by, heavy eastern woods, and then periodic copses. After some time, there were long stretches without any trees, maybe only a lonesome pine standing vigil.

The train hurtled down miles of carefully laid track, hundreds of miles, eventually speeding out across the Great Plains, a long tedious trek, alien to Cory's limited grasp. He had never seen such boundless views, miles and miles of stretched-out land, reaching out empty from horizon to horizon to the great blue arch of sky overhead. He could understand why people used to think the earth was flat. Who wouldn't? It certainly gave him that illusion, extending out to a distant point and then seemingly dropping off into nothing. So much space, vast and open, but every now and then he spotted a lone house, and wondered what it would be like to live in such remote isolation. Even in the mammoth train, he felt small and insignificant midst its limitless expanse.

After awhile, the newness wore off, and he closed his eyes for sleep, but sleep wouldn't come. So he sat there unthinking, staring out at the wind-swept plains racing by his dusty window in an all-encompassing barrenness, but it was as if someone else were watching it all. Not him. His mind was elsewhere, but where, he didn't know. It couldn't be in Sandbridge. He had shut that door, and he didn't want to think ahead, that was far too unsettling, and yet the present was incredibly painful. So he let it drift along blankly, aimlessly observing every new picture his clouded window framed. But he knew it was just waiting, the grief, that is, biding its time.

Finally, out of pure exhaustion, physically and mentally, he drifted in and out of sleep, a hazy, detached sleep as the train rolled on. At times his eyes would snap open, and he would wonder where he was for a second or two before he realized that he was in a strange land, a sudden land, it seemed. Tall buttes and flat-topped mesas appeared out of nowhere, strange sights for an eastern boy, for sure. Now and then he noticed tumbleweeds rolling across the bleak, brown landscape, blown by relentless winds, and he thought he was dreaming and that he would wake up sometime and everything would be back to normal, he, his mom, and their life by the Bay. But then it would come back, the awful reality, stark and painful, and he would seek the comfortable haven of sleep once more.

Another soldier poked him, "You gonna sleep all the way?"

He nodded and closed his eyes again. Though he knew the fellow was also headed to Vietnam, he didn't want to talk. What was there to talk about?

When the train eventually cut through the western mountains, he did sit up. They were something to see! He remembered all the stories he had heard about them, the gold rush days and the persistent pioneers who pressed through and over them for a new life. He thought of all the westerns he had watched on television and the dust kicked up by the cowboys and Indians. He peered through the clouded window. There was dust all right, but out of the vast stretches of flat land, those massive mountains suddenly rose up high and dignified. He was amazed at their awesome height and snow-capped peaks piercing the cloudless sky. And down below, the land itself was colored differently from back home, rusty looking like orange clay, it seemed, or sometimes pink or violet or even yellow. In fact, the colors changed with the day, sand hills with startling different shades and tints and magical hues. He had never seen such. He stared at it all, and caught himself thinking more than once that he couldn't wait to tell his mom, and then the old hurt would resurface.

The large Navy ship, painted a drab olive gray, sailed out of the California harbor. It floated heavily out to sea, out into the mighty Pacific, loaded down with young men just like him, some younger, some older, but they all had that same look of resignation. There were those, Cory was sure, heading out confused and lost, much like him, not knowing why they had signed the dotted line, signed away their rights and possible future. And there were those who had eagerly left their homes for quest, for excitement and adventure, certainly a male's prerogative, but now as the great ocean stretched out ahead with no end in sight, they too fell in with a look of acceptance. They couldn't turn back now.

But he didn't want to turn back, he thought, as he watched the rocky shores fade away into the distance, and the mountains swelling up from the ocean grow smaller and smaller. Though he did experience a strange sensation, one that is often common to those leaving their homeland for the first time, it was akin to loneliness, though far deeper.

But what was left for him in America?

He realized, however, that he carried his problem with him. Grief can be persistent and sometimes even patient. It can lie in wait and suddenly spring upon its victim mercilessly. Once at sea, Cory's met him head on. As they moved out into the great waters, it accosted him, coming in waves just like those beneath him—tossing and rocking the big Navy ship. First there was anguish, and then anger. Why her? She was too young to die! She hadn't finished living. They didn't get to take that trip, that trip to Maine they had planned on taking when he got back from overseas. They didn't get to taste the lobsters together or see the moose and the rugged cliffs they had talked so much about. He gripped the wet railing and looked up into the sky with its lingering gray clouds. And the heavy, salty mist covered his tears.

Why would God take his mom?

After the anguish and anger were spent, a deep abiding sorrow followed and sailed along with him over the Pacific. He studied the heavy, moving clouds above and the deep swells below, and he still couldn't believe it. His mother had been the central person in his life from the time he was born. Of course, he had loved his father, but there was a special bond between him and his mother. They understood each other. His father, though he believed he had tried, was always at odds with him, and it became more apparent as he grew older, with the gap widening to gigantic proportions during his teens. Could he help it if they always seemed to end up on the opposite ends of the stick? Was it his fault that God had not chosen to weight his psyche with Blackenstaff genes, but instead his mother's?

The passage seemed to take forever; the ship rolled and pitched, and he wasn't spared that age-old dilemma.

"Don't close your eyes. That only makes it worse," the veteran soldiers preached. However, it was easier said than done, but at least the wretched sickness forced his mind off his grief. Ironically, it made him think of his father. How in the world had he been able to live on one of these iron monsters, floating over thousands of miles of sea, miles ahead, miles behind, and miles below? He knew about his sinking ship, but preferred not to think about that. Instead, for the first time in his life, he began to wonder about his father's part in the Navy during his war, the Great War. He wondered how he must have felt as he headed into hostile fighting. It was something his dad never talked about. Maybe he should have. Maybe it would have made him more human. Perhaps he could have understood him better if he had opened up. Was he a different person back then?

Finally they arrived.

Docking in Nam, he couldn't get over the fact that the beachhead reminded him of the coast of Virginia! Not only its broad sandy beaches, but the mosquitoes and flies were there, too. Though quickly the likeness faded as the ravaged, war-torn land came into focus, and he felt as if he had been suddenly dropped into another world, another planet, a dark and bewildering maze.

He gaped at the small, isolated Vietnamese villages with no roads, no telephones, no radios, a maze of huts, thorny hedges, snorting water buffalo, bamboo clusters and lines of barbed wire. It was all so foreign! He smelled the pungent scent of fields, hay and manure. He saw the lowly people huddled in front of the huts, mostly women and half-naked children staring up at them with sometimes fear, sometimes resignation. He heard the rumbling tanks, the deep, resonant sound of helicopters, and saw the sad, torn-up land, but even more, he felt the despair of the land, its fear, suffering and death.

It was penetrating.

His unit was located near the DMZ, their primary mission was to secure and safeguard the important military installations at Da Nang. It seemed to him that everything there was a blur of drab olive—the terrain, the dust, the sky, even the Marines. He remembered the clear-blue sky over the Back Bay at home with fleecy-white clouds wafting over and felt a heaviness come over him as he listened to the whirr of helicopters overhead and the distant sound of enemy fire. Would he be up to the task? It was the question that had haunted him ever since he received his orders. Had his father felt this way, too? Or was he as confident as he always appeared to be? Maybe the Navy would have been better for him, but then his training kicked in, and he remembered *I'm a Marine—we're the best!* He smiled at his own arrogance.

Settling in, he was ever alert and cautious, following orders mechanically and methodically, and performed his duties to the best of his ability. He pushed his grief deep into the recesses of his soul to deal with later on, another day, another time. And somehow during those bleak days, his loss actually seemed to sustain him, for he didn't feel that he could hurt anymore. There was no more pain left. Instead, he moved about in a robot fashion, entirely focused on the task at hand. Occasionally, however, his mother's words, her shocking revelation, reached out to him midst the constant shelling and exploding bombs.

"*Cory…you have a sister.*"

But always he thrust it aside, refusing to hear it, refusing to acknowledge it. He wasn't ready. There was a war going on, and he was in the middle of it! One day maybe. Maybe not.

The long, hot summer slowly crawled on with its searing heat and unbearable humidity. It passed in a blurred military fashion that only soldiers understand. There were regular battalion sweeps over the rugged terrain—over the rice paddies and over the valleys, looking for Viet Cong. The sweeps were nerve-wracking, stretching one's courage to the very limit. From high above the ridges, other companies would cover them while their desperate prayers lifted up even higher, above the jungles, above the gray clouds, up into the heavens, hoping that God would hear them in all the hellish chaos.

Then it was autumn, but not the autumn of the Old Dominion, neither its mountains nor its tidewater. Instead the sweeps turned ugly as the monsoons set in with gray sheets of falling water day after day, week after week, soaking the elephant grass limp and soggy. Their canvas turned a moldy green, roads dissolved into greasy mud, and tempers flared. There was nothing but wet grayness as they fanned out, and the thick mud sucked at their boots like live organisms. Filled with water, they squeaked with every grueling step, and Cory felt the weight of them pulling him down as he ran, ducking the whistling shrapnel overhead. He could hear the rounds hitting, splashing into the flooded rice paddies all around him, and he wondered if he would ever see home again.

Then came Operation Prairie, and he headed into the jungle again. It was another search and destroy operation, and he sloshed along with a stretched column of soldiers, humped with weighty packs, slopping through the mucky paddies. A soldier fell in beside him.

"What's your name?" he asked abruptly in a deep, resonant voice.

Cory didn't feel like talking, but the big guy was glaring into his face.

"Private First Class Cory Blackenstaff," he answered curtly.

"Well, excuse me!"

Cory stared at the hefty, black soldier with dark, brooding eyes, his skin the color of copper.

"I know this ain't no picnic, soldier," he said. "But we gotta get along, seeing as how's we might be stuck together for some time." He was obviously sincere and downright personable as a broad smile spread over his face, and his brooding eyes turned merry. Cory returned a half smile.

His hand shot out. "My name's Private First Class Ernest Smith, but just call me Smith." He grinned, and they clasped hands. "I can tell you're from the South," he added as they stalked through the tall, wet grass.

"Virginia."

"Good ol' Virginny," he chuckled. "Y'all having some time down there with the likes of us."

Cory stiffened. He knew he was referring to integration, and he didn't take kindly to his assumptions. He knew well enough what was going on back home and had no intentions of discussing it now. "Where're you from?" he countered instead.

"Michigan."

"That's funny. I could've sworn you were a Southerner."

"Used to be."

"But now you're a Yankee!" Cory couldn't resist a tad of sarcasm, but the big guy just chuckled again.

"Yes, sir, Private First Class Cory Blackenstaff. I'm a Yankee…and so are you now!" He waved his hand out over the flooded rice paddy, flaunting another infectious grin.

"Just call me Blackenstaff."

"Sure thing, Blackenstaff."

The northeast monsoon was blowing in huge gusts, and it was cold and dank. The ground was completely saturated, and mud was everywhere, feeling more like sinking quicksand, but come nightfall Cory was strangely pleased to find himself hunkered down with none other than Private First Class Ernest Smith.

"Well, I declare if it ain't my buddy from Virginny!" Smith grinned, purposely exaggerating his southern accent. He sat down to pull out a spike from his boot.

Cory nodded, and they lapsed into silence.

The night was his worst dream, no moon, no stars, only a deep, black sky. He knew there were clouds up there, but they, too, were black. "It's eerily quiet," he finally remarked, seeking to break the silence.

"I figure it's better this way."

Cory nodded again. "Where did you say you come from…in the South, that is?"

"I didn't."

"That's right, you didn't."

Smith gave another one of his throaty laughs. "But South Carolina's where I grew up." He was checking his gun for mud so that it wouldn't clog up. Cory stared into the thick jungle, forgetting the banter. At least it looked like a jungle to him, a mysterious, frightening jungle. The next couple of hours were exceedingly quiet, and Cory's stomach began to growl.

Smith rummaged for a tin of c-rations out of his pack.

"How about some apricots?"

"No thanks."

"They're my favorite." He opened the can.

Cory reached for his own ham and limas.

"I betcha it ain't like Virginia ham!"

"That's for sure."

"Virginia…Virginia…yes, good ol' Virginia."

"So?"

"Ah, nothing."

Suddenly taking the offensive, Cory countered, "Well, you know Virginia's kind of like the Marines."

"How so?"

"We're the oldest of all the armed forces."

"Yeah, I know."

"And I'm proud of it."

"So am I."

"Well, the Old Dominion's the oldest, too. It all started in good ol' Virginny, as you say."

Smith eyed him curiously and then displayed that infectious grin once more. "Blackenstaff, you're all right—"

His welcomed words were cut short by a sudden explosion of enemy fire, and they dropped to the ground, grabbing their rifles. The rain had begun to fall again, and all they could see were shadows coming at them, dark grotesque shadows swaying in the tall grass, and they fired rapidly. Cory sent up clipped silent prayers as the enemy fire whistled and crackled overhead. The wretched sounds of artillery, thuds of mortar and rocket fire were all around, and he seriously questioned if they would make it out this time. His mom's silver casket swam before his eyes, and he wondered what color his might be, but after awhile all was quiet again. They stared into the darkness, afraid to move, but apparently the Viet Cong had slipped back for now. Smith slumped down, wiping his wet forehead, and Cory slid down beside him. For a long time, they were silent.

"Blackenstaff?"

"Yeah?"

"I never thought I'd die in a ditch with a white man."

Cory tried to see his face, to discern his true feelings, but all he could see was darkness.

"But I reckon if it's gotta be, then I'm glad it's you, Blackenstaff."

"We're not gonna die!" he snapped.

"How do *you* know that?"

He didn't have an answer, but he had to hold onto that thought. He had to!

"Well?"

"We have to believe it, you know!"

"Well, you believe it, Blackenstaff...for me, I ain't so sure."

The next few hours were quiet, except for the soft falling rain, eerily quiet as Cory had said. Every now and then he could hear a cough nearby, in the thick dampness, but mostly it was just still.

"Come on outa that jungle...and stand up and fight!" Smith fumed, checking his magazine. Muffled explosives could be heard in the distance, and Cory questioned this rationale. He wished it would stay quiet forever. He wished he never had to fire again!

"Come on out, Charlie," Smith dared a second time. "We know you're out there!"

Cory wished he'd shut up. He sat hunched over with the cold rain streaming down his face. He had never been so miserable.

"They're all around us, Blackenstaff...you can bet on that."

"Think so?"

"I know so. That's the first thing I learned when I was so lucky to arrive here, stupid ol' Smith. I asked that young MAC –V officer, I said, 'Where's the front?' "

Cory knew what he was going to say, but he listened patiently anyway. Sometimes a soldier just had to vent, to voice his frustrations, otherwise he might explode.

" *'Where's the front?'* that half-smart officer repeated like I had just landed from the moon. 'You're at the front, soldier,' he smirked at me. 'As soon as you stepped off that ship, you were at the front!' "

Cory shivered. That was the worst thing of all—no front and no rear. No lines drawn like he'd read about in other wars, like the one his father had fought in, the Big War. All wars had lines. They were supposed to have lines!

He remembered reading all those library books, nestled beneath the bay myrtles, with the cool ocean breezes rustling their pages. He remembered reading about the Revolutionary War and the War Between the States. And he had heard enough about World War I and World War II and the Korean War. Who ever heard of a war without lines? But this war was different. Smith was right. The Viet Cong *were* all around, all among them, a part of them even. One never knew who they were! In the daytime, they might smile at you in the villages and then kill you in the night.

And he hated these jungles!

Their dark images evoked all kinds of terror. As a boy, he had read about guerrillas in jungles, imagined them being big and black and burly. But not these guerrillas! They weren't big—most of them were barely over five feet. And they certainly weren't burly, but at night, dressed in their weird black, pajama-looking outfits, they were black all right, blending in with the dark jungle. And they were definitely guerrillas—having perfected this hideous method of warfare. They were significantly challenging the great United States Military. Cory listened to the worrisome silence and felt the fear that pervaded the jungle ooze out to him. He huddled a bit closer to Smith, and then he heard it echoing in the distance. That woeful metal sound.

"Told you…this place's crawling with them."

Cory searched all around, fear creeping up his spine like a black widow up a dark, moist crevice, ready to pounce. Smith was leaning over him, pressing his ear in its direction.

"What is it?"

"The gongs."

"The what?"

"The gongs…meant to crush a soldier's courage."

Cory nervously wiped his forehead and thought to himself that they were doing a pretty good job of it, too.

Smith hissed, "Mama told me not to join up!"

"You weren't drafted?"

"Naw, man…I gotta wife and baby back home…well, I *used* to…before that greener grass on the other side…know what I mean?"

He decided not to comment, but his opinion of Private First Class Ernest Smith suddenly climbed a few notches.

"Your mama tell you that, too?"

The sudden question was like a rug yanked out from under him, and he stared at him in the dark. "My mama's gone…she's dead."

Smith reached over to him, patting his arm in a fatherly way. "I'm sorry, Blackenstaff…man…I didn't mean to—"

"It's all right." He shoved himself up higher to survey the pitch blackness. He needed to get back to the war.

"Better watch your head!"

He slid back down. Smith pulled his canteen from his pouch and gulped a long swig.

They were silent again, and then Cory asked, "You said you have a baby?"

"Sure do…that half-pint is a chip off the old block… acts just like his old man," he bragged, carefully replacing his canteen back into its pouch. "Want a cigarette?"

"No thanks." They weren't supposed to smoke.

Scrambling around for a dry match anyway, Smith cursed the darkness, but soon the small fiery sphere glowed as he crouched over it, and the acid scent blended with the wet, pungent earth.

"My boy's name is Rayford Robert Smith. Now ain't that a whole lotta name for such a li'l fellow? But we call him Bobby anyways."

"How old is he?"

"Be five years old next month...on the sixteenth."

Cory figured he was thinking about missing his birthday for suddenly he became awfully quiet and remained that way until the shadows in black pajamas returned, coming at them through the tall, wet grass again, and shrapnel whistled overhead, lower and lower it seemed. Taking aim at the shifting, erratic figures, they fired and fired.

Weeks passed, the monsoons continued, drenching all in their path, and the wet soldiers pressed on until they either returned for a rest, or returned in black bags. But they didn't return for another operation for a while, because Operation Prairie simply wouldn't let up, continuing on through the end of 1966 and into the next year, and becoming one of the bloodiest and longest Marine operations of the war.

They were waiting for orders. It had been another one of those gloomy, gray days, and Cory didn't know which was worse, going out on the missions or waiting to go. Sometimes he thought the waiting was the worst, and time was the real enemy. Time to think, time to wonder, time to imagine the worst, time to agonize over the future, and time to fear, to be disgustingly afraid. He was a Marine, for goodness sakes! He wasn't supposed to be afraid. He was supposed to be brave. Brave Marines! Isn't that what they say? He glanced around at the others; they didn't seem afraid. But he knew how easy it was to hide it, to put up a front, to conceal it from your buddies, to press it down deep into your soul, trying to smother it. But it was alive!

Fear.

You couldn't smother it, or strangle it, or bury it, or suppress it for very long. It would rise up against all odds, just when you thought you had it covered. It would grab hold of the reins, taking charge and overriding your best intentions. Wildly and uncontrollable, it would consume you, and, ironically, Cory's worst fear was to be forever disgraced in front of his peers. It was worse than death.

"Mail call!"

He glanced up, the familiar cry breaking through his thoughts. He grabbed his knife and began whittling away at the piece of wood that Smith had given him, trying not to notice the uproar around him, trying to appear busy, hard at it. Mail call was always the highlight of any day.

"Alstad…Anderson…Arlinsky…Beckstrom…Briggs …Burnette."

He whittled furiously, pretending not to notice the happy exchanges. Smith was trying to teach him how to create a miniature rifle with his pocket knife, but it wasn't working very well.

"…Eberhardt…Etheridge…Evans…Fallucca… Fernandez…Franklin."

So what if he didn't have anyone to write him! It didn't matter. What difference did it make anyhow? Would it keep the Viet Cong from killing him? Hell…he thought of his sweet mama…Heck no!

"…Gerson…Goldman…Hahn…Humes."

The soldiers grabbed their mail and disappeared off to themselves, seeking privacy to read, to connect with their loved ones back home, leaving the others still waiting and hoping. Though Cory wouldn't look up, he could tell who received mail and who didn't, as always he could tell, and usually it was the same ones, but he pretended to be completely engrossed with his emerging miniature rifle that looked more like a wilting sea oat to him. He hated mail call! Normally he was able to keep his mind centered on the mission at hand, fixed on the war, but this was the one time the war was interrupted, taking second stage, and home was thrust back into focus. But there was nobody at home.

"...Petroskey...Powell...Quesenberry...Quillian."

Why did it take so long? Couldn't he hurry up? Or did he take pleasure in this whole depressing affair? He knew he was feeling sorry for himself, and he didn't want to feel sorry for himself. It was a sign of weakness, and he didn't want to be weak.

"...Rasmussen...Reichard...Schmidt...Smith."

He looked up as Smith strode forward with that big grin plastered across his face. He grabbed his letter and thanked the officer, but then glanced over at him. He ducked his head, but not soon enough. He had seen the look on Smith's face, and he didn't want anybody's pity, not even Smith's. He whittled harder.

"...Turner...Tyree...West...Williams."

Soon it was over, and the soldiers settled back into whatever they were doing before. Cory breathed a bit easier and glanced up into the watery sky. It wasn't going to stay up there for long, that's for sure. It would be raining soon, bucketfuls, cats and dogs.

"Blackenstaff?"

Smith was standing over him, still holding the letter in his hand, and Cory glanced away. He didn't want to hear it, the words from his mother again. The last one shook him up for days. Couldn't he see that? But his bulky shadow still hung over him, and he glanced up again, surprised to see tears glistening in his dark eyes.

"What is it?"

He dropped down beside him, but didn't say anything. Cory waited, realizing that he was struggling to get control of his emotions. He would swipe at his eyes and runny nose with his arm occasionally. Most of the guys had begun to drift off, and they were basically alone, except for a few stragglers scattered about.

"Everything okay?"

Smith nodded, and he was relieved.

"My boy…it's from my boy." He waved the envelope in front of him.

"He can write?"

"Yeah, he can write." He swiped at his eyes again. "He prints, you know. He's a smart boy. He prints real big, some of it's hard to read though, but I can make it out… 'cause he's my boy, you see. I can hear him talking to me. Know what I mean?"

Cory nodded, feeling utterly sorry for him and for this whole mess called war.

"He sent me a picture."

"He did?"

Smith pulled out a tiny photo from the envelope and handed it to him. The child looked somewhat like him, but not entirely. He appeared to be of a smaller frame with sharper features than that of Smith, but there was something that definitely bonded the two, an overall resemblance, faint though it was.

"Handsome boy," Cory handed the picture back, and Smith tucked it away in his shirt pocket.

"Looks like his mama right much."

"But I can see you in him, too," Cory said.

"You can?" This obviously pleased him.

"No doubt about it."

Smith smiled. "Maybe one day…when we get back, you can meet him."

"I'd like to."

CHAPTER TWENTY

The radio was blaring out the windows as Cory drove west. It was jamming. He let it fill his mind completely to chase away any possible negative thoughts. It pounded forth its rapturous and rhythmic sounds, and he sang along with it.

I'm picking up good vibrations
She's giving me excitations

It was happy, it was gusty, it made him feel alive, and that's what he wanted. He had seen enough death to last him for two lifetimes, and he didn't want to think of it ever again.

Never!

He had left Sandbridge early in the morning, drove on up through Virginia Beach and through Ocean View, and passed through Colonial Williamsburg, briefly enjoying its deep-rooted ambience. He was now headed toward Richmond and then on to Charlottesville. According to the map, he could get onto the Blue Ridge Parkway not terribly far from Charlottesville, and then on to the Shenandoah area.

It had been over a year since he left Vietnam, one painful year of slow restoration. Twelve months of inching forward, only to slip back every time he picked up a paper or watched the news, so he didn't watch it anymore. Instead he listened to his tapes, happy music that helped to stamp out the depressing thoughts. It had always been his refuge, as far back as his emerging teens, and now it was his trusted ally, keeping the bloody memories at bay. He thought of the old days when he had played his guitar and the piano, when he played in his little band, but it seemed so long ago. It was all before. Strange, he thought, how everything now was calculated as to before or after Nam. It was the benchmark, and probably always would be.

Maybe one day he would play his guitar again, he thought, but not yet. The lively song ended and another followed, a familiar tune, and he whistled along with its popular lyrics.

Winchester Cathedral
You're bringing me down
You stood and you watched as
My baby left town…

He had just bought an eight-track featuring it, and some days he played it over and over, wallowing in its fantasy. It didn't mean anything to him. Like most of the current songs, they were silly, some childish, some even ridiculous. But it wasn't the lyrics, it was the catchy tunes that boosted his spirits, and he enjoyed them. Suddenly it was interrupted with news—another student demonstration.

He switched it off!

His high spirits plummeted. He could feel his chest tighten up. The blasted mania was happening again. It was nationwide—and it was disgusting!

Every time he heard such things, it sent him back to Nam. And he didn't want to go! He had been proud to serve his country, and he had been proud to be a Marine—he still was. But what he had witnessed in Vietnam had disillusioned him. War was evil! Why did men have to fight anyway? Oh, he understood the fight for freedom, and he certainly stood for freedom, but why did it have to be? Why war?

However, it was too late. His mind had recaptured a piece of it, not the war itself, but those painful days when he first returned home–recounting them, slowly and arduously. He could hear those repulsive, jeering words all over again.

"Baby killer...child killer!"

Cold chills raced up his spine.

And he felt that awful sick feeling down in his gut again. He had just arrived back in the States and was strolling up and down the charming hills of San Francisco, so glad to be back in America, though the excess of affluence bombarded him on all sides, in every shop window and sprawling out onto the sidewalks, an assorted and glittering cornucopia. It seemed to mock him, and he staggered beneath its gaudy display. It assailed his shell-shocked fiber. It was a paradox, embracing, yet quite disturbing. He looked for some place quiet, and automatically headed to the water, and that's when it happened.

He was walking around Fisherman's Wharf, basking in the warm sun and gazing at the golden nuggets dancing off the San Francisco Bay. The cool ocean breezes and closeness to the salty water at last soothed his fractious spirit, and he sat down on a low concrete wall, dropping his duffle bag down beside him. He sat there for some time watching the sea come and go and soaking up the warmth of the noon-day sun. He glanced over at the large restaurant next to him. The fancy one called the Franciscan and wondered if he might fit in such an upscale place. He had the money. He knew he could afford it. Why not? It must have a fabulous view of the Bay, he thought, and he suddenly felt quite hungry. He picked up his bag and headed for it. Some hippy-looking fellows were lounging nearby, softly strumming their guitars and singing what sounded like an old Beatles' song, like the ones he used to listen to on the beach, and then he heard them.

Those damning words!

He had looked around to see who they were talking to, and suddenly realized it was *him*.

Him—the one who didn't have the courage to pull the trigger when the young Viet Cong was trying to kill him! And if it hadn't been for Smith, he probably wouldn't be here. How could they be calling him such names? Why, he would never hurt a baby…or a child! God forbid! He had felt deathly ill as he pushed away from the wharf, stumbling down the crowded streets, his duffle bag strapped to his side, banging against his leg with every step.

The beautiful city had turned sinister, a dark shade had been pulled down over its radiance, and he hurried faster and faster, climbing the steep hills, trying to escape the cruel voices, but their echoes followed after. They chased him on to the clanging cable cars that were spiraling down the narrow, vertical streets with tourists riskily hanging onto them, and laughing. Were they laughing at him? All he wanted to do was get home, back to Sandbridge, back to his peaceful Bay.

He shook off the painful memory and switched the radio on again. But another tune was playing now, one that he knew he shouldn't listen to, but yet didn't have the heart to turn off, and a hard knot formed in his throat.

Put silver wings on my son's chest
Make him one of America's best
He'll be a man they'll test one day
Have him win the Green Beret

Even after the song ended, its pensive strains still played out in his mind. Over and over, unnerving him and bringing back the cold rains, the dark jungles, the black shadows, and bringing back Private First Class Ernest Smith. His hands began to tremble, and he grasped the steering wheel harder, and then he slammed down on it. The car skidded toward the ditch, but he jerked it back just in time.

"No!"

Tears burned his eyes, and he leaned out the window. "You can't do this! Not again!" The cool, bracing air blasted him, almost too cool, but it was just what he needed. It whipped his hair, and he gulped in mouthfuls as if he were surging up from a powerful wave with his surfboard, and the haunting tune gradually left him. He sighed, realizing how close he'd come again.

He drove on up the highway, toward Richmond, a calming mood returning, slowly, a saner frame of mind, and he forced his thoughts to other things. Though he didn't relish driving through the busy city, it was necessary. He had never liked driving through cities, especially Richmond and that long Hull Street right down through the middle of it, slow and tedious. Now with his nerves so fragile, he made a point of avoiding such traffic and crowds and noise. Oh well, he could do it, and he contemplated his mission, welcomed it, in fact, yet at the same time dreaded it. But it was time—time that he found out about this sister somewhere in the Shenandoah.

He had finally come to terms with it while walking the minefields in Nam. With death looming all around him, he had decided that if he ever got out of it, he would find her. But he also recognized that the mission or adventure, call it whichever, gave him a purpose.

Everybody needed a purpose in life, something to hold onto, he concluded. A goal, a target with a straight line leading toward it, to keep you on track, a noble aspiration, a clear objective up ahead. Whether long-term or short-term, it wasn't important. If you reached the short-term goal too soon, then you just established another. He didn't know which his was, and he didn't much care. It was the purpose that counted.

However, he never realized how difficult it would be. How complicated. He had been reading up on the word *Shenandoah*, and found that it was synonymous to any number of things, including a river. One of the small towns in the Valley was also named Shenandoah, but there were many small towns in the Valley. It was a sprawling Valley, extending for hundreds of miles. She could be anywhere! She could even be in the Blue Ridge Mountains, the part referred to as the Shenandoah National Park, which also encompassed hundreds of miles of mountainous country. No, she shouldn't be in the Park itself. He understood that no one lived there anymore.

And with all this vast and unknown territory, all he had to go on was the name *Rayna*, though it was an unusual name at that.

Was he being naïve, thinking he could perhaps locate this long-lost sister with only a name? He had entertained the thought of advertising—an ad posted in the Shenandoah area, seeking a young lady by the name of Rayna, but thought better of it. Suppose she already knew and had no desire to meet him. This would give her an out, and perhaps add to the difficult search if she were to deliberately evade him. No, it was better that he find her with the element of surprise.

What did he have to lose? The idea that there was a young lady out there somewhere, who was also Lorna's child, a distinct connection to his sweet mama, urged him on. Besides, his mom wouldn't have told him if she didn't want him to find her, surely. He thought back on that day. He had thought of it a lot, analyzing each minute detail. Most likely she had been afraid that he might not make it out of Vietnam, and she wanted him to know, or she felt a need to relieve her conscience or something. She didn't want to hold the secret from him any longer, but they never would have guessed that she would be the one who wouldn't make it.

Yes, he would find her.

After several hours of driving and grappling through Richmond and Charlottesville, he was finally nearing his destination. It wasn't terribly long before he was pushing up to the Blue Ridge Mountains. And soon after, he entered the south end of the Shenandoah National Park, paid the entrance fee and headed up the long stretch of the Skyline Drive. It certainly had the right name, he thought. It was a narrow ribbon weaving around the top of the mountains, yet it calmed him like a soothing salve.

Yeah, he could live with this.

He had heard about its magnificent beauty and read about its charm. That's why he had decided to see it for himself. He figured he might as well start here as anywhere.

Its tranquility was intoxicating, and he began to whistle a tune that he couldn't even remember the name of, but it was a happy tune that he used to whistle when he was a teenager. He could understand now why it was called the backbone of the Blue Ridge Mountains. It skirted the very top of them, rising and falling, rigidly clinging to its precipitous ridges. Mileposts dotted it, but coming from the south end, they were reversed. He understood that the Drive started at a little place called Front Royal and that it was 105 miles long. Maybe one day he would have time to take the whole thing in.

The sun was almost overhead, and a faint breeze stirred the profusion of green leaves that encircled him in all their varied shades. But it wasn't the abundance of green that caught his attention. It was the vast carpet of brown decaying leaves blanketing the forest floor, spreading up its ridges and racing down the steep ravines—layers and layers of former seasons discarded and lying prostrate beneath the towering trees, patiently awaiting their fate—a return to the earth from whence they came. The circle, he remembered from his science class.

There were bright yellow plants flanking the winding road that looked like creasy salad to him. As he climbed higher, the lushness declined. The deep green subtly turned into the tender green of new life, and he had the odd sensation that he was traveling backward in time. It was more like the end of March now or the first of April instead of May! Obviously it was the cooler air and higher altitude, but it was interesting to watch, nevertheless, sort of like reversing a roll of film. And thinking of film, he wished he had brought along his camera. It had been a long time since he wanted to take a picture, but this place was made for pictures!

A blue sedan approached, pulling a long, silver camper, and passed with the glare of the sun reflecting off its smooth, rounded edges. He blinked. Silver bullets, he believed they were called. As he ascended still higher, even the tender green disappeared, replaced by a wintry landscape.

Remarkable!

There was a sign up ahead—*Loft Mountain.* As he passed by, he glanced up the steep incline, and a Ford Fairlane was slowly pushing its way up, with tents and a red and white cooler strapped to the top. Several arms were slung out the windows, catching the brisk mountain breezes. It was a happy sight, and he smiled to himself. It felt good to smile, and even if the outcome of his mission wasn't a success, he was glad he had come—glad to be up here breathing in the mountain air, glad for the opportunity to be happy.

Old apple trees showed up periodically along the way, standing out in full bloom, profusions of delicate, pinkish-white blossoms bursting forth.

Who had planted them?

They piqued his imagination, and he envisioned farmsteads with young kids climbing them, happy, laughing kids. He had heard about the mountaineers who used to people these mountains, but until now they had only been a vague piece of its isolated history. He passed Simmons Gap, recalling old western comics. He had always thought of gaps as being out west, but here he was riding through them. He glanced up at the clear, blue sky.

"Do you see me, Mom?"

A wispy cloud was drifting over.

"I'm going to find her, Mom."

And for the first time in a long time, he was optimistic, and his anticipation swelled. Would she look like him? Or like his mom? Would she be petite or perhaps a bit chubby? He had seen pictures of his mom when she was young, and she was a little that way, but not after she grew up, of course. No indeed, his mom was small and shapely the whole time he could remember. Once more, he wondered what it would have been like to have grown up with a sister. It was hard to imagine. One couldn't comprehend that which he had never experienced.

He passed through Swift Run Gap, mulling over the pleasant sound, a name that evoked images of rapidly flowing streams and cool, clear waters. It made him thirsty, and he wished he had stopped back at that wayside near Loft Mountain. Oh well, there must be something up ahead.

Old barbed wire fences stretched alongside the road, most of them boasting of only a few leaning posts now, and again he thought of the people who must have lived up here.

Gigantic, lichen-covered boulders jutted out from the mountainsides. It was a wild and wonderful country, and at first he had a hard time keeping his eyes on the road, the views were so striking. But now he was moving along rather contentedly, willingly letting it lead him on. He could do this forever and never tire of its endless curves and constant inclines. Each and every ascent brought inevitable descents, and when they did the trees began to turn green again, and he would see water spurting out from underground springs between cracks in the huge boulders—clear, cold water gushing down the stony banks, turning them a dark, shiny gray. Now he was really thirsty!

He decided he would pull over the next time he saw spurting water, but then he noticed another sign up ahead.

Lewis Mountain...Camping Available.

His hands automatically turned right, taking him into a wooded campground. A rather large picnic area was to his left. And he saw small cabins up ahead, rustic brown cabins with uneven timber boards, natural looking and very in keeping with the forest. Smoke curled up from a campsite ahead, and he spotted tents dotting the hillside. He glanced back at the cabins with their little inviting porches. They had nice, large windows and were nestled among tall, leafless oaks.

Why not?

He pulled up to what looked like a camp store, with the same rustic siding. He had planned on making it back down to the Valley, but this novel idea was too appealing, alluring actually. It fit his mood. He had never camped in his life, except for the military, but that was another story!

He gulped down the ice cold soda, quenching his thirst, and also found some bread and a can of Vienna sausages. He picked up some chips and then spotted the potted ham, just the thing. He grabbed a couple cans of it, too, for sandwiches later on, in case he got hungry and couldn't find a restaurant. Who knows what he might find or not find up here. The friendly man at the counter handed him a key to one of the cabins and pointed him to it.

It wasn't far from the store, and he pulled open the screen door, unlocked the main door and stepped inside. It was just as he had envisioned, small, rustic, and sparse. There was an undersized bed and a little square table with a couple of chairs, and a tiny, modest bathroom. Not much else, but he didn't need much else. Everything was wooden, of course, which suited him perfectly. He was tired of all the metallic clang of chrome nowadays.

He peered out the back door. A picnic table sat on the open porch, and he suddenly wished he had gotten some paper plates. He was sure they had them, but he remembered the newspaper in his car and fetched it instead, spreading it out on the table. The mountain breezes snapped at it as he sat down. He decided on the potted ham and flipped open a can and smoothed it on the bread, along with some mustard from the little packet stuck in the bag. He was about to munch down when his eyes rested on the blue sky above the tree tops, and he bowed his head. It was one of the things that he had brought back with him from Nam.

After eating, he felt a bit drowsy and stretched out on the small bed for a short nap. The window was open, and the air was growing cooler as the day waned. He pulled the light quilt up over him and fell into a contented sleep. When he awoke, the sun was sinking behind the trees, and he sprang up. He wanted to take a hike before dark.

He grabbed his jacket and walked out a ways to a narrow trail that wound in and around the trees and on out a fair distance to a rocky point. It had a splendid view. He sat down on a large rock and marveled at how peaceful it was. When he returned he was surprised that he was hungry again. Must be the mountain air, he figured. He opened up the can of Vienna sausages, but it was a little too cool for the picnic table this time. So he ate at the small, square table between the bed and the window. He pulled out the slippery little sausages, one by one, savoring their distinct taste, and washed them down with another soda.

A couple of kids were skipping by, twirling sticks and poking them at one another as they headed into the forest, and then a young man, probably their father, loped after, and he watched them disappear into the woods. It made him feel sort of sad.

Afterwards he sat out on the little porch with his jacket zipped up and read the brochures he had brought along until the light gave way. Then he just sat there, soaking up the harmony of it all, the trees, the breezes, the peculiar night sounds emerging from the darkening forest.

Before turning in for the night, however, he decided to take one last walk around the campground. It might be the only time he would ever do this. He wished there were a moon, but clouds hovered over, hiding its silvery light.

Though it was dark, he could still make out the images of tents in the flickering light of campfires and shadowy trees encircling them. He saw campers hunched over the fires, and could barely hear them talking in soft, muted tones, but he couldn't make out what they were saying, though he tried. From time to time, laughter erupted into the still night, a stark contrast to the otherwise tranquil setting, and he felt lonely, like an outsider.

He stared up at the sky. The moon was peeping through every now and then, if only for a second, appearing as if it was chasing the clouds away, instead of the other way around. Dew had fallen, and the forest exuded that pungent smell of wet, decaying leaves.

"Hello!"

He searched for the voice's owner in the dark and saw a group hovered around a dying campfire.

"Come on over and join us." The offer was certainly welcoming, and he started over.

"Here, pull up a chair." An aluminum chair was shoved toward him, and he noticed the man who had called out to him, a husky sort of fellow, broad-shouldered and bearded, though he appeared not much older than himself.

"Thank you."

He was introduced to the circle of campers, who turned out to be three different couples, all seemingly in their twenties or thirties. They each had their individual tents and were camping together.

"Where're you from?" the husky fellow named Billy asked, getting up to add more logs to the fire.

"The coast...below Virginia Beach."

Someone thrust a long stick at him, with a puffy, white marshmallow stuck to the end.

"Thank you," he repeated, and waved it over the fire. "I came up from Charlottesville."

"First time?"

He nodded, watching the flickering flames lap at the spongy marshmallow as he turned it round and round. The sweet familiar scent evoked memories of the beach and teenage days. He used to catch them on fire back then, burning them to a solid crisp.

The fellow named Billy wondered if he was alone. Not many folks camped alone, and he had always been a bit wary of them. "Like it?"

Cory looked up, unsure if he was referring to the campground or the marshmallow.

"Lewis Mountain," his wife clarified.

"Yes, ma'am, I do." And suddenly seeing an opportunity, he asked, "You all from around here?"

"Not far. Elkton."

"Well, I'm looking for someone…that's why I'm here."

They studied him more closely. "Who're you looking for," Billy asked.

"My sister."

They glanced one to another, unable to disguise their fascination.

"Her name is…Rayna," he spoke slowly and deliberately, closely observing their faces in the light of the fire.

"Unusual name," a balding fellow by the name of Ernie remarked. He was seated directly in front of him. His bushy, brown eyebrows curved together over his nose, almost touching. "Never heard anybody called that."

"Me neither," his wife added. "What's her last name?"

"I don't know," Cory answered before he thought.

Billy raked the fire vigorously, and the others suddenly seemed intent on watching him. Cory had to smile, but what else could he say? His marshmallow flamed up, burning the sticky white to black ashes just like old times, and he popped it into his mouth.

"Yuck, you just ate that whole thing all burned up!" one of the ladies cried out.

Cory laughed. "I like them that way."

"To each his own, I always say," Billy remarked good-naturedly, and the mood grew lighter. "Just like campgrounds, you said you like it here, buddy?"

"I do," he said. "It's nice."

"Most folks prefer the larger ones…you know…Big Meadows or Loft Mountain especially, but I've always been partial to this one."

"Loft Mountain—the one up the steep hill?"

"Yeah, on top of the mountain, and when I don't come here, I usually camp there. It's always cooler up there, can be pretty cold sometimes in the springtime and especially in the fall."

"Billy, remember that cold night we spent up there a few years ago when it snowed?" Ernie said with a chuckle.

"That's what I'm talking about. That was about the end of October, or maybe the first of November." He glanced at Cory to see if he was listening. "We woke up that morning and everything was white! I reckon it was about three or four inches of snow."

"In tents?" Cory asked.

"That's right, but it was mighty warm underneath all those covers."

"What did you do?"

He laughed. "What do you think we did? We turned over and went back to sleep, didn't we, Ernie?"

"Sure did, felt like Eskimos, too."

Cory smiled.

"'Course I'm partial to this one because I used to camp here as a kid," Billy said.

"Back when it was a colored campground," his wife added, and Cory glanced up.

"Nothing wrong with that, but she's right. It used to be. It was the closest one to us, and my best friend was a colored boy named Peter Jones. He and his family used to come up here once in awhile, and I'd come with them and hunker down in the truck when I saw a Ranger."

"Don't reckon he'd of done anything to you," Ernie piped up.

"Well, I wasn't going to find out either, being's I wasn't colored."

"How long ago was that?" Cory asked.

Billy scratched his head. "Lemme see, had to be before the fifties. It became integrated around that time."

"That was way ahead of most places."

"You're right. It was built in the thirties for the Negroes. They needed somewhere to go, too, you know, but then it was opened up to everybody sometime around 1950 or just before. Yeah, me and Peter used to have some time up here." He looked around nostalgically. "Don't know whatever happened to Peter Jones…once they moved away."

"Maybe you oughta look him up sometime," Ernie suggested. Billy just kept raking the fire.

"How do I get to the town of Shenandoah?" Cory asked

Billy's head shot up. "You've come too far now!"

"What do you mean?"

"You should've turned back on Route 33 at Swift Run Gap, gone over to Elkton where we're from, and then on to Shenandoah."

"So I need to go back?"

"If you wanna get to Shenandoah, you do…unless you wanna drive on up the Skyline Drive to Luray and turn onto Route 211. That'd be the long way, though."

Cory remembered reading about Luray, but it was further north and he didn't want to drive that far yet.

"But your best bet is to go back south like I said to Route 33. It's not that far back."

"You think your sister's in Shenandoah?" Ernie's wife asked curiously.

"I don't know, but I figured I'd start there."

"Good place as any," Billy said.

After awhile, they said their goodnights, and Cory headed back to his cabin. He wasn't in the mood for sleeping now and sat out on the little porch again, gazing up into the shadowy trees that reached high into the night sky. He had always loved trees, especially tall ones like these. He used to wonder why they didn't have such in their yard when he was a boy instead of the wind-buffeted scrub pines and myrtles. Of course, he had the big, live oak that the nor'easter brought down into his bedroom, but that was more wide than tall.

The trees whined as they rubbed against one another, but he couldn't see anything but blackness, and everything had grown very quiet, even the night creatures. Suddenly he was thrust back to Vietnam, and his skin prickled, and that eerie feeling flooded over him again. He was all alone in a deep, black jungle with no moon, not being able to see a solitary thing, but feeling an overwhelming sense of evil!

He jumped up, yanked open the screen door and went in, breaking the spell. He undressed and climbed into the small bed. When he pulled the quilt up over him for the night, he hoped the dreams wouldn't come back. Through the window, he could see that the clouds were shifting and fading away, and the moonlight spilled into the cabin. The skeletal trees were swaying back and forth in the steady mountain breezes, and he thought of little Bobby Smith. He figured he would be thinking of him for years to come, and he wondered if he had done the right thing. Maybe he should never have gone down to South Carolina, but he knew he could have done none other. No, he was glad that he went, glad that he was able to find the place, and especially glad to meet the little fellow. Smith would like that.

However, he was surprised at the look on his mother's face when she opened the door, and he remembered the tears that shined in her eyes when he told her who he was. Maybe she was sorry for what she had done. Who knows? He wasn't to be the judge of that, but it was the child that stuck in his memory, that little boy who looked even more like his daddy in real life than he had in the picture. It was the smile. He had his daddy's ready, all-encompassing smile.

Cory stared up at the moon and wondered if perhaps the little fellow had a new daddy by now. Would he even remember Smith when he grew up?

He pushed the depressing thought out of his mind and turned over to sleep. He had to leave the war and little Bobby Smith to the past. And the past was the past. He had a future to look to now, though it was a mystery for sure.

CHAPTER TWENTY-ONE

Early the next morning he was on his way, anxious to get on. He didn't see any sign of life from his friends' tents. Must be sleeping in, he thought as he pulled back onto the Skyline Drive. A bluish-white haze hung low over the mountains. He figured that's where they got their name, and he watched it moving ever so slowly, undulating, gradually lifting and dissipating.

The chain of mountains stretched out before him, covered with the mist, row after row, and they exuded a powerful sense of strength and solidness. It made him feel very small and insignificant in comparison. It was the same feeling he had when he walked beside the ocean back home.

He thought about the campers who had befriended him last evening and how he slept so well in that little cabin, listening to the wind as it picked up throughout the night, moaning and groaning and twisting the branches. He decided he might like to do it again, maybe next time in a tent. Who knows, this could get good to him, and one day he might be sailing along in one of those silver bullets. He chuckled to himself.

He was headed back south to Route 33, the one Billy had told him about. He should have paid more attention to the map, but it didn't matter. He enjoyed the night, and the sun was already climbing upward, warming the dew-filled forests. He felt good. Intricate silky webs glistened atop the green mountain laurel. That was one thing he had discovered already, the mountain laurel, and there was so much of it, too. Ernie's wife called it the beauty of the Park. Maybe she was right.

It didn't take long to get back to Route 33, and he reluctantly left the Park. There were only a few more miles to Elkton, though it snaked downhill as curvy as any he'd ever seen. He eased down the steep mountainside to the Valley, lurching into second gear, noticing everything turn greener and greener. Soon the foliage was lush again, and he was approaching the town of Elkton. Though pocket-sized, it was good to be in civilization once more. He drove through its quaint downtown, noticing the Elkton Theater, which immediately stirred strong emotions. He and his mom had so loved a good movie.

Well, he might as well start his search here, and work his way up the Valley and to the town of Shenandoah. He inquired as to where the sheriff's office was located. Billy had suggested this, and it didn't take long to find but turned up nothing. Neither the sheriff nor his deputy had ever heard of any Rayna, though they hadn't lived in the town all that long themselves, which didn't help any.

He stepped out of the office and glanced down at his map. The town of Shenandoah was just a hop, skip and a jump up the road. He climbed in the car and headed north, settling back to enjoy the Valley. Cattle leisurely grazed behind long, stretched-out barbed wire fences, and that same yellow plant that looked like creasy salad—but Billy insisted was wild mustard—was growing all over the gently sloping pastures. A long heap of massive mountains heaved up in the distance on his left, the Massanutten he understood, and the Blue Ridge, where he had spent the night, rose up, majestically scalloped, on his right. He smiled up at them and then passed over a bridge with an interesting name.

"Naked Creek," he chanted out the open window, imagining ways it had gotten its name. It was a mystery how so many places got their names. In no time he was approaching the sign with that word that had occupied so many of his thoughts for the last couple of years.

Shenandoah Corporate Limits.

Could she be here?

Excitedly, he pulled over next to a church to get his bearings. He looked up at the large edifice apparently constructed of cobblestone. Could she have gone here?

He followed the same plan as he had in Elkton, first the sheriff's office but again to no avail. He checked with the school office and the library and then began asking around to anybody that he happened to see.

"By any chance, do you know of a girl named Rayna?"

"Ray…what?"

"Rayna…that's her name. She would be about my age."

With a shake of the head and a curious look, the person would inevitably walk off, dashing his hopes. He did this for a good while until he began to feel downright silly and thoroughly frustrated. He finally realized that she could be in any one of the small towns in the legendary Shenandoah Valley, and this search might take some time.

He drove on.

Thoughts of Billy and Ernie sleeping up on the mountain popped into his mind, lightening his mood, and he tried to imagine them waking up in snow! That would be something. Maybe he could talk his buddy Sammy into coming up here and camping this fall—in a tent. Sammy was always game for adventure and fun to be with. They might even go up on that mountain, too, where it got so cold. What was it? Loft Mountain. They could have a blast. The two of them got on pretty well, having shared the hell of Vietnam, but that was something they didn't talk about, figured it best to let lie. He continued on north toward the next town, whistling through the rolling hills and picturesque farmland. He should have known it wouldn't be easy. Why, it was like looking for a needle in a haystack! He crossed over another bridge.

The Shenandoah River South Fork.

It must wind all through this Valley with all these bends, he thought, gazing down into the water coursing its way effortlessly beneath him and on out of sight. It was a stunning picture, and he slowed down to enjoy it. The earthy scent of agriculture lifted up to him. There were pastures with black cattle grazing nonchalantly, their tails switching lazily back and forth, and there were more pastures with black and white cattle, whatever your choice.

He came into the next town by the name of Stanley. Hedges of snowy white bridal wreath in full bloom graced the yards. He remembered his grandma having one of those bushes. The neat, little frame bungalows were quite welcoming, and he liked to imagine his sister growing up in one. He crossed over railroad tracks and again repeated his search, but still no luck.

Fighting his growing disappointment, he continued on north, wondering if he shouldn't have spent more time searching the court records before coming. He had done so as secretly as possible, but was unable to turn up anything even remotely connected. There was no baby listed with the name of Blackenstaff. Of course, he should have known that wouldn't have happened—too obvious, too risky. She would have another name, a name he didn't know. He had searched by the name of Rayna for a while and soon gave up, deciding to make the trek up to the Shenandoah, where he figured he would have better luck.

Luck?

He studied the green fields on either side of him. He didn't believe in luck. There had to be a plan. He had always believed that, even if he didn't always understand it. And things like war and Vietnam were still in His hands, after all. Man made the bad decisions and carried out the vicious actions, but He was still in control. He sighed and realized that this was a big, big land.

"If it's your will, Lord…."

The two lane road lay long and narrow ahead of him, slightly rising and dipping, with more barbed wire fences and big red barns and silos on the hillsides every now and then. It was a charming Valley, no doubt about it, and the warm sun felt especially good on his outstretched arm in the window.

But his stomach growled. He was hungry, and he decided he would eat lunch as soon as he arrived in the next town. There was still some bread and potted ham left over for a sandwich. The small towns were relatively close together, and it wasn't long before he was coming into the outskirts of the next one. It was Luray, the one Billy had mentioned, the one with the caverns that he had read about in one of the brochures.

As he approached, there were plowed fields on his right and wheat fields to the left, already a foot or more high, waving in the breeze. He drove slowly through the town, not knowing where he was going and crossed more railroad tracks. He saw a sign advertising the caverns and followed it, not that he intended on going, but it seemed like a logical thing to do, somewhere maybe to park and eat lunch.

All of a sudden he came upon a soaring stone tower just ahead, and he wondered what it was. There was a little parking area near it, just the thing, and he pulled into it. He reached in the back for the bag of food, and tore open the grocery bag to serve as a tray. While spreading the potted ham on the bread, the plastic knife snapped in two, and half of it went flying out the window. Oh well, he'd get it after he ate. He spread the mustard with the stunted half, applying more to his fingers than to the bread and kept glancing up at the tower, curious about the top of it. It seemed to be open, and it looked like huge bells hanging up in it.

He poured some coffee out of his thermos, glad that he had refilled it at the camping store before he left the mountain. It was plenty hot, and he settled back to dine, but then noticed others gradually pulling in beside him, parking their vehicles, lining up beside his. What's this?

They would get out and head over toward the tower. He saw some benches that he hadn't noticed before, strategically placed on the grassy lawn beneath the thing. The people were quietly seating themselves and staring up at the imposing edifice. He stared at it, too, while munching his sandwich. And then it started—deep ringing sounds, a beautiful, rich melody resounding throughout the area and up into the tall oak trees.

It was captivating.

Another car pulled in, grabbing his attention, a long, sleek corvette. Just what he always wanted! It was black, and the radiant sun ricocheted off it, piercing his eyes. He watched as the driver's door slowly opened, and instinctively he strained to see. An old man, quite bent over, wiggled out with a cane and then shuffled across the street to the benches.

One never knows, he thought amusedly, and quickly finished his sandwich. He got out, picked up the other half of the plastic knife and stuck it in his pocket. He walked by the shiny corvette and over toward the little gathering and found a seat among them, listening to the emerging sounds.

The beautiful strains of "Shenandoah" he recognized immediately as the bells clearly rang out, their resonate peals wafting over his head. He studied the rapt attention of the small audience, a group varying in ages, but mostly older, though not as old as the corvette driver. He, too, seemed utterly in a spell, sitting there and leaning over his cane. When it concluded, however, another tune almost immediately flowed out.

Send the Light, The Blessed Gospel Light,
Let It Shine, From Shore to Shore…

It embraced him, sending him back to his church at home. It was one of his mom's favorites. She had loved all the old hymns, but especially this one. Nostalgically, he hummed along with it, staring up at the tower. There were several small, staggered windows, apparently mounting the steps. They were all closed except for the top one, just below the massive bells. He figured that's where the fellow must be and wondered who was playing such beautiful music. Of course, it could be a lady, who knows? What a marvelous thing to be able to do.

As the song concluded, he caught a whiff of the strong, pungent fragrance of boxwoods surrounding the base of the tower, and he observed the colorful stone of the tower, stretching up into the blue sky. White clouds drifted aimlessly over, but he could see the day was waning. However, it was all quite moving, and suddenly another familiar refrain surfaced from the top of the tower, floating over their heads.

Oh Danny boy, the pipes, the pipes are calling…

The pensive song reached deep into his soul.

From glen to glen, and down the mountain side

The summer's gone, and all the flowers are dying
'Tis you, 'tis you must go and I must bide…

He started to leave but didn't want to make a spectacle of himself. Everyone was so still, completely engrossed, so he sat there and endured the brooding ballad, thoughts of the war bearing down upon him again, and he was glad when it finally ended.

A few more pieces played out, though none quite so stirring, and then it was over as unpretentiously as it had begun, and people began to amble back across the lawn to their respective cars. He followed after, the lulling strains still ringing in his ears. Now what?

The thought crossed his mind to catch up with them, to ask them his questions, but they all seemed bent on getting out of there as quickly as possible, darting across the street and hopping into their vehicles. Even the old gent was scurrying away at a fairly clipped pace. He figured they had things to do, places to go, and it was getting late anyway. And he was tired and didn't feel like any more negative replies today. He opened his door and sat down behind the wheel and watched them all leave. The black corvette peeled out and disappeared up the street.

It made him smile.

He glanced over at a motel across the way that he had noticed when he first drove up, mainly because it was made out of the same stone as the tower. All of a sudden, he felt quite drained and decided to check in and get some rest. He would be refreshed in the morning and ready to start again. He would search this town and any others left on his map. He would search until he found her!

The motel was small and quiet, thank goodness. He checked in and immediately fell across the double bed, and was asleep in minutes. The mental strain of it all was more taxing than he realized, and he didn't awaken until after dark. He was starving. The potted ham sandwich hadn't lasted long, and he was ready for something else anyhow, something heavier and more filling, for sure.

It was past seven-thirty when he set out to find a restaurant, driving slowly through the little town and scoping out everything. It was all softer, muted with the day's decline. The town was quaint, and he liked its passive atmosphere. He drove up and down the sloping hills and soon spotted a small café that looked perfect. He pulled up and went in. The place was only a third full, and he was glad of that. The waitress, a slim blond with a pencil stuck over her ear, appeared out of nowhere and immediately set a frosty glass of water down in front of him. Ice was filled to the brim, just the way he liked it.

"Come to see the caverns?" She could tell he was new in town.

"No…not really."

"That's what most people come for." She was adept at chewing gum and talking at the same time.

"Actually I'm looking for someone."

"Really?"

"A young lady named Rayna…about my age."

"Oh, that would be the Reverend's daughter probably… Rayna Ralston."

His mouth dropped open.

"Ready to order?"

He was speechless, but she didn't notice. She had grabbed a pad out of her apron and the pencil off her ear and was poised to write.

"Ah…yes, ma'am," he stammered. "But you said the Reverend's daughter?" He could feel his heart beating wildly.

"That's right. Reverend Ralston, the preacher over at the Methodist church. His daughter's name is Rayna, and she's about your age. You know, you don't hear that name much."

"No, ma'am, you don't." He could hardly contain his excitement. "And she's about my age, you think?"

The waitress began to look at him warily. "Yes…."

"Do you know where they live…the preacher and his daughter?"

"Like I said, he's the Methodist minister, and they live in the parsonage over by the church."

"Yes, of course."

"So…what will it be for you tonight?"

He was blank.

"How about our special? Hot hamburger, mashed potatoes and limas on the side, it's a favorite of everybody's, and you're lucky. We still have some left."

"Sounds good to me." He wanted to bombard her with questions but held his tongue, trying not to appear too eager.

As she turned to put in his order, she added, "Pretty little thing…the reverend's daughter, with all that curly, black hair."

His head jerked up.

"Wish I had hair like that." And she exited into the kitchen.

Curly, black hair? That didn't sound like any sister of his. Still he had to find out!

He waited for her to return, feeling confused and none too hopeful now. Nobody had curly, black hair in their family, at least none that he had ever heard of, certainly not him or his mom, nor his grandparents, not even Aunt Callie.

The waitress returned, but she seemed in a hurry when she set his food down, probably time to get off, he figured, and she slipped away before he could ask anything else. Though he thoroughly enjoyed the hamburger and potatoes, hot and delicious, he ate quickly, anxious to check out what she had told him.

He strode up to the cashier and asked for directions to the Methodist church. It was dusk now, and his hands were sweating as he drove back through town. In a way, he wished it was daytime, but somehow it seemed more appropriate, more suitable for the task at hand.

There it was.

A beautiful, old church, but it seemed formidable as he pulled over to the side of the street, staring at it and the parsonage adjacent to it. There were lights on in the parsonage, dim lights or lamps most likely. And he wondered if it were possible!

Could she be here?

He got out and headed toward it, then stopped abruptly. He retraced his steps, his hands shaking visibly, and slumped back down on the seat as darkness fell about him. The church and the parsonage became shadows in the half moon, and he noticed a silhouette before the window shutting the blinds. Was that her or the preacher? It was difficult to tell with the overhanging tree branches swaying in front. He tried to muster the courage to go back but instead grew more and more apprehensive. After all his planning and plotting and anticipating, he had lost his nerve!

He drove back to the motel.

He would try again in the morning. Things always seemed better in the morning. He could wait. He had waited this long, and wait he did as he counted the hours throughout the night. He couldn't sleep. The long nap hadn't helped any, and his excitement only mounted as the time dragged on. Finally in the wee hours of the morning his eyes closed, only to find himself back in the wet, gray jungles of Vietnam with Private First Class Ernest Smith at his side, and they were on a battalion sweep to search and destroy. It wasn't the first one they had performed together, but this one was different. He knew it was not the same from the moment they started out—something told him—something foreboding. It was his turn to lead out. Knowing the area was perhaps laden with mines, he was more edgy than usual, jittery in fact. And then there was that copper face in front of him.

"I'll lead out, Blackenstaff...it's my turn."

Did it show that bad? But he was glad to let him lead. His skin crawled with raw nerves, and all he could think of was the dark, shadowy forms of Viet Cong in the bush, hiding, waiting—waiting to kill him and the whole battalion. Suddenly the hazy, gray dream erupted in color—lightning yellow crisscrossed with ebony black and red, a bloody red—a red the mind never forgets. There was a monstrous explosion—ear-splitting, and he was sailing through the air. And the blast and colors were all jumbled together like some abstract art mixed with falling soldiers—soldiers with missing body parts and cold, staring eyes. And one of them was Private First Class Ernest Smith.

He sat up in a cold sweat!

Wiping his brow, he realized it was a dream, another one. Sunrays fell diagonally across the bed, and he looked out the window at the golden glow of morning. Once again he wondered when they would stop. Maybe never, maybe when he was old and gray-haired with grandchildren or great-grandchildren, maybe then. At least he had a chance to grow old.

He held his aching head, and then glanced at his watch. Nine o'clock!

Though the dream was gone, its mood hung on, and he vehemently pushed its fragments off. He heaved himself up and hurriedly showered and dressed and hopped in the car. His headache was gone, but he didn't feel like eating. He would skip breakfast. Whether it was the dream or his task, he couldn't eat!

Just like he knew it would, everything did look brighter. When he drove up, the church was bathed in the morning sun, and the stained glass windows were lit up with familiar Bible scenes. Even the parsonage looked inviting as he walked up to it now with his daring spirit, and before he could back out, he lifted the bronze knocker and let it drop.

He waited.

Silence.

He lifted it again and let it fall harder this time. Still no sounds from within, and then he looked around. There were no cars in the driveway. He hadn't noticed before, and he felt like kicking himself. Why had he overslept?

They were gone now!

And he would have to wait. Just when he'd gotten up the courage, now he would have to wait and perhaps lose it again. He glanced around at the two white rockers and pleasant swing and green spray of fern in a planter—such a hospitable place, but of course, a parsonage should be. Shouldn't it? He stepped off the porch, noticing the flawless grounds and flagged walkway leading around to the side, to a willow tree just turning green. An empty bench sat beneath it, inviting, and he felt like sitting down on it, but that would be presumptuous. Instead he started to flop down on the front steps and wait but felt foolish doing that, too; besides, he was feeling like breakfast now.

He returned to the same café, but the slim blond wasn't there, probably not her shift. Afterwards he headed back to the parsonage, but still no sign of anyone. Annoyed and not knowing what else to do, he drove out again to the singing tower in hopes of hearing more of its pleasing music. Maybe it would help his mood, but it stood alone and quiet. He glanced over toward the caverns. Well, he had to kill time one way or another. He had been in a couple before, but the clerk at the motel had informed him that Luray's were the largest and most popular in the East. He figured he'd find out.

The lobby was modest and so was the entrance fee. Soon he was being led through a small doorway and down some brick steps, seventy of them, to be exact, at least that's what he was told, and the further he descended the cooler it became and the more slippery the steps. He clutched the sturdy iron railing, surrounded by about twenty other tourists chattering excitedly.

It was not one of his most favorite things to do, going down under the earth. It reminded him too much of death and the grave, but it would possibly take his mind off other things until he could face them, and he certainly hoped that would be today! This waiting around was getting to him. He would ride back to the parsonage once he finished up with the caverns, and if they still weren't there, he would continue riding back and forth until somebody was there. In fact, he was already considering calling his friend Sammy to let him know that he might be gone longer than expected and not to count on him to help with that wallpapering job, at least not until later.

The guide was admonishing them not to touch any of the formations, as if he wanted to. Everything looked wet and sticky. It got cooler and cooler as they descended, and there was a thick dampness in the air, but still not uncomfortable. He heard her say that the caverns had a constant temperature of fifty-four degrees, but it actually felt a little warmer. They landed in a spacious room or whatever it was called, and already she was expounding the virtues of the place. He was amazed at all the shimmering color, carefully illuminated by strategically placed lights.

He looked up overhead and thought to himself, there's grass growing up there or maybe trees or perhaps even buildings. One never knows what you might be walking on top of, he mused.

"...and these caverns were discovered in 1878 by three men," she was saying. "One was a tinsmith, and another was a local photographer. They were actually searching for such a cavern when they stumbled upon this one, a marvelous discovery, don't you think?"

You could say that! He glanced up over his head and all around cautiously, remembering the bats he had seen in the others. That was the other thing he didn't like.

"...and since then, countless numbers have descended into this subterranean wonderland," she narrated, and he wondered if she got tired of repeating the same thing over and over again, hour after hour, day after day, month after month, and he found himself mentally mocking her. He could never do that job! Suddenly a large drop of water plopped down on his nose, and he figured he deserved it.

The group shuffled through almost reverent-like, stopping to snap pictures every now and then and standing in awe of its splendid artifacts. Cory couldn't help but fall in step with them, not only physically but emotionally. They were certainly the most stunning caverns he had ever seen. Of course, he wasn't any expert, but he figured the motel clerk just might be right. Though he lagged behind, he could hear the guide pointing out what she called Dream Lake, and when he got there, he was unquestionably impressed. The lake, as she called it, was so clear that it looked exactly like a mirror and reflected the cavern's ceiling just that way. He stared down into it and felt completely disoriented, and then he heard her mention a *ghost.*

Now, that was appealing!

She was saying that the three explorers in fact believed there was a ghost, and as they explored the caverns, it kept popping up in front of them. Apparently they thought it was following them, and they actually left their exploration for about a week because of it. She explained that it was due to all the linking tunnels, and they just kept running into it over and over. When she finally pointed out the presumed ghost, he could understand their dilemma. It was a huge white column formed by connecting stalactites and stalagmites. He could see how the enormous pillar could appear ghostly in the dark. Such columns were throughout the caverns, but this particular one was so pristine white that it actually gave off an eerie ethereal effect. He could only imagine how unnerved the explorers must have been with nothing but candles down here, flickering candles at that. He smiled at the thought, but was secretly glad for the hidden lights.

The group wound in and out of the colorful chambers, and Cory's attention was temporarily diverted from his mission. He was intrigued by all the magnificent sculptures but still wondered how much longer it would take before they saw the light of day again.

Was that music?

Very faint music like an organ playing somewhere, yet it was different, almost like a part of the caverns, a beautiful but haunting sound. They kept walking, and the guide was explaining various things, but it was difficult to hear everything she was saying and look at what he wanted to see at the same time, so he trailed behind, preferring the sights to instruction. He could read about it later, but then he happened to hear her say, "Hear the rocks sing."

He zoned in.

"It's the world's largest musical instrument…the Great Stalacpipe Organ." He searched all around for it.

"It was dedicated some years ago in the summer of 1957," she added and then explained how such unique tones were created by a one-of-a-kind instrument from the surrounding stalactite formations covering over three acres.

No wonder it sounded like some concert underground, Cory thought to himself. And then they were in a magnificent room rising to extreme heights with massive crystalline cascades in absolutely breathtaking colors. There was a man sitting before what looked like an elevated organ. A hush fell over the group as he played…

A mighty fortress is our God
A bulwark never failing…

They stood there as if they were in some grand cathedral, and they were, Cory decided, as he listened to Martin Luther's age-old words. When finally they continued the tour, he was glad, though he had to admit the stillness of the caverns, the undeniable aspect of time, and the lingering strains of the old hymn had lessened his anxiety. Leaving the sober melody behind, he thought maybe he would start back to church soon, back to Nimmo.

He glanced at his watch, but couldn't see it, so he skirted up from the rear to ask the guide exactly how much longer it would be. He waited impatiently for her to stop gabbing. She was one of those who seemed to take great pride in her own wealth of knowledge, and then there were those in the group, so full of enthusiasm, they kept shooting up their hands with more and more questions. He wished they would just shut up and get on. He was about to shove on past them when the light overhead reflected off her name-tag.

Rayna

He caught his breath.

"You had a question, sir?"

He was gaping, speechless.

"Did you have a question, sir?" she repeated.

He shook his head.

She looked at him curiously and continued explaining the difference between the stalactites and the stalagmites. He remembered studying about them in another world, grade school maybe. He tried to see beneath her cap, and sure enough, there were some black ringlets sticking out. Was it the underground, the darkness, or the guide? Suddenly he felt like he was hyperventilating? He had to get out! But his feet were solidly stuck to the damp floor, not physically, but emotionally. They wouldn't move.

She kept talking, explaining every detail of the caverns while his mind catapulted, trying to make sense of everything. She seemed to be about his age, but she didn't look at all like him! She certainly didn't look like his mom, but, yet, there was something. He couldn't quite put his finger on it. The other tourists moved around him, hanging onto her every word while he just stood there.

"Coming, sir?"

He looked up, and she was waiting for him. Awkwardly, he scrambled forward and took up his position in the rear. They were almost to the end of the tour, but it seemed like eons as he followed after, edging closer and closer in order to get a better look at her, and then it hit him. Though extremely vague, something about her reminded him of his granddad. Maybe it was the wide forehead or the slight, protruding chin. When finally she led them back up the steps to daylight, he breathed a sigh of relief and waited for the crowd to disperse, which took another ten minutes or so, with all their tedious post questions.

They were in what appeared to be a gift shop with black, rubber bats bouncing from the ceiling. He glanced around impatiently. At last it was just the two of them standing there facing one another. She pulled off her cap and ebony curls fell out, tumbling down to her shoulders. She looked even less like a Blackenstaff, but, of course, she wasn't a Blackenstaff!

"You have a question?" she asked again in her inquiring school-teacher tone.

"Yes…I do." He cleared his voice. "Could we go somewhere and talk…maybe?"

"Pardon?"

Immediately he realized he had said the wrong thing. She thought he was coming on to her, and her expression had suddenly changed.

"I'm sorry. I guess I didn't phrase that quite right. What I really mean is that I need to get some information…."

Relieved, she responded, "Yes?"

"Not about the caverns…though they're very nice. I know this will sound strange to you, but I need to find out…do you have a mother?"

The look on her face was so startled that he realized again how stupid he must sound. "I'm sorry," he repeated. "That's a crazy question…but…." He was nervously shuffling from one foot to the other.

"Why do you ask?" She was frowning, and her brow was completely furrowed.

"Because I'm here…looking for someone."

"Who?"

Now that he was faced with the inevitable, he couldn't get the words out, and it didn't help any that he was being shouldered by another group of tourists ascending the stairway and flooding into the gift shop.

She waited, her frown deepening.

He gave her an imploring look and blurted out, "My sister."

She stepped back.

The shock on her face was disturbing, and he rushed on, "I guess what I'm trying to say is…I'm on a mission to find—"

She interrupted, "Where did you come from?"

"I live on the coast…the Back Bay below Virginia Beach." With this she spun around and walked off. He stood there wondering whether to call her back or what, and then she turned.

"How old are you?"

He told her, and she looked oddly puzzled.

He didn't know what to say or do next. She was just staring at him. Suddenly she motioned for him to follow as she made her way through the crowd and on out the front door. She walked over toward a bench.

He came up behind her. "You never answered my question."

She glared at him, and he began to feel utterly foolish. What was he doing here in this strange place, facing off with a strange girl, who must think he's nuts?

But then she spoke softly, "I don't have a mother…I never had a mother. My father raised me."

Grasping the full weight of those words, he motioned to the bench, "Mind if we sit down?"

They eased down on opposite ends, staring off into the distance to the Blue Ridge, seemingly afraid to look at one another now. There was a nice breeze blowing, and the sun was warm and soothing. They sat there quietly for a few moments, awkwardly, as others crossed back and forth in front of them.

"You think I'm your sister, don't you?"

He nodded.

And she was quiet.

Two days later he was on his way back home with a bounce in his step, a joy he hadn't felt in a long time with the events of the last few days playing out over and over in his mind. No longer did he feel alone. No longer did he harbor self-pity for the loss of his mother.

He and Rayna had decided to spend some time together, to get to know each other, and he couldn't wait. They had a lot to catch up on—years, a lifetime, two lifetimes, in fact. And he hoped her father was all right with it. The preacher had been very courteous, but restrained. He tried to put himself in his shoes and figured he might respond in like manner given the same set of circumstances. Oh well, in a few weeks, he was to visit with them again, and then he would have the opportunity to get to know him. He wasn't sure he really wanted to, but he knew he must if he were to become a true brother to his new sister.

Greyson and Rayna sat out on the porch. The night was cool but comfortable. He watched her push the swing back and forth and remembered how she had insisted that they needed one when they first moved into the parsonage.

It had been several days now since Cory's visit, and still they hadn't discussed it as openly as they both would have liked. His sudden appearance was like a rock thrown into their calm pond, the ripples had widened, growing larger and larger while creating newer ones, until the pond was completely unsettled.

"So he'll be back later…in a few weeks?"

She nodded. "He'll be staying at the motel again."

"Rayna, you know I don't mind him staying here."

"I know, Dad."

"He could stay in my room…I'll sleep with Grandpa."

"I told him that, but he said he'd feel better staying in the motel, that it would give us all some space."

Greyson made no comment, but he was secretly glad. He felt that they would all need that space.

"Plus he likes staying across from the singing tower apparently." She laughed softly, pulling her legs up and hugging her knees just like she had when she was six years old. "I still can't believe it."

He watched her in the light of the full moon, and listened to her go on and on about his visit. He saw her animated expressions and ready smile. Clearly she was as happy as he had ever seen her, so why was he so thrown off balance? He supposed it was because the young man embodied the past, a past he had tried to forget.

"Dad, are you okay with all this?" her question read his thoughts.

He shifted in the rocker. "I only want what's best for you, Rayna…and if you're happy, I'm happy."

"I know that, but you seem somewhat indifferent, that's all."

"I'm sorry, honey, if I do. It's just been a big surprise, and it will take some getting used to."

"Did you love her, Dad?"

Shocked by the blatant question, he couldn't answer immediately but thought on it first and then carefully measured his words. "Well, it was the love of youth, I guess, mixed with a lot of infatuation. Whether or not that's true love, I'm not sure. But one thing for certain, it was not the love, the deep abiding love that I have for you."

"I wish I had met her now."

"Maybe I was wrong in never making that possible…but life seemed so good for us, and I guess I didn't want to take a chance of messing it up, and then life just sort of moves on, you know, creates its own momentum, and time fills in."

"Oh, I'm not blaming you, Dad. I would never blame you, and I certainly didn't want to initiate a meeting myself. I always sort of figured that…maybe she would come to me."

The knife twisted in Greyson's heart once more.

"But I never thought about her dying."

He searched the uneven planks on the floor. "She did come…once."

"She did?"

Shock registered on her pretty face, and it broke his heart. "It was a long time ago."

"When?"

"You were small...and she just wanted to find out about you, to see you and make sure you were okay. You were sick, getting over a virus or something...but you came to the door, and she saw you."

"I don't remember...why didn't you tell me?"

"I was afraid...."

She stared at her dad in the darkness. She stared in disbelief. It was more than hard for her to understand, but she could see that it was pure agony for him. He had stopped rocking and was staring down at the floor, nervously rubbing his hands together. She couldn't imagine her dad being afraid, and she wondered about all the secret pain that he must have endured throughout the years.

"I guess I was afraid of losing the most important thing to me in the world," his voice was barely above a whisper now. "And I guess Lorna was afraid of the same thing."

Rayna sat on the edge of the swing, trying to digest this new revelation, trying to comprehend the full meaning of it, but it was all so complicated. Suddenly she spilled out of the swing and plopped down on his lap as she had done so many times as a child.

"I love you, Dad."

And he held her against him as the full moon climbed higher.

CHAPTER TWENTY-TWO

It was one of those late spring days that beckon you to the outdoors, to the woods or someplace away from the ordinary, away from the plastic and metallic world of man's kingdom, away from the complex society of mounting technology, to some place akin to nature where one can slide transparently into its magic cocoon. It was one of those days when Cory Blackenstaff and Rayna Ralston headed up to the Skyline Drive.

They planned to have lunch at the popular restaurant at Skyland. Rayna was playing the gracious host and driving her white Mustang convertible. It had been a gift from her dad upon graduation from college, and she dearly loved it, especially on days like this. The top was down with the bracing wind blowing her dark curls away from her face, and as they climbed up the mountain, Cory stared at the puffy white clouds overhead. He had arrived back in the Shenandoah the night before, called her, and scheduled the day.

"I'm glad you suggested this…the mountains, that is," he said.

"My favorite place."

"I can understand."

"Didn't you say you came up here on your last trip?"

"I did and spent a night, too."

"Where?"

"In a cabin…at Lewis Mountain."

"No way! Did you like it?"

"It was rather poignant, you might say."

"Really? In what way?"

"I don't know…touching is perhaps a better word. It was a special night."

"Dad and I have stayed there several times, but it's been awhile."

"He didn't want to come along today?"

"I asked him, but I think he had something else to do."

Climbing slowly up Route 211, scaling the steep mountainside, they at last entered the Shenandoah National Park at Thornton Gap, and Rayna paid the entrance fee.

"My treat."

"As you say, little sister."

"We could eat there at the Panorama." She pointed in the direction of an attractive building to the right. "But I really want you to experience Skyland."

"That good, huh?"

"Well, there probably wouldn't be a Shenandoah National Park if it weren't for Skyland."

"Oh?"

"It was here way before and was called Stony Man Camp. It was built just before the turn of the century, around 1895, I think."

"That's a long time ago."

"Yeah, and some of the cabins still stand that were built way back then, but most have been torn down. It was quite a fashionable place in its day. Dad said they used to hold masquerade balls and sunrise parties and moonrise parties and such, and a number of notable people came to it, some staying for months at a time, spending their whole summers. Dad's older brother, Jack, used to work there when he was a teenager, and he could tell you some stories."

Cory had never heard of a moonrise party, but it did sound rather appealing.

"The name was changed to Skyland later on."

"Sounds like you know your history."

"Well, if it weren't for the folks back then, who worked hard convincing the powers that be to establish the new park here in Virginia...in our mountains, instead of someplace else, we wouldn't have it."

"Good for them."

She smiled and wheeled the Mustang around the curves. "I can tell you're really captivated with all this."

"No, no...I am. Don't get me wrong. It's just that I'm more interested in getting to know my little sister."

"Well, there's not much about my life. It's been pretty boring by most standards, I'm sure, but it has been a happy life, a very happy life."

"I'm glad."

She detected a hint of compassion. Already she had sensed a measure of guilt, though subtle, perhaps because he had had Lorna Blackenstaff for his mother, and she had not. Did he feel bad about it?

As if he had read her mind, he blurted out, "I'm sorry about everything, Rayna...not that I had anything to do with it, at least not directly."

"There's no need to be sorry, Cory...like you said, you didn't have anything to do with it."

He nodded, happy to change the subject. "Sure is beautiful up here."

"I love it in the springtime."

"What's the tallest peak?"

"Hawksbill...4,050 feet up, but another one is my favorite, and it's almost as tall."

"Oh, yeah?"

"You'll see him in a minute."

"Him?"

"Stony Man."

"Didn't you just say that was the name of the old resort?"

"That's right. You *were* listening."

He grinned. "Care to elaborate?"

"Stony Man is the name of a mountain, and the old resort was named after it."

"I see."

"Not yet, you don't…and Stony Man has character, too."

"Hm-m-m-m…character." He was beginning to see a side of this sister that he hadn't seen before. Obviously, she was very ingrained in these mountains.

"Ever since I was a child, Stony Man's image has been a part of my life. Dad and I spent so much time up here, and we've hiked most of these trails, but Stony Man was always my favorite. You'll see."

He cleared his throat. "What do you mean…you'll see?"

She smiled mischievously and drove on. After awhile she whipped off the road, onto a pull-off and stopped. She was staring straight ahead at a sizable mountain, and he followed her gaze.

"There he is…see him?"

He strained to see, and then stood up, clutching the windshield, peering up at the majestic mountain. Sure enough, its outline resembled the face of an old bearded man, seemingly reclining on the slope of the mountain.

"That's pretty neat."

"Told you so."

He smiled.

"Stony Man is the most prominent of all these mountains."

He continued to stare up at it.

"Looks like he's gazing out over the beautiful Shenandoah Valley, doesn't it?"

He nodded, recalling the awesome, rugged mountains that he had seen out west. "I suppose it's a nice enough mountain."

Rayna frowned.

"No offense…and we're going to climb him?"

"You guessed it."

When they arrived at the restaurant, the dining room was almost full, but fortunately there was one more window table left. They ordered their food fairly quickly and settled down to enjoy the view.

He pushed back in his chair, staring at the Valley down below.

Rayna was pleased that the day was turning out so nice.

"I don't know which is prettier, the mountains or the Valley."

She smiled in agreement.

A black and white clad waiter placed two frosted glasses of water before them, and Cory thanked him. Then he turned to Rayna a bit uncomfortably. "Your father…has he ever dated?"

She shook her head. "No, never…well, once way back when I was little, but not since then."

He looked at her questioningly.

"He feels that his calling is wholly to serve the Lord."

"I see."

"Except, of course, for me," she added.

"Of course."

She unfolded her napkin and spread it out on her lap.

"What about you? Any serious boyfriends?"

She shook her head.

"That's hard to believe."

"Well, there was Kent, but it wasn't right between us, if you know what I mean. So, I'm concentrating on my own future now."

"Don't blame you."

After lunch, they headed for the trail.

It was a well-worn trail, being such a popular one. Lots of timber and fallen trees scattered about. They hopped over dry ditches that had been dug out at an angle to allow for the frequent heavy rainfalls, and Cory caught a strong whiff of evergreens.

"I was reading about the trees last evening," he said, breaking the silence, "that one out of every three used to be a chestnut."

"Well, that was before my time, but Dad used to talk about them. He remembers seeing them die. The white ghosts—he called them, and he hated seeing the CCC guys cutting them down."

"That's a shame."

"It had to be done, still Dad hated seeing it."

Cory fell in behind her, weaving up the mountainside, dodging the occasional rocks and trees in the narrow path.

"He felt it was sort of sacrilegious cutting them down and hauling them off."

"Sounds like your dad's a fine person."

"The best."

They skirted between bright green ferns that carpeted the dark forest floor, some as high as two feet, thick clusters waving softly in the mountain breeze. The afternoon sun dappled the trail, and only a few clouds passed over now and then, stealing its warmth.

"You realize what tomorrow is?" she asked suddenly.

He tried to remember. Her birthday? His? George Washington's? But he couldn't think of a thing.

"The first day of summer!"

"I knew that."

She laughed as they pushed on uphill through thick stands of twisted mountain laurel now in bloom. Bees buzzed about, and Cory suppressed his nagging questions. Why hadn't her dad come with them? He wondered again what he thought of him tracking them down. Did he dislike him? He hadn't noticed any hostility, but then he was a preacher.

"Look!"

An old, fallen tree lay beside the trail with a small hole in one side of it, and a chipmunk stared out at them. He grabbed his camera, but it vanished.

"Shucks."

"Quick little characters."

"I'd say."

They trudged on as the incline grew steeper, winding through masses of rocky boulders. "This will get you in shape."

"But the view at the top is worth it!"

"How long is it?"

"Not long, about a mile and a half up and back."

He was glad. Hiking reminded him too much of Nam, though, he had to admit, the two couldn't be more different. The mountain laurels thickened, sandwiching them in on both sides, and their fragile blossoms showered the mossy earth with a fine spray of pinkish-white. Rayna stooped to pick one up.

"Little teacups," she said softly.

"Excuse me?"

"Dad says my namesake used to call them little teacups."

"Your namesake?"

"Dad's twin sister, Rayna Rose. I was named after her. She died as a child." Cory figured he had a lot to learn about this family.

She fingered the delicate blossom.

"They are pretty," he acknowledged.

"Most people think they grew here naturally, but the CCC boys planted them and a lot of other things, too."

"You said you and your dad have hiked most of the trails up here?"

"Well, I exaggerated. There are over 500 miles of trails, including 101 miles of the Appalachian Trail, but we've hiked quite a few. We'll soon be on top of Stony Man…so watch your step."

Watch your step!

He felt like he was back in the caverns and experienced a tinge of irritation. She *was* his kid sister, for Pete's sake.

"We're 4,010 feet above sea level."

"You don't say," he mocked good-naturedly.

She looked back.

"Just kidding, though I'm surprised at your knowledge of the mountains."

"I've a lot to learn yet." She pointed out the small, gnarled trees. "Ice and wind—they catch it hard up here."

"They aren't the only ones," he joked.

Soon they were there.

"We're standing on top of Stony Man's forehead," she announced proudly.

He pushed up beside her. "Wow!"

The summit was sheer cliffs, but the view was spectacular as they maneuvered cautiously over the gigantic outcropping of huge boulders. Rayna was glad that no one was up there but them, which was not always the case. She could not have ordered a more perfect day. She watched Cory step guardedly over the precarious rocks and closer to the edge. A pool of water lay in the midst of the boulders, left from yesterday's rain, though it would soon evaporate in the hot sun.

"Windy up here."

"Usually is."

The sweeping Shenandoah Valley spread out below with fertile squares of farmland and rolling pastures. He recalled all the grazing cattle he had seen on his search from town to town just a few weeks prior.

Rayna was staring out toward the range of mountains.

"I will lift up mine eyes unto the hills, from whence cometh my help," she uttered.

He suddenly felt a true kinship to this preacher's daughter and was glad that she was his sister. A strong updraft swept up from the Valley, and she wrapped her arms about herself. "Psalms," she explained.

"I figured." He sat down on one of the large boulders, and she joined him, pointing over to their left.

"That's Skyland."

"It looks so small."

They were silent for a while, observing the massive chain of distant mountains, rows and rows of them.

"Does make you feel closer to heaven up here," he said and then felt silly for sounding so melodramatic. It was out of character for him, but she nodded understandingly. A raven soared in the distance, a gentle flight on the constant updrafts, and then it did a sudden flip.

"They like to show off."

"Is it always this way, so windy?"

She nodded, and her face brightened. "The wind can do strange things at times."

"Like?"

"Well, there's a statue in a little cemetery at my alma mater, and its hand was carved in such a way that when the wind passes through, it produces a high-pitched whistle, just like a scream."

"You don't say."

"But people believe it's the ghost of a little girl that's screaming. She's buried there."

"That must have been comforting at night."

"I never actually heard it myself, but my roommate did." She had to smile just thinking about Norma's escapades.

Cory leaned back contentedly, clasping his hands behind his head. "It sure is peaceful."

"Climb the mountains and get their good tidings. Nature's peace will flow into you as sunshine flows into trees…."

"That's not Psalms."

"No," she smiled, "John Muir."

"I've heard of him." He shifted more comfortably. "You're definitely a mountain girl…I mean you know a lot about them," he quickly added.

"I hope to know a lot more."

He looked at her questioningly.

"As a Park Ranger."

"No kidding?"

"It's what I've always wanted, but it has taken awhile to get here."

He waited for her to explain.

"I mean it's taken me some time to decide. Besides, they just started letting us girls in, you know. There was an old law years ago, around 1870, that prevented it."

"How so?"

"By allowing federal agencies to offer jobs according to sex, and it wasn't changed until a couple of years back. But even then, it wasn't taken seriously, not until they had a discrimination suit last year. I don't know why, but they seemed to think that guys were better at interpreting nature than us girls. And I'm here to tell you they're wrong!"

Cory admired her feisty spirit. It reminded him of his mom.

"Who better than a female to understand the sensitivity of nature?" she asked passionately.

Cory shot up his hands. "Hey, I'm with you!"

She laughed.

"I can see you now in that green and gray uniform... Smokey bear hat and all."

"Not yet, you won't. We have to wear those silly-looking polyester knit things with a pillbox hat! I guess they want us to look like Jacqueline Kennedy tromping through the woods. But one day we'll wear the regular uniform...and the official badge. Just watch and see!"

"I admire your grit, little sister."

"Thank you."

"Well, I guess that means no more leading chatty tourists down under the earth?"

"That's right."

"I'm sure you'll make a good one, too."

"I hope so. The Park is very special to me, not only because I love the mountains...but also because of my heritage."

"That's what surprises me. I'd think you'd feel a bit...well somewhat disenchanted with it. From what you've told me, you might be living up here if it weren't for the Park!"

"Grandpa sure does, but then he lived through the take-over, both he and Dad. Don't get me wrong, I'm not glad that we lost the mountain place, not in the least. And all of this came with a terrible price...a sacrifice."

"That's what I mean."

"But if it hadn't happened," she grew quiet for a moment, "we wouldn't have all this!"

He made no comment.

"And I feel that it all belongs to me now," she concluded. "To all of us...and I want to spend the rest of my life sharing it."

"I understand...I think."

She twisted around on the rock to face him more directly. "Are you familiar with the climbing plant that turns a bright red and orange in the fall...called *Bittersweet?"*

"I am. We have it on the coast, too."

"Well...it's sort of like that."

He nodded understandingly, and they were silent for a while.

"What about you?" she asked suddenly.

"What about me?"

"Your dreams?"

His countenance instantly darkened. "I don't know. Ever since I got back from Nam, I've sort of been floundering, living for the moment, just happy to be home."

She studied him, and he shifted uncomfortably. "Though I have been giving some thought to going back to college. I know that's what Mom would want."

"Why did you leave?"

"I don't know…tired of school, and all my friends were joining up. It sounded cool, you know, exciting."

"And patriotic."

"Yeah. That was part of it, and I don't regret it, really. It's just that…"

She waited, anxious to learn more.

"…just that war isn't something you can ever imagine, ever prepare for, or ever forget."

"I'm sure things will get better for you."

He shrugged.

"Was it that bad?"

How could he tell her? How could he tell her about the fear, the smell, and the death? How could he tell her what it was like to witness your buddies being blown up by mines all around you? And how could he tell her about Private First Class Ernest Smith? And about vomiting all over himself, how could he tell her it was pure hell? He couldn't, so he was silent.

"I'm sorry. I guess that was a stupid question." She stood up and gazed out over the Valley as the wind buffeted her dark curls. "But…maybe your trips up here to the mountains will help, like John Muir said."

"Maybe."

"Dad says it gives God a chance to speak to us."

His reserve lessened, and he found comfort in her tender efforts to help him.

"And perhaps you will share your memories of your mother with me," she added a bit hesitantly.

"Our mother," he corrected.

And they smiled at one another.

Greyson slowed down as he neared the familiar spot. He hoped he'd done the right thing in refusing Rayna's offer to accompany her and Cory. But somehow he felt it was important for them to be alone, to get to know each other and the shared blood that coursed between them. His mother had certainly done a good job of raising the young man, and he was looking forward to getting to know him. He only regretted that Lorna had never been able to know Rayna, but one cannot change the past.

He pulled up and shut off the engine. He glanced over at his pa, who was staring straight ahead, oblivious to where they were, all his former fight gone. He didn't even turn his head to look at him. Greyson couldn't help but remember the other times, year after year, when they had driven up here, and a flood of memories washed over him—like the strong winds blowing his pa's hat off that day. He climbed out and walked around the car.

"Want to get out, Pa?" He pulled open his door.

The old man's watery eyes stared blankly at him.

"The home place, Pa…remember?"

Slowly he looked out the door at the weeds blowing softly in the wind, and then out to the crumbling remains of the cabin. Greyson thought he caught a glimpse of a faint smile, but he made no effort to move.

"I'll just take a walk around, Pa…be back in a bit."

His pa didn't answer, so he pushed on through the high weeds, walking around looking at first one thing and then another. Finally he sat down on a stone left from the old porch steps. He remembered his pa anxiously looking for the front stoop that day and how upset he had been. He glanced back to the car. Maybe it was best that his mind was gone, and he was set free from his sorrow now. He sighed and leaned up against a splintered log, absently stroking the crumbling stone beneath him. A tiny, brown and white butterfly landed on a bright orange weed nearby and tenaciously clung to it as it swayed back and forth in the warm sun.

"Make mud pies with me, Greyson…please."

The familiar voice whined through the tall swaying trees, as much a part of the mountain scene as the sun and the breeze. Of all God's creations, he thought, the memory had to be at the top of the list. Here he was in his forties, and it seemed like yesterday that he and his sister were playing in the mud together.

He sat there thinking about his life and all his mistakes and troubles, his epilepsy, the cross he'd had to bear, and about his call to the ministry. He glanced up the hill to the little cemetery overtaken with tangled weeds, and thought sadly that she had never had the chance to experience life. It was cut off too short. But then all of our lives are short in the scheme of things, he concluded, sitting there on the solid, aging mountain. First we're here, and then we're gone…just as the lives of the people that once claimed these mountains.

He stood up and brushed the dirt from his pants.

'For what is your life? It is even a vapour, that appeareth for a little time, and then vanisheth away.'

Not just our lives, he thought, but the old home place was fast disappearing, too, overtaken by the winds of time, erasing all signs of the past. It wouldn't be long before people wouldn't even know that there ever was a home here, a family, laughter and tears….

ACKNOWLEDGMENTS

I give my heartfelt thanks to all those who have supported me in the writing of this book. As always to my family: My loving husband who has patiently but happily accompanied me on our numerous trips to the mountains, to the Shenandoah National Park to research, to hike its wooded trails and discover the "jewels" of its past. We have spent many a night along its poignant and wind-swept ridges in our trusty camper.

Also to my understanding and sweet children and their families: Troy, Tara, Bethany, Geanna, Will, Justin, Robby, Laura, Sarah, Will, Caroline and Alexandra—for their caring and encouragement, plus diligent reading of this and other manuscripts in the past.

Thanks to my brothers, Richard and Bennie, for their assistance: Richard, for his first-hand account of Vietnam and many helpful documentary books on the subject; Bennie for his historical information and original Current Events of that period; also to my sisters, Rita and Linda, for their continued encouragement.

A sincere thanks goes to the great staff of the Shenandoah National Park, especially to Greta Miller, Executive Director, for her continued support and guidance, and to Karen Michaud, Chief, Interpretation and Education, for taking the time to read the lengthy manuscript and to guide me in the process, and to those helpful Park Rangers who have answered my many questions.

As always, I thank Joyce Maddox and Amy Moore, of Warwick House Publishing, for their expertise and fortitude in working with me to get this book complete, and Dr. Peter Houck for making it possible.

I cannot begin to list all of the sources from which I gleaned to recreate this important period in history, which also includes much time on the amazing and valuable Internet. However, I want to especially acknowledge the following sources.

American Chronicle: Six Decades in American Life, Lois Gordon & Alan Gordon

This Fabulous Century – Time/Life Books, *The Great Depression: America in the 1930s*, T. H. Watkins

Current Events - The National School Newspaper

The Undying Past of Shenandoah National Park, Darwin Lambert

Shenandoah Secrets: The Story of the Park's Hidden Past, Carolyn & Jack Reeder

Shenandoah Heritage: The Story of the People Before the Park, Carolyn & Jack Reeder

Herbert Hoover's Hideaway, Darwin Lambert

Herbert Hoover– Fishing For Fun - Hoover Presidential Library

Memories of a Lewis Mountain Man, John W. Stoneberger

The Tree Army, Stan Cohen

Everything Was Wonderful, Reed L. Engle

Shenandoah: Its National Park and Neighbors, Anne Frederick

In the Light of the Mountain Moon, Reed L. Engle

The Greatest Single Feature—A Sky-line Drive, Reed L. Engle

The Anguish of Displacement, Katrina M. Powell

Shenandoah: The Story Behind the Scenery, Hugh Crandall/ Reed L. Engle

Discovery Of Luray Caverns, Virginia, Russell H. Gurnee

John Muir's Wild America, Tom Melham

The Vietnam War (An Almanac) - A World Almanac Publication

Armies of the Vietnam War 1962-75, Osprey, Men At Arms Series
The US Marine Corps Since 1945, Osprey, Elite Series
The Illustrated History of Marines: The Vietnam War, Edwin H. Simmons
13/13 Vietnam: Search and Destroy, Gordon Baxter
Young Man in Vietnam, Charles Coe
The Beach: A History of Virginia Beach, Virginia, Virginia Beach Public Library
A Naturalist's Guide to the Virginia Coast, Curtis J. Badger
From the Beach to the Bay: An illustrated history of Sandbridge in Virginia, Chris Jennings & Hank Gardner

LITERATURE AND SONG CREDITS:

Quote from "For Whom the Bell Tolls" by Ernest Hemingway, p. 14
President Hoover's speech– *Herbert Hoover's Hideaway* by Darwin Lambert, p. 80-82
Quote from President Roosevelt's speech – SNP Dedication – July 3, 1936, p. 129
Quotes from John Muir, p. 314-315 and 319 and 404
Quote from *John Muir's Journal*, July 27, 1869, p. 320

"She'll be coming 'round the Mountain"– Mother Jones, p. 109
"How Are Things in Glocca Morra?"– Finian's Rainbow Musical, p. 152
"Blue Suede Shoes"– Elvis Presley, p. 255
"Rock Around The Clock"– Bill Haley, p. 257
"Whole Lotta Shakin' Goin' On"– Jerry Lee Lewis, p. 270
"Poison Ivy"– The Coasters, p. 282
"Good Vibrations"– Beach Boys, p. 352
"Winchester Cathedral"– The New Vaudeville Band/Geoff Stephens, 1966, p. 353
"Ballad of the Green Beret"– SSgt. Barry Sadler & Robin Moore, 1966, p. 355
"Send the Light"– Charles H. Gabriel, p. 377
"Danny Boy"– Frederick Weatherly, 1913, p. 378
"A Mighty Fortress Is Our God"– Martin Luther, 1529, p. 387

All Biblical quotes are taken from the King James Version and the New King James Version of the Holy Bible.

About the Author

Carolyn Tyree Feagans is the author of six novels. The others are listed in order on the back cover of this book. She lives in Virginia with her husband and enjoys their three children, Troy, Tara and Bethany and their families. For more information, visit the author's official Web site at www.carolyntyreefeagans.com or write to P.O. Box 10811, Lynchburg, VA 24506.